A Band of Roses

Book One in the Band of Roses Trilogy

PAT McDERMOTT

For Dolly

Also in This Series

Fiery Roses
Salty Roses

Preface

In 1002 A.D., the chieftain of an obscure Irish clan rose to claim the High Kingship of Ireland. Brian Boru united Ireland's warring tribes under one leader for the first and only time in Irish history. A scholar as well as a warrior, King Brian rebuilt churches, encouraged education, repaired roads and bridges, and roused the country to rise against the Norse invaders who had ravaged Ireland for centuries.

On Good Friday in 1014 A.D., Brian's army challenged a host of Vikings and their allies on the plains of Clontarf. Though his troops were victorious, Brian's son and grandson perished in the battle. Brian himself died as he prayed in his tent, murdered by fleeing Vikings who stumbled upon his camp.

Many historians have speculated that Ireland would be a different place today if Brian Boru and his heirs had survived the Battle of Clontarf. *A Band of Roses* presents one possible scenario.

The Irish Royal Family

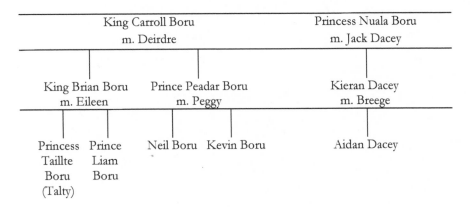

King Carroll Boru m. Deirdre			Princess Nuala Boru m. Jack Dacey
King Brian Boru m. Eileen	Prince Peadar Boru m. Peggy		Kieran Dacey m. Breege
Princess Taillte Boru (Talty) Prince Liam Boru	Neil Boru Kevin Boru		Aidan Dacey

The English Royal Family

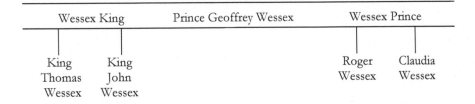

Wessex King	Prince Geoffrey Wessex	Wessex Prince
King Thomas Wessex King John Wessex		Roger Wessex Claudia Wessex

CHAPTER ONE

Fargan

The Twenty-first Century...

The *Fancy Annie* plowed through waters speckled by midmorning sun. A fine catch of groundfish filled the hold, all gutted, sorted, and iced. The yellow-slickered crew, eight weathered fishermen who'd worked the sea together since boyhood, had already hosed the decks and stowed the gear. Matt Foley kept a tidy boat.

The smaller boats couldn't handle the winter seas, but these men would risk the rugged weather on trawlers like *Fancy Annie*. They had families to feed, and the big boats could command high market prices for a winter catch.

Fancy Annie had hit some chop this time out, but the weather held and the fishing was good. When the crew talked of being home with their families for Christmas, Matt cut the ten-day trip to eight. On that brisk winter morning, he radioed his wife to say that the wind was on their tail and they'd make Killybegs by eight o'clock that night. Her response was the same as it had been for over forty years: a squeal of joy and a promise to have his supper ready. After a week at sea, thoughts of Annie's cooking—and Annie—had Matt smiling.

He left the wheelhouse and planted his six-foot frame on the forward deck. The sunny skies offset the cold salt air that stung his cheeks and blew at the curls his old wool cap hadn't covered. His hand shaded his eyes while he scanned the horizon. We'll pay for such a fine stretch of weather, he thought, and then he saw it.

The men had seen it too. After a week of hauling nets and dressing tons of fish, they cheered the sight of the salt-sprayed rock. They were on their way home.

The tip of the ancient volcano rose eighty feet above the rolling ocean. Named for its single granite ledge, Fargan served as a navigational guide in the Irish Sea lanes two hundred miles off the Donegal coast. The ocean around it provided some of the North Atlantic's finest fishing, at least when the oil companies and their sonar weren't scaring all the fish away.

Matt was about to give the order to turn southeast when he caught sight of a vessel drifting north of Fargan. He sprinted to the wheelhouse and snatched his binoculars. The boat was too far away to decipher her markings, but he knew her for an English gunboat, one of the fast attack craft used for coastal patrol and training exercises—but not in Irish waters.

He lowered the binoculars, though his gaze remained fixed on the gunboat. "Keep your ear to the radio, Eddie. That boat might be in trouble. Ronnie, cut the throttles."

Fancy Annie slowed until she rocked in the swells. A dinghy drifted from behind the gunboat. One of three men sitting in it started an outboard motor and steered the craft to the edge of the rocky outcrop. Laden with backpacks, the other two jumped onto the tiny island.

The dinghy returned to the gunboat, leaving the men to scale the rock and hoist themselves onto the ledge. One man drove a pole into a fissure and raised an English flag; the other set up a small survival tent.

Matt stared in amazement. "What in holy hell are they doing? Anything, Eddie?"

"Nothing, Matt."

The gunboat glided toward *Fancy Annie*. Her name was clear now: HMS *Coulter*. Armed men stood gathered on her deck.

A voice boomed through a bullhorn. "This is Captain Andrew Mayne of HMS *Coulter*. Heave to, *Fancy Annie*, and prepare to be boarded."

Matt had no bullhorn and didn't care if Captain Mayne heard his bellowed response. "The hell I will, you bastard. What do you think you're doing? These are Irish waters!"

Concerned now for the safety of his crew, Matt shouted to his first mate, "Get underway, Ronnie. Full speed ahead!"

The engines growled. *Fancy Annie* turned to starboard and cut through the swells. Smoke wafted from *Coulter*'s forward-mounted gun turret. A moment later a loud boom thundered over the water. A shot had crossed the trawler's bow.

Matt grabbed the handset from Eddie and called out to any and every nearby vessel, though the nearest, according to the radar screen, was more than two hundred miles away. Switching from frequency to frequency, he shouted into the radio as if the mere loudness of his voice could get his message through.

He slapped the top of the receiver and flung the handset back to Eddie. "Keep trying, lad. Reach anyone you can and tell them what's happening here."

Heart thumping in his ears, Matt flew down the stairs to his quarters. Pistols couldn't defeat a gunboat, but he'd be damned if he'd cower before pirates.

As he always did when he entered his cabin, he glanced at the photograph of his wife hanging over the gun cabinet. "Keep my supper warm, darlin'. I'll be a little late."

He'd just snapped magazines into two of the pistols when a thunderous impact knocked him down. The guns went flying.

"Feck and bedammit!" He seized the nearest pistol, shoved it into his belt, and raced up to the deck. *Fancy Annie* was listing to port. Her burst of speed had placed her in *Coulter*'s path. Unable to stop, the gunboat had rammed the trawler. Now ten English marines, all armed, stood on *Fancy Annie*'s slanting deck.

A pallid man in his mid-forties swaggered before them. His choice civilian attire failed to conceal the flabbiness around his waist. He glanced about the trawler, plainly seeking whoever was in charge.

Matt wasted no time obliging him. Fists clenched, he charged across the swaying deck and confronted the intruders. "I'm the captain here. Who the hell are you?"

The man's strange eyes—one was blue, the other brown—focused on Matt. "We didn't mean to hit your boat, Captain. I'm Prince Geoffrey Wessex, Regent of the Kingdom of England. These men are my royal marines, and you're trespassing. We will, of course, escort you safely out of English waters."

"English waters because you say so?" Matt spat on the deck. "Never happen."

Prince Geoffrey's face reddened. Before he could reply, Matt's first mate came running from the stern.

"We're taking on water, Matt. If we don't seal her and start the pumps, she'll go down!"

Matt thought of the fine catch of groundfish in the hold and started chuckling. The chuckling grew to wild laughter. The laughter stopped when he tore the pistol from his belt and fired a round into the air. "Get the hell off my boat."

His first mate seized a gaff hook and hefted it with deadly precision. The

3

rest of the crew grabbed gutting knives. All stood ready to fight.

The sight encouraged Matt. Still, they were sinking. "You gobshites will patch my boat, and learn some manners in the process." He raised the pistol to add weight to his demands.

Prince Geoffrey's different-colored eyes widened in alarm. He pointed his weapon at Matt and fired, crying "Shoot!" as he did.

The marines obeyed. A pistol and gutting knives were no match for semiautomatic weapons. Before the gunshots ceased to echo over the ocean, *Fancy Annie's* crew lay dead on her deck.

CHAPTER TWO

Matchmaking

Rain blew into London on New Year's Day. Beyond the grounds of Southwick Castle, motor vehicles inched through the gridlocked streets like crawling ants. Andrew Mayne turned from the diamond-paned window and glared at his royal cousin. Geoffrey had made a muck of what should have been a simple matter.

Andrew now regretted telling Geoffrey of the maritime law concerning territorial claims. Once Geoffrey had learned that anyone who could set up permanent house on an uninhabited island could lawfully lay claim to it, he'd set out to prove Fargan fit for human habitation. He intended to annex the tiny island and the waters surrounding it to the Kingdom of England.

At first Andrew had thought Geoffrey's plan brilliant, but how brilliant had it been to board a commercial fishing boat with ten armed marines? Andrew should have forbidden it, should have forbidden Geoffrey even to come along, though he'd learned long ago that no one forbade Geoffrey Wessex to do anything.

Andrew filled two snifters with brandy and handed one to his royal cousin. "Happy New Year, Geoffrey. I hope this Fargan affair is worth the effort."

Geoffrey sat reading at his food-strewn desk, a slick smile above his chin-and-a-half, a superior glint in his different-colored eyes. He set down his reports and clinked his glass against Andrew's. "You aren't losing heart, are you?"

"You had no business boarding that trawler. We should have warned those fishermen off and let them go."

Savoring a sip of brandy, Geoffrey leaned back in his chair. The unbecoming position showcased his budding paunch. "I fully intended to

5

release them at the nearest port. They'd have hurried things along by reporting the success of my ingenious plan to the Irish authorities. How was I to know there'd be a bit of a glitch?"

"A bit of a glitch?" Unable to keep his voice from trembling, Andrew slammed his glass on the desk. "You shot them all! How will we explain it?"

"Is it my fault the Irish are so hotheaded? Besides, no one can connect us to the missing boat. Men are lost at sea all the time, and your crew saw to the trawler."

"Yes, but I didn't like the look in my officers' eyes."

Geoffrey reached for a heel of bread and tapped it on the scattered pages before him. Crumbs bounced over the timeworn desk. "Don't worry. Those men are loyal to me. All will be well, you'll see. Soon we'll never have to negotiate for fuel again."

Calmer now, Andrew lifted his glass from the desk and mulled over Geoffrey's words as he sipped. "Do you really think there's oil beneath Fargan?"

"I do, but I'll tell you a secret: I never intended to keep Fargan. It's too impractical to drill for oil so far out in the Atlantic."

"What?" Andrew sputtered in disbelief. "Then why did we go to all that trouble?"

"To obtain and control our own fuel supply. One closer to home. And to further our plans for my dear nephews."

Andrew agreed that both young King Thomas and his doltish brother John were unfit to rule. Geoffrey had been plotting to position Roger Wessex, his oldest nephew and Andrew's own godson, as heir to the throne. That was the important thing, more important than oil.

"In the week since I claimed Fargan," Geoffrey said, "King Brian has filed a petition with the World Court to ban all maritime activity in the area until the ownership of Fargan is decided. The ban will keep us from drilling for oil, but it will also cripple the Irish fishing fleet. I feel badly about that, Andrew. I'm going to return Fargan to Brian—for a price."

Struggling to follow Geoffrey's reasoning, Andrew swirled his brandy and stared into its amber depths. "What price?"

Geoffrey lifted a printed page from his desk. "This is the royal physician's latest report. Thomas is deteriorating, and I believe his imminent demise might benefit us."

Though tempted to remark that Thomas's death would benefit everyone, Andrew kept the thought to himself. "What does Thomas have to do with oil?"

"I intend to send an envoy to the Irish court to tell King Brian that in exchange for a few of Ireland's offshore wells, England will surrender its claim to Fargan. I'll even throw in an extra incentive or two to show our good will. A simple marriage treaty will seal the bargain."

"Are you mad? Who would marry a drooling idiot like Thomas?"

Geoffrey's slick smile returned. "King Brian's daughter, of course. The oil wells will be part of her dowry."

Andrew downed his brandy in one quick gulp.

* * * * *

Ireland's royal family conducted their day-to-day business from Tara Hall, a centuries-old neoclassical landmark built on the south bank of Dublin's River Liffey. The first decree signed in the King's Chambers after the Hall's completion had been the Act of Heritance, the law that made Ireland one of the few monarchies in the world where the throne passed to the firstborn child, male or female.

Only three regnant queens had ruled the Emerald Isle in all the years since, all efficient, effective monarchs. Taillte Rosaleen Boru would be the fourth. Since early childhood, Talty had endured private lessons that enabled her to graduate from secondary school far ahead of her peers. Admission to Ireland's Naval School in Cork followed, and she'd flourished there.

The Irish Constitution mandated that the king's heir must be ready to accede the throne on his or her eighteenth birthday. Talty was already twenty and doubted she'd ever be ready. She had so much to learn! Still, an Air Corps Dauphin flew her from the LÉ *Alastrina* to Tara Hall's helipad each Saturday morning to meet with her father for a review of the week's events. His request for a midweek meeting worried her.

Praying that the dark blue of her navy uniform hid the wrinkles in her skirt, she smoothed her pinned-up hair and stepped from the private elevator to Tara Hall's fourth floor. The rapid click of her regulation military heels echoed down the corridor leading to the King's Chambers.

Though she'd told no one, Talty hated being Crown Princess. The prospect of spending her life preparing for her beloved father's death depressed her. She wouldn't have to worry about that for years, however. Silver might speckle King Brian's russet hair, but he was only fifty, and still strong and healthy.

She hurried past the reception area, where her father's no-nonsense assistant rose from her desk and opened the carved oak door bearing the royal lion of the Boru clan. With a nod of thanks, Talty stepped into her father's chambers.

Like old friends, the dark wood panels and their oil paintings welcomed her. The plush oriental rug cushioned her feet. Her father stood before the blazing hearth, a gold pen in one hand, a communiqué in the other.

He set them down and lifted his hand toward her. "Talty! How's my favorite junior executive naval officer?"

"I'll do, Dad." She caught his fingers in hers and kissed them, a gesture of affection offered by members of the royal family to those who outranked them. Once she'd properly greeted her king, she stood on her toes and greeted her father, pecking the cheek above his well-groomed beard and snagging him in a firm hug. His subtle cologne, an exclusive concoction of citrus and sandalwood, never failed to comfort her. Neither did the sturdy arm that dropped over her shoulders.

"Lunch will be here soon," he said. "Uncle Jack is joining us."

"Uncle Jack? I thought he was in Brussels, at the World Court."

"He was. I called him home." Brian nodded to the black leather chairs before the fireplace. "Shall we talk a little before he arrives?"

Their talks were usually a cozy routine. Today, Talty detected tension in her father's eyes, the same chestnut brown as her own. Since Uncle Jack was coming, she suspected her curious summons to Tara Hall involved Fargan. Brian had been on edge in the month since England had staked its ludicrous claim. Whatever had possessed Geoffrey Wessex to seize part of Ireland's crown territory and upset the neighborly relations England and Ireland had enjoyed for centuries?

Talty filled two china cups from a silver teapot. The task complete, she sat back, locked her ankles together, and waited to hear what was on her father's mind.

"How's the Fian training coming along?" he asked, stirring milk into his tea.

"I spar with Neil on weekends, and I work with two fellas on the ship when there's time."

"You'll have your pin before you know it."

Talty couldn't wait. Since she'd been a child, she'd longed to wear the Fianna pin on her collar, to be part of the elite group of two hundred warriors whose dedication to protecting Ireland hadn't changed since the days of Finn MacCool and his valiant men. For the last ten years she'd trained under the tutelage of Brian's younger brother, Prince Peadar, the leader of the present-day Fianna.

Yet even if she passed the grueling initiation trial, her status as a Fian warrior would be nominal, a mere enhancement to her status as Crown Princess. Brian had made that clear when he'd first allowed her to train with her male cousins: her royal duties must come first. She wished it weren't so.

Tea in hand, Brian settled in his chair. "You'll be going off to California soon. Looking forward to it? Mendocino is a long way from home."

"Not so far these days. Mendocino has some of the finest military research programs in the world. I won't be treated as a princess there, just as another officer. I can do my job better that way."

"From what I hear, you do your job well now. *Alastrina*'s captain told your Uncle Peadar that you more than contribute to the efficient running of our flagship."

Talty raised her tea to her lips and sipped. "Ah, but would he say that if I weren't your daughter?"

"Peadar thinks so. So tell your old father. Is there any special fella you'll be leaving behind when you go off to California?"

"Just you, Daddy," she said in a little-girl voice.

Brian's eyes narrowed, though he grinned. The click of the door handle cut short his response. A spry, spindly white-haired man stepped into the room.

Talty set down her cup and stood. "Howya, Uncle Jack!"

"Talty! It's fine to see you, Lady Princess. I was delighted when your father said you'd be joining us."

Jack Dacey caught her hand and kissed it. His pale blue eyes twinkled with affection. The ready smile that people said was the result of his marriage to Brian's aunt, the feisty Princess Nuala, blossomed on his face. As Ard Brehon, Prince Jack embodied the highest legal authority in the kingdom. He'd been a kind and steady mentor to both Brian and Talty, a nurturer of ideas whose counsel they treasured.

Once Jack was seated with tea before him, he pulled an old briar pipe from his pocket and rubbed it between his hands. For years Talty had watched her granduncle perform the ritual. The pipe had belonged to his father and grandfather. Jack himself had never smoked it. He claimed he only had to hold it to hear the sage advice of his wise old forebears.

As Jack fiddled with the pipe, Brian fidgeted in his seat.

Talty folded her arms. "All right, fellas. What did you bring me home in the middle of the week to discuss?"

"Some developments with the Fargan matter," Brian said.

Jack selected a strawberry scone and set it on a plate. "We've learned that before the court imposed its ban, Geoffrey Wessex leased a ship to conduct seismic testing in the area."

"So he means to drill for oil around Fargan?"

Her father shook his head. "No one can drill for oil around Fargan. I commissioned three different geological surveys. Each stated the Fargan

9

Trough is more than six miles deep. No oil platform can get down that far. If Geoffrey tries to drill for oil, he'll not only fail, he'll foul the ocean and kill the fish."

"The fish are safe enough for now," said Jack. "No one can fish in that area until the World Court completes its review and schedules public hearings. It could go on for years."

"But if we can resolve the Fargan matter now," Brian said, "the World Court will throw out the case. Our fishing fleet can work those waters again." His fidgeting increased. He attempted to smile, but his lips and eyebrows twiddled in ambiguous contortions that finally settled into his "this is a hard one" frown.

Talty braced herself. *Here it comes.*

Her father leaned forward and looked her in the eye. "In exchange for a few oil wells in the Irish Sea, Geoffrey will waive his claim to Fargan. He's also offering several shipping lanes and access to England's oil refining facilities." Brian lowered his head for a moment, apparently to study his knuckles. "The catch is, he wants to seal the agreement with a marriage treaty." Again, he peered straight at her. "Between you and King Thomas."

"What? Thomas Wessex? You're joking!" Talty's heart thumped. She clawed at the arms of her chair and turned her head in disbelief from Brian to Jack and back again. Would he do this to her, her own father? Had he been asking about her plans and dreams only to dash them?

Brian seemed oblivious to her distress. "You know poor Thomas isn't well." He glanced at Jack as if seeking support, but Jack seemed content to study his scone and let Brian handle the matter.

Talty swallowed hard. She'd never met Thomas Wessex, but she'd heard the pitiful stories. "Yes. Some sort of degenerative disease."

"His family claims it's a neural disorder," Jack said, his eyes on the jam pot, "though they won't say what, exactly. Their legal advisers insist he's competent enough to function as head of state with Geoffrey acting as Regent. But Geoffrey tells us Thomas won't live much longer."

Brian's mouth tightened into a thin line. His white-knuckled fingers gripped his knees. "This might sound callous, Tal, but if you knew it would only be for a short time, could you marry Thomas?"

Still gaping at both men, Talty clasped her hands to still her trembling fingers. "You're really serious! You want me to marry Thomas Wessex? As in husband and wife?"

"He'd never touch you, darlin'," said Jack. "That would be part of the deal. The marriage would be a token thing, though the benefits would be great for both our countries."

Brian shifted in his chair and spoke with a clearly feigned buoyancy. "I've been studying some new technology, darlin'. Plans are in the works to build drill ships that can reach deeper into the ocean than ever before. I'm thinking of investing in one. They're building them to be careful of the environment these days. If that's so, our fishermen and oilmen can work in the same areas. I think we can afford to give away a few oil wells if we know we can produce others."

Did he really expect her to share his enthusiasm? Though she came close to telling him and Jack to take their oil wells and go to the devil sideways, she mustered all the dignity she possessed and walked to the window. Arms folded tight, she glared down at the river, fighting to keep her tears at bay and her temper at a simmer.

The door opened again. Talty turned. A harried looking woman dressed in the black and white uniform of the royal catering staff wheeled a cart into the room. Setting the cart before the fireplace, she started uncovering soup tureens and assorted platters.

"Why, Daisy!" Jack said. "I haven't seen you for months."

Daisy Cleary removed the tea tray from the table and set out fresh linen napkins, china, and silver. "You're very kind, sir. My old mum's been ill. It's been hard looking after her, but I got someone now who'll come in and see to it she don't hurt herself while I'm working."

"That's too bad," Brian said. "Let us know if you need anything."

Daisy set a bowl of soup before Brian. Jack didn't want one, and so the woman nodded and departed. Talty stared after her until she'd left the room. The break had given her a chance to process her father's proposition.

If the marriage didn't interfere with her career plans, it might be all right. If she agreed to marry Thomas knowing he'd be dead soon, what harm would there be? Shuddering at the ghoulish thought, she ambled to the cart and helped herself to some parsnip soup. Though she was far from hungry, ladling out the fragrant concoction helped calm her.

She set her steaming bowl on the table to cool and reclaimed her seat. "What do you think of this marriage thing, Uncle Jack?"

"I've looked over the proposed treaties. I think we can work it out."

"Treaties? Do you need more than one?"

Having finished his scone, Jack selected a croissant and buttered it. "We need three. The first has England relinquishing its claim to Fargan. The second details the terms of the marriage itself. Which oil wells will be part of your dowry, things like that."

Talty broke open a cinnamon scone. "I'm expensive, I think."

"You're more precious than any oil well, girl." Brian spooned a chunk of parsnip into his mouth. He took his time chewing.

Talty waited. Neither man spoke, though they traded uneasy glances.

"All right, fellas. Let's have the third."

Jack bit into his croissant, a calculated move that rendered him unable to speak. Despite her growing dread, Talty admired the old fox.

Brian set his spoon down and sighed. "I don't like it, but Geoffrey insisted on it. The third treaty stipulates the removal of your title as Crown Princess. Since you'd be Queen of England, he won't risk giving Ireland any advantage over England if by some misfortune you should become Queen of Ireland at the same time." He looked away, into the fire. "If we agree to all of this, I'd have to declare Liam my heir."

No! She wanted to throw the scone at him. All her life she'd trained to take his place. Had it been for nothing? And what would Liam think? Her sweet bookworm brother wouldn't want to be Crown Prince, she was sure of that. Yet something tugged at her, something she couldn't let escape. Crumbs bounced over her navy blue skirt as she tore the scone to pieces trying to capture the elusive thought.

Brian's hands covered hers. "We don't have to do it, Tal. We can refuse."

If her father and Uncle Jack hadn't caught her off guard, she'd have seen it right away. If she were no longer Crown Princess, she'd be free of the tedious responsibilities being heir to the throne demanded.

And what about Liam? If her father had already thought this through, he must think Liam wouldn't mind. Her brother wouldn't be the first scholar who'd sat on Ireland's throne. Yes, it just might be all right.

She brushed away a blur of tears and sucked in a deep breath. "Only until Thomas dies? Or forever?"

"Even after Thomas dies," said Jack, "you'd still be a member of the Wessex family in name. Geoffrey wants no loopholes to challenge his power. I suspect he means to continue to act as Regent even after his nephew John takes the throne."

Talty would have obeyed her father in the end, yet self-interest more than filial duty prompted her compliance now. Unused to dishonesty, she waged an inner struggle.

I'm licking honey from a thornbush.

"When would this marriage take place?"

"In June." Brian almost smiled. "When the roses are blooming."

"So in five months, I'm to be the Queen of England. In name, anyway. Will I have royal duties there?"

Brian nodded. "Nominal perhaps, and only until Thomas…leaves us."

Again, Talty shuddered. "I'll agree to your treaties, Dad. If it's all right with Liam."

"Liam will agree, and you'll help him."

"Of course I will, and you'll have a son for an heir." She'd meant it in a lighthearted way, and so Brian's anger surprised her.

He slapped the arm of his chair. "Is that what you think I'm doing this for? Listen, young lady. Liam is a good boy, but he'd rather learn about kings of old than be a king himself. He'll be a mediocre king, though he'd be a brilliant adviser, which is what I thought he'd be to you one day." Brian jumped from his chair, punched the top of it, and began pacing. "No, you're the stuff thrones are made of, girl. I don't like this third treaty one bit, but unless Jack can find a way around it, we'll have to agree to it."

Talty sat stunned. Though she'd seen the volatile Boru temper often— and had displayed it herself on occasion—her father's sudden fury shocked her. "I'm sorry, Dad. I didn't mean it that way. I was only trying to lighten things up."

The sparks vanished as quickly as they'd appeared. Brian slowly shook his head. "I'm sorry too, Tal. I'm a mediocre king myself, I'm afraid. Just promise me you'll look after your brother."

"I always have. I always will."

Jack smacked his pipe against the palm of his hand. "Then you're all right with this marriage treaty, Talty?"

She decided she was. "Yes, Uncle. What do we do next?"

Her father sat and found his spoon. "Finish lunch. Then we'll call the English ambassador."

Trusting as she had all her life in her father's gentle, reassuring tone, Talty believed it would all work out.

✳ ✳ ✳ ✳ ✳

The village of Howth sits on the northern cusp of the crescent that forms Dublin Bay. Upscale shops and restaurants line the main street. Fishing trawlers bob in the water beside a private yacht club. Splendid homes adorn the small peninsula, from the waterfront to the top of Howth Head, a lofty bluff that overlooks the Irish Sea. Foremost among these grand abodes is Garrymuir, a majestic estate that had been in the Boru family for generations. Prince Peadar, King Brian's only sibling, lived there now with his wife and two sons.

A special wing of Garrymuir housed an airy gymnasium dedicated to training Ireland's next generation of Fianna. Neil Boru, Peadar's elder son, expected to join their elite ranks soon. While he waited for Talty to change, Neil stood beneath the skylights twirling his bata in practiced circles, swinging the lethal hardwood staff at imaginary enemies.

For years he and Talty had trained to become Fian warriors. Neil's father had paired the cousins as partners years before, after Neil had emerged as the only boy in the training class unafraid to trounce Talty.

Her midweek call had surprised him. Since her assignment to the *Alastrina*, Neil had only seen her on his weekend leaves from the Air Corps. Still, he'd had no trouble obtaining permission from his commanding officer to rearrange his flight-training schedule so he could take her to Garrymuir. Being the king's nephew had its privileges.

"Ready, Neil?" Talty marched in from the lockers dressed in padded workout clothes, as was he. She hefted a six-foot bata from a rack.

A pretty enough girl, he thought, though thin to the point of being wiry. Her ivory skin and auburn hair proclaimed her Boru heritage. Neil's own blue-black hair and azure eyes were constant reminders, at least to him, that he only bore his royal surname through the kindness of the man who'd married his mother shortly before his birth.

He stepped toward Talty. "*I'm* ready. You're not."

"What do you mean?"

Neil loved her tiny pout, the last vestige of the little girl who'd grown up with him and become one of his closest friends. "I mean this." He tugged her hair, a ritual he'd performed since their first training class, after a fellow Fian student had tried to defend himself against her by grabbing her chestnut locks and yanking too hard.

Pulling something from her pocket, she shook her head and ensnared her dark red tresses in a ponytail. "All right. Let's go."

She banged her bata three times on the floor, the signal to start. Neil approached her as he always did: with caution. His father's voice whispered in his ear: *A pretty little girl can kill you just as dead as a big, ugly man.*

Talty never began a training bout the same way twice. Today she started pacing. Neil concentrated, tried to sense her battle spirit, and barely managed to parry a lightning-fast shot to his chest. She jabbed her bata at his head. He had a split second to decide whether to ward a strike that might be a feint, or wait and parry the real attack.

Thwack! The blow might have broken his thigh if he hadn't deflected it. What was going on? He darted behind her.

She whirled to protect her back. Fury blazed in her chestnut eyes. He decided he'd better find out what was going on before he got hurt. "What's up, Tal? Uncle Brian got you flustered again? Taking it out on me again?"

"Nothing's up!" With a furious swing, she cracked her bata against his.

He countered the assault by a whisker. Talty would be a fine addition to the Banfianna, as the female Fianna were called. She might be lagging behind Neil—her royal duties had cut into her training time—but she knew her moves and possessed a strength that belied her slender form.

Thwack! Thwack!

Neil danced back, his bata raised in defense. "All right, Tal, what's wrong? Tell me before you kill me so I can die happy."

Thwack! "Nothing's wrong."

Her glistening eyes said otherwise. Neil flung his bata down, twisted hers from her hands, and slammed his thigh behind her knees.

She toppled in outrage to the shock-absorbent floor. "You big dope!"

Turning so she wouldn't see him grin, he sauntered to a nearby alcove and drew two bottles of mineral water from the mini-fridge. "You should learn the Fian motto, Tal."

"I know it as well as anyone!" She rolled to her feet and stomped after him. "'Truth in Our Hearts, Strength in Our Arms, Dedication to Our Promise!'"

He plunked himself down on the bench against the wall. "All right. Let's start with truth in your heart." Two quick twists removed the bottle caps, which he pitched them into a nearby wastebasket. He raised one bottle in a gesture of truce.

She accepted it and sat beside him. A swig of water seemed to calm her down. "Thanks, Neily. You're always looking after me."

"It's my duty to look after you. I'm your Shivail."

"An honorary title you take far too seriously. I can look after myself."

"My father's always taught me to protect you. 'As long as you live, neither for gold nor for any other reward in the world abandon one you are pledged to protect.'"

"You're full of Fian mottoes today. How about this? 'A pig's arse, and that's pork.'"

He pretended to be shocked. "That's not a Fian motto."

She drew the bottle to her smiling lips and chugged. "Get a life, Neil. You have more to do than baby-sit me. You're going to be the best pilot the Air Corps ever had." The pride in her voice pleased him. "And then there's the girls."

"What girls?" He couldn't keep from grinning.

"Truth in our hearts, Neily. I've heard how you and our rascally cousin Aidan have the girls swooning all over Ireland." She poked his shoulder. "Strength in our arms."

"How about you, Lady Princess, off on a ship full of randy sailors?"

Her cheeks blazed. That such a strong young woman could blush so easily had always amused Neil. "I'm not interested in such things, Neil Boru. Anyway, it wouldn't matter if I had tons of lovers. I'm to marry Thomas Wessex."

Neil froze, unsure he'd heard correctly. "Thomas Wessex? He's the King of England."

"Aren't you a feckin' genius." She drank until her bottle was empty.

"I don't believe it. You can't marry Thomas Wessex. He's...he's not well."

"That means nothing in the grand scheme of world politics." She swatted a tear away.

Unsure what to do, he leaned toward her. "Don't cry, Tal."

"I am *not* crying!"

"No." A gulp of water hid another smile. "That would be ridiculous. Can't you refuse?"

"I could have, but I didn't. I want to do it. If I marry Thomas, I won't be Crown Princess anymore."

"What? How can you not be Crown Princess anymore?"

Talty explained the treaties, and how Geoffrey Wessex had insisted she relinquish her title to her brother Liam. Her declaration that she hated her "king lessons" and despised sitting about like a delicate doll while everyone else had all the fun astonished him.

"So I agreed," she said. "But as I thought about it, I felt like a cow being sold at the fair. I love my father, but sometimes I wish I were someone else's daughter."

She was afraid, though she'd never admit it. Neil set his water down and squeezed her hands. "Your father would never hurt you, and no one's going to harm you while I'm around."

"This politics stuff is all codology." She sighed and slipped her hands from his.

"Arranged marriages between England and Ireland are nothing new. My father was supposed to marry Claudia Wessex, remember?"

Talty's quicksilver temperament cast its spell. Like sunshine bursting from behind a dark cloud, a smile lit her face—and Neil's heart.

"But he didn't." She pecked his cheek. "The smartest thing your father ever did was marry your mother and adopt you the day you were born."

Her unwitting reminder that he wasn't a born Boru overshadowed the compliment. He tugged a wayward wisp of her hair. "Come on, Tal. Let's get changed for dinner."

CHAPTER THREE

A Thorny Wedding

In the clothing-strewn dressing room of an upscale hotel's penthouse suite, Roger Wessex assessed his muscular physique in a gilded mirror. Not bad for a man approaching thirty-five, he thought. He'd make a fine show at the wedding. His military haircut had grown out, and his light brown hair appeared more regal in the new style. He decided he'd keep it.

The hotel's central air conditioning battled the rare June heat wave baking Dublin. The gentle hum from the vents blended with the opera music serenading Roger and his former army colleague and closest friend, Philip Leverington. The reverse image of Philip's prematurely gray hair in the mirror reassured Roger that his plan would succeed.

"Why is a king a king simply because of his birth, Philip? We're not the only ones who want Thomas off the throne."

Philip helped Roger into his dinner jacket and picked lint from the lapel. Whether seeing that Roger's nails were buffed or negotiating for illegal arms, Philip looked after Roger well. "You mustn't be bitter. Thomas won't last forever." Philip's hooded eyes scrutinized the outfit.

A quick shrug settled the jacket properly on Roger's shoulders. "He's lasted too long already. Then we go from dumbnuts Thomas to John the genius. We should strike while the throne is in transition. If only I had more time. And money. Guns are so tediously expensive."

"Patience, Roger. The timing will work well, you'll see."

Roger pivoted to check his back in the mirror. "I still can't believe Uncle Geoffrey is stooping to dickering with the Irish over oil wells. I've never understood why he insists on doing things by the book when he could take more direct and effective action. Andrew is disgusted with him. Hand me the blue cummerbund. I think it would add the proper touch."

Holding the jacket aside, Philip helped Roger fasten the garment around his waist. "You're right. It's perfect."

Roger agreed. "Thank you for your help, my friend. I want to look my best for Cousin Thomas's wedding."

"I can't believe we're really doing this." Philip donned his own dinner jacket and straightened his black bow tie. "Do you think he understands what you told him about marriage?"

As Roger admired his image one last time, he imagined himself in a king's attire. "Oh, yes. It took some persistence to get through to the poor cretin, but I'm confident he now has a thorough understanding of his wedding night responsibilities. Shall we go?"

* * * * *

Helicopters bearing the call letters of Ireland's news stations hovered over the single granite spire of St. Columcille's Cathedral. Ignoring the jostling horde of onlookers, a steady stream of royalty and international celebrities alighted from limousines and paraded into the medieval church between a military honor guard and a circle of police barriers.

When the limousine bearing the king and his daughter arrived, a roar of cheers erupted from the crowd. Grateful for their affection, Talty maneuvered from the car in her stiff white wedding gown. She stood in the warm Dublin sunshine, hefting her bridal bouquet in one arm and waving with the other.

Splendid in his full dress naval uniform, her father waved with her. At last, he tapped her arm. She turned as quickly as the weighty dress allowed. Afraid she might trip on the train, or on her ridiculously long bridal veil, she gripped Brian's proffered arm. Together they climbed the church stairs.

Inside the foyer, a party of six Boru bridesmaids in a rainbow of gowns waited beneath stained-glass windows. No King's Piper would lead them down the aisle today. Geoffrey Wessex had deemed the Irish Great Pipes inappropriate for the marriage of an English king. To preserve good will, Brian had agreed. Talty hadn't, though she'd bowed to her father's wishes. The solemn organ music that accompanied the procession into the church offended her Irish pride.

Though no stranger to public scrutiny, she cringed at the ocean of staring eyes. The statues perched amid the tombs and plaques seemed to peer down at her. What was she doing? She'd always thought that when she married one day, she'd marry a man she loved. As if he sensed her hesitation, Brian squeezed her arm. She squeezed back, rearranged her bridal bouquet, and sought comfort in her roses.

In a centuries-old family tradition, the Borus planted a rosebush to mark the birth of each child born into the clan. The pink Princess Taillte roses bred especially for Talty not only rode in glory on her arm today, they graced every altar in the church. She inhaled the flowers' spicy perfume and stared straight ahead at the archbishop waiting at the altar—and at the grinning young man beside him.

She had met Thomas Wessex only once, at an engagement party thrown by his family at London's Southwick Castle. The stocky young king had been pleasant enough, and had proudly shown her his tabletop battlefield of soldier-dolls dressed as Crusaders and Saracens. The few words he'd spoken had sounded rehearsed—and he'd never stopped grinning.

He was still grinning, standing at the high altar wearing some sort of faux-military suit and a diamond neck order. Except for that grin, he looked like the king he was.

Despite the heat, Talty shivered. Only when she and her father reached the pews filled with familiar faces—she made no attempt to scan the groom's side of the church—did she breathe more easily.

In the front rows, her closest family members offered fond smiles. Peadar Boru, the big, bearded bear of an uncle she adored, held hands with Peggy, his spirited wife. In the row behind them, Neil and Kevin stood raven-haired and handsome, looking more like twins than half-brothers. They all offered encouraging smiles, and Neil's quick wink did wonders for Talty's spirits.

In the front row, her brother Liam stood beside their mother. The blond-haired, blue-eyed Eileen Mandeville Boru bore little resemblance to either of her redheaded children, though Liam seemed to have inherited her serene demeanor. Talty and Eileen couldn't be more different, yet they were friends who'd soon be speaking, as Eileen had joked that morning, queen to queen. Eileen's lip quivered now, but Liam stood straight and tall, his usual mischievous grin buried in his public mask.

Talty smiled bravely at them and realized that she and her father had reached the end of their formal walk. She curtsied to her king, as was proper, though it was her father who smiled and kissed her cheek before he joined his wife and son.

On her own now, Talty clutched her bouquet and stepped up to the altar. All through the long, grueling ceremony she stole little glances at Thomas. His grin never wavered, and he seemed oblivious to the proceedings. When at last the archbishop called out, "I pronounce you husband and wife," the finality of what Talty had done hit her like a two-ton anchor gouging the ocean bed.

Horrified that she had to guide Thomas down the stairs, she held his arm as loosely as she could and led the bridal party down the aisle. The organ music she despised kept everyone but Thomas in step. Again she sought the comfort of her roses, breathing in their spicy fragrance until she stood outside the cathedral, where limousines waited to convey the bridal party to the reception.

* * * * *

In Clontarf Castle's bustling kitchen, Daisy Cleary donned the black and white uniform of the royal catering company and began polishing trays. She'd spent more than twenty years looking after Ireland's royal family, and she'd grown to resent it. Why should a spoiled young girl receive such attention when Daisy herself had been forced to work so hard?

She set down her cloth and sighed. Princess Taillte didn't deserve her ill will. The years Daisy had spent looking after her bedridden mother had worn her out, that's all. Her guilt at the relief she'd felt when the old woman died the month before hadn't lasted long. Once the solicitors settled the estate, Daisy would heft no more trays of champagne and hors d'oeuvres. For the first time in her life, she felt free.

* * * * *

Built by the order of the first Brian Boru to memorialize his victory over the Vikings, Clontarf Castle endured on Dublin Bay's northwest coast. The old stone fortress, a medieval jewel set in a ring of mature trees and gardens a short distance from the Clontarf Yacht Club, had always been the Boru clan's favorite gathering place.

Electric light glowed from crystal chandeliers and iron wall sconces now, yet the great hall's granite walls still displayed their original tapestries. Despite the addition of central heat, wood burning hearths still warmed many chambers. The old stone steps, deliberately laid at random intervals to thwart attacking swordsmen, still tripped those unfamiliar with their irregular slope. And all over the castle, hidden doorways still led to the secret passages where Talty and her brother and cousins had played as children.

Hundreds of formally attired guests took their seats in the great hall. Talty sat at the head table between her parents and Thomas Wessex. Her mother shot her a reassuring smile and tapped her own cheek, the signal to remind Talty to smile.

Her father stood and lifted a glass of sparkling champagne. When the murmuring crowd grew silent, his deep voice rang through the hall.

"Dear family, dear guests. Eileen and I thank you all for coming. We're in high hopes that this wedding will mark the beginning of an even deeper friendship between England and Ireland. The motto of the Boru clan is old: 'The Strong Hand Rules.' But my father told me once: 'There is no strength without unity.' Treasured clan, dear friends, may our hands be ever united, and may the blessing of each day be the blessing we need most." He raised his glass to Talty.

She beamed proudly at him and acknowledged a round of polite applause—one in which the ever-smiling King of England did not participate. Brian's words reaffirmed Talty's sense of clan, a sense strong enough to overcome any political ploy. All would be well.

After a succulent dinner of roast beef, salmon, and countless side dishes, the diners retired to various lounges while the catering staff cleared the hall for dancing. Soon strains of music beckoned everyone back to the hall.

At any family gathering Talty had ever attended, the tail of the day brought the loud, hard kicking reels and jigs that were the soul of the clan. Tonight, out of deference to guests unfamiliar with the traditional dances, the Borus would two-step and foxtrot. They'd even forego the magnificent, roof-rattling Siege of Dublin, the grand set dance that commemorated the first King Brian's victory over the Vikings in 1014.

Talty endured several starchy dances with members of the English nobility. After an awkward waltz with Prince John, her shy new brother-in-law, her godfather came to her rescue. Kieran Dacey gracefully danced her through a simple two-step that gave her a chance to catch her breath. His six-foot-plus frame, still solid though he'd passed his forty-fifth birthday, cast an air of protection wherever he went.

As head of Ireland's Intelligence Sector, Kieran arranged the royal family's security. He was Jack Dacey's son, Brian's first cousin—their hair was the same dark red—and one of Talty's personal heroes. Not only had he encouraged her to join the Fianna, he'd inspired her to serve with International Security Forces, as he had.

In his early twenties, he'd done a tour of duty with an ISF peacekeeping mission in North Africa. During a mortar attack that had left one side of his face torn from cheek to chin, he'd saved another man's life. Brian had pinned the Medal for Gallantry on his collar for it. Kieran wore it now, beside his Fianna pin.

He smiled at her, and his hawk-like eyes, ever on guard, softened. So did the jagged scar on his jaw. "How are you holding up after such a long day?"

"I'm running out of steam," she said, "but I expect I'll last the night. The English are an odd lot, aren't they?"

"They are," he agreed, "and you've been gracious enough to them. We'll keep you occupied for the rest of the night."

She wondered what he meant, though she didn't have to wonder for long. The dance ended, but he stayed with her until a waltz began, and then she found herself in the perfectly poised arms of her brother Liam. He spun her into a hidden alcove and stopped.

The gleam of mischief Talty knew so well shone in his myopic brown eyes, fortified today by contact lenses instead of the gold-rimmed glasses he preferred. "I thought you could use a respite from the dancing, Tal."

"You thought right. Thanks. It isn't even the dancing, y'know? I had to wear all this Lady Muck wedding stuff"—she waved her hands over her opulent gown—"because Geoffrey Wessex said it was a formal occasion, as if we didn't know what that meant."

"You look fine in that dress." He held his breath, pretending to choke. "Too bad you can't breathe in it."

Talty laughed and thought that Liam looked fine himself. Though a year younger, he towered over her. Not a strand of his chestnut hair was out of place. His signature rose, the off-white Alba, graced the lapel of his black dinner jacket. Brilliant, kind, and delightfully witty, Liam was Talty's coconspirator, the ally who understood what being a royal child entailed.

Suddenly Aidan Dacey, Kieran's high-spirited son, stepped from behind Liam. "Why, the dress is only as lovely as the princess it contains!" Aidan snatched Talty's hand and kissed it. "Forgive me, Beauty. I meant, as lovely as the *queen* it contains. I'm privileged, mere mortal that I am, to be basking in the glow of such divine splendor."

"What codology, Aidan Dacey! Give me back my hand!" Talty yanked her hand away, though she gazed fondly at her roguish cousin. He'd inherited his father's ginger hair and cinnamon eyes, though Aidan's hair was a lighter red. Despite his propensity for blarney—he wore the aptly named Yellow Rascal rose in his lapel—Aidan was a gentleman, an athlete who'd trained for years with her and Neil to be a Fian warrior.

"Where's Neil?" She looked for him, her special cousin, sworn from childhood to protect her. A tap on her shoulder announced his arrival. She turned and smiled at him. He smiled back, dazzling in his black silk suit. His dark good looks counterpointed the auburn hair of the Borus around him. His signature rose, the deep red Ace of Hearts, gleamed on his lapel.

Enjoying the conspiracy, Talty eyed her brother and cousins. Only Kevin was missing. "I suppose Kevin will be along any minute?"

As if on cue, Kevin wobbled into the crowded alcove, a crystal beer mug in his hand, his apricot Derry Rose askew on his jacket. "Waltzes, waltzes, and more waltzes. I've never seen such a dull party in my life! When are we going to start *dancing*?"

Neil wrenched the glass from his brother's hand. "You've had enough."

"Kevin's right," Aidan said. "We need a good dance. I don't think our English guests like to have fun."

"I don't think they like us much, either," Liam added. "Earlier my father stopped the chef to tell him what a fine job he'd done with the dinner. I overheard some fella named Mayne say how disgraceful it was that a king would let himself be seen speaking to a servant. I'd love to see the look on Mr. Mayne's face when the old fella starts dancing with them!"

Aidan lifted a glass from a passing tray and sampled the wine. "I suppose they wanted King Thomas married in *veddy* proper English style. Still, this has to be the stuffiest wedding I've ever seen. Anything would be better than the rigor mortis we've been subjected to today."

"To remedy the situation," Kevin said, pointing a finger in the air, "I've set up a sound system in the basement. Our cousins and friends are waiting. Change out of that concrete dress and join us, Tal."

Talty shook her head. "I can't get away. Everyone's looking for me."

Just then, the Queen Mother, Deirdre Boru, glided toward them, regal in a silvery gown that matched her pinned up hair. A hint of the doting smile she reserved for her grandchildren and grandnephew fluttered over her lips. "What are you rascals up to?"

Aidan's eyes grew as round as an angel's. "Nothing, Auntie Dee. Just wishing Talty all the best."

"Horsetails!" Deirdre folded her slender arms. "Your parents don't call the five of you a band of roses for nothing. I overheard your party plans"— her indulgent gaze took them all in—"and I intend to help."

Talty's heart filled with affection for her grandmother. "You're a love, Grannie. But how can we do it?"

Deirdre bent her head. Intrigue tinged her lowered voice. "You're exhausted, Talty. You want to retire. I'll offer to sit with you. We'll get you out of that horrid dress, and you can slip down the secret staircase. I'll deny any collaboration in the matter, so be sure none of you are caught."

Delighted with the plan, Talty made the rounds, bidding her family and guests good-night in her most courtly manner. Much to her relief, Thomas was nowhere in sight. Impromptu honor guards Neil and Aidan escorted her upstairs to the changing room reserved for the bride, where Talty's lifelong aide, a plain young woman named Jenna, waited to help remove the cumbersome wedding dress.

Deirdre slipped into the room. "We'll get that gown off straightaway. Jenna, go to Talty's rooms and get her some suitable dancing attire."

Talty lifted the hated white skirt and kicked off her heels so fast they flew across the room. She'd done it! Done her duty and rid herself of her repressive Crown Princess title. Now she could relax—and dance! "My blue pantsuit, Jen. And the black strap pumps with the suede soles."

Smiling in understanding, the young woman hurried out. Deirdre lifted a hairbrush from the vanity and motioned for Talty to sit. As she often had, Talty plopped down and surrendered to her grandmother's soothing touch.

A rap at the door broke the spell. Before either woman could respond, Thomas Wessex entered the room, mumbling and grinning his perpetual grin. Talty gasped and sprang to her feet.

Her grandmother puffed with indignation. "What are you doing here, sir? Where are your minders?"

Thomas neither responded nor stopped. His mumbling grew clearer as he approached.

"Why, he's telling you a poem, love." Deirdre relaxed and set the hairbrush down. "There's no harm. It sounds as if he's practiced for weeks, poor fellow. We'll let him say his poem. Then I'll call his minders."

Thomas stepped closer, reciting what sounded like a lover's declaration of devotion. When he was within arms' reach of Talty, he raised his hand as if to touch her cheek.

Because she cringed, she didn't see the dagger until after he'd stabbed her twice. An explosion of pain drove her to her knees. Her hands flew to her chest. Blood pulsed over her crisp white wedding gown.

Deirdre screamed and ran to the door. Just as she reached it, two men burst in. English men. Talty had danced with one of them. His name was Roger. Roger Wessex. He'd been nice. He'd help her.

Roger jerked the dagger from Thomas and slapped his face. "You really are hopeless, Thomas. You can't do anything right." Thomas mewled like a frightened child.

"Talty is hurt!" cried Deirdre. "Get help!"

Roger's hand shot toward Deirdre's throat. Blood gushed over the dagger. Deirdre collapsed to the floor in a lifeless heap, a look of utter astonishment on her face.

"Let's get it done," Roger said, sounding bored.

He intended to finish what Thomas had started, but Talty didn't want to die. Tears blurred Roger's approach, yet she knew when he was near enough.

"No!" she cried. Hurt as she was, she clawed at him, fighting for her life.

His cold-blooded detachment erupted into rage when she struck him. He attacked in a frenzy, cutting her again and again.

She cried out once more. Then there was nothing.

CHAPTER FOUR

Controlled Chaos

The door of a private office at St. Brigit's Hospital opened. Brian's grip on Eileen's hand tightened. He stared stupidly at the sparse metal furniture and dingy green walls, unable to focus on the exhausted face of the trauma surgeon whose words were breaking his heart.

"I'm sorry, sir," the doctor said in a faraway voice. "We've done all we can. If you'd like to call the priest..."

Eileen wept. Fighting back tears himself, Brian held her close and steeled himself. "I want to see her," he said.

Hand in hand, they followed the surgeon to the waiting area, where Brian's aunt Nuala sat near a rain-spattered window with Jack. Breege Dacey, Kieran's wife, sat with them. Peadar's wife Peggy sat crying next to Kevin. Face averted, Liam leaned against the wall.

Brian approached Jack. "Where are Peadar and Kieran?"

"Seeing to Deirdre's arrangements." Jack's voice croaked when he spoke.

"Aidan and Neil?" Brian asked.

His uncle nodded toward a nearby door. "Inside with Talty. The doctors won't allow more than two of us in at a time."

"Neil says it was his fault," sobbed Peggy. "He was her protector."

Brian crossed the room and slid his arms around her. "She'd already be gone if not for Neil and Aidan."

Deirdre's scream had brought the boys running back to the bridal room. They'd torn sheets from the bed and ripped off their shirts to stem the horrible bleeding. Shaking off the gruesome memory of his mother's maimed corpse, Brian stepped into Talty's hospital room.

Beeps and blips from the jungle of medical equipment taunted him.

Aidan stood on one side of it. His clothes were wrinkled. His ginger hair needed combing. He nodded when Brian came in, peering through swollen eyes that begged for a word of hope.

Unable to offer any, Brian glanced at his gauze-enshrouded daughter and saw her dressed in her blood-soaked wedding dress. Distraught, he shook his head to banish the image.

Neil sat beside the bed holding Talty's hand. Uneven patches of black stubble covered his cheeks and chin. His red-rimmed eyes focused on Brian. "I'm sorry, Uncle Brian. I'm not a good protector."

"Don't do that to yourself, Neil. If anyone's to blame... Both of you go and get some rest. I'll sit with her a while."

After the boys left, Brian forced his gaze to the bandages covering Talty's ruined face. He slid his hand over her still white fingers and closed his eyes.

"Please forgive me, Talty."

✳ ✳ ✳ ✳ ✳

Roger Wessex lifted a crystal decanter from the bar in his hotel suite and filled two tumblers with whiskey. "Uncle Geoffrey is appalled that Thomas could have perpetrated such a horrendous crime. Thomas knows he did something wrong, though he doesn't know what." Roger smiled. "Just as I planned." He touched his glass to Philip's, and both men sipped. The whiskey warmed Roger from mouth to belly.

The lines on Philip's forehead deepened. "Will the Irish allow Thomas to leave?"

"They can't detain him. He's incompetent to stand any legal proceeding. My sister Claudia is taking him home to seek medical attention for his despondency."

"And John?"

"The entire matter has befuddled poor John. Claudia is bringing him home too."

Philip let out a relieved breath. "All's well, then."

"This is only the beginning. Despite its unfortunate outcome, the marriage took place. We're entitled to the oil wells and everything else in our dear Talty's dowry. Now we'll have it all without the ignominy of a bogtrotting queen on our throne. My way is so much more effective than Uncle Geoffrey's, don't you think?"

Raising his glass to Roger, Philip smiled and sipped again. "Shall I pack?"

"Yes. Geoffrey wanted me to stay for Queen Deirdre's funeral. I insisted that Claudia couldn't manage both Thomas and John without my help."

"Queen Deirdre's funeral?" Philip started for the closet. "What about the princess? She must have succumbed to her injuries by now."

"Not as of an hour ago. That could be a problem. She saw what happened. We can't risk her surviving and proving Thomas innocent of his dreadful crimes. I think we should pay a sympathetic visit to the hospital and speed her on her final journey."

"What?" Holding the suitcase he'd just pulled from a shelf, Philip stood motionless. His puzzled expression amused Roger. "But how? People will be there. We can't just walk in and pull a plug."

"Do be optimistic, Philip. I always finish what I start. You'll distract whoever is there while I slip into her room." Roger downed his whiskey and smiled. "A pillow will leave no marks."

* * * * *

A little past midnight, the soles of Roger's handmade shoes whispered over the hospital floors. Philip's footsteps made no sound at all. Only an occasional muffled announcement over a distant loud speaker broke the silence. Well-dressed and aristocratic, Roger talked his way past the guards in the hall and the nurses at the intensive care station. He and Philip continued on as if they had every authority to do so.

Roger eyed the deserted waiting area with contempt. "The devoted family isn't even here. Keep watch for me, Philip. A moment is all I need."

He'd just reached the door to the girl's room when a black-haired young man toting a tray of beverages stepped into the hall. He set the tray on the nearest table. The undisguised hostility in his bearing caused Roger to step back. "What do you want here, Wessex?"

Angry with himself for allowing Neil Boru, not even a true Irish royal, to intimidate him, Roger held up his head and forced himself to be civil. "Good evening, sir. We find we must return to London. We wished to offer our condolences to your family before we go. Too bad about the girl."

Boru glared. "She might have been all right if you'd helped her."

"No one could have helped her. Indeed, we thought her already dead."

Boru's forearms rose. His fingers curled. "You didn't even try, you scut! You just stood there, afraid to get your fine quality hands soiled." He stepped toward Roger.

Bolstered by Philip's presence, Roger glowered at Boru. "Really, sir, I resent your tone. I've come to offer sympathy, not listen to the insults of a lowborn commoner. Anyway, it would have made no difference. The girl will die soon enough."

Boru swung. His fist smashed Roger's ribs. Roger had barely registered the assault when an elbow sent him tumbling against the wall. Too late,

Philip leapt to help. Boru sent him sprawling too.

Roger sat on the floor gasping for breath. An opening door drew his watery gaze.

Kieran Dacey stepped into the lounge from the girl's room. His scowl accented the jagged scar on his jaw. "What the hell is going on out here?"

Boru's frosty eyes never left Roger. "Nothing's going on. Lord Roger and his friend were just leaving."

Philip rolled to his feet and helped Roger up. Roger opened his mouth to denounce the attack, but stopped. The Irishmen's hostile glares left no doubt they'd joined forces against him.

"And with great pleasure," he said, "if this is the reception we receive for coming to offer our wishes for Princess Taillte's recovery."

Dacey's right eyebrow shot up. He scrutinized Roger for a long, nerve-wracking moment. "You're too late," he finally said. "She died a few minutes ago."

Roger could barely contain his delight. As for the insults he'd endured here tonight, the anguish on Neil Boru's face was almost all the revenge he could ever want.

✳ ✳ ✳ ✳ ✳

The church bells that had pealed for Talty's wedding now tolled the death knell. Outside the cathedral, Brian sat with Eileen in the same limousine that had transported him and Talty there only days before. He peered at the murky Dublin sky, black with pending rain. But the rain held off, sympathizing, perhaps, with the brokenhearted kingdom.

Brian ordered the driver to start the somber cortege. The hearses rolled, bearing two rose-covered caskets—one of them empty—through winding, crowd-lined streets to the Clan Boru burial grounds north of the city.

That evening, Tara Hall hosted a grim reception. Cordial but reserved, Brian and Eileen thanked the hundreds of compassionate guests who'd come to Dublin for a wedding and stayed for a funeral.

Heads turned when Peadar Boru marched into the room. Dressed in a dark suit that offset his silver-flecked beard and moustache, he strode with a grace unusual in a man his size. He also wore a scowl so fierce, no one moved to greet him.

Kieran matched Peadar step for step, a tad taller, a shade leaner, and no less intimidating. Together they worked their way toward Brian.

He kissed Eileen's hand. "Excuse us, darlin'. It's time."

She responded with a ferocious smile: she agreed with what they were doing. Yet he couldn't smile back at her. Numbly, he led his brother and cousin to his fourth-floor suite, where Jack waited in a chair by the fire.

Brian slammed the door behind him. "Is he coming, Uncle Jack?"

"He's on his way. Too bad Roger slipped through our fingers."

Kieran punched the wall so hard the pictures shook. "That gobshite! Slithering in to offer his condolences in the middle of the night. I should've let Neil fry the little hog's turd altogether!"

Peadar's smile bore no humor. "From what you said, Neil gave him a good clipping anyway. The boy's instincts are good. Yours aren't bad either, Kieran. You bought us time."

"If I'd known then, I wouldn't have done it. I'd, why I'd—"

"You did what you thought best," Brian said. "We'll deal with Roger in time."

A brisk knock announced the arrival of Geoffrey Wessex. Dapper, cocksure, and emphatically inconvenienced, he stomped into the room. "You just caught me, gentlemen. My private jet is waiting at the airport. How may I assist you?"

Brian's cheeks burned. Struggling to contain his rage, he said nothing.

"By understanding this," Peadar said, growling like the bear he resembled. "Your marriage treaty is in the cesspit."

Geoffrey glanced from Peadar to Brian to Jack. His different-colored eyes narrowed with suspicion. "What do you mean? I'm as appalled as anyone by my nephew's unspeakable actions, but we acted in good faith. The marriage took place—"

"We've annulled the marriage," Jack said from his chair.

"That's impossible!" Geoffrey spun on Brian. "Regrettable as it might be, your daughter died a married woman. You can't annul a marriage after one of the parties has died. We're entitled to the dowry!"

Brian's nails dug into the palms of his hands. "My daughter was alive when I ordered the annulment. She lived long enough to tell us it wasn't Thomas who attacked her and my mother, but your nephew, Roger."

"Roger?" Geoffrey stood stunned. "I don't believe it. It was Thomas!"

Peadar's fists swung ominously. "Was it? Even if Thomas had the sense to draw the guards from their posts, he'd need help to hit them from behind and lock them in a closet."

"Where is Roger?" Kieran asked.

"You know very well he escorted Thomas home to London days ago."

"Send for him," Peadar said.

"So you can accuse a Wessex of murder?" Geoffrey raised his chin and eyed Peadar up and down. "I'll do no such thing! You can't level your ridiculous charges at anyone unless they're on Irish soil. Really, I resent this interrogation!"

Brian shoved Geoffrey against the wall and twisted the collar of his overcoat. "Resent this, Geoffrey. If Roger ever sets foot on Irish soil again, we'll not only charge him with murder, we'll hang him, Wessex or not!"

Geoffrey squirmed in a futile effort to free himself. "You wouldn't dare. Why, you don't even have a death penalty in Ireland!"

"True," Jack said, as if he were discussing the weather. "Still, the king can condemn a convicted criminal to death if he so chooses. In this case, I expect he would so choose."

"Damn right I would!" Brian's grip on Geoffrey tightened. "One way or another, I'll smash the little gick like the slimy maggot he is!"

Again, Geoffrey tried to heave Brian away. "You're only trying to evade your legal obligations. Princess Taillte died a married woman. The marriage is valid!"

"The marriage is annulled! My daughter was never your queen. No marriage, no oil wells. But you give us Roger, and maybe we'll make a new deal." Brian released Geoffrey and wiped his hands on his own suit jacket.

"How dare you touch me, sir!" Geoffrey huffed, brushing himself off. "Since there's no chance of discussing the matter civilly, I suggest you prepare for another round of visits to the World Court. We'll see about your attempts to invalidate lawful treaties."

"We're only invalidating the marriage treaty," Brian said. "We keep Fargan."

"Keep your miserable rock, for all the good it will do you." With a toss of his head, Geoffrey fled the room.

After the door slammed, Jack pulled out his pipe and held it as if he were praying. "He's right about one thing, boys. Unless Roger's on Irish soil, we can't indict him for anything, and England won't extradite any English citizen facing a death penalty."

"The cacks on the man!" Brian roared. "Thinking he could simply walk in and hurt Talty. As if he hadn't hurt her enough already."

Leather creaked as Kieran plopped into the chair beside Jack. "He can't hurt her anymore, Brian. She's safe for now—and she's a strong girl."

Peadar took a third chair. "We'll get Roger in time. Kieran's idea has a few flaws, but it will work if we keep our heads."

Brian pounded the wall beside the mantle and kicked the nearest chair. "The devil take my eyes if I ever understand how I let the three of you talk me into this mare's nest!"

CHAPTER FIVE

Suitable Arrangements

High over the Scottish Highlands, a bird of prey drifted on currents of air. Talty shielded her eyes from the sun to watch. Envious of the bird's freedom, she wondered what kind it was. She'd read about raptors. She'd read about so many things in the last six months. Books lay all over her hospital room, waiting to nourish her hungry mind.

A quick knock sounded behind her. Dressed in blue jeans and a light wool sweater that matched his azure eyes, Kevin stood in the doorway.

"Kevin! What a surprise!" Talty combed her fingers through hair damp from her shower and touched her face, hating the bandages on her ruined cheeks. This latest round of reconstructive surgery would be the last, the doctors had said. They'd done all they could.

Kevin looked so much like Neil, and yet so different. His ebony hair had more curl, his smile more boyish charm, and his eyes lacked the constant vigilance in Neil's. Though thrilled to see Kevin, Talty missed Neil.

Dragging a chair from a corner, Kevin explained how he'd come for a family birthday party. "We thought since we were in Inverness anyway, we'd stop by to see you. Neil and Aidan are downstairs parking the car."

"Neil and Aidan are here too?" Delighted, Talty shifted in her chair and arranged her robe to hide the dramatic amount of weight she'd lost. "And here I am with nothing to wear. I'll have the sister dry my hair." She reached for the call button.

Kevin touched her hand. "I can dry your hair for you, love. It really isn't much longer than my own, y'know? Why did they chop it off like that? Where's the dryer?"

She pointed to the bathroom. Soon the dryer's drone filled the room, and much to Talty's relief, masked the sound of her sniffling.

"What are you doing to her?" Aidan shouted from the doorway. He held a shopping bag overflowing with books. Neil stood grinning beside him. Both were dressed sweaters and jeans, though Talty wouldn't have cared if they'd come in spacesuits. She wiped her eyes and smiled.

From behind her, Kevin turned off the dryer. "I'm not doing anything, you big lug! I'm helping to get her hair dried, is all."

"Big feat!" Aidan tramped in and set the bag on a table. "She doesn't have much. What did they do to your hair, Beauty?"

After Kevin set the dryer down, he glanced at Talty. She hadn't wiped the tears away quickly enough. "What is it, Tal? Did I hurt you?"

"Oh, no." She dabbed at her eyes again. "It's nice to have someone touching me without poking me or prodding or sticking me with something." Aidan made a theatrical attempt to kiss her. "I don't see any tubes or wires. How will you get good radio reception? Where is there a bare spot for kissing, I wonder? Any place with no bandages?" He pecked her mouth with a quick cousin kiss. She rewarded him with a smile.

"That's better, Beauty. These fiendish Scottish nuns will chuck us out if they think we made you cry."

"I am *not* crying, Aidan Dacey! And I think you'd better find a new name for me."

"Ah, Lady Cousin, the beauty I'm referring to emanates from your very soul. We mere mortals can only stand back and be dazzled." He reached for the box of tissues on her bedside stand and held it for her.

She plucked a tissue from the box, dabbed one last time at her eyes, and shook her head. "Do you never stop being so daft, Aidan?"

"No," said Neil and Kevin together.

Neil moved in beside her then. He held onto her hand after he'd kissed it. The pain in his fine blue eyes disturbed her. Since they'd been children, he'd taken his duties as her Shivail seriously, had always watched over her. She could only imagine how he must feel each time he saw her now.

"Kieran says you'll be coming home soon," he said.

Home. After six long months. But who'd want to look at her? She pulled her hand from Neil's.

Aidan put the tissues back. "You're healing fast, Beauty. Look how—"

"Don't call me that! I'm a fright, and it isn't just my hair. You haven't seen my face without the bandages. I have. I'll have to hide all my life."

"No, you won't, and I'll call you what I please. We'll take you to one of those fairy doctors in the country. He'll put a bag around your neck with a few spider webs in it, and maybe some dried dragon's blood and a donkey ear or two. You'll be prettier than ever, and dancing with everyone before you know it."

He ruffled her hair, and she smiled sheepishly at him. "Sorry, Aid. Find some chairs and sit down, all of you. Catch me up on the latest gossip. Tell me how you and Liam are doing at law school, Kev." She smiled at Neil and Aidan. "And I want to know all about the Military College you two rascals are turning upside down."

"How did you know?" Aidan asked with round, innocent eyes.

For the next half hour, they talked and laughed. The boys left Talty in good spirits, but that night, she cried herself to sleep.

* * * * *

Fresh from a routine kickboxing session, Roger Wessex left his private club and waved his driver on. He wanted to walk today. He did his best thinking while walking, and today he had much on his mind. Humming a favorite opera tune, he raised his collar against the December drizzle and crossed the park.

A month had passed since Thomas had at long last succumbed to his illness, and Geoffrey had reneged on his promise to support Roger's claim to the throne. Roger had bitten his tongue and publicly sworn his allegiance to his dimwitted cousin John. It seemed Geoffrey had no intention of relinquishing the power he'd come to enjoy as Regent. He would regret his betrayal.

Just last night, Roger had dined with Andrew. They'd discussed their plan to usurp King John, a plan that would succeed now that Andrew's recent promotion to Staff Admiral had given him access to critical naval resources. They only had to keep outwitting Geoffrey. A few details still required attention, but things were moving along well.

"Lord Roger! Here you are."

The raspy voice had always annoyed Roger. He glanced behind him. MI6 Chief Bert Benson was strolling toward him.

"Benson. What do you want?"

"Prince Geoffrey is asking for you, sir." Benson, a lanky man with thinning hair, raised a lit cigarette to his lips.

Roger's nose wrinkled in disgust. "Put out the cigarette."

Benson bared his yellowed teeth in a semi-smile and blew smoke through his nostrils. He tossed the cigarette to the ground and crushed it beneath his foot. "A filthy habit, sir. I try my best to stop, but I'm a terror when I do." He waved his arm. "If you please, sir."

Assuming an air of indifference, Roger followed Benson to a waiting limousine. They reached Southwick Castle a quarter hour later. Benson escorted Roger to Prince Geoffrey's private study and left.

Roger seldom visited his uncle these days, though each time he did, the clutter in the room repulsed him. Today would be no different. He closed the door behind him.

Geoffrey sat at his desk reading food-stained reports and nibbling meat pasties. He looked up, set the papers aside, and smiled. "Roger! How delightful to see you. Sit. Have a glass of wine. We have things to discuss."

Settling into the chair before the desk, Roger poured himself some wine and swirled his glass, enjoying the burgundy's ruby red tones. "Whatever is it now, Uncle?"

"I've been hearing disturbing things about you. 'Lord Roger is planning to usurp the throne. He means to overthrow his cousin John and have himself declared king.'"

Roger's fingers tightened around the glass. Who could have betrayed him? No one. Had he underestimated his uncle's spies? No. Geoffrey was guessing. "Really, Uncle. I know you consider me a bother, but you're talking about treason."

"Yes, and civil war perhaps." Geoffrey's pleasant tone belied the gravity of his words. "It's so tiresome having a disgruntled member of the royal family trying to oust the lawful king."

He selected another pasty and chomped. His different-colored eyes gleamed like those of a cat toying with a mouse. He wasn't guessing.

Roger would seek out and crush the informer. For now, he would bluff it out. "Who's been telling you these fairy tales? Benson?"

"I'll let you wonder about that. Let's just say it would be in your best interest to cease your subversive activities."

"Really, Uncle—"

Geoffrey leaned forward and pointed his fork at Roger. "Listen, boy. We must abide by our agreements with foreign countries. Proper treaties don't happen overnight. They take a great deal of work."

Roger set his wineglass down. "You and your proper treaties. Six months have passed, and we still don't have those oil wells. We should have seized them instead of stooging about while some foreign court decides our fate. We're entitled to that dowry."

"And we'll have it, but we must move with sensitivity out of respect for our dear, departed Taillte." Sensitivity forgotten, Geoffrey speared another pasty.

"So the girl had a sticky finish. Why should we forfeit our due simply because Thomas became overzealous with his bride?"

Grinning widely enough to reveal the gold caps on his molars—and the food stuck between them—Geoffrey leaned on his elbows and dangled his fork. "Shall we tell the Borus how you helped with his overzealousness?"

What? Only Philip knew about that, and Philip wouldn't...

"Let me tell you something, boy. Something I've kept to myself these past few months. Something I wanted to save until I needed it. I've been keeping tabs on your friend Philip's travels back and forth to the continent to buy guns. Perhaps what I'm going to say will make you return those guns and get your money back." Leering now, Geoffrey set his fork on the desk and sat back like a glutted swine. "It seems before Princess Taillte died, she named *you* her murderer, and the murderer of Deirdre Boru."

"That's a lie!"

"Is it?"

Heart pounding, Roger heard Geoffrey's gleeful description of his meeting with King Brian and his kinsmen after the funerals. Geoffrey ended the dissertation with a sinister chuckle. "I'd really hate to see you hang, Roger."

Roger stood. His quivering hands enraged him further. "This is pure slander. If you think I'm going to carry the can for Thomas—"

"You had no idea I knew anything about it, did you? You're arrogant enough to believe you can get away with it. If I were to leak this little scandal, you'd be ruined, guilty or not."

"You wouldn't!"

"Try me. Stop your scheming *now*, boy."

"John is incompetent. He might not be a slobbering imbecile like Thomas—"

"John might be slow, but he can grasp an idea if it's explained to him properly. I believe you found the same true of Thomas when you taught him to wield a knife."

Roger flung his wine against the wall. The glass exploded. Burgundy splattered everywhere. He stormed from the room, leaving Geoffrey chuckling behind him.

* * * * *

A turf fire blazed in the den of the King's Residence. Phantoms lurked in the dancing flames, bewitching Brian until Kieran's voice pulled him from his ugly reverie.

"All right, Brian?"

Brian rubbed his eyes. "Sorry, lads. Where were we?"

Peadar poured himself more brandy. "We were discussing updating our security to ensure Talty's safety when she comes home." He tilted the bottle toward Brian's snifter.

Brian shook his head. "I should be shouting from the rooftop that my daughter is coming home, not trying to hide her like some—"

"Things will fall into place." Peadar's gruff voice rumbled with kindness. "Don't forget. You aren't alone in this."

"I never forget." Brian smiled. "You two don't let me. All right, who do we have?"

"Our best bet is Mamoru Services," Kieran said. "A Japanese company that recently opened an office down in Blackrock. The CEO owns different companies. Computers, helicopters, even a sports team. His specialty is telecommunications security."

Brian stifled a yawn. "Talk to them, Kieran."

"I'll be on it first thing." Kieran rose and bade his cousins good-night.

* * * * *

Eric Yamada had come to Ireland to supervise the start-up of his latest hobby, Mamoru Services, Ltd. He couldn't have chosen a better springboard to ensure his company's success in the European market. Ireland's tax benefits, dependable work force, and friendly business environment overruled any other choice.

Eric ducked beneath the window frame to admire the view from his newest office. He'd acquired his height from his Canadian mother, his dark hair from his Japanese father, and his business savvy from a desperate need to prove to the censorious Japanese society in which he lived that he was more than just a half-breed.

He'd found that Ireland and its amiable people appealed to the western half of his heritage. Already he'd purchased a house in Malahide, a small coastal town north of Dublin, so he could feel at home whenever he visited.

Behind him, his business manager and friend, Kiyoshi Sasaki, waited for him to finish his contemplation. Eric turned from the window and followed Kiyoshi to the nearby room that served as a dojo, the workout room that his offices all over the world included.

Dressed in pajama-like white training outfits with black cloth belts around their waists, Eric and Kiyoshi bowed and began their exercises. At the end of the hour-long session, they bowed again, changed into western business suits, and prepared to review the day's agenda.

His assistant's knock drew Eric's attention from his notes. "What is it, Keiko?"

"A gentleman named Kieran Dacey wishes to see you, sir. He had no

36

appointment."

Eric glanced at Kiyoshi. They knew who Kieran Dacey was.

"Bring the gentleman in."

✳ ✳ ✳ ✳ ✳

Kieran scolded himself when the young woman made the introductions. Expecting Eric Yamada to be Japanese, his attention had been on the Asian man. Having had much practice with blunders involving prejudgment, Kieran recovered with grace.

As he shook Yamada's hand, he assessed the man. Yamada was only forty, yet silver dusted his dark brown hair. Nearly as tall as Kieran himself, the round-eyed, broad-shouldered businessman didn't look Japanese, or even Asian. Nor did he sound Asian. Despite its clipped American rhythm, his English was polished.

And as Kieran released Yamada's hand, he smiled. He had a knack for recognizing another warrior.

Two warriors, he thought as Yamada introduced his business manager. After the thin-haired and deceptively stout Sasaki melted from the room, Yamada waved Kieran to a round table, stopping at a credenza first to pour whiskey into crystal glasses.

For a polite moment, Kieran savored the pure malt liquor. Then he outlined the royal family's need for enhanced security. He didn't mention Talty.

Yamada turned his glass in his hands as he listened. He barely paused before responding. "I'm sure you already know that my companies have provided such services for governments from Japan to South Africa, Commander. May I ask if this is a routine security analysis? Or do you wish to protect something sensitive in nature?"

Nowhere in the introductions had Kieran's military title been mentioned. Yamada not only knew the players, he understood that something unusual was afoot. Kieran warmed to the man.

"We have specific concerns, yes. You'd be evaluating the security we have in place on several sites. The King's Residence, Tara Hall, Clontarf Castle, and perhaps others. We'd like Mamoru to upgrade our systems, should you find them lacking. How soon can you start?"

Yamada swallowed the whiskey he'd been rolling around his mouth. "It would be my pleasure to start at your earliest convenience."

"Brilliant. Might it also be your pleasure to spar on occasion? I couldn't help noticing your fine training room."

Kieran was a great believer in the old Fian saying that a single session of sparring revealed more about a man than a lifetime of friendship. He reached across the table. Yamada smiled and clasped his outstretched hand.

* * * * *

Despite Kieran's ironclad security precautions, rumors from Inverness reached Prince Geoffrey. He slammed the telephone down and scowled.

Rumors. That's all they were. The Highland Scots in his employ were unreliable. Their blaggering English was unintelligible at best. They must have misunderstood whatever they'd heard from their friends who worked in that private hospital. That, and their passion for romantic endings, had them imagining things.

Geoffrey had seen the girl after the attack. No one could have survived such injuries. Still, if she were alive, her existence would invalidate his challenge to the annulment. If Roger had bungled it, Geoffrey would have to deal with it.

He'd call Andrew and say he'd heard some ridiculous gossip concerning Roger. Andrew wouldn't hesitate to protect the godson he practically worshiped.

* * * * *

A week later, a helicopter landed at Clontarf Castle's helipad in the early hours of the morning. Talty nearly cheered when she saw the old castle's towers from the air. She was home.

During the flight from Scotland, Kieran had described how Mamoru Services had updated the castle's security system. Until they finished updating the other royal residences, Talty would stay at Clontarf. He smuggled her in through the old drawbridge room.

"I know it's the middle of the night," she said, "but I'm hungry."

"Hospital food." Kieran rubbed the scar on his cheek. "I tried it myself once. No wonder you're as thin as a leprechaun's walking stick. I'm sure there's food in the place. Your parents brought Aggie up. She'll fix you something to eat. They brought Jenna too, to look after you."

Talty touched the scars on her cheeks and wondered what Jenna would think of her princess now. "How long am I to stay hidden away?"

"Until we decide it's safe," Kieran said simply. "Just promise me, Talty. Promise you'll mind me about it, even if you don't agree with me."

"I will. I don't want to go back to that hospital." She jumped up and flung her arms around his neck. "I'm just so glad to be home!"

* * * * *

Days later, Andrew met Geoffrey at Southwick Castle. As they strolled to

Geoffrey's offices, Andrew relayed his report. One of the men he'd sent to Dublin to investigate the rumors Geoffrey had heard about Princess Taillte had gone to the betting office to place a wager on a dog race. A woman there was in a flat spin, telling the bookmaker she couldn't pay him.

Andrew's man knew from photos that the woman worked in the Boru family's catering operations. He'd stepped over and slipped a hefty wedge of cash into her hand, telling her he hated to see a lady in distress. She'd been grateful. She still was.

"The woman says they have the girl at Clontarf Castle."

"Incredible." Geoffrey rubbed his chin. "Do you believe her?"

"I expect she's smart enough to know that if she gives us bad information, her funds will dry up. She's already gambled her recent inheritance away, and the bank is about to foreclose on her home."

"I don't care a pin for her troubles. Can she get your friends into Clontarf Castle?"

Andrew nodded. "She did say that for this one, she was entitled to a bonus."

They'd reached Geoffrey's private apartment. Geoffrey didn't invite Andrew in. "I agree, Andrew. Arrange something suitable."

* * * * *

While she'd been recovering in Scotland, Talty had dreamed of the roaring hearth and lace-canopied bed in her Clontarf Castle rooms. Now she was here, having tea with her mother.

"Scotland's mountain air has done wonders for you," Eileen said. "I believe you've put on a pound or two since you've come home, and that makeup is doing a wonderful job."

Talty disagreed. The horrid paste did no good, and never would. Her nose was uneven, her cheeks thick with scars. She avoided mirrors and refused to even glimpse at the nightmare of purple welts on her chest.

She wouldn't burden her kindhearted mother with useless complaints, however. "Aggie's a great cook."

"Yes, she is. I hear you're having company for supper tonight."

Talty could hardly wait. "Yes. Neil and Aidan are coming."

"That should keep you busy." Eileen finished her tea and rose. "And now, I have to go home and dress."

Remembering parties at Tara Hall—parties she'd always taken for granted—Talty walked her mother to the door. "I wish I were coming with you."

"So do I. You'll be dancing with us before you know it."

Eileen's smile held no trace of pity. Talty almost believed her.

* * * * *

The royal family was entertaining the Crown Prince and Princess of Belgium that night. Most of the catering staff would be at Tara Hall. Clontarf Castle was nearly empty.

Daisy placed the call. Getting the two Englishmen past the guards would be easy if they did as she told them.

CHAPTER SIX

Outnumbered

Kieran had just finished waltzing with the Belgian Princess when one of his men told him Jimmy Gallagher wanted him to call right away. Jimmy was Kieran's second-in-command, a capable man who wouldn't interrupt a state dinner without good reason. Worried, Kieran returned the call in a nearby room.

"Get up to Clontarf," Jimmy said. "Your friend Yamada's equipment is picking up things we never could have heard before. I'll meet you there."

Kieran called for his car, took the steps two at a time to his office, and . withdrew a holster and semiautomatic pistol from a concealed safe. In moments, he was racing to Clontarf Castle.

* * * * *

Jenna's joyful welcome for Talty had quickly dissolved to a horrified stare. Yet the loyal aide had pulled herself together quickly and buckled down to work. In the two weeks since Talty returned to Ireland, Jenna had altered her clothing, polished her nails, and trimmed the hair the nuns had chopped to pieces.

In preparation for tonight's supper, Jenna finished applying the heavy concealer—Talty called it "undertaker's stuff"—and handed Talty the hand mirror. She wouldn't take it. Even Jenna's artistry couldn't restore her face, and she refused to let another round of self-pity spoil her happy mood.

"Your cousins will be here soon," Jenna said. "I'll walk down with you."

The first time Talty had ventured from her castle suite, every shadow had filled her with irrational fear. Little by little, the fear had dwindled, though she still treasured Jenna's company.

41

Chatting about winter wardrobes, the women reached the bottom of the rear staircase. Two men stood in the back hall between the cellar door and the corridor to the reception rooms. Both wore workmen's attire. Arms folded, the short, bald man leaned on the dark oak table beneath the medieval tapestry. Coarse blond hair spilled over the tall man's forehead. A folded racing form jutted from his jacket pocket.

"Who are you?" Jenna demanded. "What do you want here?"

"We'd like a word with the princess here," the short man said.

Talty gasped at his English accent. She shrank against the wall. "Jenna, call the guards!"

Wild-eyed now, Jenna opened her mouth, though her voice wouldn't work. Suddenly Daisy ran into the hall.

Her arrival clearly boosted Jenna's courage. Hands on her hips, she glared. "How did you scuts get in here?"

"Why, I let them in," Daisy said.

The short man drew a gun from his pocket.

Jenna shoved Talty toward the cellar door. "Run, Talty!"

But Talty couldn't move.

Jenna kicked the short man and pummeled his chest. Cursing crudely, he whipped the gun at her head. The tall man grabbed her from behind and threw her headfirst against the table. She collapsed beside it, blood flowing over her face.

"Jenna!" Talty's scream echoed down the hall. Her bloody wedding dress sprang at her, a dizzying image that quickly vanished. In its place, the two intruders stood shoving each other to get to her.

She yanked the cellar door open and ran for her life.

* * * * *

Neil's blue Jaguar coasted to a stop in Clontarf Castle's courtyard. Inhaling the heady aromas of roasting meat and baking bread, he and Aidan traipsed through the kitchen door and hung their jackets in the mudroom.

Old Aggie beamed when Aidan handed her the bouquet of flowers they'd stopped to get when they realized they'd be late. "Hey there, Aggie. Where's our girl?"

"Not down yet, young sir, and you're late. My food is going to spoil. Be good lads and fetch her down, poor thing." The cook set the flowers in the sink and returned to her gravy.

* * * * *

Still weak after her hospital stay, Talty struggled to breathe. Pain pounded her chest. She had to slow down—but the rapid footsteps behind her grew louder and closer. Her only hope was to reach the secret passage to the chapel. If she could unbolt the door behind the hunting tapestry, she could escape. She turned out the lights and trusted her memory to guide her down the hall.

"Come out, girl! No sense trying to run away. It won't take long, I promise."

Daisy's voice coiled through the murky cellar like a serpent. Talty nearly surrendered at the hideous sound. Had she passed the tapestry yet? If so, she'd have to go back and slip behind it to reach the door. But what if it were still ahead? Moving as fast as she dared in the dark, she ran her hands over the walls.

Seconds later, she touched the old holy water font. The tapestry was just ahead. Holding her breath, she listened. Where were they? Were they listening for her?

Picturing the part of the hall she was in, she ran. Her fingers found the edge of the tapestry just as the lights came on.

* * * * *

Neil and Aidan were halfway down the kitchen hall when Kieran charged in from a side corridor. He was clad in formal attire. Urgency shone in his hawk-like eyes.

"Where's Talty?"

Neil stiffened. His heart thumped in his throat. "Aggie sent us to fetch her for supper. Is something wrong?"

"Jimmy picked up a suspicious call made from here an hour ago. It might be nothing, but let's find Talty." Kieran plucked the pistol from his belt. "You say she's not in the kitchen. I've just come from her room. She's not there either. Let's try the back stairs."

The men spread out and hurried down the hall. They turned the last corner and found Jenna lying beside the overturned table, her face streaked with blood.

Kieran handed his pistol to Neil and bent over the senseless woman. Her eyes opened when he touched her neck.

"Talty," she moaned. "They're after Talty."

"Easy, love," Kieran said. "Where are they?"

"The cellar. Stop them, please stop them!" Her eyes closed.

Gripping the pistol, Neil bolted toward the cellar stairs. Aidan was right behind him.

* * * * *

Daisy dragged Talty into a storage room and pushed her against the wall.

The cold, damp stone scraped her back. She lashed at Daisy's throat. Daisy swore and pulled Talty's hair, and she yelped.

"No need for that," the tall man said. "We'll finish and be on our way."

Releasing Talty, Daisy backed against the opposite wall. Her smug expression disappeared when the short man aimed his gun at her. "No! I've done what you asked!"

"Sorry, old girl. No loose ends and all."

His muted shot pierced Daisy's forehead. A burst of blood sprayed the wall behind her. She dropped to the floor. The short man raised his gun again.

Smothering a sob, Talty tensed to tackle him, for all the good it would do. Another shot thundered through the air. Her eyes squeezed shut. Why hadn't it hurt? Was she already dead? She opened her eyes in time to see the short man drop.

Neil stood across the room, a pistol raised in both hands.

"Damned Irish bastard!" cried the tall man. Too late, he swung his gun. Neil fired again. The tall man fell beside his partner. Aidan appeared and kicked the guns from their hands.

Talty's knees buckled. Tears streamed down her cheeks. Leaning against the wall, she slid to the floor.

Neil knelt and held her face in his hands. "Are you hurt, Talty?"

The gunshots had deafened her. She could read his lips, but she couldn't answer.

He carried her away from the carnage and set her down on a chair. "Tal, are you all right?"

This time she heard him. She nodded.

Suddenly Kieran was there, draping his dinner jacket over her shoulders. "Well done, Neil. Take her upstairs and stay with her." He slapped Neil's shoulder and shouted orders at the men who'd come running from their posts around the castle.

Aidan's fingers brushed Talty's hair. "What about me? I helped too."

"Forget it," Neil said. "He only gives out one compliment a day."

"Don't I know it." Aidan pecked Talty's forehead and joined the cleanup crew.

Neil peered down at her. His smile seemed at odds with the anguish in his eyes. "Good thing you don't weigh too much. I could hurt my back carrying you around so." He helped her up and led her down the hall.

* * * * *

The men guarding the King's Residence nodded with newfound respect when Neil arrived the next day. He entered the queen's suite and found his great aunt Nuala knitting on a couch. Her clacking needles fell silent. She put her project down and reached up to pat his face.

Neil kissed her hand. "Howya, Auntie Nuala. Is it all right if I see Talty?"

"She'd like that, Neily."

He followed her into the bedroom. Talty sat near the window. The navy blue sweat suit she wore looked so huge, he thought she must have borrowed it from someone. The chest patch displaying the Defense Forces logo over a pair of crossed silver anchors declared it hers, though. It would have been in her closet, of course.

Her mother sat with her. Neil crossed the room and kissed Eileen's cheek. "Howya, Auntie Leenie," he said, and then he turned to Talty. She wore no makeup, but he barely noticed the scars. "Hey there, sleepy."

She smiled up at him. "Hello, Neil. Are you all right?"

"Am *I* all right? You're something, girl. How are you feeling yourself?"

"Hungry."

"Aggie is sending something up," Nuala said. "You look like you could use a cup of tea, Eileen. Let's go clear that table." The women retreated to the sitting room.

Neil sat beside Talty. Her shoulders relaxed. "How's Jenna?" she asked.

"A bad bump and a few stitches, but she'll be all right."

"I feel awful about it. If she hadn't been there, and if you and Aidan hadn't come…"

He took her hand. "Don't think about it." He didn't want to think about it himself.

"But Daisy! All this time. What if there's others?" Glittering tears marred her lovely Boru eyes. "Why do they hate me so much?"

A sudden urge to hold her and comfort her confused him. Of course he'd want to comfort her. They were the best of friends, and he was her protector. "It isn't personal, love. It's the politics. The oil wells."

Biting her lip, she looked out the window. "The old fellas are going to send me away, aren't they?"

The idea shocked him. Why would she think that? "I don't know, Tal. I hope not."

Both their heads turned at the sound of the outer door opening and closing. Subdued men's voices melded with the women's, and then Brian and Kieran entered the bedroom. Neil stood and greeted them.

Peadar arrived a moment later. "Neil, we'd like to speak to Talty. Can you visit later?"

"No!" Talty frowned at each of them in turn. "I'm outnumbered here.

Neil stays."

Brian sighed and nodded, and then he sat opposite her.

"What happens now?" she asked. "Won't someone miss Daisy and those men?"

"No," Kieran said. "Daisy had some serious money trouble. Her disappearance will surprise no one. The men will turn up as robbery victims, but that isn't important, Talty. What is, is someone suspects you're here."

"Are you going to find out who so I don't have to keep hiding?"

Brian seemed to shrink beneath her withering glare. His eyes clamped shut. "Hiding isn't the same as protected."

Peadar's gentle growl intervened. "We have to find out who's trying to hurt you, love. We suspect one of the Wessex lads. Each has his reason."

"Until we do," Brian said, "I've decided it would be best if you continue your recovery away from Ireland. It won't be for long. Only until we can set things right."

Kieran reached over and squeezed her hands. "Have faith, Talty. Remember the old saying: 'Don't show your teeth until you can bite.' When we're ready to bite, we'll bite big. Now listen. I know a fella, the very fella whose security caught Daisy and her friends. We haven't spoken to him yet. We wanted to speak to you first. If he agrees, you could go with him."

"Where?"

"He lives in Japan."

Neil's heart broke for her. "How well do you know this man, Kieran?"

"Quite well. He's a strong, honorable man. We wouldn't even consider this if he weren't. I also have a friend with ISF in Tokyo. He'll help look after you while you're there, Tal."

Talty stood, and though her lip quivered, she set her shoulders back and clenched her fists. "All right, I'll go. Now get out, all of you, and leave me alone. I don't want to see any of you any more than you want to see me."

Brian reached for her arm. "Talty—"

She slapped his hand away. "Why didn't you just let me die, Dad? Go on, get out!"

The older men winced, and then they left. Talty ran into the dressing room and shut the door. Her muffled sobs infuriated Neil. He thought he should go in and comfort her, but Talty hated to have anyone see her cry. Instead, he tore past his apprehensive aunts and hunted his elders down.

He found them in Brian's book-lined study, sitting before the fireplace, his father and Kieran on either side of Brian. "How can you do this, Uncle Brian?"

Brian shook his head. "I have no choice. We want her safe."

"Safe? If you can't keep her safe in her own home, how can you keep her safe halfway around the world? What kind of king are you if you can't take care of your own family?"

"Neil!" Peadar bellowed. "You'll not speak to your uncle so!"

"Someone should speak to him so. One day you'll find you've thrown her away too many times!" He waited for an argument. None came. He left, slamming the door behind him.

* * * * *

Early the next morning, Eric Yamada welcomed Kieran into his offices. His Irish friend hadn't come to work out today. Instead, he asked for Eric's ear. Eric listened in stunned silence to the royal family's request that he bring a young woman everyone believed dead to Japan with him.

After giving the matter the same brief but serious consideration that had won him major business deals, Eric agreed, with one condition. The girl must come with him as his wife, albeit a temporary one. In return, he'd protect her until he could bring her safely home to her family. He cited strict Japanese propriety as his reason. That was true, yet Eric neglected to mention that if he returned to Japan a married man, the unkind whispers about him and Kiyoshi would stop.

Speaking through Kieran, King Brian conveyed his reluctance to subject his daughter to another arranged marriage. Yet for her protection, he agreed to Eric's terms.

Late that night, Eric met the king at Tara Hall and heard the disturbing story of Princess Taillte's wedding night. Soon she came in, escorted by a boy on the verge of manhood who held her arm as if to keep her from falling. Her loose-fitting pantsuit couldn't disguise her frailty. No cosmetic concealed her horribly scarred face. Any misgivings Eric had about helping her vanished.

He studied the boy, a serious young man with ink-black hair and sky-blue eyes. From what Eric knew of the royal family, he guessed this was Neil Boru, Prince Peadar's son.

When King Brian introduced them, Princess Taillte held her head high as if to show Eric what he'd be getting. "Mr. Yamada," she said in a soft, sad voice. "I understand you're the gentleman whose gadgets allowed me to cheat death again."

"I'm delighted they found such auspicious use, Your Highness."

His words drew no reaction. "Dad, may I speak to Mr. Yamada in private?"

King Brian nodded. He and his nephew left the room.

Eric followed Talty to the fire, where they sat studying each other. Her soulful eyes fascinated him. He couldn't quite place the look. Haunted? Yes. Afraid? Maybe. Nervous? Definitely. And humiliated, perhaps, at being sold away by her father yet again.

"May I call you Talty?"

"Why not? We're practically engaged. You would really do this, Mr. Yamada?"

"Eric. And yes, I'd really do this. I'm glad to help." He touched her hand.

She drew it back. "My father marries me off easily, it seems."

"No. The marriage was my idea. Japanese society is quite strict. I can't simply bring a young woman to live in my house. And the marriage is only temporary. When the time is right, we'll dissolve it and I'll bring you home."

"I'm sorry for the trouble," she whispered.

"I'll make a deal with you. A business deal. In return for giving you a safe and comfortable environment in which to recover, you'll never again speak about being sorry."

She pressed her lips into a tight line. "All right, but I'll insist on one thing. I was training to become a warrior before I was...hurt. I want a trainer to help me continue, so no one will ever hurt me again."

Eric smiled. It seemed no one had told her that he and Kiyoshi were warriors. He found himself looking forward to surprising her. "I think we can arrange that."

"All right. It's a deal." She held out her hand.

He squeezed it gently. So fragile, he thought.

They were soon joined by several members of the royal family: King Brian, Queen Eileen, Prince Peadar, and Kieran. Neil returned as well. He came in with Kieran's father, Prince Jack, who'd not only prepared the necessary documents in great haste, but would also conduct the barebones ceremony.

No flowers graced the wedding, no photographs, not even a ring. When the ceremony, such as it was, ended, Talty said good-bye to her family and left Tara Hall with Eric.

CHAPTER SEVEN

Japan

Wall vases in the jet's cabin overflowed with roses. They weren't my Princess Taillte roses, but since I wasn't me anymore, I supposed any old rose would do.

I sat in a daze, contemplating the wedding ceremony, such as it was. The formalities had included the usual components: the bride and groom, the officiator, the scowling father of the bride, the crying mother of the bride, and assorted, somber relatives to act as witnesses. Right after the hasty good-byes, Eric spirited me away to his private hangar at Dublin Airport, where I first met Kiyoshi Sasaki. A reserved, unreadable man, Kiyoshi grunted more than he spoke. They settled me into a comfortable seat, and we flew off into the Irish twilight.

I stared out the cabin window and watched the clouds slip away beneath the jet. Only a few weeks before, I'd been so happy to leave Scotland for home. How did I end up bound for Japan with a new husband?

Eric hovered over me at first, though once I assured him I was fine, he snapped a fold-down table into place and began pulling things from his briefcase. I must have slept for some time. We'd stopped in Alaska to refuel when he tapped my arm.

"Kiyoshi has been busy in the galley. Are you hungry?"

"I usually am, Eric. Thank you."

He led me to the dining area, where the furnishings matched those in my father's Gulfstream for elegance and comfort. Another fold-down table was set with china and crystal. The sight of chopsticks on the place mats panicked me, though I relaxed when I saw silverware beside them. Eric held my chair for me, and I sat down to an excellent meal of pasta primavera and hot, fresh bread.

Kiyoshi served the food with efficient politeness, and then he joined us. He said little, and his face betrayed nothing. In all the time I've known him, I've rarely seen Kiyoshi's expression change.

I waited for a signal of some sort to begin eating.

"*Itadakimasu,*" Eric said. He and Kiyoshi raised their chopsticks. "We don't expect you to learn these things overnight, Talty. Saying this at the start of a meal is customary. It means 'I receive this food gratefully.' And we are most grateful to Kiyoshi for his fine work."

I agreed, and said so. Since Kiyoshi was a close associate of Eric's—and more important, an excellent cook—I decided to try to make friends.

"The food is excellent, Kiyoshi."

He looked to Eric as if asking for permission before answering. "*Domo arigato, Hime-san.*"

The first part I understood. I wondered what he was calling me, though I wasn't sure I wanted to know. "How do I say, 'You're welcome'?"

"*Do itashimashite,*" Eric said.

I tried it, with acceptable results. Kiyoshi nodded and turned his gaze to his plate. I wondered if he suffered from shyness or if his reticence was simply a cultural thing. Then it occurred to me that my appearance might be upsetting him. I'd applied some undertaker goop over the scars before we left, but I knew it didn't conceal the whole multitude of sins.

Eric filled my glass with mineral water and poured wine for Kiyoshi and himself. Someone must have given him a crash course on my medical condition: no alcohol while I was taking the drugs I'd need for a little while longer.

I dabbed my mouth with a linen napkin and tasted the water. "Eric, all my life I've learned about etiquette and protocol. I know the way things are done in Ireland isn't necessarily the way they're done in other countries. I've read a little about Japan, but this is all happening so fast. You'll help me, won't you?"

"Absolutely. We all will, won't we, Ki?"

Kiyoshi answered with something like a grunt and continued eating.

Eric smiled. "And I expect to learn more about Irish culture."

"When I'm better, I could teach you a few dance steps, if you like."

He laughed. My Irish ears heard music. If I had to leave the music I loved behind, I thought I could find new music in Eric's laugh.

"Tell me, Talty. Was there some significance to the hand kissing your family bestowed upon you at the end of the...the marriage ceremony?"

Apparently he'd been as impressed with our slam-bang wedding as I had been. "Yes. What they were doing was an abbreviated version of the formal obeisance to a ranking royal person. I get the Obeisance to a Lady Princess."

"Even from your elders? Kieran and Prince Peadar offered this obeisance to you."

"I'm the king's daughter and rank first, after my parents. Once upon a time, I was the heir to the throne. My brother Liam is Crown Prince now, and technically I should make the obeisance to him, but he refuses."

"Liam. He wasn't there, was he?"

No. I didn't get to say good-bye. "No. Not enough notice, I suppose."

Eric reached across the table and patted my hand. "We'll find a way to have you communicate with your family. It's what I do, after all."

I tried to smile my thanks. Clearly sensitive to my distress, Eric chatted to distract me. "They each kissed your hand twice before they kissed your mouth. Is there some significance to that?"

"Yes. In the full, formal version, you kneel and kiss the person's hand once, saying, 'I will kiss your hand as you are the heart of this kingdom.' Then you get up and kiss her hand again and say, 'I will kiss your hand as you are my own heart.' Then you kiss her on the mouth and say 'And I will kiss your mouth to show my everlasting love and devotion, beloved Princess of Ireland.' My brother and cousins and I all hated it when we were little and had to learn it."

Neil hadn't minded last night. Neil, my Shivail, a protector who now had no protectee. He'd given my hand an extra squeeze when we said good-bye.

Eric chuckled. More music. "You gave this obeisance to your father."

I did. We'd reconciled, I think. Never in my life had I spoken to him so disrespectfully. Once I'd calmed down and thought things over, I felt terrible and asked my mother if he'd speak to me. He'd come flying.

"Yes," I said, "though that usually happens at formal occasions, with slightly different words." I remembered the last time, at the start of the "Thomas" wedding, before hundreds of people. I'd been proud to show my love for my father.

Small talk rounded out the remainder of the meal. After dinner, Eric gave me a tour of his jet and its amenities. He opened wall cabinets beside a long sofa in the living section to reveal an impressive collection of books. "I understand you like to read. Make yourself comfortable. Let Kiyoshi know if you need anything. We'll arrive at Narita in a few hours. I'm going to try to get some sleep."

I thanked him, and he disappeared aft. I poked at the various volumes until the faded cover of an antique caught my eye. The book was a treasure, an English translation of samurai adventure stories, but I fell asleep on the sofa before I finished the second page.

Soon Eric tapped my arm again. We were landing at Narita Airport and must buckle in.

A short helicopter ride brought us to the Tokyo Heliport, where Eric's limousine waited. The silent chauffeur hefted the luggage into the trunk and saw to the doors while we got in, Kiyoshi up front, Eric in the luxurious back seat with me. As we drove west toward the hills of the Musashino Plateau, Eric pointed out several landmarks. While he focused his attention on the sites, I stole a few glances at him.

Kieran had mentioned mixed heritage, yet I saw little Asian in him. He was old enough to be my father, I thought. Sitting so close, I could see grains of silver in his thick, dark hair, a very distinguished look. I wondered if he'd ever been married before, and if he had any children.

"We'll be home in twenty minutes," he said at last. "My aunt will have our best rooms ready for you."

"Your aunt?"

"Yes. Imi is my father's sister. She never married. My parents weren't given the gift of long life. Imi came to look after me many years ago. I think the two of you will get along well."

I hoped so.

We were up in the hills now. Soon we approached a black gate that opened with a whirr when we approached. Eager to see my new home—the word "prison" flashed through my mind—I edged forward on the seat. The car finally stopped. The driver opened the door.

I don't believe I've ever fallen in love with a place so fast.

Eric explained that it was an old rice plantation. "I had it restored about ten years ago. Everything is modern inside. We have privacy here, a precious commodity in Japan."

"It's beautiful, Eric. I've never seen anything like it."

High up as we were, I could see Tokyo and its polluted air in the distance. Huge walls of glass on the main house promised breathtaking views from inside. And the gardens! Little bridges and ponds beckoned. I couldn't wait to explore them.

"Let's go inside," Eric said. "I'll introduce you to Imi."

"Could I have a minute to fix my face before I meet her?"

He smiled with the pity I saw on the faces of everyone who looked at me now. I hated it.

"I'll show you to a powder room," he said.

I received another lesson in Japanese etiquette when we entered the main door. A bamboo cupboard waited to receive our shoes. Following Eric's example, I kicked mine off and set them on the bottom shelf, exchanging them for a pair of slippers. Kiyoshi repeated the ritual. Japan must have lots of cold toes, I thought, until my feet detected heat radiating through the floors.

Eric ushered me into a reception hall. I caught the subtle fragrance of incense. Plum, or perhaps musk. My first impression of the place was that it reflected his diverse heritage. Low tables and tatami mats coexisted with sofa and coffee table groupings without conflict. Some of the lovely heirlooms and treasures had to be centuries old.

And then I found myself trying to fix my face before a bathroom mirror. I was about to make my first impression on a lady with whom I wanted very much to live in harmony, and I missed Jenna. From now on I'd have to decide for myself if my appearance would pass inspection.

Imi Yamada had no trouble passing *my* inspection. Eric's elderly aunt offered a nimble bow when he introduced us. Not sure how to respond, I nodded and said hello. It might have been my imagination, but she seemed a bit suspicious of me—I would've been—though her impeccable manners prevented any discourteous scrutiny. Petite, proper, and hospitable, Imi instructed her servants to prepare tea and welcomed me into her home.

* * * * *

Each day Eric set aside time for us to talk. One day we'd walk through the gardens, another through the maze of connected outbuildings. His descriptions of the two-hundred-year-old structures transported me to an earlier time. Long departed builders had constructed the walls with mud from the bottom of the rice paddies that had once flourished there. Buildings that had provided housing for laborers and storage space for farm tools and crops now served more modern purposes. Eric showed me his office and pointed out the apartment over the old barn where Kiyoshi lived.

One afternoon we sat before the fire in the living room. Consistent with the theme throughout the house, the room held an eclectic mix of furnishings, each piece carefully chosen and displayed for admiration. Eric poured tea from a silver pot and told me about his parents.

"My mother was the daughter of a Canadian scientist who worked for the Ontario branch of Ibaraki Technologies."

"There's an Ibaraki Laboratories in Dublin. They do something with computers, I think."

"That's them. Many years ago, my Canadian grandfather came to Tokyo with his family to develop some sort of analytical instrumentation here at Ibaraki's home offices. They were to stay a year or two and then return to

Canada, but one project led to another. My grandfather was a brilliant man, and the company kept him as long as they could. My mother met my father while both attended Tokyo University. When my grandfather finally took his family back to Canada, she stayed."

I suspected that Eric didn't share his personal history with everyone. Feeling honored, I wondered if he'd tell me what had happened to his parents. He spent a few moments inspecting the wooden beams in the ceiling before he continued.

"Even after all these years, I still miss them. They took special care with me, to help me fit in. Growing up in Tokyo a *konketsunohito* was difficult." He answered my unspoken question. "A mixed race person. A half-breed. The people were polite, but I always knew I didn't quite belong."

He set his teacup on the tray. "One day, my father and mother went to visit her family in Ontario. I stayed behind to attend school. Their plane went down in British Columbia."

"I'm so sorry, Eric. How old were you?"

"Fifteen. Nearly grown, though I'm sure I could have benefited from their continued guidance. For that final polish, you know? And with that, my young friend, I must get back to work. I have a day full of meetings tomorrow for which I must prepare. I'll see you at dinner."

I was on my own for the rest of the afternoon. A servant, as they referred to the house staff in Japan, came to take the tea things away. The woman seemed shy, though she smiled at me. Despite the language barrier, I was already developing a rapport with Eric's house staff. I have to admit I hadn't minded their coddling since I'd arrived. Still, I resolved to become more independent once I grew stronger.

My parents had taught my brother and me to appreciate the helpers we couldn't do without. They were part of a circle. We were simply another part. The idea was that they'd take care of mundane tasks so our princely minds could soar to higher plateaus. I wondered, thinking that I was developing a rather smart-ass attitude, if that included the Musashino Plateau.

Thanking the woman, I left her to her task and wandered through the maze of rooms, admiring priceless collections of antique porcelain and lacquerware. Soon I found myself in the atrium, a delightful open area at the center of the house where stepping stones led to a rock garden and a small, bubbling pond. I looked up when I entered the courtyard, a victim to my deep-rooted habit of checking the Irish skies to see if it would only shower, merely rain, or out and out bucket. Growing used to the scant rainfall here would take some time.

Imi sat reading in a carved wooden chair beside the pond. I turned to leave, reluctant to intrude on her quiet time, but she caught me.

In one deft move she removed her reading glasses. "Hello, Talty."

"*Konnichiwa*, Imi-san."

She nodded, pleased by my stumbling attempts to learn basic Japanese—Imi had polished her own excellent English as a professional interpreter—and then she pointed to a matching chair. Before I sat, I moved the chair to keep the late afternoon sun from my eyes.

Imi frowned. "Perhaps you should not be lifting chairs."

The usual pity appeared in her eyes when she looked at my face, which she had to do to carry on polite conversation. If nothing else, Imi was polite. I wouldn't dare appear before her without a proper coat of paint. "I'm fine. It's not heavy, and it's good exercise."

"Are you finding your rooms comfortable?"

"Oh, yes." They'd given me the entire second floor of the east wing, a western-style guest suite with every convenience. Each window offered a spectacular view of mountains, valleys, forests, and lakes. I had no complaints there.

"Eric has told me a little about you," she said. "I have met many high-ranking people in my day, but I have never met a princess."

"I've met a few. It's nothing special."

A smile blossomed over her venerable face. "I think you must be special, or Eric would not have brought you here. He has instructed me to keep your secret. Please tell me if you find anything lacking here."

"I lack nothing here, Imi-san. You and Eric have been very kind. My only wish now is to regain my strength."

She seemed unsure about proceeding. She spoke in a softened voice. "Eric said you had an accident. I am very sorry."

I wasn't about to elaborate on my "accident." "Please don't worry about me, Imi-san. I'm feeling stronger every day, and I'm not shy. If I need something, I'll say so."

"Please do. Now, I must supervise dinner." She put her book down and stood.

I rose with her. "Maybe I could help."

A look of horror replaced her serene expression. "No, Hime-san. The servants will take care of everything. Please, enjoy the remainder of the afternoon."

I'd learned that *hime* meant princess. One could be called worse things, I supposed. After Imi glided from the atrium, I went upstairs to rest before dinner.

Mealtime had started to fill me with dread, though I'd die before I'd tell Imi I didn't like Japanese food.

$$* * * * *$$

Living among strangers, I longed for my own tribe. When Eric's departure for a series of business meetings in Tokyo left me with extra time on my hands, I spent some of it tracking the news from back home and monitoring my family's public appearances. I wondered if they missed me as much as I missed them.

I had to keep busy. Exploring Eric's extensive library helped. Reading about Japanese culture and etiquette gave me a greater appreciation for my new home.

I roamed the gardens until I knew every nook and started picturing how some plantings would look in different spots. From watching the workers in my family's gardens—I'd often seen my father and Uncle Peadar jump in with spade and hoe—I knew that garden work would be good exercise. The gardener, a crotchety old gentleman named Takumi-san, resisted my attempts to sign on as his apprentice. Undaunted, I tried a technique I'd seen my mother and aunts use to great effect: I glared.

Soon Takumi-san and I became good friends, united in our passion for shrubs and flowers. I learned much from him, including several Japanese expletives. He came to love the prime gardening rule I'd learned as a little girl: 'Leave a little room for the fairies to dance.'

$$* * * * *$$

A week later, Eric returned from his meetings and asked what I'd been doing. We strolled through the gardens, enjoying the sunshine, the trilling birds and splashing carp. I pointed out the azaleas and dwarf trees I'd helped relocate.

He seemed pleased. "You've kept yourself busy, I see. I've been busy myself. Several of my associates have learned of our marriage. As we agreed, I told them you had an unfortunate accident just after our wedding. They send their wishes for your speedy recovery and look forward to meeting you."

"It won't be long, Eric. I'm feeling much better, and already I've gained nearly five pounds."

His lips curved in a smile that spread until the corners of his eyes crinkled. "Imagine how much you'd gain if you ate food you really liked."

I stopped and gasped. Had my dislike of sashimi and natto been so obvious? I didn't think so. I was learning that Eric possessed an amazing ability to perceive even the subtlest nuance.

He chuckled, and we continued walking. "Don't worry. Your secret is safe with me. I've already asked Imi to incorporate more western dishes into our diet, since I myself have acquired a taste for Coq au Vin and Veal Piccata."

Just the mention of such dishes had my mouth watering. "I'd like to learn to cook things like that. Someday I will."

"Talty, you can learn anything once you set your mind to it. In the short time you've been here, you've learned some rudimentary Japanese and stolen your way into Imi's affections."

We passed the sentinel stone and turned onto a path that led to a grouping of low, leafless shrubs. The branches looked familiar, though in their dormant state I couldn't identify them.

Eric waved to a wooden bench. We sat with plenty of space between us, and I began to worry. I'd never seen such a serious expression on his face.

"While I was in Tokyo," he said, "I found a doctor to monitor your general health, as your parents requested. I also found a specialist I'd like you to see."

My heart pounded. For all I owed them, doctors weren't my favorite people. Eric must have noticed my anxiety, though he didn't coddle me.

"I want you to have those scars fixed. I know you worry about the effect they have on the people around you. Even those of us who've grown somewhat accustomed to them still find them distressing. What will happen when you meet strangers?"

Locking my hands together didn't stop them from shaking. Angry and afraid, I sucked in a deep breath. "The plastic surgeon in Scotland said my face would always have scars because they waited too long to fix it."

"I'm sure he did his best. But you can't remain hidden away once you return to Ireland. And what about your dream of working with International Security Forces? Listen to me, Talty. The doctor I want you to see is an eminent Tokyo surgeon. He'll meet with you for a private consultation. You'd have no obligation to undergo any treatment."

"I don't know. Doctors really make me nervous."

He reached for my hands. I pulled them away so he wouldn't see my trembling fingers.

"Talty, I can't pretend to know what you've been through or how you feel. I only know those scars can't hide the beauty in your heart. The kindness you show to everyone around you has reassured me that I was right to help you. If we can improve things for you, I think we should try.

"What if we could not only reduce the scars on your face so you could stop using that chalk cosmetic, but we could also change your appearance?

Just enough so you could come and go anywhere unrecognized."

"I—you mean, like in a spy story or something?"

"Yes. Don't answer now. Just promise me you'll think it over."

I wanted to hit him. I wanted to run away, but all I did was cry. He seemed to expect it and didn't get flustered at all.

Then he pulled me to my feet and led me to the hibernating shrubs. "Have you ever seen tree peonies?"

Ah, that's what they were. "Yes. They grow in our gardens back home."

"These plants are dormant now, but soon their leaves will sprout. Takumi-san will cultivate them and fertilize them with ashes and manure. He'll dust them against insects, and for all that work, these bare-branched, skeletal twigs will reward us with the most majestic blooms in the garden. You are such a flower, Talty. With the right care, you'll become the finest of blooms. Let me give you that care. You'll be my special *hana*."

I choked back another sob. "*Hana?*"

"Flower. *Hana*. That's what I'll call you to remind you that you will bloom. I know that even without further surgery, you'll bloom and be beautiful. Still, it wouldn't hurt to speak to the doctor. Please consider it."

The dinner-plate-sized flowers I remembered from Uncle Peadar's garden seemed to appear on the branches before me. I brushed my fingers over my eyes. I really hated to cry in front of anyone. "Yes, Eric. I'll speak to him."

"That's all I ask." He took a handkerchief from his pocket and dabbed my cheeks. "We can't have Imi think I made you cry. She'll chase me out of the house with a broomstick."

Smiling at the comical image, I took the handkerchief and wiped away the evidence.

* * * * *

A month after Dr. Takahashi carved the heavy scar tissue from my cheeks, changed a contour here and resected a bit of cartilage there, ISF Lieutenant Colonel Ron Chambeau, Kieran's "friend in Tokyo," came to call. He didn't seem to notice the facial bandages I still wore. As it turned out, he knew all about my ongoing alterations.

A handsome, sandy-haired man from Boston, Massachusetts, Colonel Chambeau was an American version of Kieran. They'd shared a hospital room after artillery fire had injured Kieran during his African peacekeeping mission. Colonel Chambeau had come down with appendicitis at the same time. I knew from Kieran's stories that they'd been in cahoots ever since.

He'd already chosen my new name: Christy McKenna. The "McKenna" gave me an Irish background, he said. I thought I could pull that off all right.

"You made lieutenant in the Irish Navy, Princess. You'll be a major with ISF."

"Please call me Talty. Or Christy. Major seems like a very exalted title for a lieutenant."

"Christy it is. Might as well get used to it. Major is the rank ISF would've assigned if you'd joined Research and Development on schedule. You went through the schooling and officers' training."

I'd never keep all my different names straight. "Am I going to California after all?"

"Yes, but you'll work with me until you're comfortable with your new identity."

"Yes, sir." A tad confused, I sat blinking at his rapid-fire discourse.

"That paper trail of ID papers I put together for you should hold up, but I want you to lose that brogue. Think you can do it? Kieran says you're a pretty sharp kid."

Surely something had been lost in the translation. "I'll try my best, sir." How hard could it be to learn American?

"Mr. Yamada has no objection to starting your diction lessons while you're recuperating. I'm sending someone to work with you. A dialect coach. He works with actors in Hollywood, but we keep him on retainer for special assignments. He'll come here for a few sessions and give you some recordings to listen to. You have a few more surgeries scheduled, so you'll have plenty of time to study. You'll be ready for duty before you know it."

Despite the soreness it caused, I couldn't help grinning. More than anything, I wanted to work with ISF. That and earning my Fianna pin. One thing at a time, though. "Yes, sir. I'll look forward to it."

Colonel Chambeau left me some sample assignments ranging from requisitioning and tracking food and medical supplies to providing backup and defensive weaponry for the peacekeeping troops. I was on the other side of it all. I could feel it.

* * * * *

My continuing education reignited my passion to learn new things. Or perhaps I'd simply had my fill of fried tofu. Causing a hardship for the staff was the last thing I wanted, however.

I spoke to Eric. "I want to learn to cook. Can you find me a cooking class in Tokyo?"

Before I knew it, a European chef and his retinue arrived at the house, returning each Tuesday and Friday for a month to introduce me to a world of culinary adventure. I'd soon gained enough confidence to prepare some of Eric's favorite dishes.

Fortunately, he had a sense of humor. After a few over-lemoned starts, I mastered the techniques well, and I believe Eric received a good return on his investment.

Three months later, Dr. Takahashi removed the final round of bandages. I almost kissed him when I looked in his mirror. His scar revisions had removed the uneven bumps and ugly welts. Although he said it would take up to a year to see the complete results of his work, I was thrilled with what he'd accomplished so far. The scars left behind this time were mere red streaks that blended with the expression lines on my face. Ordinary makeup would cover them until they disappeared.

I held a private ceremony in my bathroom to flush away the heavy war paint.

I don't know if I'm more vain than the next girl, but I'd avoided mirrors after "it" happened. When I looked in the mirror now, a stranger looked back at me. Excising the welts had tightened my skin and given my cheeks the chiseled look of a high-fashion model. Even my nose looked chiseled, which of course it had been. The only remnants of Talty Boru I recognized were, as Uncle Jack called them, my "Beautiful Boru Eyes."

Yes, I looked different, but I was so grateful I wasn't a freak anymore I didn't mind. I'd been given a gift. I remembered the old Irish tales of the deities who could transmogrify themselves into crones, young girls, crows, or cows. Perhaps I couldn't change shape at will, but between my speech training and my appearance, a dramatic metamorphosis was underway.

As for the scars on my chest, I'd had enough. I'd keep my shirt on, thank you.

* * * * *

Feeling quite fit now, I reminded Eric about the training he'd promised, thinking he'd hire a trainer as he had the chef. Instead, he brought me to the barn beneath Kiyoshi's apartment. He could have knocked me over with a cherry blossom when I saw the dojo, the archery range, the kendo sticks and swords, and the soundproofed outbuilding that served as a firing range.

By now I knew Eric well enough to realize he'd relished springing his surprise, and he wasn't done yet.

"Kiyoshi and I are samurai, Hana. We await your command."

* * * * *

From the first day I'd begun my Banfian training, Uncle Peadar and Kieran would say things like "Cunning is better than strength," and "You are the deadlier of the species." They demanded that I practice harder than the boys. They taught me that whether I fired a gun, threw a knife, or merely pitched a rock, I mustn't miss. If an opponent broke through the boys' defenses, they could put up a sustained fight. I'd never have male muscle. That didn't mean I was helpless.

Eric and Kiyoshi agreed with this philosophy. After much debate, they decided that rather than try to teach me new skills that could take a lifetime to learn, they'd work to improve the skills I already had. I'd been given yet another gift.

My new mentors began my lessons with an excursion to Imabari via Eric's private helicopter. We then took a ferry to Omishima Island to view a fine collection of armor and weaponry that emperors and samurai had donated to the island's ancient temple over the centuries.

I fancied hearing the artifacts call to me: *Here I am, Talty! Come see me!* Of course, I didn't mention this imagined communication to anyone.

As a Fian novitiate, I'd always respected the spirit of any weapon I touched. I always felt some acknowledging spark snap from the weapon to me, creating a synergy between us. I hadn't felt this strange communion since my last sparring session in Kieran's training room.

After the trip to Omishima Island, the sparks returned.

* * * * *

I still knew my Fian exercises by heart. Each day I spent hours in the dojo trying to regain the level of ability I'd achieved before Roger Wessex so rudely interrupted my training.

Eric acted as my trainer when he was home. He showed none of Kiyoshi's lenience when he put me through my drills. In fact, he had me grinning at his tricks, and I do believe I pulled a few surprises that had him grinning as well.

When Eric left again for business, Kiyoshi took over as trainer.

Kiyoshi never grinned.

I intended to change that.

Kiyoshi gradually introduced me to the equipment, and soon he and I were sparring with kendo sticks, a Japanese bata of sorts. As much as I prized his patience and skill, his polite constraint had me longing for Neil, who'd never hesitated to knock me on my duff.

One morning as I swung my kendo stick at a hanging bag of straw, I realized that Neil must be flying with the Air Corps by now. An elusive image of him kissing some faceless girl interrupted my attack.

Naturally he'd be kissing her. They'd all be kissing the girls, rogues and rascals that they were. I, however, had never gotten a real kiss from any fella. Ever.

I whacked the bag with the kendo stick.

I thought I must really be healthy again to be wondering about romance.

Sex, actually.

Eric treated me like his foster child, but I began to wonder if I could change that. He was my husband after all, and I was curious to know what romance would be like.

Sex, actually.

I needed my mother.

I whacked the bag again.

I'd try speaking to Imi.

* * * * *

As an offshoot of my bata training, Eric and Kiyoshi introduced me to the *naginata*. Samurai brides often received the *naginata* as a wedding present, and wasn't I a samurai bride?

A long pole that looked like a cross between a sword and a spear, the *naginata* had once been employed by samurai women and warrior priests not only for defense, but also for the development of desired virtues. Nowadays the emphasis was on the virtues, though my boys made certain I could handle the thing effectively as a weapon. They assured me that my virtues would develop along the way.

Between sparring and thrusting, Kiyoshi taught me the value of blank expression. "Poker-face" we called it back home, though no card player I knew had anything on Kiyoshi.

"Make your opponent wonder," he'd say. "Never show surprise or anger. Never give the slightest clue. This defense is as important as any weapon you'll ever wield."

Kiyoshi insisted I spend extra time practicing with knives. The smaller ones that fit my female hand could be just as deadly as any sword, he said. I got to the point where I could throw a ball of paper in the air and slice through it several times before it hit the ground. When I could toss the paper ball behind my head and spin around and slice it to shreds, he presented me with an antique tanto knife.

For throwing the lighter knives, Kiyoshi taught me variations of the grips I'd learned in Ireland. I practiced until I instinctively knew how many times the blade would rotate when I threw it from different positions, even while running by the target.

"Keep your wrist stiff, Hime-san. Use your hip to add force to your throw. Keep your elbow up! The point you are aiming at is in your mind, not on the target board."

At the end of three months, I was fairly proficient in several traditional combats he and Eric had mastered. Swordplay and spear throwing weren't my cup of tea, though I knew the basics well enough to defend myself. I'd learned about firearms back home and had great respect for the power of even the smallest gun. The image of the bullet tearing through Daisy's forehead was still quite clear in my mind.

To keep my shooting eye sharp, I practiced in Eric's indoor firing range. Small-scale and well ventilated, the innovative range offered a choice between lasers and live shooting. I had great fun with the simulated and pop-up targets, one of which I nicknamed "Roger."

Kiyoshi's tutelage of Kyudo, the art of Japanese archery, led to what was perhaps my greatest enlightenment. More a philosophy than the mere launching of an arrow at a target, Kyudo taught archers to seek the truth. I learned that if you got the philosophy down, hitting the target just sort of happened.

The sound of the bowstring being plucked was supposed to strike fear into the hearts of evil spirits.

I liked that.

As for the philosophy of seeking the truth, I came to understand that I was as interested in hunting down Roger Wessex for revenge as I was in being able to protect myself. The realization surprised me. I thought I was a nice girl.

* * * * *

One evening during dinner, Eric poured wine instead of water into my glass. "I've been slipping a few hints that my wife is ready to venture out of the house. I don't think any of my associates believe you exist, Hana. Are you ready to start socializing?"

Calculating quickly, I added my time in the hospital to the month I'd spent at Clontarf Castle and added it all to nearly eight months so far in Japan. Even if I were back in Dublin, being out among people again after such a long time in relative seclusion would be a brutal test. In Tokyo it would be terrifying.

"Oh, yes," I said.

"Then we must prepare you for an outing or two, especially since the Tokyo Journal of Technology has named me CEO of the Year. The dinner is in two weeks. I'd like you to accompany me. This would be a perfect opportunity to test your new persona."

I detected something akin to pride in Kiyoshi's inscrutable face. Proud of Eric myself, and more than a little impressed, I agreed to attend his award dinner.

"Except I have nothing to wear."

Eric kept a flat near Tokyo's business district for times when he needed to be at his offices for days at a stretch. He and Kiyoshi brought me there and treated me to a three-day shopping spree. When Eric's business required his presence at the office, Kiyoshi escorted me to the Ginza's most fashionable stores. I obtained a variety of outfits complete with matching shoes and bags and ranging from training duds to the formal gown I'd wear to the dinner.

Selecting the gown was easy. Only a few had fronts high enough to cover a girl's chest.

Finding a decent hairstylist was next. Nearly a year had passed since Jenna trimmed the chopped mess that now sat in untidy chunks on my shoulders. I asked the stylist to leave enough to tie back. With a sad sort of happiness, I remembered the day my distraught mother caught me as I was about to hack it off so the boys couldn't pull it during training. It was then that Neil began tugging my hair to remind me to tie it up at the start of our exercises.

Neil, my Shivail and lifelong friend. My thoughts always seemed to drift back to him.

* * * * *

If my father and Eric had negotiated the consummation of the marriage as part of their business arrangement, I knew nothing about it. I'm sure my physical condition at the time precluded such discussions. However, I wondered. Though Eric was nearly twenty years older than me and had never even hinted at such things, I wondered. The scars on my chest would repulse even the most dedicated suitor. Still, I wondered.

One evening after dinner, Imi consented to my request for a private talk. When she answered my knock, I slid open the rice paper door and entered her private world. I expected conservative quarters, in keeping with the lady herself. The explosion of colors nearly knocked me down.

"*Konban wa,* Imi-san."

"Good evening to you, Talty-san. Please, come in."

I closed the door behind me and stood transfixed. Chinese rugs covered the floors. Carved wooden chests had me guessing what prizes they held. Then I looked up.

Magnificent antique kimonos adorned the walls, each stretched to display embroidered designs ranging from simple to elaborate. Cranes in flight graced the back of a gorgeous black garment to my right. A majestic phoenix suspended over red and gold flowers hung to my left. Silk robes embedded with metallic green and blue chrysanthemums shone from their perches. Embroidered peonies blazed everywhere.

"Your collection is lovely, Imi. I've never seen such fine things in a museum."

Imi lowered her eyes. "They are my one indulgence. Especially the wedding kimonos. Sometimes I imagine wearing them to the wedding I never had."

Wedding kimonos. What a great opening. I sat, determined to end my wondering. "I've been thinking about weddings myself. Mine and Eric's, to be precise. You know that Eric married me as a favor to my family."

"Yes. I think he made a wise decision."

I smiled at the compliment. "Imi, what happens when girls in Japan marry?"

Her face scrunched in question.

"I mean, how do they know...what to do? Do their mothers talk to them?"

None of Imi's kimonos matched the brilliance of her smile. "Girls from wealthy homes can go to special marriage lessons. Men treasure more a bride who has this training."

Well, of course they would. Even I knew that. "How do you get this training? Can only Japanese girls go?"

"You want to be Eric's real wife?"

I nodded. If Imi was beside herself with joy, I was behind myself with embarrassment. I'd started this, however. I'd finish it. "If he's amenable. I don't know, though. He doesn't—"

"I can arrange these lessons, *Aijou*. It would be my wedding present to you and Eric."

Calling me "beloved daughter" was a recent development. Technically, I was her niece-in-law, and Eric her nephew. However, I'd often heard her call him *Aisoku*, "beloved son."

"I don't want Eric to know. Not yet. I'm not sure he'll like the idea. I'm not sure he even thinks of me that way."

"All he needs is one night with you. Everything will be fine then."

I let out a breath and thanked her. Talking to her hadn't been as hard as I'd thought.

* * * * *

As was proper, Imi accompanied me to the establishment where the marriage lessons took place. She enjoyed tea with the older ladies while I met with my classmates. *Gaijin* that I was, they stared at me, though only for a moment. I suspected they felt just as awkward to be receiving these instructions as I did.

The sessions were basic, though graphic. Boys of about eighteen entered the room wearing silk robes until several older women disrobed them to provide various demonstrations. We weren't supposed to touch the boys, only watch. After five classes, I knew more about boys and their privities than I ever thought there was to know.

Now all I had to do was find the right moment to show Eric how much I appreciated everything he'd done for me.

✱ ✱ ✱ ✱ ✱

On the night of the award dinner, the ballroom at one of Tokyo's finest hotels oozed the cream of the business world. Some had flown in from the Americas and Europe. Black dinner jackets and Middle Eastern headdresses complemented a rainbow of elegant gowns. Gold and precious gems glittered everywhere.

Comfortable in my green silk frock, I stood smiling beside Eric while he worked his way through clusters of admirers. As he introduced me to his business associates, I recalled the tricks my father taught me about remembering who was who, and hoped who would still be the same who I thought he or she was the next time I met him or her. The affair really wasn't much different from the gala events at Tara Hall, except here I spoke Japanese, and American English when so addressed. I thought I pulled off both foreign languages well.

Eric's speech followed the sumptuous banquet. I sat at the head table with eminent members of the Tokyo business community and their spouses and listened.

"Thank you for the honor of selecting me as the recipient of this year's award."

While Eric spoke about the changing economy, I sensed curious eyes on me. I sat up straight, daring them all to take a good look. Almost two years had passed since I'd attended such a function, and I was loving it.

"...access to the global marketplace for both large and small businesses..."

Kiyoshi sat at a nearby table with a young couple. Earlier in the evening he'd introduced the gentleman as Ryota Sasaki, his younger brother. The lady was Ryota's wife.

"…provide the proper environment to foster growth on both local and global levels…"

Imi's personal maid had fussed over me and my new face until I hardly recognized myself. Twenty-three now, and didn't I look grownup and gorgeous. Eric had not only presented me with emeralds set in earrings and a bracelet to match my gown, he'd given me a box that held a gold wedding ring. He'd had it for some time, he said, but my fingers were so thin it wouldn't have fit.

Tonight would be the perfect night to speak to him, if I could find the nerve.

"…and nurture the proper conditions for investments from the private sector…"

I could nurture the proper conditions. I knew I looked exceptionally lovely, and he *had* given me the ring. I decided tonight would be the night.

"Thank you."

You're welcome.

* * * * *

At midnight, we returned to the house, and the servants relieved us of our coats. Imi had waited up to hear all about the dinner. While she went to see about tea, Eric loosened his tie and made his way into the sitting room.

My gown and I swished along behind him. "I was proud of you tonight."

"Thank you, Hana. I was proud myself, though I know these awards are usually political. I must say that I was just as proud of you. You enchanted everyone. So lovely."

We sat on the couch. He didn't attempt to touch me. Even my cousins would have squeezed my chin or tugged my hair. This might be harder than I thought. "I've been thinking about something since you gave me this ring, Eric. I want to be a real wife to you."

In my preconceived notion of what would happen next, he would smile, take me in his arms, and kiss me. We would live happily ever after.

I waited.

He didn't even smile. "Why would you think such a thing, Hana?"

His stern, incredulous tone confused me. "We *are* married. I just thought…"

"Did you?" He folded his arms across his chest. "Did you also think that one day I'll return you to your father? What will we tell him, hmm? You've overstepped your bounds here, young lady."

I fought to hide my injured feelings. "I don't have to go back to my father. I've been learning to be a good wife."

"Oh? And how have you managed that? More reading?"

"Well, no. I attended...sessions."

He slammed a fist on the arm of the couch and bolted out the door. A moment later I heard him shouting—at Imi, whose pitiful cries as she tried to defend herself resounded through the house.

I ran to find them. Eric Yamada was about to learn that his temper was no match for mine.

$$* * * * *$$

I'd always found solace in the gardens. Not now. Maybe never again.

For months I'd been speaking American English exclusively to lock it into my head. Last night I'd been so angry I couldn't remember any of it. My defense of Imi had been pure Irish, and savage. It wasn't that Eric had rejected me—well, maybe a little. I simply couldn't bear to hear him bashing Imi, a generous, delicate lady who'd seen to my every need from the first day I arrived.

His counterattack had been just as ferocious, though strangely he hadn't directed his wrath at me. He'd blasted Imi for meddling in his personal affairs, and had only stopped when, still resplendent in my evening finery, I'd physically stepped between them.

"Leave her alone, Eric. She only did as I asked."

"This is none of your affair, Hana."

I set my hands on my hips to keep from shoving him. "Isn't it? I won't stand by and watch you eating the head off her. You want to give out to someone? Have a go with me!"

"Stay out of it, Hana!"

Imi's hands covered her face. Her weeping enraged me.

"She's not to blame. The idea was mine, though now I can't understand what I was thinking. Let her be or get out. Leave! We never want to see you again!"

He turned and left the kitchen. I'd thrown the man out of his own house. Now I sat bleary-eyed on a stone bench in his garden bemoaning the trouble I'd caused. Once I apologized, I'd call Colonel Chambeau and ask to stay in the officers' housing at ISF headquarters in Tokyo. My self-pitying thoughts took up so much of my concentration, I didn't hear Eric approach.

"Talty."

No more Hana. Embarrassment kept me from looking at him, or even responding. I didn't know what to say.

"Please, Talty. If you won't speak to me, at least listen."

I stood and faced him. "I'm sorry for what happened, but the fault was mine, not Imi's."

He looked away and sighed. I wondered if my father would get a full refund.

Glancing around as if he were seeking an escape route, Eric sighed again and nodded toward a nearby bench. "Could we sit?"

We did. The early morning sun warmed the air. Birds chirped contentedly, oblivious to the catastrophe below them.

"Talty, I'm as sorry for this argument as you are. I'm worried you're blaming yourself for it." He paused. He seemed to be having a hard a time finding words too.

I waited.

"Don't misunderstand," he said at last. "I'm devoted to Imi. She's my elder, my only living relative, but she shouldn't have encouraged you to compromise yourself. Not with me, anyway."

"I don't understand."

He patted my hand. "No, you don't. How could you? I thought you might have known, but it's obvious now that you don't. Imi thought that if you...gave yourself to me, I'd enjoy the experience and be cured."

That I had no idea what he was talking about must have shown on my face.

He sighed again. "Fixed. A normal man. A man who likes to be with women. That's why I was angry with her. She knows I love someone else. She disapproves and doesn't treat him very well."

As his words sank in, it all fell into place. How could I have been so oblivious? "Kiyoshi. You and Kiyoshi?"

He nodded. His hand returned to his lap. He waited for me to speak. What could I say? I realized what an intruder I'd been here. I thought about the late-night work sessions over the barn, how Imi seldom dined with us when Kiyoshi was present, and how happy she'd been when I'd said I wanted to be Eric's real wife.

"I didn't know, Eric. I'm sorry. I'll go now."

"Where would you go? To a military barracks?"

"I can't stay here."

"Yes, you can. Neither Kiyoshi nor I want you to go. Nothing would change. You'd still have your own quarters and access to the dojo."

"Things have changed already. You're calling me 'Talty' instead of 'Hana.' And I'll be leaving at some point to work with ISF."

"But not yet—Hana. I wasn't sure you'd feel the same as Imi about my...partnership with Kiyoshi. He is dear to me. So are you, in your own way. You've brought a vibrancy here, shaken us from our day-to-day routine."

"I've shaken you, all right."

He smiled. "Come back to the house. Kiyoshi is making breakfast."

"And Imi?"

"I've spoken to Imi. All is as well as it can be." He stood. "Can we agree to remain friends—Hana?"

"Is it all right if I hug you?"

He pulled me close. I hugged him tight and he hugged me back. Though it wasn't the sort of hug I'd been hoping for the night before, it meant the world to me now.

We returned to the house and found Kiyoshi preparing my favorite breakfast: scrambled eggs and bacon. He looked up from his stirring when we came in.

"Good morning, Kiyoshi-san."

"*Ohayo gozaimasu*, Hime-san." He glanced at Eric in question.

"Hana will be staying, Ki. Everything is fine."

Kiyoshi grinned.

* * * * *

Whether Eric and Kiyoshi started behaving more like a couple because I knew their secret, or because I started seeing them so, they seemed more relaxed around me. For my part, I felt more like an intruder than ever. Despite their objections, I called Colonel Chambeau's private number and let him know I was ready to work.

Eric insisted I stay in his downtown apartment, which wasn't far from ISF Headquarters, rather than at the officers' residence halls. I agreed to please him, though I refused his offer of having his chauffeur shuttle me back and forth to the base each day. The chauffeur would bring me home on weekends, however.

Home. I'd come to think of Eric's place that way.

Ron Chambeau, my new commanding officer, set me up in an office right beside him. He'd promised Kieran he'd keep an eye on me. I didn't care that I'd simply traded one watchdog for another. At long last I was serving with ISF. I still hoped to get to their research center in California one day, but for now I'd be helping the peacekeepers through my work with Ron's requisitions operation.

Tokyo was a jump off point for the ISF peacekeeping missions in the eastern hemisphere, and the international troops stationed around the area required provisions. ISF Tokyo manned a central depot that flew supplies everywhere by helicopter or plane, depending on the distance. Ron supervised the distribution of those supplies. No one could obtain ordnance, medicine, or even silverware for their mess halls without his signature.

He could get anything anyone wanted. Seeing how he worked—and turning a blind eye to many things he did—I came to understand how he'd managed to create false identification papers for me so easily. He and Kieran certainly were kindred spirits.

When I joined his team, his staff was shipping supplies to a tiny new nation near Australia, half of a large island that had recently declared its independence. The government was volatile, the people prone to rioting. Their new leaders had requested ISF peacekeeping troops, who'd arrived to patrol the border and police the area.

My first assignment was to help Ron equip a helicopter-carrying ship that was moving a small fleet of Bellwether Sachems into the area. The Sachem, a versatile, multi-mission helicopter, could handle the varied demands of peacekeeping. Its crew could arrange the modular seats for VIP or troop transport, or remove them for heavy cargo. These shiny black helicopters would haul humanitarian provisions around the island during the upcoming monsoon season when the rains washed out the roads.

The Sachem could also carry detachable weapons. Though the peacekeepers couldn't take offensive action, they had every right to defend themselves. We always had weaponry ready for installation on the helicopters in case hostilities broke out.

"Can't keep peace without teeth," Ron said.

And so I met Kiyoshi's brother Ryota again. Ryota, a private arms contractor, could provide armament more quickly than the military could, given the distance the weaponry would have to ship.

Ryota had only met me once, when I'd been all decked out in evening clothes and sported a formal hairdo. I was sure that when Ron introduced me with my new name, Ryota never guessed I was his brother's lover's wife. He came in, conducted his business, and left.

For two months I was a glorified requisitions clerk, ordering crates of ketchup and mustard. When Ron decided I was ready for the big test, he started sending me out of the office to "really get it through your head that your own mother wouldn't know you, Major Princess."

I delivered sensitive dispatches as far away as New Zealand and Australia, and despite minor hassles—my wedding ring did nothing to thwart male advances—I loved the work, and the freedom. I could go anywhere a plane or helicopter could take me.

I wanted to go home.

An opportunity to do so presented itself sooner than I expected.

CHAPTER EIGHT

A Small Conspiracy

The first sailors sought protection from the ocean's perils by offering blood sacrifices to their gods. The Babylonians butchered oxen, the Ottomans, sheep. The Vikings, believing that sea gods who received a blood offering now would spare the lives of warriors later, crushed slaves and innocent maidens to death on the hulls of their long ships.

As mankind became more civilized, water and wine replaced blood in maritime rituals. One overcast afternoon in Ireland's Cork Harbor, a bottle of champagne waited to christen the massive drill ship looming beside the dock, ready to start her seagoing life.

The mist couldn't dampen the spirits of the spectators on the quay. A military band complete with Irish pipers accompanied the cheers that greeted King Brian and Queen Eileen as they strolled side by side to the sponsor's platform.

Brian beamed with pride when Eileen stepped up to the bow of the ship. Her gloved hands tugged at the ceremonial ribbon.

"I christen thee *Kincora*," she shouted. "May all who sail her sail in safety!"

The magnum exploded against the ship's hull, triggering hearty applause and a brass band fanfare. Champagne sprayed Eileen, wetting her blue silk suit, her ivory face, and her upswept hair. An attendant handed her a linen towel. She thanked him and patted her cheeks.

Brian hoped he was the only one who realized she was wiping away tears as well as champagne.

★ ★ ★ ★ ★

Once Ireland had reclaimed Fargan, the World Court lifted the fishing ban.

Ireland's fishing industry regained its former prosperity. Brian saw no reason the fishing trawlers couldn't coexist with oil rigs. He believed he could harvest the hydrocarbons that lay beneath Irish waters equitably and efficiently. The big rigs would enhance, not undermine, the wealth Ireland derived from her lucrative fishing trade.

Brian charged his ministers to pass strict legislation that enforced superior ecological and safety standards on every oil rig operating in Irish waters. Consequently, Ireland's offshore hydrocarbon facilities boasted some of the highest production and lowest accident ratings in the world. The economic growth resulting from these stringent management policies promised further prosperity to the already thriving kingdom.

Having tightened the reins on the hydrocarbon industry, Brian invested a hefty portion of his personal fortune in the construction of a state-of-the-art drill ship. Built by Irish shipbuilders in an Irish shipyard—workers had to dredge an area of Cork's biggest shipyard to construct the 38,000 ton ship—the *Kincora* slid into the deep waters of Cork Harbor. Her captain and crew would conduct four months of final tests before she began her maiden voyage to the Fargan Trough, where her biggest challenge waited. Could her ability to drill seven or more miles beneath the surface of the ocean tap the wealth of hydrocarbons resting there?

Brian believed it could. Still, not everyone agreed with his energy policies. The Minister of Finance had refused to back *Kincora's* first mission. Not only was he reluctant to risk the kingdom's treasury on an expedition that might turn up empty, he cited studies stating the kingdom already had more than enough oil and gas.

Brian disagreed. He'd commissioned his own studies. No immediate crisis loomed, but production from the older wells had declined. Though tempted to override his minister's decision with a royal mandate, he chose a different course of action: he quietly committed the remainder of his fluid assets to finance *Kincora's* first endeavor. The gamble was great, but Brian's faith was greater.

According to tradition, the godmother of the new ship would impart her spirit to the vessel for all time. If Eileen's spirit graced the *Kincora,* what could go wrong?

* * * * *

Eileen laughed about her champagne shower, yet Brian suspected some underlying problem. He cornered her during a private moment before the post-christening reception.

"What is it, Eileen? Were you hurt when the bottle exploded?"

The tiniest pout, one he knew well, appeared on her face. "Talty should be doing these things. She should be christening ships and cutting ribbons on new hospital wings. I haven't seen my daughter in donkey's years. When are you going to bring her home?"

"She's my daughter too. Don't think I don't care."

"Then bring her home. I don't understand what you're waiting for. The girl needs her family. She needs her mother!"

"Kieran is—"

"Is Kieran the king, then? I want my girl!"

An aide called through the door that the reception was about to start.

"We'll be right there," Brian said, and then he kissed Eileen. "Mmm. Fine champagne. Don't cry, darlin'. I'll find a way."

* * * * *

Early the next morning, Peadar welcomed Brian to Garrymuir. Sunshine beckoned them outside for a tour of the lofty gardens overlooking Howth Harbor. As they strolled past the spring-flowering shrubs and perennials, Peadar pointed out his newest botanical treasures. He enjoyed the tour until his brother stated the reason for his visit.

Brian turned his face to the sun and inhaled the salty breeze. He wore that smug look that said he'd thought things out and no one would stop him. "Look at this garden! It's a feast for my poor, daughter-deprived eyes."

"Kieran won't like it. He'll stamp his foot down."

"Is Kieran the king, then? Anyway, we can't let Kieran know. He's the very one we'll have to convince. You still supervise the Military College, don't you?"

"You know I do." Peadar stopped on the path. A moving cloud left him shielding his eyes from a sudden flash of sunlight. "Just what do you have up your sleeve?"

Slipping his hands in his trouser pockets, Brian smiled and sauntered on. "When does the summer semester start?"

Peadar hurried after him. "In a few days. Why?"

"Talty always liked military history. In fact, she was quite good at it. Send one of your instructors on leave for the semester. We'll say he got sick and we need a substitute teacher. We've looked everywhere, and the only one we can find is Talty."

"Be serious. No one will believe that, especially Talty. She'll know."

"I spoke to Eric Yamada this morning. He says she's come a long way. He put me in touch with that friend of Kieran's she's working for. A fella named Chambeau who said in no uncertain American terms that my timing stinks." Brian smiled. "Said he doesn't like the idea of sending her off when he has a ton of work for her. Sounded very impressed with her."

Peadar gazed down at the Irish Sea, where a fishing trawler inched toward Howth beneath a flock of circling seagulls. The peaceful scene clashed with his growing agitation. "You shouldn't be interfering with her military duties."

Brian's smile widened. "What's the fun of being king if I can't pull a few strings? I coaxed a little, and Chambeau finally said he'd give anything to see the look on Kieran's face when he finds out who she really is."

"You're taking a chance bringing her home just now. What if there's trouble?" Recalling Talty's ruined face, Peadar stopped again and closed his eyes. "Has she really changed that much?"

This time Brian stopped with him. His smile vanished. "He and Yamada both said so. What harm can it do? She'll be at Curragh Camp, surrounded by our finest soldiers. When will we not be taking a chance? It's time to bring her home."

The brothers reached the part of the garden that offered the finest view of the harbor. Peadar gazed over the piers and fishing smacks and considered the possibilities. "I'll want extra security in place. We'll have to be discreet if you don't want Kieran to know."

"What do you suggest?"

"Aidan's been talking about taking a turn at training the new cadets. We'll have him teach something at the college too. He'll keep a close eye on her, all right." Peadar chuckled. "And I think he'd kill to play such a fine joke on his father."

Brian laughed. "So would I. Where's Neil?"

"On search and rescue training with the Rangers."

"That's all right, then. Aidan will be enough. Call this Colonel Chambeau, Peadar. Work with him to make it sound real. If we can pull it off, we'll have a party and dance all night."

"Now, that's an idea I like!"

"We'll have it here, so we can enjoy the gardens. Look at those azaleas!"

Peadar loved his azaleas, though he considered them standard garden fare. "Come this way and I'll show you a sight I wait all year to see." He led Brian to the hedges that sheltered his roses from the temperamental Irish weather.

May was too early for the roses. The bloom on the tree peonies, however, had never been more spectacular.

✳ ✳ ✳ ✳ ✳

Talty was packing her briefcase when Ron called her into his office. "Glad I caught you, Major Princess. I just got this and thought you might be interested."

He handed her a dispatch. While she scanned, he summarized. "A history instructor at Curragh Camp's Military College needs immediate surgery. The other instructors have full schedules. They need someone to fill in for the semester."

Talty glanced up from the typed page. "Why are you giving this to me?"

"I shouldn't be. I need you here. But it's only for nine weeks, and teaching military history would be a cinch for you. And maybe you could sneak home for a visit."

"Home? But...but this says the new semester begins in three days. I'd have to leave right away. And what will my father say? And Kieran—"

"How will they know? You talk like a Yank, your face looks different, and you've put on weight since I met you. Think about it. If you pull it off, you can go home anytime you like."

Home. "Are you sure you can do without me for a few weeks?"

A delighted grin lit Ron's face. "Hell no, but go pack, Major Princess. That's an order."

With a joyful squeal, she hugged him and hurried to the waiting limousine.

* * * * *

During the long flight to Dublin, Talty reviewed the class syllabus. She knew the material well. Not only had military strategy been a favorite part of her mandatory training as Crown Princess, she'd also devoured the lessons Uncle Peadar had taught in his Fianna classes. As she recalled those lessons now, the words of one in particular played over in her head:

All warfare is founded on deception, false appearances, and disinformation. The ruler who understands this principle, and the principles of careful defense and bold attack, will conquer.

The old fellas had created an astounding deception when they'd declared her dead. She knew the hoax had protected not just her, but the kingdom as well, yet her exile had hurt. Her family seemed to have forgotten her. She meant to remind them she was still around.

* * * * *

By the end of the first class, Talty had reviewed the course objectives and given her students a brief introduction to the siege equipment used by the Greek leader Dionysus in 300 B.C. Alone in the room, she sat reviewing the next day's lesson. A knock on the doorframe drew her gaze to the sparkling brown eyes of her cousin Aidan.

"Beg pardon, ma'am. I'm looking for Major McKenna. They told me she was in Room 241, and here it is, and here you are. I'm guessing I've found you."

It took all the willpower Talty could muster to maintain her American accent. "Yes. Please, come in."

Aidan swaggered to the desk and extended his hand. "Major Aidan Dacey, at your service. They've asked me to look after you."

Fighting to hide her joy, she shook the hand of her ginger-haired kinsman. His grip nearly crushed her fingers. The boyish face she remembered had changed. He looked more manly now, but she'd have recognized him anywhere. She wanted to jump up and hug him. "That would be great. I just got in. I don't know my way around."

"I'll see you to your quarters." Before she could protest, he picked up her briefcase and stood aside while she walked through the door.

The game had Talty tingling. "Are you teaching too?"

"Yes. Marksmanship. Indoor and out."

On the way to her quarters, they chatted about the new rifle range. Talty wondered about his presence at Curragh. She didn't believe in coincidence.

* * * * *

After a week of entertaining her students with stories of Roman and Viking invasions, Talty thought the time had come to let her family know she was home.

As it happened, Aidan was headed to Dublin for the weekend. He stopped by her classroom and invited her to join him. "I'd hate to leave you here all alone when you could be eating decent food."

"Thanks, Aidan. I'd love to come. I have a favor to ask anyway. I'm trying to make my class more interesting for the cadets. I understand your father and uncle both know a lot about the old Irish warrior ways. I hear they even train young men and women in the techniques."

"My father and my uncle are Fian warriors." He proudly added, "I've recently become a full-fledged member of the Fianna myself."

Neil must have too. Talty didn't intend to be left behind.

"Congratulations. Do you think your father or your uncle would agree to present a live demonstration of traditional Fian skills for my class? I'm sure it would liven things up." Talty knew very well—as did Aidan—that Kieran and Peadar would both refuse such a request.

Aidan only hesitated for a moment. "They conduct presentations for those who aspire to the training, but they don't do it for the public. I can ask, though."

"Thanks. That's all I can hope for."

* * * * *

The Dacey family's Dublin home stood on the site of an ancient fort whose ruins had rested undisturbed for centuries. A medieval Boru prince had taken a liking to the verdant setting and built an estate there for his bride, naming the ten-acre property Duncullen: the "fort in the holly."

After spending several weeks in cramped quarters at Curragh Camp, Aidan delighted in Duncullen's open spaces. Despite the late afternoon rain, twelve-foot bay windows let in enough light to brighten the book-laden alcoves in the drawing room, where he sat having tea with his father. The fire dancing in the ornate hearth would have cheered the room if Kieran wasn't scowling.

Talty's request had provoked the scowl, as Aidan knew it would. The Fianna were the elite of the military, and his father wouldn't make a circus act of them.

"And you know it, boy! Why didn't you tell her so?"

"She's only trying to make her class more interesting. What harm would it do to show them a bit of fencing and sparring?"

Just then the arched oak door opened. Breege Dacey entered the room, her dark hair frizzy from the rain. Her blue eyes glowed when she saw her son. "Aidan, love. It's fine to have you home." Then she cast a glance at Kieran's face. "Hmm. Looks like I got here just in time. What's going on?"

After Aidan rose and kissed his mother's cheek, he repeated Talty's request. Breege had once been an army lieutenant, and as Aidan expected, she shared Kieran's opinion.

"When we see your friend at dinner," she said, "your father will explain his position. Kieran, you might think of another suggestion that might satisfy the young lady without compromising the dignity of the Fianna. It is, after all, your area of expertise."

Plainly pleased by the compliment, Kieran grunted.

"Your parents are coming for dinner," Breege added. "Aidan, if all the shouting down here hasn't frightened your friend away, I'll have dinner prepared for eight o'clock."

* * * * *

Standing before the bedroom mirror, Talty tied back her hair. The dark pantsuit she'd chosen from her meager wardrobe was the one that least restricted her ability to move. She checked her appearance one last time and decided she'd pass inspection.

"How do I address your parents and grandparents, Aidan?" she called out to the sitting area. "So many titles!" She hadn't expected Uncle Jack and Auntie Nuala tonight. This would be a real test.

"We aren't quite as stuffy as other royal families," Aidan said. "'Ma'am' and 'sir' will do well enough."

Moments later, they were down in the drawing room. Aidan introduced her to his parents and grandparents as Major Christy McKenna of ISF's Special Services. She greeted everyone in turn.

Uncle Jack took her hand and kissed it. "A pleasure, Major. A very great pleasure indeed."

From the twinkle in his eye, Talty realized that Jack not only knew her, he was going to play along. She squeezed his hand. "You're very kind, Your Highness."

Kieran took Nuala's arm and led her to the dining room. Aidan walked with Breege. Uncle Jack and Talty lagged behind.

"What gave me away, Uncle Jack?"

"I've been looking into beautiful Boru eyes since I married Nuala. I'd know them anywhere. What are you up to, girl?"

"If I can prove to Kieran that no one knows me, maybe he'll let me come home sometimes. Don't give me away just yet. Please?"

Jack chuckled and offered his arm. "Your servant, Lady Princess."

* * * * *

Eating only small bites of a home cooked Irish dinner was difficult, but if things went as planned, Talty didn't want mashed potatoes bogging her down. "I understand your position, Commander," she said at the end of the meal. "Perhaps you could grant me a small consolation. I noticed some very old weapons on the walls. Could I have a tour?"

Kieran seemed disappointed that she'd surrendered so easily. "It would be my pleasure."

"He means that," Aidan said, grinning. "He'll go on for hours over it."

Talty smiled. She knew Kieran well. "Just the highlights would be fine."

Aidan joined Kieran and Talty for the impromptu tour. Kieran warmed to his role as guide, describing this axe and that scabbard, telling Talty stories she knew by heart. She also knew he kept his most prized items locked in a case in the training room, and she counted on him to show them off. He didn't disappoint her.

They descended the stairs to the basement. Aidan switched on the lights in the small-scale gym. He leaned against the wall while Kieran showed off the rare daggers and short swords in the glass case. Talty admired the relics long enough to be courteous. Then she pretended to notice the wooden staffs in the corner of the room. She stepped to the rack and hefted a bata in her hands.

"A bit like Kendo sticks, aren't they? Do you spar, sir?" She tossed the bata to him.

He caught it easily. "I'm not dressed for sparring, Major."

Ignoring him, she selected a bata and twirled it in a warm-up pattern. "Come on, let's see a few moves." She assumed a combat stance and banged the stick three times on the shock absorbent floor, the signal to begin.

Kieran didn't question how she knew it, yet something in his eyes changed. "As you're the challenger, the rules allow me the first strike." He swung the bata at her shoulder as if he were swatting a fly.

Talty dropped her bata into both hands and deflected his blow with a loud crack.

Lightning fast, he swung at her thighs. She jumped over his bata, landed on one knee, and poked the tip of her bata into his chest. Before he could respond, she jumped to her feet. Repeating the maneuver he'd just tried, she swung at his thighs.

He went down. She straddled his chest and pressed her bata against his throat.

Her American accent disappeared. "A pretty little girl can kill you just as dead as a big, ugly man."

Dumbfounded, Kieran stared up at her. "Mary and Joseph! Talty? Get up, girl! I'll have you over my knee in a minute!"

Her laughter welled and bubbled over. "What, you haven't had enough? Here, old fella. Let me help you up."

He pushed her away. She fell over, laughing even harder. A moment later he was laughing with her. At the door, Aidan, Jack, and Peadar laughed as well.

Kieran's scowl reappeared. "So you came for the show, Peadar? I'm thinking you knew about this all along."

"I did. So did Aidan. We had to know if Talty could come home without anyone knowing her. I think we have our answer."

Peadar barreled across the floor. He seized Talty's underarms, picked her up, and shook her. "Well done, Talty! Well done! You look different, but you look fine! Doesn't she look fine, lads? It's great to see you, love! Your father will be beside himself!"

"All right, Uncle," she giggled, "put me down." He kept shaking her. "Uncle Peadar, put me down." He did, but caught her again in a hug that took her breath away. She loved it, loved that she'd proven herself completely recovered and very, very well.

* * * * *

Two enormous wolfhounds lay before the fireplace in Kieran's study. Gentle flames bathed the room in a dreamy glow. Peadar sat beside Kieran on one side of the hearth, content in its warmth. Talty sat on the other, facing her kinsmen.

Over the edge of his teacup, Peadar studied his niece. Her new face amazed him. Her request to speak with him and Kieran in private did not.

She crossed her legs and smiled. "Have you forgiven me, Kieran?"

"You're a bad girl to play such a trick on a poor, unsuspecting fella," he grumbled. "I'll do, I expect. Now, what's on your mind, girl?"

"I'll be here for eight more weeks. I want to complete my Fian training. I'll have time when I'm not teaching, if you can find time to work with me."

"It's been years since you've trained," Peadar said.

"I've been training in Japan."

Kieran scowled. "Do you think that Japanese stuff is enough to get you back to where you were before—"

"My accident? I don't know, but I have to find out. Please consider it. That's all I'm asking." She rose gracefully, kissed their cheeks, and said good-night.

Peadar watched her go. He'd always taken his responsibility to produce the next generation of Fianna seriously. Talty had been a promising candidate until her "accident."

"She's lost too much time," Kieran said. "She'll never catch up."

Peadar shook with silent laughter. "She didn't look too far behind tonight. I'll speak to Brian and send for Neil. She'll need her training partner. They can work at Garrymuir."

"Maybe she fooled me, but she didn't fool my father."

"Your father aside, no one will know her. She's changed a great deal. Besides, we've seen no indication that anyone is even looking for her anymore. I'm tempted to announce that she's back and let Geoffrey Wessex go to the devil."

Kieran snapped his head toward him. "You know better. Geoffrey still insists England is entitled to her dowry. He'll never get it if she turns up alive, and that letter I have leaves no doubt that the murdering bastard would go after her."

Peadar had seen the letter. Kieran had only received it recently from the niece of a man he'd met in North Africa. If what it claimed were true, Geoffrey had murdered innocent men in his greedy quest for oil. "What about Roger?"

"Right now Roger believes that *we* believe Thomas murdered your mother. If he knew Talty was still alive to say otherwise, he'd send someone after her before you could spit. We have to get rid of Roger."

"What? What are you suggesting?"

The scar on Kieran's jaw caught the firelight. His smile chilled Peadar. "Don't worry, Pead. I'm not talking about assassination. My friend at MI6 says Roger's plot to overthrow King John is drawing more high-ranking followers than they first thought. The instant Roger tries something, they'll arrest him and his gang of traitors. He'll be in prison for a long time, if they don't hang him. Talty will be safe enough then."

Roger's machinations baffled Peadar, though he supposed the ambitions of such men were what had kept the Fianna in existence for centuries. "It's a bad bird that dirties its own nest. John Wessex is a decent fellow. With the proper people behind him, he'll do right by his country. Meanwhile, I don't think it would hurt to have ourselves another Banfian warrior."

Kieran stood and stretched. "Agreed. And now, we'd better get to our girls if we want them to be good to us tonight."

The cousins walked down the hall, Kieran limping, Peadar smiling.

CHAPTER NINE
Favorite Pastimes

Hunkering down in the Trinity College Library archives on a rainy Saturday morning suited Liam Boru well. Dressed in comfortable old clothes appropriate for treasure hunting through cobwebs, Ireland's Crown Prince was just another student translating the annals that depicted life in ancient Ireland.

Though his Early Irish Law class required him to conduct such research once a week, Liam could be found in the dusty basement storage room more often. He loved touching the old vellum documents. Knowing that others had touched them long before he was born enhanced his appreciation of history—and his own fleeting place in it.

Once he'd finished deciphering a battered manuscript that detailed a long-ago land transaction, he made his notes, removed his gold-rimmed glasses, and rubbed his tired eyes. Then he picked up what should have been another land record. He chuckled as he translated the words.

So erotic poetry is nothing new. A few lines later, he decided this wasn't poetry, but downright pornography. He grinned with delight as the poem fueled his imagination. He'd take no written notes from this one.

"Excuse me," said a female voice behind him. "I need to reach those shelves."

Like a twelve-year-old caught with an obscene magazine, Liam flipped the paper over and adopted his well-practiced air of angelic innocence. His shrewdly widened blinked in disbelief at an emerald-eyed beauty with flaming curls. It seemed he'd somehow conjured up the personification of his randy fantasy.

He adjusted his glasses and gave her his best smile. "Oh, sorry. I'll move over here."

"What are you reading?" She plucked the parchment from his hand, leaving behind a trace of flowery perfume.

She'd never understand the old thing. He might offer to translate it, though he'd tell her it described cattle dealings. Perhaps she'd agree, and they'd become great friends.

"It's very old stuff," he said. "I'd be happy to help you read it."

As she studied the paper, her lovely face reddened. "I'll bet you would, you lecherous pig! Enjoying your reading, are you? Is this what you come here for?"

She could translate the old words as well as he could! "Well, I didn't write the thing, did I? I found it with the land records."

"I'm sure you did! Well, I'll leave you to your *land records* and come back when the place is safe for decent people." She tossed the paper at him and flew from the basement.

Liam imagined a trail of smoke in her wake. He was sorry for what she thought, and sad that they wouldn't become great friends after all. The smart ones were the best company, especially when they were so pretty.

The alarm on his watch buzzed. His guards would want their lunch. He entrusted the poem-gone-astray to the curator on duty and set out in the morning rain. He'd just reached the main intersection of the campus paths when a young woman with tied-back chestnut hair stopped him.

"Can you point me to the Ballsbridge bus?" she asked in a snappy American accent.

Another pretty one. Ah, Liam, you're a magnet for them. Or a bull's-eye.

"It's right on Nassau Street. I'm going that way," he fibbed. "I'll walk with you."

Liam's protectors fell in behind them. They kept their distance and wouldn't interfere unless he called them. "I'm thinking you're a long way from home," he said. "Is this your first visit to Ireland?"

"No." She stopped. "I'm really not lost at all. I wanted an excuse to speak to you."

Disappointed, and more than a little resentful, he stared at her. She was a reporter or something. "Call Tara Hall for an appointment, why don't you? If you'll excuse me, I'm running late." He turned to retrace his steps.

"Would you turn your back on your sister, Li?"

Her American accent had vanished. The familiar voice puzzled him at first. When he grasped what she'd said, he gawked at her. "Talty?"

She glanced at his guards. "Don't give me away," she said, though she smiled.

He almost picked her up and swung her around. "Not that I'm not happy to see you, but what are you doing here? And why are you playing tricks on your own darlin' brother?"

"I'm sorry, Li. I had to know if you'd recognize me."

"How could I? You look so different. You look wonderful! Are you going home to see Mum and Dad?"

"Home. Yes. Aidan is waiting to take me there. I'll explain everything when I see you."

She hurried off to Nassau Street. He watched until she was out of sight. Then he practically jig-stepped to the car that brought him home.

* * * * *

Aidan's daredevil navigation delivered Talty to the King's Residence in record time. Liam met them in the front reception room. After properly kissing Talty's hand, he hugged her hard enough to make her laugh.

"Dad's in his study," he said. "Go easy on him. He's nervous."

Talty was nervous herself. When her father answered her knock, she turned the doorknob, but stopped until Liam and Aidan whispered words of encouragement. She nodded and stepped into the familiar, oak-paneled room.

Brian stood by the fire. His beard and hair sparkled with more silver than she remembered. Uncertainty flickered in his eyes. "Come here, girl. Let me see you."

Remembering Liam's warning to go easy, she crossed the room. "Hello, Dad." She took his hand and kissed it.

He touched her cheek, as if to prove to himself she was really there. "A kiss for your king is fine. How about one for your Daddy?"

She nearly wept when she sank against him, secure in his fatherly embrace. At last he set her back and inspected her again.

"Talty. You don't look like my Talty, but I could feel that spirit of yours right across the room." Abruptly he switched to his stern, authoritarian tone. "You took a big chance coming home without telling anyone."

"Get out of it, Dad. I happen to know you were part of the conspiracy to bring me here."

He responded with a sheepish smile. "Your mother threatened to leave me if I didn't. She's afraid you'll forget your dance steps."

She laughed, and he laughed, and then he stopped laughing. "Let's talk, darlin'."

They sat before the fire. "You've been through a terrible ordeal," he said, "thanks to my treaty mongering. I've thought more than once you'd never forgive me."

"I agreed with your treaties, didn't I?"

"Treaties be damned. I'm your father first, or I should've been."

She touched his hand. "There's nothing to forgive. You couldn't have known what would happen. I love you, Dad. All I want is to come home."

"I'm not convinced you'd be safe here right now."

"Why not? Because Kieran says so? I can't believe—"

He bent and kissed her forehead. "Be patient, daughter of my heart. Never forget that I love you well. I miss you and I want you home as much as you want to be here."

For now, she'd accept his decision. She'd made this much progress. Soon she'd make more. She pulled him from his chair, and they went to find Eileen.

✱ ✱ ✱ ✱ ✱

Rain pelted the multi-paned windows of King John's Southwick Castle apartments. Inside the rooms, the fragrance of hot cinnamon scones melded with the scent of linseed oil, a soothing mixture that had become a familiar part of John's Saturday afternoons. The twenty-three-year-old king touched the tip of his sable brush to his palette, alternating dabs at his canvas with swats at the unruly light brown hair falling over his eyes. John Wessex hated haircuts.

His cousin, Lady Claudia Wessex, sat beside the fire. Her silk-stockinged, rain-soaked feet rested on an ottoman to dry. Her slender fingers combed her damp, dark hair. At forty-five, Claudia was the oldest of the current generation of Wessex cousins, and John adored her. She'd always looked after Thomas and her brother Roger, but she doted on John. She'd supervised his private tutoring after his parents died in a yachting accident. His favorite lessons by far were his art lessons. Painting helped him feel significant and capable.

Claudia constantly told John he was gifted, though he didn't see himself so. She'd convinced him to exhibit his best paintings at an upcoming charity luncheon. The prospect both pleased and terrified him.

"You've been painting for an hour, darling. Have some tea."

Wiping his hands on a linen cloth, he sat beside her and asked a question that had bothered him all week. "Why won't Uncle Geoffrey let me read the speech, Claudia? I'm the king. The king is supposed to announce the government's intentions for the year at the opening of Parliament. It's an ancient custom, one I'm well able to conduct."

Claudia passed the scones to him. "Uncle Geoffrey took over many duties for Thomas. I suppose he's used to it."

John set the plate down and clasped Claudia's hands. "But I'm not as bad as Thomas. I've never killed anyone. Am I really so...so brainless that Geoffrey must continue to act as Regent? Am I?"

"Certainly not. It's just that you're so young. Uncle Geoffrey doesn't want you overwhelmed, and I'm sure he's concerned for your safety."

John considered that in his slow, insightful way. "My safety? Am I in danger?" He frowned. "I've heard things when they think I'm not listening. They say Roger is going to depose me so he can become king instead."

Claudia's head jerked up. "Whoever said such a thing? Why, that would be treason!" She looked away, as she often did when she was thinking, and then she lifted the teapot and poured. "I'm going to speak to a man who works hard to keep you safe. He's with MI6."

"That's our military intelligence."

"Yes. His name is Bert Benson. I'm sure he'll tell us that what you're hearing about Roger is rubbish."

"Thank you, Claudia. Sometimes I feel you're my only friend."

"Nonsense." She handed him a cup of tea. "You're the king. Everyone loves you."

John thanked her and tasted his tea. Claudia always put in just the right amount of lemon and sugar. "I've read our history. The English didn't love all their kings. If only I weren't so pudding-headed."

"You aren't any such thing. You mustn't listen to Uncle Geoffrey."

"Would Mr. Benson keep me safe if I attended the opening of Parliament? I only want to watch. I promise I won't do anything to make Uncle Geoffrey angry. I know how he upsets you when he's angry. Do you think Mr. Benson would agree?"

"Why wouldn't he agree? You're the king. Now let's discuss that charity luncheon."

They reviewed John's speech and selected what he'd wear. Claudia assured him his paintings would raise a hefty sum. As always, she left him in better spirits.

* * * * *

The vehicles clustered in Garrymuir's courtyard put Neil on guard: his parents were entertaining. He groaned and asked the limousine driver to continue past the front entrance and drop him at the kitchen door.

He meant to steal up the back stairs, but waves of enticing aromas lured him to the kitchen. Tossing his Air Corps duffel bag into a corner, he popped a canapé into his mouth and was reaching for another when a pair of scurrying caterers banged through the swinging kitchen door. His hand froze in midair.

The open door let strains of Irish dance music into the kitchen. More curious than hungry now, Neil headed to the great hall, where family and guests whirled to a hard kicking reel.

A hand smacked his shoulder. Liam stood smiling beside him. "Good to see you, Neily. We wondered if you'd come in time."

Their backslapping hug ended with Neil automatically grasping and kissing his cousin's hand. "Is this why my father sent for me?"

"Absolutely. We need able-bodied men to keep the women dancing."

Neil shook his head and grinned. "Who's that girl dancing with Aidan?"

Before Liam could answer, Kevin rushed over and caught Neil in a hug. "Neil! We've missed you!"

Neil tousled his brother's hair. "I've only been gone a few days, Kev. What's going on?"

"A dance, what else? Everyone's here."

"Just so," Liam said. "Auntie Connie wanted to throw a party to announce Sandy's engagement to that yellow-haired girl talking to Kieran. She called your mother, and before you could blink, they flew over from Scotland."

Neil eyed his Scottish cousin's fiancée with approval. "They'll be after you to marry now, Li."

"I'm far too young, and in no way deserving of such an esteemed privilege."

Peggy Boru approached them. "You're a rogue and a rascal from what I hear, Liam Boru, and the girls aren't safe around you. About time you got home, Neil. Everyone is here, love. Come dance with us."

Neil kissed his mother's cheek. "I'd like to get cleaned up first."

Peggy inspected him. "Hmm. Good idea. Don't be long. Everyone's asking for you."

Grabbing snacks along the way, Neil returned to the kitchen and raced up the back stairs. Fifteen minutes later, he returned to the kitchen, deserted now but for a young woman helping herself at the water cooler. Her back was to him. He ogled the curves and the tight little rump beneath her silvery pantsuit.

Water in hand, she turned. Her brown eyes widened. Whoever she was, she was pretty.

He affected his most charming smile. "Hello. I'm Neil Boru. Are you here with my cousin Aidan? I saw you dancing with him."

"Yes. He was kind enough to invite me." She offered her hand. "Christy

McKenna."

Her skin was soft, her grip firm. Neil's thighs pulsed with pleasure. Reluctantly, he released her hand. "A Yank, are you? Aidan should know better than to leave a pretty girl like you alone. Some disreputable fella might come along and steal you away from him."

The thought seemed to amuse her. "Some disreputable fellow like you?"

"Me? Oh, no. Not until I'm sure I've fallen in love with you. Right now I only think I have. How's a beautiful American girl getting along in a house full of mad Irish dancers?" He lowered his voice. "Perhaps some private lessons would help."

Grinning gorgeously, she hurried toward the door. "I'm getting along just fine, thanks. See you later." She headed toward the lav down the hall.

Neil braced himself and joined the party. Waving and chatting, he worked his way across the room. Delightful Scottish burrs drew his attention to the windows, where his Edinburgh cousins stood laughing. Talty would love to be here, he thought.

"About time you got back," Liam said. "You were the only one of us missing."

"Not unless your sister is here I wasn't."

"She's here." Liam nodded. "Over there, talking to Aidan."

Too flabbergasted to speak, Neil gawked at the girl he'd met in the kitchen. No wonder his flirting had amused her! "Why didn't you tell me? She looks great. I can't believe it! Does everyone know who she is?"

"No. We're to say she's a friend of Aidan's from the Military College."

Jubilant as a hurler who'd just scored the winning goal, Neil patted Liam's arm and carved a path through the crowd. "Hey, Aidan. How's the teaching going?"

"Great." Aidan's eyes twinkled with mischief. "I get to meet lots of pretty girls, like Christy here. Christy McKenna, my cousin, Neil."

Mindful of the crowd around him, Neil resisted the urge to hug her. He squeezed rather than kissed her hand and lowered his voice. "Hello, Talty. Enjoyed your little joke, did you?"

Her smile warmed his heart. "I did, Neil. You're a frisky fella. A credit to the family."

"And you're a bad girl, putting such thoughts in a fella's head. Stand still."

He marveled at the subtle changes in her. She wasn't simply an older version of the Talty he remembered. Her imperceptibly altered face bore no scars. Her clear brown eyes—how had he missed those eyes?—wore a touch of makeup, and her glorious chestnut hair had grown back.

He touched her arm. "Walk outside with me."

Leaving Aidan chuckling, they strolled through Peadar's gardens until they reached the lily pond. Neil stopped and inspected her again in the twilight.

"What's going on, Tal? Are you home to stay? I can't believe how fine you look! Never mind, come here to me!" He pulled her close and hugged her tight. She felt wonderful in his arms, sturdy and strong, not at all like the thin, fragile girl he'd seen off two years before. He said so.

Her cheeks reddened. She nudged him away. "I've spoken to your father and Kieran about earning my Fianna pin while I'm home. That's why they've sent for you."

"Oh? I'm not sure we can get you your pin in just a few weeks. It's been a long time since we've worked together."

"Please say you'll try. Please? It's important to me."

"You know I will. You have my word."

A quick cousin kiss sealed his promise. Again, she blushed, and he laughed and tugged her hair.

They walked on, chatting and catching up, until the music for the next set dance drew them back to the house.

CHAPTER TEN

Crossroads

Arms folded over his chest, Neil leaned against a wall of Garrymuir's airy training room enjoying a dynamic fencing match. Clad in protective masks, gloves, and form-fitting jackets and pants, Talty and senior Banfian Treasa O'Donnell had been lunging and parrying for five electrifying minutes.

Petite, blond, and effervescent, Treasa had been training aspiring Fian candidates, including Neil and Talty, for more than twenty-five years. Though still agile and muscular, she was struggling with her opponent. Her épée hadn't touched Talty once.

"Touché!" Treasa cried for the fifth time. "Halt!"

She raised her sword and stood gasping, as did Talty. Both women lifted their masks. The grins on their faces had Neil grinning too.

Treasa sputtered before she could speak. "Jakers, Tal. I'm done in and I didn't get one touch on you! They'll be putting that pin on your collar in no time." Merrily chatting about her current young Fian pupils, she helped Neil and Talty stow the fencing gear and said good-bye.

Neil opened a bottle of water and handed it to his hard-working cousin. "She means it. You're ready to go a few rounds with my father."

Talty shook her head. "I'll never be ready for him."

"You did all right sparring with Kieran, didn't you?" Neil wished yet again that he could have seen her trounce Kieran. Aidan never tired of talking about it.

"I caught him unprepared. He puts me through my paces here."

"Let's ask this, then. Where do you think you're weakest? What should we work on?"

She shrugged. "I don't know. I can't pinpoint anything."

"Neither can I. It's time for your trial with my father."

"Just so!" Peadar bellowed behind them. "I met Treasa on her way out, Tal. She says you're ready for your challenge."

Talty's face paled. "I need a few more days. I don't mean to be a bother, but, well, there's lots of little things. Yes, that's it. I was about to tell Neil that when you came in."

Neil caught his father's eye and winked.

Peadar winked back. "Today's Friday. Neil will train with you until Tuesday. We'll have your trial combat Wednesday. I can't have it go on any longer than that. From what I hear, you're wearing everyone out!" Chuckling away, he left the room.

Neil might have missed Talty's bout with Kieran, but he suspected her initiation trial would be a great treat. "Let's put the boots on it for today. We'll have tomorrow and most of Sunday to work. Let's go out tonight."

"No, Neil. You can't take me out. I'm married. People will talk."

"We'll be fine if your husband doesn't find out." He dodged her playful smack. "I was thinking of your parents' house for dinner. I've already arranged it. Kevin and Aidan are coming too. We'll sit upstairs and listen to music, just like we used to."

He'd said the right thing. Her eyes lit up. "Oh, Neil!" She practically dived on him to hug him, but quickly backed away, her cheeks flaming. "I'll, um, I'll go change."

While Neil locked up the weapons, he tried to reconcile the timid girl embarrassed to hug him with the fierce creature who'd been knocking him around the training room all week. She'd more than kept her resolve to regain her strength. He told himself again that he was fond of her because he was proud of her.

✳ ✳ ✳ ✳ ✳

Sunshine streamed through the training room windows on Wednesday morning. Talty sat with Eric, who'd flown in from Munich. The invitation to the private event had delighted him.

The small audience fell silent. Peadar had stepped to the center of the room.

"I have to go," Talty whispered. "Wish me luck."

Eric patted her hand. "When we next speak, you'll be one of the Fianna."

At Peadar's summons, she crossed the room, assessing her beloved uncle as an opponent. The padded jumpsuit he wore was identical to hers, though much larger. The contrast in their sizes had her wondering if she could ever best the bear-like man.

He'd show her no favoritism. As Ard Laoch, the High Warrior, he had to decide the worthiness of each Fian candidate, and he took that responsibility seriously.

"Taillte Rosaleen Boru," he began, "you seek to join the Fianna today. You must prove yourself worthy of this honor. As you know, the initiation standards have changed. We no longer require our candidates to pull thorns from their heels while running through the woods. We won't be burying you to your waist and throwing spears at you today. And we'll leave the recitation of twelve books of poetry to the poets."

A soft chuckle rippled through the room.

"Our ways have changed," he continued, "but our basic function remains the same: we guard the Kingdom of Ireland. We might have more sophisticated defense systems than Finn MacCool's beacon fires and relay runners, though I'm not sure they're more effective."

He asked the ritual question: "Who sponsors this Banfian candidate?"

Treasa shouted the traditional response: "I do, and right proudly, Ard Laoch."

"Who is this Banfian candidate's trainer?"

"I am, and right proudly, Ard Laoch," said Neil.

"Do you both deem this candidate fit for trial combat?"

"We do."

Peadar peered at Talty through unblinking eyes. "Your trainer and sponsor assure us of your proficiency in the use of many weapons. We have no need to test you in all of them. We'll choose the bata for your challenge."

At Peadar's nod, Neil plucked two of the long wooden poles from their rack. He passed one to his father, the other to Talty. She and Peadar accepted masks from Treasa and slipped them on.

Talty had no way of knowing that since Peadar Boru had been Ard Laoch, no Fian candidate had ever beaten him in a bata match. He would let them work long enough to display their mastery of the weapon, and then he would call a halt. The Fianna witnessing Talty's trial expected him to do the same today.

Kieran stepped forward to review the rules. The emphasis would be on accurate hits. Each combatant would attempt to touch his or her bata to four of the eight target areas: the head, throat, wrists, shins, and sides of the torso. Kieran and Treasa would decide the winning points.

Peadar rocked on the balls of his feet, twirled his bata, and assumed the classic fighting stance. Despite her earlier nervousness, Talty settled into the inner calm she'd come to know so well. In addition to proving her skill with the bata, she planned to display some *naginata* techniques practiced by the *onna-muscha,* the women warriors of ancient Japan.

Three bangs of Peadar's bata on the floor granted Talty the first move. He presented a broad target, but Talty knew she'd be lucky to get one point on the nimble giant, let alone four.

She whirled the bata and held it horizontally in front of her. Focusing to sense her uncle's—no, her opponent's—battle spirit, she gripped the pole firmly with her left hand and loosened her right thumb to create a spring-like tension in the stick. In a blur of speed, she bent her knees and snapped the bata at Peadar's left shin. She'd scored the first point.

No smugness tainted Talty's concentration. She'd poked a hornet's nest. Peadar would come after her from every which way now.

As she expected, he tried several feints. The trick was to know which move would be the real attack. She sensed and circled.

For his part, Peadar watched her every move. Her lightning strike had not only stunned him, it had hurt. Vowing not to let her get to him again— at least not so quickly—he searched her eyes for a hint of her intentions. He found nothing to help him. She'd "gone off," and though this match was no life or death situation, the girl had his hackles up.

He hadn't enjoyed a sparring session like this for ages.

His bearded face settled into a look Talty knew well. The old rascal was having fun. His bata whizzed at her left side. She banged hers into it and barely managed to deflect it. Her arms burned from the blow. She'd received a potent reminder that she couldn't match his strength.

Then the swarm of hornets came at her.

His swinging bata forced her back. The bata became a cue stick in his hands. He jabbed it through his fingers and poked her right side—a poke that earned him a point—as if she were a ball on a billiard table.

She danced sideways, feinting as she moved. Peadar tore toward her and twisted his bata, neatly catching it under the left end of hers. She couldn't move her arms.

A hard kick to his shin let her chop the right end of her bata into his left side. Another point, though neither Peadar nor Talty cared about points anymore.

Though she'd begun in the mindset of an anxious neophyte, Talty's confidence soared. She became one with the bata, and the bata became a *naginata* in her hands.

Peadar took a moment to admire the grace of her movements. He regained his concentration just in time to deflect the swing she aimed at his throat.

Talty grunted at the impact of his defensive blow. Like a mosquito, she darted behind him and tapped the side of his head.

Whipping his bata in a figure eight motion, he kept her from closing in on him while giving him a chance to think. If they'd been genuine enemies, she'd have killed him by now. Of course, he'd have fought to kill as well. For the first time, he wondered if he could best this girl.

This woman. He'd been coddling her and had broken his own rule: "A pretty little girl can kill you just as dead as a big, ugly man."

His next charge smacked her left side hard enough to make her spin. When she did, he came at her from behind, raised his bata over her head with both hands, and trapped her arms and shoulders. He had her. Kieran and Treasa would call the match now.

They didn't.

Talty sucked in a deep, audible breath. Her hands shot up and gripped Peadar's bata. She squatted down, twisted, and drove both elbows into his gut.

Peadar dropped his bata and released her. Gulping air, she backed up to the center of the room and dropped into a defensive stance, leaning hard on her bata.

Peadar's face broke into a huge grin. Treasa and Kieran halted the match.

"It appears the girl beat you soundly," Kieran said, "though the rules say we must go by the points. I came up with a tied score."

Treasa nodded. "So did I. You each got your fourth point at the same time. Dead even."

Searching their faces, Talty surrendered her bata to Neil. "That's good, right?"

Peadar roared with laughter. "I'm not so sure I like the use of 'dead' even, but yes, darlin', it's good. Congratulations, Banfian."

The observers cheered. Talty's cheeks warmed at the attention, though she didn't mind. She'd earned her pin.

Peadar raised his arms. "All right everyone. We aren't quite finished. Kieran?"

Pulling a set of keys from his pocket, Kieran unlocked a glass case in the corner. Legend said the iron swords it held had belonged to the first Fianna. Kieran removed a short sword from the collection and passed it to Peadar. Wide near the hilt, the blade narrowed to a sharp, thin point. An ancient artisan had worked the intricate knotwork designs of the early Celts into the handle, which was small enough to fit a woman's hand.

The Ard Laoch before Peadar had initiated Treasa with this sword. Now Peadar carried the weapon to Talty. It hummed in her hands.

As the old weapons on Omishima Island had called to her, so too did this one: *I have been waiting for you, Banfian. Hold me. Many warriors have held me. Touch me and add your spirit to theirs, and I will make you strong.*

No one said a word. No one had to. Talty was one of them now.

***** * *****

The following afternoon, Talty watched the few guests invited to the pinning ceremony take their seats in Garrymuir's largest reception room. Her father stood in suit and tie behind a small dais. Dressed in her dark blue ISF uniform—her old Irish Navy uniform no longer fit—Talty took her place before him.

He winked. She smiled and glanced at the stand beside him, where her priceless pin waited to be tacked to her collar.

Barely an inch in circumference, the full-circle gold brooch resembled an archaic shield. The fastening pin crossed the back of the shield. A tiny sword lay across it. Three diamonds graced the hilt of the sword, one for each component of the Fian motto.

As he often did, Brian put his notes aside and spoke from his heart. "I'm proud to be part of this important occasion. Talty, we salute you. Despite the interruption in your training, you've shown resilience and dedication—and you've successfully met the challenge of the Ard Laoch."

Talty glanced sideways at Peadar, who nodded and grinned.

Brian continued. "This isn't the elaborate ceremony we would have liked for you, though it's unique in its own way. It's the only time we've ever pinned one solitary warrior. Still, the intent is the same.

"As I told the rest of you young fellas at your own ceremony a few months ago, you are our new Fianna. Remember your motto: 'Truth in Your Heart, Strength in Your Arms, and Dedication to Your Promise.' You've had the finest Fian training in Ireland's history. Because of this, we expect much of you, from keeping Ireland safe to preparing the Fianna who will come after you. I know I can count on you, as every king before me has counted on your predecessors.

"Talty, the oath you swear today distinguishes you as a member of an elite society of warriors. No invader has ever defeated the Fianna. A tough act to follow, but that's why your training is tough, and why this pin is so precious. By wearing it, you tell the world that you are a daughter of this fine circle of warriors."

Brian pinned the brooch on her collar. Applause and cheers erupted in the room.

***** * *****

Early the next morning, the fickle Irish sun shone on Peadar's majestic gardens. Talty strolled beside Eric and pointed out the landmarks in the distance. Beyond Howth Harbor, Ireland's Eye and Lambay Island stood guard over the choppy Irish Sea. Seagulls squealed above a trawler cruising toward the pier.

"It's lovely here, Hana. As lovely in its own way as the gardens in Japan. I'm glad your uncle invited me to your pinning ceremony."

"I'd never have won my pin if not for you and Kiyoshi. *Arigato.*"

"Thank *you* for giving us the honor of helping you. What did you want to discuss?"

Sure her news would please him, she smiled. "Ron Chambeau called. On my way back to Tokyo, I'm to stop in California for a brief orientation and a physical at Fort Pinard."

"A physical? You dislike doctors. Why are you so happy?"

"It's a prerequisite to working with Research and Development. I have two weeks to finish up with Ron, and then I'll be stationed at Fort Pinard for six months."

The crease between Eric's eyebrows deepened. "Your father will allow this?"

"Yes, and Uncle Peadar and Kieran agree."

"But your enemies across the Irish Sea—"

"That doesn't matter, Eric. Talty isn't going to California. Christy is, and she can't wait. And when the assignment is finished, I'm coming home for good. Kieran says things here will be straightened out by then."

Eric stopped as if she'd slapped him. "Is it so bad in Japan?"

He walked on. Appalled to think she'd offended him, she hurried after him. "I'm sorry, Eric. I thought you'd look forward to having your life in order again. I've enjoyed staying with you, and I'm grateful for what you and Kiyoshi have done, but I really, really want to come home."

She wished he'd say something, anything, but he only kept walking. She tried again. "If dropping me off in California isn't convenient, I can take a commercial flight. Or my broomstick. I'm really sorry."

Chuckling gently, he slowed his step and linked his arm through hers. "I'd welcome a break in such a long trip. I've always wanted to see northern California. I've thought about establishing a division there. And now," he said with a bittersweet smile, "you must show me your uncle's tree peonies."

CHAPTER ELEVEN
Fragile Layers

Excited as she was to be in California, Talty already missed Ireland's green vistas. Mendocino was dry and brown. She and Eric settled into the separate bedrooms of their hotel suite, she to unpack, he to catch up on his telephone calls.

The next morning, she donned her ISF uniform. Refusing Eric's offer of the rented limousine, she took a taxi to Fort Pinard, a complex of low, modern buildings tucked away in Mendocino's wooded hills. An aide escorted her to the medical wing of the Research and Development building and introduced her to Dr. Samantha Reed, a lady in her mid-thirties.

Talty instantly liked the doctor, whose stiff white lab coat offset her smooth, mocha-colored skin. Warmth and humor flowed beneath her crisp demeanor. Her accent wasn't as Bostonian as Ron Chambeau's, but Talty would bet she had spent some time there.

Meekly following Dr. Reed to an examination room, Talty fought her growing panic. She cringed at the sight of the exam smock. Despite her assurances to Eric, she dreaded the impending physical.

I'm a Fian warrior, she repeated to herself. *I'm not afraid. I'm not.*

"You're a major," Dr. Reed said once they were ready to start the exam. "I'm a doctor, and a captain too. Too many titles. Any objection to us getting on a first name basis?"

Talty appreciated the woman's attempt to put her at ease. "I don't suppose we'd be breaking any rules—Samantha."

Samantha started checking this and that with an unusual device. When Talty asked about it, she learned it was one of Dr. Nathaniel "Creek" Martin's newest inventions.

"We named it a 'Creek Unit' after him," Samantha said.

"What does it do?" The gadget didn't poke or prod Talty at all. She relaxed.

"It registers your vital signs and gives us a picture of your general health. I've only been using it a month or so. We're not sure it will completely replace more conventional examinations, but trying new things is the reason we're here."

The unit hovered over Talty's chest. Samantha frowned. "This thing must be malfunctioning. I know from your records you had an accident, but the scar tissue it's reading is off the scale. Mind if I have a look?"

Talty minded. "If you like."

Samantha slipped the smock past Talty's shoulders and gasped. "I'm sorry. Do you want to tell me what happened?"

As she and Ron had discussed, Talty only said she'd had an accident. "I'm fine now. What else do we need to do?"

"Nothing for now." Samantha told Talty to expect more specific testing over the next few days and left her to dress. She returned to the hotel in time for lunch.

* * * * *

Worlds away from the wild, rocky shores of his native England, Richard Gale hiked the cliffs above northern California's coast. By midafternoon he'd reached an overlook where a salty breeze blew wisps of dark hair over his eyes. From the shade of a cypress tree, he gazed out at the ocean, still and blue beneath feathery clouds. Below him the thundering surf sprayed a herd of harbor seals contentedly barking on sunlit rocks.

Despite the peaceful setting, Richard constantly scanned his surroundings for trouble. His work with International Security's Research and Development Division had taught him that his fine English manners were only a fragile layer from barbarity. Though the realization had disturbed him at first, he now considered his ability to instantly shed his civilized veneer a crucial lifesaving skill.

The shadows changed. Richard committed the tranquil scene to memory, an image to resurrect when he needed solace, and headed home.

The house was quiet with Nick in the hospital. After filling and switching on the electric kettle, Richard hit the blinking button on his answering machine.

Samantha Reed's efficient voice crackled from the speaker. "Hey, Richard. Call me when you get in. We might have a new candidate for the project. I'll brief you when I see you. Bye."

Richard thought Samantha brilliant, professional, and one of the most beautiful black women he'd ever met. She'd served with the United States Army's medical division and now called Fort Pinard home, as he did.

She answered on the second ring. "Talk to me."

"Hello, Samantha. I'm keen as mustard to hear about the new applicant."

"I'll tell you all about her over dinner tonight. My treat."

Surely he'd misheard her. "Did you say 'her'?"

"I did. I'll swing by at seven o'clock."

*****

Over dinner with Eric in the hotel restaurant, Talty recapped her meeting with Samantha Reed and described the Creek Unit. "Compared to most of the medical experiences I've had, this one was a snap."

Eric's expression remained neutral. "Dr. Reed wants to see you again?"

"Yes. To do more tests. She said they'll take about a week. I'm to meet the officer in charge of the division tomorrow morning."

"Then you'll want to rest. And I must pack."

Talty's heartbeat quickened. She wasn't ready to be alone. "You're leaving?"

"Yes. A business matter has come up. I must return to Tokyo." He topped off her glass of Chablis and smiled. "You'll be fine here, Hana. It's what you wanted, after all. Call me when your tests are done. I'll send the Lear for you."

*****

By the dessert course, Richard's subtle admiration of Samantha's good looks had given way to anger. He remained silent until a waiter poured the last of the Chianti and departed.

"Her medical records show all the numbers are right." As she spoke, Samantha fingered the rosebud in the crystal vase between them. "We only need to verify them. I've arranged for her to meet you tomorrow."

"I don't want to meet her. You know what happens on the other side of that portal. All the fun of the fair. Nick and I can't baby-sit a woman there."

"You won't have to. This lady works with our Logistics and Ordnance Division in Tokyo. She's proficient in self-defense and knows a variety of weapons."

"Don't give me that equal rights nonsense. Look what happened to Nick!" If Richard held the stem of his glass any tighter, he'd break it. He downed the rest of his wine.

"We have to try," Samantha said. "We're going to lose our funding if we can't add travelers. This project is too important to have only two—"

100

"Guinea pigs?"

"Travelers sounds nicer, and Nick is fine. He's already nagging to leave the hospital."

"He's lucky he's alive!" Richard lowered his voice. "I'm all for visiting these places for research, but fighting off primitive people who think we're monsters is another pair of shoes. Those tribesmen tried to kill us!"

"We didn't know that would happen."

"My point exactly! Bloody hell, Samantha!" He signaled the waiter to bring the check.

* * * * *

Talty had no trouble locating the R&D building the next morning, though once inside she found the corridors confusing. She soon suspected she'd taken a wrong turn. Being late for her meeting with the man who might be her new commanding officer wouldn't do.

Footsteps echoed in the hall behind her. The approaching officer was as tall as Kieran, yet dusky-haired, younger, and a lieutenant colonel, according to the insignia on his uniform. He'd point her in the right direction.

He stopped and smiled. "You look to be in a right flat spin, Major. Can I help?"

His English accent startled her, but she scolded herself. He couldn't know who she was. "I hope so, sir. I'm looking for the admin offices."

"I'm going that way. I'd be happy to escort you. Richard Gale, at your service."

They shook hands. "Christy McKenna. I have a meeting with you, sir."

His smile vanished. He dropped her hand. "This way, Major."

Colonel Gale said no more until they reached his office. He opened the door and told her to sit. She complied, wondering what switch had flipped to turn her charming rescuer into such a rude boor.

He sat back and crossed his arms. "So. You've come to work with R&D, have you?"

"Yes, sir. As requested."

"I did not request you, Major. I want that understood."

"Yes, sir." She offered silent thanks to Kiyoshi for his "blank expression" lessons.

"What did you understand you'd be doing here?"

"Studying new technology. Non-lethal weapons, warning systems—"

"That's a different division, one you're most welcome to attend. You're here today to help our scientists gather the data they need to further their biomedical research. Help them and go."

A quick rap on the door interrupted her intended response. A lanky, silver-haired man in a stained white jumpsuit entered before Richard invited him in. His nametag read "Colonel Nathaniel Martin, Bioengineering." His shoulder twitched nonstop when he saw Talty.

"You must be Major McKenna," he said in a lazy southern drawl. "Creek Martin, Major. Happy to meet you. Samantha's told me amazing things about your brain."

Though the comment puzzled her, Talty rose and shook his hand. She couldn't help smiling at the enchanting old gent. "Hello, Colonel."

"Please, sit. Don't let me interrupt. I hope you two are getting to know each other. I know you're going to enjoy working with us."

"Major McKenna won't be staying," said Gale. "She'll be cutting along to another division as soon as Dr. Reed finishes with her."

Talty had already tuned him out. "If you have time, Colonel Martin, I'd love a tour of the place."

Creek was grinning like the mad scientist she suspected him to be. "Delighted, my dear. You're done with Richard?"

"Oh yes, I'm done with him. Thanks for your time, Colonel Gale."

✳ ✳ ✳ ✳ ✳

Empty pizza containers and root beer cans littered Creek's office. Accustomed to the eccentric scientist's habits—and absorbed in Christy's test results—Samantha ignored them.

Creek peeked over his reading glasses. "I see my diagnostic unit even picked up the scar tissue. I really must be a genius!"

Smiling fondly at her boss, Samantha flipped to the next page. "It picked up more than that. Your miniature EEG got us some good preliminary readings."

Creek's shoulder hadn't stopped twitching since he'd reviewed those readings. He'd theorized that Richard's and Nick's unique brain wave patterns were the prime factor in their successful ventures through R&D's top-secret Peregrine Portal. Christy McKenna's electroencephalography was nearly identical to theirs. Further testing would determine her suitability as a traveler. That, and convincing Richard to accept her.

Samantha set another page on Creek's desk. "You know he doesn't want her here."

Shoulder twitching away, Creek chugged his root beer and smiled. "That's understandable. She's only twenty-four years old, very young to have such experience and attain the rank of major. I'll order him to want her if I have to, but first let's do the rest of those tests."

* * * * *

After the final medical test, Talty returned to her empty hotel suite and snapped on the lights. She'd only seen Richard Gale twice since she'd met him, and both times his behavior had irritated her. Why didn't he want her around? Samantha wouldn't elaborate.

Earlier that afternoon, the genial doctor had prepared Talty's arm for an intravenous needle. "If the test results are good, we'll want you to stay on with us."

"Colonel Gale doesn't want me," Talty had bluntly stated, focusing on the photographs of underwater sea life hanging on the walls. "And I have no desire to enter a hostile relationship."

Samantha only said, "Richard's a good guy," and the needle went in.

Wincing at the memory, Talty rubbed the tiny bandage on her arm. Except for the fleeting queasiness caused by the intravenous dye, today's tests hadn't been bad. Now she was hungry. She ordered a room service meal, changed into a sweatsuit, and rested on the couch in the sitting room. After she ate, she'd call Eric and ask him to send the jet for her.

A loud knock roused her from a nap she hadn't intended to take. Ready for supper, she opened the door. Instead of the room service cart, Samantha stood in the doorway. Richard Gale was with her.

Smiling to hide her disappointment, Talty invited them in and led them to the sitting area. Their stern expressions worried her.

"I'm afraid we have some bad news," Gale said. "I received a call a while ago from a man called Kiyoshi Sasaki. Do you know him?"

Why would Kiyoshi call Gale? "Yes. He's my husband's business manager."

Gale leaned forward. "There's been an accident. A helicopter carrying your husband hit some power lines and went down. There were no survivors. I'm sorry."

The weight of the words buried Talty beneath them. She never remembered walking to the window, only that when she looked out, Eric's face smiled back at her. His gardens filled the sky around him: the flowers and dwarf trees, the ponds and bridges.

And the tree peonies.

She wouldn't cry in front of Richard Gale. Steeling herself, she turned to him and Samantha. "I'm sorry for the distress this must have caused you. I must return to Tokyo at once."

"I've taken the liberty of arranging transportation for you," Gale said. "Colonel Martin wants us to accompany you."

"That's not necessary."

Samantha stood. "We're coming, okay? Let's get your things together. Call the front desk, Richard. Get her checked out." She followed Talty into her room and closed the door.

Talty pulled two suitcases from the closet and tossed them on the bed. And then she sat weeping beside them. "Eric flies everywhere in his helicopter. How could they hit power lines?"

"Mr. Sasaki said something about heavy fog disorienting the pilot. I'm so sorry, honey." Samantha busied herself in the closet.

Talty emptied dresser drawers, haphazardly throwing things into the nearest suitcase. "Why is Colonel Gale here, Samantha? I thought he...I mean...I don't understand. And you. Why would you come with me? You hardly know me."

"I like what I do know, and I told you. Richard's a good guy. Besides, Creek asked us to look after you. Period."

The closet was empty. Talty zipped the suitcases shut. "I need to make a call before I leave. Do you mind?"

Samantha started for the door. "Take your time."

Still sobbing, Talty calculated the time in Dublin and called Kieran's private line.

CHAPTER TWELVE

The Gardens

Three chanting Buddhist priests concluded the funeral and left in a nebulous haze of incense, gongs, and swirling saffron robes. A throng of mourners lined up to offer their condolences to Eric Yamada's aunt and young widow.

Richard pulled Samantha into one of the *saijou's* nooks to escape the stampede. A ripple in the crowd caught his attention. "Well, look at that."

"What?" whispered Samantha. "I can't see. I'm not as tall as you."

"Our friend Christy moves in high circles. The Crown Prince of Ireland just arrived. See those four westerners walking toward her and Imi?"

Samantha stood on her toes. "Yeah. I haven't seen such expensive suits since I graduated from medical school. Which one's the prince?"

"The one in the middle, that's Liam Boru. Don't tell anyone, but the man behind him is one of my personal heroes."

"Get out! *You* have a hero? Who is he?"

"The Chief of Ireland's Intelligence Sector. His name is Kieran Dacey. He's the King of Ireland's first cousin. The other two might be bodyguards, though the red-haired one has the look of a Boru. I don't know the black-haired one."

"Well, let's get introduced." Samantha stepped toward them.

Richard tugged her arm and smiled. "I think we can wait until they pay their respects."

* * * * *

Neil strode in step with Aidan to create a path through the curious crowd for Liam. Kieran guarded the prince from behind. They stopped before the casket, closed and afloat in a sea of lilies and chrysanthemums. A portrait of

Eric Yamada hung above it.

Talty and an elderly Japanese lady stood nearby greeting mourners. Talty's simple black dress set off her pale skin. Her dispassionate expression was one all members of the royal family learned to don in public, yet tears shimmered in her eyes when she spotted her kinsmen.

Liam took her hands and kissed her cheek. "I'm sorry to see you again under such sad circumstances, Christy." He repeated his condolences when Talty introduced Imi Yamada.

"You have eased our grief by coming all this way," Imi said. "Please honor us by staying at our house for as long as you wish. Christy, your friends have had a long journey. Offer them some refreshment." Imi bowed and returned to acknowledging condolences.

Neil caught himself staring at Talty. She glanced at him; and her sad smile tugged at his heart. She seemed so fragile. He longed to offer her his strength. He was her protector, after all.

Flanked by Liam and Kieran, she started across the room. With Aidan at his side, Neil followed. She suddenly waved to a couple standing against a wall. A dark-haired man as tall as Kieran waved back, as did the alluring black woman with him. Then Talty was introducing everyone, saying that she and Aidan had taught classes together in Ireland.

As the handshakes progressed, Neil tapped Talty's elbow. "Is there somewhere I can make a phone call?"

Excusing herself, she brought him to an office and closed the door. "There's the phone."

"I don't need it. Come here to me." Neil hugged her and set her back to inspect her. "Are you all right, Tal? You could use some sleep, I think."

"I am tired. It's been hard. You have no idea how happy I am to see all of you."

"Sit for a minute while I call Dan." He drew his cell phone from his pocket. "That colonel's a big fella. Did you notice he's English?"

She raised her hand to hide a yawn. "Aren't you the clever one. Dan Joyce?"

"Yes. Kieran finally trusts us to fly his esteemed self around. Dan's at the hangar scheduling maintenance for the Gulfstream."

At the age of fourteen, Neil had taken his first flying lessons at the Limerick helicopter company owned by Dan's father. He and Dan had been friends ever since. They'd received their Fianna pins together.

Dan had attended Talty's pinning ceremony, and she was fond of him. "He's not staying in some drafty old hangar. Have him come to the house."

Neil nodded. A few words with Dan reassured him that all was well.

With Talty's help, he relayed the Yamadas' address and flipped the phone shut. "All set. Can you get through the next few hours?"

"I have to. Eric and I weren't really husband and wife, but he was good to me. I hope he never knew what happened. That he didn't suffer."

Her words surprised him. Despite the agreement between Talty's father and Yamada, Neil hadn't expected the marriage to remain celibate. Reluctant to ponder Talty's sexuality, he sought to offer proper comfort. "Crashes like that happen fast."

"That's what I keep telling myself." She sighed. "We'd better get back."

He reached for her hands and pulled her to her feet, wondering why a man wouldn't bed such a fine young wife.

$$* * * * *$$

Talty had asked Imi's staff to lodge the guests in bedrooms with western furnishings. After she saw the boys to their rooms, she walked with Kieran to his suite.

He asked her to come in. "I know you're tired, but I want to know what's going on with California."

Stifling a yawn, she said she wasn't sure. "Whatever I do, I won't be working with Colonel Gale. He doesn't like me."

Kieran's right eyebrow arched. "Then why did he come all this way?"

"His CO asked him to. A few days ago he told me to go home, that he didn't want me. I'll talk to Ron. He'll straighten it out. Please don't worry."

"It's my job to worry about you, darlin'. Now get to bed."

$$* * * * *$$

Creek's call infuriated Richard. The persnickety old boffin was no dictator, yet Richard always knew when his commanding officer was pulling rank.

You all left in such a state, I never got to speak to the young lady. Get her back here. I want her on our team.

The unmistakable mandate wasn't the only cause of Richard's agitation. The events of the last ten days gnawed at him, from his first meeting with Christy McKenna to her husband's funeral. For some irrational reason, he felt responsible for her now.

Wondering what he could say to her to undo the damage he'd done, he dressed and stole downstairs for a nightcap. Kieran Dacey sat before the smoldering fireplace, a brandy snifter in his hand.

Dacey glanced up, and then he gazed at the glowing embers. "Hello, Richard. I had a feeling I wouldn't be the only one who couldn't sleep. I have the bottle and another glass here. Can I interest you?"

"Thank you, sir. I wouldn't mind." Richard eased into a chair next to an ebony table. He did his best to conceal his awe of the brooding Irishman.

Even at rest with a drink in his hand, Dacey radiated power. The scar on his left cheek created the illusion of a dangerous man, though Richard knew from his days at MI6 that it was no illusion. Dacey not only ran Ireland's Intelligence Sector with a tight rein, he'd earned Ireland's highest military honor for saving an English life, a feat that had won him English respect.

Their glasses clinked. Richard savored the brandy's burn going down. "I expect the time difference from Ireland is a bit more drastic than it is from California, sir."

Dacey rolled the snifter between his hands. "It's not the time change. I can't sleep because I can't stop thinking about Christy McKenna. I'd heard she might be working for you in California, but she tells me those plans have changed."

"I'll admit I've done my best to dissuade her from joining us. The work is…complex. However, I've received orders that she's to join our R&D division after all."

Dacey's right eyebrow shot up. His grin bewildered Richard. He'd expected a rebuke akin to those he'd already received from Creek and Samantha.

"It takes a woman to beat the devil," Dacey said. "From what I've seen, Christy McKenna is the one to do it. One sparring session with her taught me that."

"She sparred with you, sir?"

"I can't be comfortable if you keep calling me 'sir.' It's Kieran, all right? And yes, she sparred with me. Beat the stuffing out of me, though I'll admit I gave her a handicap, her being a little bit of a thing. A big mistake."

Little Christy McKenna had thumped one of Ireland's elite Fianna?

"So you're of the opinion that she can handle herself—Kieran?"

"If my opinion counted, she'd be working for me at Tara Hall. Her current CO told me today he'd be sorry to lose her, but she's wasted behind a desk. Give her a chance. We'll be returning to Dublin tomorrow morning. I'd like to know she has a place to go."

Richard wondered about Dacey's interest in Christy. She must be a close family friend to bring him and the others halfway around the world for a funeral. "I'm still not convinced she belongs at Fort Pinard."

Kieran downed his brandy and smacked his lips. "You may be right. A lion isn't a safe companion for all men." He stood and arched his back. "Bedammit, I'm not looking forward to another long trip sitting in one place. If you've a mind, meet me in that barn first thing in the morning. We'll have a proper workout."

Richard's pulse raced at the invitation. "I'll be there."

* * * * *

Sparkling in the sunrise, the manmade waterfall trickled over moss-covered rocks. Its fine mist moistened Talty's face. She pulled her jacket tight against the cool morning breeze and walked into the lower gardens, imagining Eric strolling beside her, hearing him speak to her. No particular words, just the soothing sound of his voice.

She entered the crisscross tunnels and emerged near the little wooden bridge. The breeze followed her. Then it blew ahead to rustle the blooming tree peonies. Unable to bear the sight of the flowers, she crossed the bridge to return to the house.

Neil waited on the path, hands tucked in the pockets of his jeans. The sunlight behind him set off his blue-black hair and cast shadows over the stubble on his cheeks and chin. Talty had never seen her well-groomed cousin unshaven. He looked rugged, fierce even.

"Sorry to intrude, Tal. I didn't know anyone else was awake."

"You're not intruding at all. I'm on my way back. How did you know where I was?"

"I didn't. I couldn't sleep, so I came down for a walk. I'd be wandering in this maze forever if you weren't here. Which way is the house?"

Talty pointed. They strolled in silence until they reached the herb garden near the kitchen door.

Neil raised her hand and kissed it. "I wish you were coming back with us. I don't like leaving you here alone."

"I'm not alone. I'll be fine." Already missing him, she slipped her hand from his.

"Kieran spoke to Colonel Chambeau at the funeral yesterday. Said he was losing you to Colonel Gale, but now you're saying that won't happen. I'm—we're worried. Will you stay in Tokyo if you don't go to California?"

"I don't know, but you shouldn't worry. Things will work out."

His eyes were so blue. She wondered if he had a girl back home, wondered if he liked kissing her. The thought warmed her cheeks. She turned away so he wouldn't notice.

"Come inside, Neily. I'll make you a cup of tea."

* * * * *

Richard rose at dawn, eager for his workout with Kieran. The spectacular sunrise drew him to his bedroom window. He looked down and saw Neil Boru kiss Christy's hand.

She seemed flustered. The idea that he might be pursuing a new young widow roused Richard's protective instincts. He hoped the Irishman was simply being gallant. Having no wish to intrude on a private meeting, he left the window to dress.

* * * * *

Later that morning, Talty knocked on her brother's door. "All packed, Li?"

"All packed." Liam pulled her inside. "I haven't had much time to speak to you."

She hugged him, surprised to feel such strong, hard muscles in her scholarly brother. She poked his stomach. "You're keeping in shape."

"My duty to the family, love. Uncle Peadar says we'll meet girls who'll like our money, and girls who'll think we're smart. However, it's the girls who appreciate the fine physical condition of the human body that we want to marry. Says he."

Talty was still giggling when Aidan came in. "Ah, a private party. So sorry to interrupt." He grinned and shut the door behind him. "Do you need help with your luggage, Li?"

"I do, frail fella that I am."

"Liam is hardly frail." Talty missed the boys' clowning, and now they were leaving. She sat on the bed, determined to keep them with her a few precious moments longer. "I was just telling him what fine shape he's in."

"If Liam's in fine shape, I must be one of the wonders of the world!"

Aidan struck hilarious poses that had Talty laughing harder than she had in years. The comedy continued until Dan knocked and called from the hall that the car was ready.

"We'll be right down, Danny," Liam said.

Talty jumped to her feet. "They can wait a few minutes, can't they?"

"They aren't likely to leave without us, love." Aidan crossed the room and hugged her. "You're a fine one to be talking about your brother. You're a good sturdy girl yourself, all nice and round. Give us another hug!"

Aidan got a shove for his daring words, though he got his hug as well. He put his teasing aside then. "Your father asked us to see that you don't forget who you are." He reached for her hand and kissed it twice. Then he pecked her mouth, completing the abbreviated version of the Obeisance to the Lady Princess.

"My turn." Liam repeated the ritual.

Talty bit her lip. Tears blurred her eyes. "I need a little air. I'll see you downstairs."

* * * * *

Braving the tangle of garden paths, Neil stopped at the sentinel stone to get

110

his bearings. He spotted Talty near the pond. "There you are. We'll be leaving soon. I wanted to say good-bye."

She straightened her shoulders as he approached. "I was just coming to see you off."

As he suspected, she'd been crying. How could he leave her behind? Heart aching, he tugged her hair. "Tell me you'll be all right here, Tal."

"I'll be all right here. What will you be doing yourself?"

"Didn't I tell you? Aidan and I volunteered for duty in the Middle East."

"Neil! You really did? With the peacekeepers? Do you know what your duty will be?"

The pride in her voice had quickly turned to worry. She'd told him about her work with Colonel Chambeau. Neil did his best to reassure her. "Border patrol and civilian support. It's not a combat zone."

Her smile returned, though concern lingered in her eyes. She reached up and tousled his hair. "They'll cut all that fine black hair away."

"It will grow back again, I expect. Please send me a note or something once you know what you're going to do."

"I will. I—"

He snatched her hand, kissed it twice, and then he kissed her mouth. A delicious heat pulsed in his groin. The taste of her lips tempted him to really kiss her, though he caught himself before such a disaster could occur.

"Thank you for coming, Neil." She bussed his cheek.

Then his arms were around her, hugging her, holding her. Telling himself he felt this way because he was her protector no longer worked.

She hugged him hard and then broke their embrace. "We should get back. They'll be waiting for us."

The courtyard bustled with friendly farewells and thumping luggage. Soon the limousine drove away. Neil glanced out the rear window in time to see the electric security gate close firmly shut.

✳ ✳ ✳ ✳ ✳

The Gulfstream's engines hummed. The control tower had approved the flight plan, and Neil and Dan had finished reviewing their pre-flight checklists. While he waited for Kieran to board the aircraft, Neil retrieved a soft drink from the galley's refrigerator. The sound of clowning in the cabin had him looking in on the fun.

"I'm glad you made Talty laugh," Liam said to Aidan, "but I thought she was going to hit you when you told her how nice and round she was."

Aidan flung his jacket down and rolled his eyes. "Oh, that sister of yours is a beauty, Li. I'll be having dreams about her."

"Get out, you demented idiot. You don't have dreams about your own cousin."

"Why not? She's a fine-looking girl, all soft and curvy. Why, just thinking about her has Mr. Mickey acting up. You know what they say: 'Incest is best!'"

Liam threw a pillow at him. "You're a depraved degenerate. A reprehensible pervert!"

"You have a command of the language, I'll give you that." Aidan tossed the pillow back and turned toward Neil. "Hey, Neily. Are we all set?"

"Yes. Just waiting for your father."

"What's wrong, Neil?" Liam asked, catching the pillow. "Not more bad weather?"

"Nothing's wrong. We're good to go."

"Glad to hear it." Kieran bounded into the cabin and plopped into his seat. "Let's go home, lads."

Neil raised the air stairs and returned to the cockpit. The Gulfstream taxied to its assigned runway and took off.

CHAPTER THIRTEEN
Extraordinary Ideas

Peadar and Peggy were out at a charity luncheon. Final exams would keep Kevin at Trinity Law School for hours. The house staff had finished their upstairs chores. Neil was alone in the family wing.

He stole into Kevin's rooms, deeming the unthinkable violation of his brother's privacy a necessary intrusion. Asking Kevin—or anyone, for that matter—to check the Irish laws concerning incest was unthinkable. Neil had to learn for himself if he could marry Talty.

Gently closing the door behind him, he padded past the sitting area into Kevin's bedroom. Sunshine brightened a mix of grownup toys and childhood treasures. On the shelf above a messy desk sat a framed photograph of Kevin with his arm around a honey-haired young lady. Neil smiled in admiring approval before returning to his quest.

Kevin had been reviewing contract law all week. Ignoring the notebooks and law texts littering the desk, Neil searched the shelves in nearby bookcase and found a text titled *Irish Family Law*. He sat and opened the book to the table of contents.

"Capacity to Marry" seemed a good place to start. He scanned "Free Consent to Marriage," glossed over "Domiciles of Prospective Spouses," and closed his eyes in dread at "Prohibited Degrees of Relationship by Consanguinity or Affinity."

Bracing himself, he started to read the ancient Law of Consanguinity. He'd just finished scanning how the law allowed certain consanguineous marriages in order to keep the cattle in the family when the door opened and Kevin came in.

Neil snapped the book shut. "Hey, Kev. How'd the exam go?"

"Not bad, I hope. Only one left." Evidently unfazed by Neil's intrusion, Kevin set a leather-bound notebook on the desk and tossed his jacket over a chair. He glanced at the book Neil held and grinned. "Got yourself in a jam, Neily? Some little Boru popping up where you didn't expect? If you're looking for anything special, Liam's better with family law than me."

"No, nothing special. Just curious about what you're studying. I'm impressed. This stuff's pretty involved. I don't think I could do it." He nodded at the photograph on the shelf. "Who's the girl?"

Kevin's raised eyebrows conveyed his recognition not only of Neil's fib, but also of his attempt to change the subject. He pointed to the book in Neil's hands. "I'll tell if you will."

For a brief moment, Neil considered confiding in his brother. His courage failed him. He decided against it and slid the book back on the shelf. "I have to pack."

"That's right, go off and abandon me. I hate when you're away. It's no fun being the only one here for Mum and Dad to pick on."

Smiling in sympathy—and frustrated by his thwarted search—Neil clapped Kevin's shoulder. "Better you than me. See you at supper."

✱ ✱ ✱ ✱ ✱

Christy was out in the gardens again. Her gloved hands picked spent blooms from a hedge of pink camellias. The setting sun played up the bronze in her free-flowing mane.

A lion isn't a safe companion for all men.

Richard swallowed and sauntered over. "Samantha and I are leaving after dinner. I thought you and I might discuss the Mendocino assignment before we go."

Eyes wary, she looked up from her task. "There isn't one, remember?"

He opted for a light approach. "I've been giving the matter some thought. I was hoping you'd reconsider your refusal."

"*My* refusal?" Looking quite vicious, she stared him down.

He had no choice but to throw in his cards. "I deliberately bodged things with you, Christy, and I'd do it again in a minute. But Creek overruled me, and there's bugger-all I can do about it. He ordered me to tell you about the work, if you'll listen."

"I won't work where I'm not wanted."

"It's not that I don't want you. I don't want you hurt. Before you set foot in the Bioengineering Division, I intend to find out if you really know your onions, Creek or no Creek."

She removed her garden gloves and nodded to a nearby bench. "I can see

I'll need to learn a few English idioms as well."

They sat with their backs to the sun. Richard sighed and began. "As an officer with International Security Forces, you're bound by the rules of classified and restricted information. What I tell you now, you'll repeat to no one, is that understood?"

"Yes, sir."

"Creek Martin has been director of ISF's Bioengineering Division for years. He and his people have developed some extraordinary ideas. You saw his Creek Unit."

"Yes. It's amazing."

"Indeed. Creek is a brilliant man, if a tad eccentric. Sometimes I wonder if the old boffin is batting on a full wicket."

"I'm sure he knows his onions, Colonel."

The twinkle in her eyes made Richard smile. He'd grown fond of her in the short time he'd known her, though he'd have to curb that fondness if they were to work together.

"We humans can perceive three dimensions," he said. "Creek believes there are others."

"Superimposed spatial dimensions. I've read about it."

"I'm impressed, darling. Creek wanted to adjust the human brain to recognize more than three dimensions. He needed healthy individuals to help calibrate his readings. I volunteered. Soon he and his team were popping me inside a metal cocoon. I must admit I was nervous when they retreated behind a glass wall to conduct their tests." Richard paused. The nightmare came alive for him again.

"Something went wrong, didn't it?"

"Let's just say things didn't go as expected. When they pulled the switch, I disappeared. They scrambled to reverse what they'd done. When they did, I reappeared in the middle of the room. It seems that instead of simply perceiving different dimensions, I actually visited one."

Those incredible brown eyes darted everywhere as she processed what he'd said. Alarm showed on her face, and something else. Skepticism? No. Curiosity. "You don't have to make up this bizarre story so I'll turn tail and run, Colonel. I already said I'd go to another division."

"I'm not making it up, darling. Sometimes I wish I were."

"Where were you?"

"I don't really know. Creek thinks it was a parallel world, a place that physically occupies the same space as our world."

"A parallel world. I'll bet he couldn't wait to try again."

"You're catching on. Research and Development launched the Peregrine

Project. I became a permanent member of ISF, and Peregrine is now a classified military operation."

"Have you returned to this parallel world?"

"Not the same one. We've never been to the same place twice. The portal's controls are too willy-nilly just now."

"So others have gone?"

"Besides me, only Nick. Good man, Nick. You'll meet him later. Let's walk a little, shall we? It's a lovely time of day."

They ambled past rustling cherry trees. She seemed upbeat and inquisitive, yet her tightened jaw and pale face betrayed a degree of fear. At least she had some sense. She also had a keen mind, one that apparently had something in common with his and Nick's.

"Creek believes some unique component in our brains, mine and Nick's, allows us to make the transition. For the last six months he's been hijacking every newcomer to R&D and testing them for the same components."

"I see. And I'm the latest hijackee. What's he looking for?"

"I'll let him explain that. I couldn't repeat it if I tried. All I know is, Nick and I are the only ones to date whom Creek will allow through the portal. On the other side, we've met Native American sorts, Egyptian sorts, and sorts bearing no resemblance at all to any sort I know."

"Egyptians? How do you know you aren't going back in time?"

"We don't. Perhaps you'll help us determine that."

"It sounds exciting."

"It's not all beer and skittles, darling. The work is dangerous."

"So is crossing a busy street."

Richard stopped. "Listen, Christy. Most of the natives we've met have been friendly. This last time, we did more than observe. We got caught up in their affairs, and ate some horrid food—true torture for Nick, as you'll learn. The superstitious among them accused us of sorcery and tried to drown us. Nick got hurt. He'll be fine, though he'll be limping for a while. It could have been a lot worse—and *that's* why I don't want you to go."

She seemed offended, indignant even. They walked on in awkward silence until they reached a small ornamental bridge. She rested her hands on the wooden rail and stared at the stream beneath her.

"Nick and I train constantly to ensure our survival. If you join us, darling—"

She spun so fast, he cringed. "If you really want to ensure your survival, stop calling me 'darling.' How soon do you need me back in Mendocino?"

Richard suddenly realized he'd have been disappointed if she'd gone to another division. "How much time do you need to wrap things up here?"

116

"Is two weeks acceptable?"

"Yes. If you need more time, that's fine too. Be prepared to work when you come. Your friend Kieran assured me you're well able to look after yourself, that you bested him in a sparring match. I sparred with the man myself before he left. If you can stand up to a man of his abilities, I'm impressed. Still, I need to know what you can do and what your weaknesses are." He smiled. "Provided you have any, that is."

* * * * *

As he had every night since the funeral, Kiyoshi knelt before the chrysanthemum-filled alcove where the urn containing Eric's ashes rested. Talty had come to speak to him, though the sight of his stooped back convinced her that tomorrow would do.

Before she could tiptoe away, he rose gracefully and bowed to her. "How may I assist you, Hime-san?"

She should've known he'd hear her. "I'm leaving soon, Ki. I want to know if you'll be all right. Will you stay here, or leave?"

"I will stay for the thirty days until the interment. After that, we will see. And you, Hime-san? Will you go to California after all?"

"Yes."

"Wherever you go, you will find green hills, and I will be your friend. If you are ever in need of anything, please let me know."

"*Arigato, gozaimashita.*" *Thank you for all you have taught me.*

Kiyoshi bowed again. The proper response was to bow in turn. Instead, Talty kissed his cheek.

His dignified bearing faltered, though he quickly regained his composure. "To teach is also to learn, Hime-san. Good-night." He padded down the hallway.

Talty touched the urn and went to bed.

* * * * *

While Talty slept, the sun burned the fog from Hoy's Neck, a small peninsula on England's west coast that jutted into the Irish Sea. The humidity had left Catherine Dolliver's hair frizzed beyond hope. She smoothed her blond curls and prayed her makeup was intact. Roger Wessex had his pick of women, and Catherine's orders were to be his first choice.

As she strolled beside him on the beach, she thought she'd done well so far. Still, she and Roger were far from new lovers enjoying a casual ramble in a romantic ocean setting. Their walk had taken them through a complex that once housed a sporting facility. It now harbored Roger's growing cache of munitions.

117

They stopped at the largest of the buildings, where Gordon Randolph, Roger's "fix it" man, stood guard at the door. Catherine had run into hatchet men before, but something about Randolph's private little smiles sickened her. A former street gang leader, the balding thug's illegitimate relationship to the royal family had saved him from prison more than once.

Roger nodded to the stony-eyed sentry and ushered Catherine inside. Strains of opera drifted from somewhere, incongruous with the crates of rifles, small arms, submachine guns, heavy machine gun ammunition, and rocket-propelled grenades.

Once Catherine finished inspecting the deadly stock, she made a deliberate show of inspecting Roger. The task wasn't difficult. His athletic build and dark good looks—attributes of which he was very much aware—had proved a bonus on this assignment.

"This is quite a setup, Roger. You really are quite clever, darling."

"I've prepared well, haven't I? I haven't had to tap my principal cash reserves, and Philip knows the proper markets. He's with a specialty dealer in France now."

They entered the adjoining room. Catherine blinked at the rockets and mortar rounds. "Will subjugating Ireland really help our cause?"

"Yes. Steal money and you're a thief. Steal a country and you're a king! The outing won't even require much in the way of munitions. The Irish are too complacent to have proper defenses against real attack craft."

"Then why so much ordnance?"

"It's not just for Ireland. I won't tolerate any interference when I put John aside."

Bert Benson suspected that Roger meant to do more than put John aside. "I see. I do hope you're taking steps to protect all this treasure. You wouldn't want anyone stumbling across it."

"No one but us knows about it, pet. There's an alarm system in place, and Gordon always has men on guard."

Catherine linked arms with Roger. "I'm excited to be part of your plans. Knowing the kingdom will soon be in your hands makes me tingle."

Roger ran a finger under her chin. "Come up to my private quarters, Cat. I'll show you some real firepower, and we'll see about that tingling problem you're having."

✳ ✳ ✳ ✳ ✳

Two weeks later, Talty arrived at San Francisco International Airport on a late afternoon flight. Richard met her in the arrival area. Nick Tomasi was with him.

118

Nick's leg injury had apparently healed. He moved like a stalking tiger, one that stood just under six feet. His swarthy skin and dark, wavy hair proclaimed his Mediterranean heritage. Richard had told Talty that Nick retired from the U.S. Air Force a captain. For two years, he'd worked as a helicopter pilot for a small San Francisco company that offered transportation to tourists and business clients. Now he was a major with ISF—and his smile was infectious.

"Aw, man!" Nick squeezed her hands in greeting. "Look at this beautiful woman. You didn't tell me she was beautiful, Richard. Welcome to sunny California, *bella donna!*"

The men toted Talty's carry-on and overnight bag to Richard's car. They headed north out of the city, Richard driving, Talty beside him, Nick in the back seat. Just after six o'clock, they stopped at an Italian restaurant, where Talty learned more about Nick.

"The marinara sauce here isn't as good as my grandmother's," he said, "but it's better than my mother's. Now *my* sauce is a masterpiece." He kissed his fingers to emphasize the superiority of his "gravy." "Maybe I'll make some for you sometime."

Talty decided she liked Nick Tomasi. "Will you share the recipe?"

Nick's fork stopped halfway to his mouth. "Hey, that's a state secret! What, you cook?"

"A little."

"Hey, Richard! She's beautiful *and* she cooks. Have more eggplant, Christy. Have more wine. *L'appetito vien mangiando!*"

Richard was grinning. "He says that a lot. It means—"

"Appetite comes with eating!" Nick reached for a plate of ziti. "Have more pasta!"

By eight-thirty, Richard and Nick had delivered Talty to her tiny apartment in Fort Pinard's Officers' Quarters. The trip from Tokyo had exhausted her. Tomorrow she'd unpack—the rest of her things would arrive in a week or so—and contact Kieran to let him know she'd arrived safely. She would also remind him of his promise to have things in Ireland straightened out by the time her assignment here ended. Tossing her clothes on the back of a chair, she tumbled into bed.

✳ ✳ ✳ ✳ ✳

The following morning, the Peregrine Team met in Creek's office. Mysterious, humming machinery filled the sunny room, as did empty pizza cartons and dozens of opened soda cans.

Sitting at a round conference table, Talty shared a pot of tea with

Richard. Samantha and Nick sipped coffee. Creek chugged a can of root beer and shuffled untidy stacks of paper over his desk like a madman playing a strange game of solitaire.

At last the gangly scientist interlaced his fingers on the table and greeted his team. The twitch in his shoulder increased when he welcomed Talty. "Let's talk a little about our work."

The others in the room appeared bored. Talty, however, set her tea aside to listen.

"I'll keep it as simple as possible," Creek said. "We humans interpret the world around us as three-dimensional. That's an illusion. The universe is really hyper-dimensional in nature. There's a constant flux of energy through the space-time continuum. This energy flows in patterns we call superimposed energy domains. These domains are the building blocks of the universe, like the way atoms form molecules."

He stopped for a swallow of soda. No one made a sound. "Each domain has its own unique frequency. Human brain waves have frequencies too. If we adjust the frequencies of the brain to match the frequencies of the domains, we should be able to see them."

"So far it only works with certain brains," Samantha said. "Like Richard's and Nick's."

Creek was grinning like a kindly grandfather. "We're pretty darn sure it will work with yours too, Christy. The portal will cycle to the next loop in a few weeks. We'll try a test run when it does, something real short to see if we're on the right track."

Richard reached for the teapot. "Meanwhile, Major, we'll see if you know your onions."

* * * * *

Talty's Peregrine training took place in the house Richard and Nick co-owned. Nick's massive, modern kitchen impressed her, as did the view. The rambling building, once a communal home for artists, overlooked the ocean and California's north coast. Though they'd renovated the place, and even added a modest gym, the men had done nothing with the outside areas. The neglected gardens broke Talty's heart.

"I'm jealous," she said. "Maybe I'll get a place myself."

"We got tired of the Officers' Quarters," said Nick. "A guy can't cook there, y'know?"

When Nick wasn't cooking, he and Richard tossed hypothetical scenarios at Talty, working out various outcomes until they were confident they could meet trouble as a team. When they tested her unarmed combat skills, she didn't hesitate to clobber them.

She learned about the leather pouches both men fastened around their waists during missions, kits that contained basic survival tools, emergency rations, and small weapons. When she prepared hers, she included the tanto knife Kiyoshi had given her.

After six weeks, Creek announced that the portal had reached its transport cycle. He'd send his team through in full gear for a pre-mission test run that would allow him to fine-tune his coordinates for the actual mission. Samantha gave Talty a final checkup and embedded a contraceptive implant beneath the skin of her upper arm, a routine procedure that Talty cynically regarded as a waste of time.

The day of the test, she rose at dawn, her favorite time to dream and think things out. The sunrise held the promise of the day.

While making tea, she thought how far she'd come since her disastrous wedding to Thomas Wessex. Now she was about to undertake an important mission, one where her abilities, not her name, were all that mattered. Eager to prove herself, she sought something to keep her from becoming antsy until she had to report to the lab.

The rest of her personal effects had arrived from Japan. She started putting her books away. A history text she'd used to teach the class at Curragh Camp found its way into her hands. She flipped it open.

Hannibal smiled up at her. Caesar waved. And there were the Vikings, who'd always set her imagination spinning.

In 1014, her own ancestor, the first Brian Boru, ended decades of Viking attempts to invade Ireland at the Battle of Clontarf. In the years that followed, King Brian brought stability to the kingdom and firmly established the dynasty that ruled Ireland to this day.

Her eyes grew moist with longing for her family. Setting the book aside, she opened her top bureau drawer and unlocked the gold box that held her Fianna pin, the badge of honor she couldn't wear, not yet. She held it to her collar, admiring it in the mirror before returning it to the drawer. Neil had worked so hard to help her earn it.

Neil. He was far away in the Middle East, but she felt his gentle tug on her hair. An unbidden memory of his strong arms around her had her longing for the protection she'd so often scorned. Wondering how long it would be before she'd see him again—and Aidan too, of course—she tied her hair back and left for the lab.

* * * * *

Richard's claustrophobic cocoon no longer existed. The Peregrine Portal was now a glowing, humming rectangle that looked like a freestanding doorframe.

The lab itself seemed to hum. Samantha stood behind a glass partition with two staff members who monitored a wall loaded with instruments. Creek hovered around the portal reading dials and displays. The twitching in his shoulder had progressed to turbulent spasms when the readings reached the proper levels.

"It's time!" he shouted. "Let's do it, people!"

Talty's heart fluttered. Readjusting the leather toolkit that hung securely at the waist of her mottled gray jumpsuit, she followed Richard and Nick, clad in similar attire, to the portal.

"We'll be back in time for supper!" called Nick.

Creek yanked the transpulsion switch. The glow around the portal surged. Richard ran through first. Talty followed him into a buzzing black maelstrom.

CHAPTER FOURTEEN

Clontarf

Richard and Nick had taught Talty to roll to her feet prepared to defend herself the instant she crossed through the portal. Instead, she lay helpless and retching in ferns flattened by her undignified arrival. The slicing pain in her head not only blinded her, it rendered her indifferent to her fate. Somewhere between salvos of vomiting and desperate gasps for breath, a man's voice—Richard's—called her name. He knelt beside her and gripped her shoulders.

"Go away!" she sputtered, adding a few choice expletives she'd learned in the navy.

"Let's get out of the open, darling. If you can't get up, I'll carry you."

Mortified, she wiped her mouth on her sleeve and staggered to her feet. The pounding in her head eased. "I can get up myself, and I'm not your goddamn darling! Where's Nick?"

"I don't know. I hear water running nearby. Come on, we'll get you cleaned up." He sounded calm, yet he pivoted as he spoke, scanning nonstop and poised to spring into action.

"I hear it too. I'll get myself cleaned up, thank you."

Nevertheless, he slipped an arm around her waist and tugged her along. At the edge of a bubbling stream, she knelt and splashed cold water over her face, hating him for not suffering as she did. He'd told her that he recovered more quickly with each trip. This was only her first. Still, she hadn't expected to be so pathetically sick.

Feeling better, she leaned back on her heels and surveyed her surroundings. The stream rushed down to a large, winding river. The land on either side of it was green and rolling. Mist diffused the sunlight trickling through the surrounding treetops. Hazy mountains nowhere near as high as those in California or Japan loomed in the distance. Still, their tops pierced the cottony clouds.

"Where are we?" she asked. "Will we go back soon? And where's Nick?"

Richard's pinched expression worried her. "I don't know where the bloody hell he is. Either he didn't make it through, or he's somewhere nearby and we'll meet up with him later. But we should already be back. Test runs never take more than a minute. Let's find cover and sit tight."

He pulled his commando knife from his toolkit and slid it into his boot sheath. Following his example, Talty slipped her tanto knife into her own boot. They rested in a copse of oak trees, sipping water from their canteens.

Richard soon grew restless. "It won't matter where we are when Creek calls us back. I don't like sitting in one place too long. Let's see if we can make friends with the natives before dark."

They found a deer track and set out through the woodlands, hearing only bird calls and rustling leaves until crashing branches and stumbling footsteps announced a desperate flight through the woods. Talty dashed behind a tree, as did Richard, just as a boy of no more than fourteen emerged from the undergrowth. Richard signaled Talty. Together they stepped from behind the trees.

The boy froze. Curly black hair framed his pallid face. The torn crimson cloak covering his shoulders tumbled to leather-clad feet. Beneath the cloak, he wore a belted blue tunic that reached his knees. Yellow leggings completed the colorful outfit.

Richard held his hands palms out. "Can we help you, lad?"

Frightened blue eyes flashed over Richard's fatigues. The boy didn't seem to notice Talty. His response sounded like gibberish to her, though an instant later the words made sense.

"Please, can you? The Danmarkers have my mother. I'm afraid Brother Marcan and the others will be too late!"

"Which way?" Richard asked.

The distraught boy ran off.

"You go first, darling. I'll take the rear."

Talty set her hands on her hips. "Don't you think you should've asked how many attackers there are before you agreed to help?"

Before he could answer, she grinned and jogged after the boy.

"Bloody hell," Richard muttered behind her.

A distant babble of voices quickly grew to angry shouts. The woods thinned. The boy stopped, and then he crept to a line of shrubs at the edge of a glade. Talty squeezed beside him, Richard at her sleeve. She peeked through the greenery to see a round thatched cottage, the main building of a small homestead. Four brawny men stood before it. Armed with swords, clad in wool and leather, they'd tucked their long hair into their weapon-laden belts…

Vikings!

They weren't the only ones shouting. From inside the cottage, a woman barraged them with piercing insults.

"Curse all of ye! I'd send ye to the devil, but ye'd be in too good company! Death and smotherin' on ye, and may ye die roarin'!"

"Come out, Leesha!" called one of the men. He lifted a flaming torch from a fence post and stood grinning with his flaming prize. "If you don't, we will burn you out!"

"Come out, Leesha!" called another. "I will keep Leg-Biter in his scabbard." His companions made lewd jokes about the swords that would make a scabbard of Leesha.

"Don't listen to them," called the apparent leader. "We only want to talk. Come out now, or we will set the place afire!"

"Pig snouts on your children, ye miserable dogs!"

At the leader's nod, the torch man swung his arm in ever-widening arcs.

"No, ye filthy pagans!" Before Richard and Talty could stop him, the boy charged into the clearing. He slammed into the torch wielder, who fell backward and raised his hands against the boy's pummeling fists. The burning torch rolled harmlessly to the ground.

"The bitch will come out if we kill her pup!" shouted one of the other Vikings. They drew their swords and closed on the boy.

Richard slid his knife from his boot. He nodded toward the standing Vikings. "The one on the right is yours. I'll take the two on the left."

Tanto in hand, Talty shrieked to divert her target's attention away from the boy. The Viking swept his sword at her. She ducked beneath his arm and drove her knife through his leather jerkin, up and under his breastbone. The shock on his face stirred no sympathy in her. Taking care to avoid his falling sword, she set her foot on his corpse, yanked back her knife, and coolly wiped the blade on his shirt.

The cottage door burst open. A sword-swinging blaze of red hair exploded into the clearing and screamed at the boy. "Get out of it, Carney!"

Carney scrambled away. The Viking he'd been bashing sprang to his feet. The woman screeched and beheaded him.

Talty checked on Richard. He'd lost his knife, but he'd whacked the sword from his adversary's hands and begun a nonstop assault of rapid-fire punches. The Viking, used to hacking with weapons, couldn't counter the skillful clobbering.

The fourth Viking spun and thrust his sword at Richard's back, but the red-haired woman's blade smashed the sword to the ground. Her repeated jabs forced the man back. He seemed to trip, but then he lunged and tackled the woman down. As he rolled away, he pulled a dagger from his belt and twisted toward Richard.

Talty's warning shout saved him from catching the dagger in his back. The weapon nicked his arm however, distracting him long enough to allow his opponent to retrieve a fallen sword.

The Viking swung the sword at Richard's head, though he suddenly dropped the weapon to clutch at the tanto knife lodged in his throat. He fell choking to the ground.

The surviving attacker bellowed his rage. The boy snatched up a sword and flew at him, the force of his young body an unstoppable missile. The Viking had no chance. Impaled on the sword, he smashed into the wattle fence, the boy atop him.

Richard lay unmoving on the ground. Talty ran and knelt beside him, worried that he'd received more than a nick to his arm. His erratic breathing unnerved her.

Furious shouts boomed from the woods. Grabbing the nearest sword, she dragged it beside her, ready to rush the sturdy man who broke through the brush with a sword in his hand.

As he stared at the Viking corpses, he slid his sword into the scabbard on his belt. "By God, Leesha. Young Carney said you needed help. I'd say you've got things well in hand here, woman."

"What would you expect, and you taking your sweet time, Marcan?" Despite her harsh tone, Leesha smiled at the brown-robed friar and the six armed monks behind him. "Please see what's wrong with this man."

Brother Marcan knelt beside Richard and cursed. He tore off Richard's sleeve and tied it tightly above the gash on his arm. "Vile cowards and their poison! We must drain as much as we can." Wasting no time, he snatched a dagger from his belt and sliced the wound twice.

"Poison?" Talty's heart beat in her throat.

"What do ye need, Marcan?" asked Leesha.

"A warm fire and God's help, sister. Have you any all-heal?"

She asked Carney to go to the shed and fetch the all-heal. The boy ran, leaping over a corpse on his way. Leesha charged into the cottage.

Fighting panic, Talty touched Richard's wrist. His pulse was rapid and weak, his skin cold and moist. "Don't you dare die on me," she whispered.

Carney came running from the shed with a clay jar in his arms. "There's enough for a poultice, Uncle Marcan."

"Bring it to your mother. Tarlach, return to the abbey and get more. Aron, help me get him inside. The rest of you do something with those pagans. I don't expect they'll be rising on Easter Sunday."

Talty rushed into the cottage to help Leesha. She found the woman setting small caldrons over a turf fire. "What can I do?"

The woman cast a kind eye her way. "What's your name, girl?"

"I'm Christy. Christy McKenna. I expect you're Leesha."

"I am. Fetch the bed coverings from the chest in that back room. We must keep him warm." She paused. "Is he your husband?"

"No. A friend." Talty went to find the blankets.

Brother Marcan's poultice used up most of the all-heal, though enough remained for a bowl of tea. Richard swallowed enough to satisfy the friar.

"It's up to him now," Marcan said to no one in particular. "We'll make a fresh dressing when Tarlach returns and get more tea into him. By morning we'll know if he'll live. I'll stay the night, if I won't be in the way."

Leesha set her stoker down and rubbed her hands on her bloodstained clothes. "And how could you ever be in the way? Watch my cook pots while we wash up. Then we'll see about supper. Christy"—she nodded at Talty's toolkit—"put your *criss* over there with your friend's."

Talty glanced down in horror at her gore-encrusted clothing. For a moment, the jumpsuit turned to her bloodied wedding dress. Hands shaking, she unbuckled her toolkit. She placed the pouch beside Richard's and hurried after Leesha to a pond surrounded by trees and shrubs.

Desperate to banish the nightmare the bloody clothes had evoked, she tore off her jumpsuit. She gave no thought to the scars on her chest.

Leesha gasped at the sight. She said nothing, but disappeared into an outbuilding. When she returned, she laid two blue cloaks over a boulder. "We have a proper bathtub, but I think this would be easier tonight."

The women waded into the water and soaked away the harrowing events. Afterward, they donned the cloaks. Talty bent to gather the filthy clothing.

"Leave them," Leesha said. "My people will take care of them. I sent them running when the Danmarkers came. They'll be back soon." She laughed. "I hope. Let's find something to wear."

Inside the outbuilding, Leesha opened a wooden chest. She handed Talty dark leggings and a red tunic and selected a yellow outfit for herself. The garments were fine-spun wool, thin and soft. The swirling, unmistakably Celtic designs sewn into the collars and sleeves astounded Talty.

Where was she?

"What's your friend's name?" Leesha asked while they dressed.

127

"Richard. Richard Gale."

"Come from far away by the sound of ye. Picked up some fighting skills along the way as well, did ye?"

"A few. And you? Not many women are so comfortable with a sword."

Leesha's chin rose. "I am. I am Leesha Ni Lorcan, trainer of warriors."

None of Kiyoshi's blank expression exercises could have kept the grin from Talty's face. "I've trained with a warrior or two myself. Perhaps we could teach each other a few tricks."

"I'd enjoy that, Christy. Now let's feed the men before they start grumbling. We've had enough trouble for one day." She laughed again and sauntered up the path.

* * * * *

Brother Tarlach soon returned with the precious all-heal. A second sack held a contribution to the evening meal: early spring vegetables, honey, and oatcakes. The food joined the bread and cheese Talty had set on the table.

She inspected the cottage while she set out wooden bowls. She'd seen such structures reproduced in Ireland's tourist parks. Beneath the thatched roof, the sod and wattle walls shone with a lime whitewash. The rough-hewn furnishings were sparse and practical, set in areas separated by simple wooden planks. A ladder led to a small loft beside the hearth. Carney's sleeping quarters, no doubt. The shutters on the unglazed windows were open to let the twilight air in and the smoke from the turf fire out.

When supper was ready, the monks sat in silence. Brother Marcan blessed the Lord's gifts and said a prayer for Richard's recovery. The burly friar's hair, a darker red than his sister's, showed no gray, though his beard was shot with silver.

Talty experienced the strange sensation of being among kin. "How did you know what poison was on that knife, Brother Marcan?"

"Despite all the Druids have taught me, I didn't. I've known the Danmarkers to use anything from wolfsbane to berry concoctions. All-heal is an antidote for most poisons. I pray for its success here."

Marcan seemed too polite to inquire about Talty's origins, yet she sensed his scrutiny. Apparently Leesha sensed it too.

"This is Christy McKenna, Marcan. She and her companion Richard are travelers. I've invited them to stay and visit."

"Travelers? You're a long way from home, I'm thinking." Marcan raised his ale cup. "Welcome, Christy McKenna." He saluted his nephew then. "A toast to you as well, Carney. The man of the house now, aren't you?"

Carney turned scarlet. He remained as silent as the friars.

"A bit more practice will polish him off," Leesha said. "I am proud of ye, darlin', though I should be scoldin' ye. I told ye to wait for Marcan before ye came back."

Marcan drank and set his cup down. "What happened, Leesha? Where did those Danmarkers come from? What did they want?"

"They were with those lice-ridden Danmarkers we met at Kincora a few days ago."

Talty stopped chewing the bread in her mouth. Kincora was the royal ringfort of her ancestor, the first Brian Boru. Had she and Richard arrived in ancient Ireland?

The lines in Marcan's forehead deepened. "Ospak and his crew."

"Those heathens who were here today deserted Ospak," Leesha said. "They claimed that Ospak betrayed his fellow Danmarkers by siding with King Brian. They meant to steal one of Ospak's ships and sail to Dublin to warn Sitric of Brian's plans, and they stopped by to invite me along for sport. Filthy swine! The devil take them by the heels and roast them!"

Two of the friars choked. The rest crossed themselves. Marcan and Carney only smiled.

Then Marcan's smile vanished. "Their comrades will come looking for them. You and Carney must come to the abbey."

Leesha tore a chunk of bread and waved it at the sword hanging on the wall. "We'll be ready if any more of them come slithering around."

Talty wanted to know if the Brian under discussion was her ancestor, but she couldn't just ask. She must find another way. The Irish history she knew taught that Sitric led the Viking forces defeated by the first King Brian. A test was in order to see if the facts matched. "Who's Sitric?"

"Why, Sitric is the King of Dublin," Marcan answered.

That was wrong. How could a Viking be King of Dublin?

"The poxy swine joined forces with the King of Leinster against Brian," Leesha said. "Last autumn, Brian laid siege to Dublin, but returned to Kincora when his stores ran low."

Carney's eyes lit up. "But now he's gone back. He'll show them this time! Gayth is going to join him. I wish I could go too."

Leesha cast a sad look her son's way.

"Yes, Brian has gone back," Marcan said. "I'm hearing talk now of the biggest battle ever. Ospak warned Brian that many Norse warlords are coming from over the sea to join Sitric. We're not sure who will help Brian, though. Some feel he's too old to lead anymore. Others resent his power and wish to see him defeated, and so we see Irishmen allying themselves with Dublin Norsemen while Norsemen like Ospak side with Brian."

None of this sounded right to Talty. "What date is this?"

Leesha stared at her. "Monday. The fifth day of April."

"What year?"

"Why, it's 1014," answered Marcan. "Do you travel so much you don't know the year?"

"Maybe." She thanked Leesha for the meal and went outside.

This couldn't be her Ireland. The pieces didn't fit. The Irish chieftains hadn't allied themselves with the Vikings. They joined forces with King Brian and his Fianna to rout the invaders. Was it possible that history had overlooked the intertribal bickering Marcan had described to make her ancestors appear more honorable?

Marcan said some thought Brian was an old man. Yes, Brian Boru had grown sons with him when he defeated the Vikings at the Battle of Clontarf, but he'd been far from an old man. He'd lived for years after the battle and brought peace and prosperity to the kingdom.

Talty strolled across the courtyard, avoiding the blood that still stained the ground. Despite the late hour, sunlight glowed in the sky. This Ireland was as far north as hers.

Was it hers? She wanted it to be. If the Brian Boru Marcan and Leesha mentioned really was her ancestor, she had to meet him. Her history taught that the Battle of Clontarf took place on Good Friday. Today was April fifth. Good Friday was only a few weeks away.

Carney came running up behind her. "Your friend is askin' for ye, miss."

She hurried back to the cottage and found Richard cursing the all-heal Marcan was coaxing him to drink. Then he cursed Marcan.

The monk didn't seem to mind. "Your friend is strong, Christy. I didn't think he'd wake before dawn." He carried the empty bowl to the sideboard.

Talty sat in his place. "How are you?"

Richard's eyes were closing. "Still here. What happened? I feel awful."

"A Viking cut you with a poisoned knife. I'll tell you all about it in the morning."

He fell asleep. She pulled the bedcovers to his chin. "He seems better, Brother Marcan."

"God works in his own way. I'll sleep here to tend him during the night. Carney and the others have retired to the warriors' hut. Leesha, you and Christy will sleep in the back room."

Leesha folded her arms. "Are ye done getting my house in order, rascal?" She cuffed him playfully and retired to the back bedroom.

Talty claimed an adjoining bed and fell into a dreamless sleep.

* * * * *

After Marcan and his friars left the next morning, Leesha's attendants returned. They swept out the cottage, tended to the laundry and gardens, and fed and milked the animals. In the midst of this domestic activity, Talty and Leesha carried staves resembling batas from the warriors' hut and tested each other's sparring skills in the courtyard.

Once the friendly warm-up period ended, the women engaged in some serious competition. Leesha finally called a halt. "Mother Mary, girl! I haven't had this much fun in years! Who taught ye all that?"

"I've wondered about that myself," Richard said from the cottage door.

Leesha's mouth fell open. "What are ye doing there? My brother said ye'd be abed for days!"

Happy to see him, yet worried by his unhealthy appearance, Talty set her stave on the ground. "He might be headed back there from the looks of him. How do you feel?"

"Hungry. I hate to impose, but—"

"Ye'll eat!" Leesha shouted. "Orla! Where are ye, woman?"

A gray-haired woman came running from the pond, wiping her hands on her apron. She smiled when Leesha asked her to heat some food.

Talty offered to help. Feigning relief that the sparring ordeal was over, Leesha agreed and excused herself to see to her own chores.

Inside the cottage, Orla rewarmed the breakfast porridge and set out oatcakes, honey, and buttermilk before returning to her laundry. While Richard ate, Talty munched an oatcake.

"Something went wrong with the portal," she said.

Richard looked up from his porridge. "Yes. I'm guessing Nick didn't even make it through. Your neural patterns must have altered things. Creek will call us back as soon as he fixes it. Now, what happened to my arm?"

"A poisoned knife nicked you. I told you, but I guess you don't remember."

"This is no nick, darling. My arm is well-sliced."

"Brother Marcan sliced it to get the poison out. Otherwise, you wouldn't be here enjoying your porridge."

"Nothing wrong with porridge. That all-heal rot is beastly, though."

"The kettle is on to make more. You need it for a few more days to counteract the poison."

"What the bloody hell is it, anyway?"

"Mistletoe, Colonel. The cure for all ills. It isn't doing you any harm."

"It's filthy stuff! And how do you know about it?"

"I read it in a book. Marcan learned about it from the Druids." She waited for his reaction.

He put his spoon down and stared at her. "Druids? Where are we?"

"In Ireland, apparently. That river we saw was the Shannon. We're in Killaloe, at the home of Leesha Ni Lorcan, trainer of warriors, cousin of King Brian Boru. It's 1014, four weeks before Good Friday." How good was he with history?

He looked away somewhere. "1014. The Battle of Clontarf. It would be something to see, wouldn't it?"

Talty smiled. She was starting to like Richard Gale. "If we could see it, we'd know whether we're in our own past or in a parallel world." She explained the historical deviations she'd encountered. "If this is the past, King Brian will win at Clontarf."

Richard nodded. "Perhaps it will happen that way. I've never believed I was in the past on my other trips. But I agree. We must try to see it. How can we get there?"

"First of all, Colonel, you're not going anywhere until you're well. We have four weeks, plenty of time. Even if we walked, it would only take a week. On horseback, a few days."

Richard's blue eyes gleamed. He must be feeling better. Still, Talty knew something about relapses. She fixed him some tea. "This will top off your breakfast, Colonel. Cheers."

"All right, I'll drink it—if you stop calling me Colonel."

"Stop calling me darling and it's a deal. Now drink up."

He complied, though his face scrunched in revulsion. "This disgusting tea isn't the only reason I'm still sitting here," he said after he'd swallowed half of it. "You're damn good with that knife of yours. Your professional abilities continue to amaze me."

Talty wished she could control her blushing cheeks. "Get some rest. Later I'll show you around the place...Richard."

He downed his tea and smiled.

✳ ✳ ✳ ✳ ✳

A regimen of rest and long walks enhanced Richard's recovery. While his health improved, Talty familiarized herself with the round warriors' hut, the building where Leesha's students learned their art.

The loft served as sleeping quarters for visitors. The ground floor housed the tools of war. Leesha explained that many of the weapons had been gifts from King Brian, the spoils of victories against Vikings and hostile neighbors.

One rainy morning, Kane the Blacksmith hammered metal pegs into the wall and hung the swords and knives that belonged to the Vikings who'd tried to kidnap Leesha. Kane set the fierce looking sword called Leg-Biter at the end of the impressive collection.

Leesha's husky laugh echoed through the hut. "Leg-Biter will be needing a good Irish name, I think."

Talty agreed. She cast an appreciative glance at the rest of the display. A magnificent bow caught her eye. Had it whispered her name? Unable to resist, she stroked the knotwork designs carved into the yew wood.

"We Irish aren't much for bows and arrows," Leesha said. "We prefer our swords and axes. That's a fine bow, though. Brian presented it to me after he sacked Limerick years ago. It's smaller than most, made for a woman's hands. Do you know the bow, Christy?"

"I can pass myself with it. May I try this one?"

Leesha nodded. Kane lifted the bow from the wall. Talty accepted it with reverence. The grip fit her hands perfectly. After testing the weapon's tension, she selected an arrow with a leaf-shaped iron head from the quiver Kane held. A line of straw "men" Leesha used for practice sessions stood against the opposite wall. Talty's arrow whooshed toward a straw head and spit into the center of its face. A second arrow followed, penetrating the chest with a neat thud.

"Mother Mary!" Leesha cried. "I would learn that, Christy."

"All right. When you have time, we'll practice." Talty retrieved the arrows from the straw man and returned them to the quiver.

The blacksmith returned bow and quiver to their place on the wall. He gathered his tools and turned toward the door.

Leesha slapped his back. "A good day's work, Kane. You're well worth your honor price."

Talty's requisite training as Crown Princess included the study of Ireland's early laws. If the laws were the same here, she might have another indication that she and Richard were in the past. After Kane left, she asked Leesha about honor price.

"Everyone has an honor price, Christy. Whoever violates a person's honor must pay a fine. The higher a person's rank, the higher the honor price, and the higher the fine."

"So an injury to a chieftain would bring a higher price than the same injury to a farmer?"

"That's right."

So far, the laws were the same. "Are all crimes dealt with this way? Even murder?"

"Most often, yes."

"What happens to murderers who can't afford to pay the fines? Or just don't want to?"

"That's up to the murdered man or woman's next of kin. They can declare the murderer a slave or have him put to death." Leesha's eyes narrowed. "Does your wanting to know have anything to do with those scars on your chest? Is the one who did that to ye still alive? Is that why ye became a warrior? To have your revenge on him?"

Talty's fists tightened. She hated Roger Wessex for the shambles he'd made of her life. Still, she'd decided that the best revenge would be to return home one day laughing at him. "No. I was training to be a warrior before…it happened."

A knowing smile bloomed on Leesha's face. "Most young women learn spinning and churning, and perhaps a little embroidery. I myself despised such boring pastimes. Not that they aren't valuable, mind, but when my father's champion taught me the warrior ways, I felt as if I possessed some ancient power. No one could hurt me."

"Does your father's champion still serve him?"

The sound of rain pelting the roof grew louder. Leesha's voice grew softer. "Dunlan went with Brian to fight the Danes in Limerick nearly thirty years ago. I never saw him again. He left Gayth in my belly."

"I'm so sorry. And Gayth?"

"He lives at Kincora now. He leads the Dalcassian guard that protects King Brian's home while he's away. Now Brian has sent for them all. They'll be leaving for the east soon." She paused and frowned. "Maybe it will be over by the time they get there, hmm?"

The Dalcassians were Talty's own ancestral clan. However, when the Vikings attacked, King Brian sent for the Fianna, not the Dalcassians. She asked the question that had troubled her since Marcan said he wasn't sure who would help Brian.

"Are there no Fianna to keep the country safe?"

An incredulous laugh prefaced Leesha's response. "Fianna? Men from long-ago tales. The legends say that the last of them—Finn MacCool's own son—came back from the Otherworld a very old man to tell the tales of Finn and the Fianna to St. Patrick. Tales, Christy. We don't even know if the Fianna were real, though the poets say the first Dalcassian married Finn MacCool's daughter."

No Fianna? This couldn't be Talty's Ireland!

Leesha's hands flew to her hips. "All right, girl! Who are ye? Are ye one of the Fianna? Is Richard? Have ye come here from the Otherworld?"

She must say the right thing. Her head spun to find ambiguous words. "Richard is a great warrior, but he isn't one of the Fianna."

"I see." Leesha's eyes narrowed to slits. "Does he know that you are?"

Talty's cheeks burned, but she remained silent.

"The fairy women sometimes come for husbands. They bewitch our young men and lure them off to the Otherworld. Are ye here so?"

Leesha's sudden hostility—the volatile Boru temper?—had Talty's guard up. "I'm no fairy woman, and I'm definitely not looking for a husband. I'm not really sure why I'm here."

Leesha's rage melted as quickly as it had appeared. "I think I know. Ye've been sent to help Brian fight the Danes. Are the Fianna so great that he only needs one of ye?"

"Hardly, but I'll help if I can. As for Richard..."

"I'll keep your secret, Banfian. In return, ye'll teach me great things, like bow shooting."

That seemed a fair deal to Talty. "My father told me once: 'An hour of play teaches more than a year of lessons.'"

Leesha howled with laughter. "What else is there to do on this miserable day but play?" She lifted the Viking bow from the wall. "Pull out two of those straw men, girl. We'll send them on their way to hell!"

* * * * *

Late one rainy evening, Talty sat with Richard and Leesha enjoying a supper of vegetable stew and grainy bread. She sensed a change in the air, something between her dinner companions, though before she could decide what, Orla rushed in to announce the arrival of Leesha's older son.

Gasping with delight, Leesha rose from her chair just as a rain-soaked young man swept in like a king coming home to his castle. Gayth MacDunlan lifted his elated mother from the floor and kissed her cheek.

"I stopped to say good-bye, Mam. I'm leaving in the morning." He set her down, unpinned his cloak, and handed it to Orla. "Isn't it just my luck to be in time for supper?"

Leesha's smile faded at the news of his departure, though she swiftly recovered her merry mood. "When are you not looking to be fed? Sit, Gayth. Meet my guests."

Gayth settled himself onto a seat beside Leesha. He greeted Richard cordially, and then his dynamic, brown-eyed gaze locked on Talty. An electrifying intimacy shot between them. Bewildered, she lowered her head.

He helped himself to a cup of ale. His vibrant eyes hunted the room, darting from Richard to Leesha. A worldly smile lit his handsome face. Feeling like a cadet in a room full of admirals, Talty realized that Gayth had seen at once what had eluded her: Leesha and Richard were lovers.

Apparently concluding that such a situation left Talty available, Gayth turned his bewitching smile on her. She was ready to play—but Leesha had noticed her son's winning smile.

"Christy is a holy woman, Gayth. She's traveling on a pilgrimage to visit Ireland's holy wells. Richard is her protector."

Talty nearly laughed out loud at the confusion on Richard's face. He had no way of knowing that Leesha was trying to protect her son from an Otherworld romance.

No such confusion marred Gayth's virile face. Undaunted by his mother's words, he reached for the bread, his chocolate eyes never leaving Talty. "Is that so? Many such wells can be found along the way to Dublin, holy woman. You and Richard would be safer if you journeyed with us, and having a holy woman along will bring us luck. We have extra horses. Can you ride?"

"Yes," Richard said, interrupting Leesha's stammering.

"We leave at first light. Be ready."

Talty bit back a joyful cheer. She must try to meet King Brian, if she could. For now, she'd convince Leesha that Gayth had no place in her plans—even if his smile did entice her. "It's time for us to leave Killaloe. Richard has recovered."

Leesha sighed. "Yes, I know. I'll miss ye, though. Orla, see that our friends have proper provisions for their journey."

Averting her attention from Gayth, Talty stood. "Since we must rise early, I will go and say my prayers."

The befuddled look returned to Richard's face. Leesha, however, smiled at Talty with gratitude.

*****

Talty stood near the edge of the pond. Lost in fanciful dreams of Brian Boru and the Battle of Clontarf, she didn't hear Gayth approach until he stood beside her. "Gayth! You have found me at my prayers."

"Forgive me, holy woman." He stepped closer, bringing with him delicious scents of wet wool, turf smoke, and heather. "Tomorrow I go to battle. I might never return. I do not wish to sleep alone tonight."

Talty nearly melted, though thoughts of Leesha cooled her down. Expecting lightning to strike any minute, she said, "I have taken vows."

"Perhaps I can convince you there is no sin in the flesh Our Lord created." His fingers slid down her cheek.

Her knees buckled. She wanted him to do it—or something like it—again.

He lowered his head toward hers. "My mother speaks highly of your fighting skills. You would be a fitting mate for a warrior. What fine sons you would bear!" He stroked her other cheek. "Can I convince you?"

"I don't know. Can you?"

Leesha forgotten, she stepped into Gayth's open arms. He pulled her against him and kissed her. She'd wondered so long how a real kiss would feel. Now she swayed in his embrace, yielding the intimacy he demanded. At last he took his mouth from hers. Again he ran his fingers over her cheek, this time continuing downward to linger at her neck. Then he was teasing her breast. An exquisite burning pulsed in secret places.

"Lie with me, Christy. The grass is soft beneath the hawthorn trees."

"Yes. I will. But I must tell you—"

He kissed her again, his busy hands undoing the ties of her tunic. She combed her fingers through his thick, dark hair, and then she nudged his face away. "Gayth, I must tell you…"

"Tell me later. Lie with me now. I will fill you with fine sons."

He slipped her tunic down with a finesse that stunned her. She couldn't get it off so fast herself. Then he stared—not at the beautiful woman he'd surely thought to see, but at the scars.

He turned away. "Truly you are a holy woman. Your great suffering will assure your place in heaven. Please forgive me for this…this violation."

"No, Gayth. It's not like that. Please—"

"I will make my confession and do penance for my lust."

And he was gone. Miffed at his rebuff, Talty drew her tunic up and retied the laces. If only she could have prepared him. If only the night had been darker. If only…

Richard and Leesha had crossed a line she'd never know. She suspected they'd be saying their good-byes in the warriors' hut tonight.

Gayth would sleep in the cottage, on the spare bed by the fire. Perhaps she'd have another chance to convince him she was no saint.

A sudden sense that someone was watching her had her peering into the shadows. She shook off the feeling and made her way back to the cottage, envisioning sexy scenarios.

* * * * *

Brother Marcan sat near the fire with Carney and Gayth. The genial friar looked up when Talty entered. "Here's our friend Christy now."

Talty wouldn't have Gayth to herself tonight, but she couldn't help smiling. "Hello, Brother Marcan. What brings you here so late in the day?"

"We came to wish Gayth Godspeed. I'm glad we did. He tells us you and

Richard are leaving as well. I would have regretted not seeing you off."

"I could go with you, Gayth," Carney said. "I can fight!"

Gayth ruffled his brother's black curls. "I know, and I'm proud of you. But I need you here to protect Mam and Uncle Marcan while I'm away."

Marcan frowned. "Where is Leesha, anyway? Richard is missing too. We thought the place deserted when we arrived."

Talty and Gayth traded smiles. "Out walking, I expect," said Gayth.

Marcan's frown deepened, and then he grinned. "I see. Well, Carney. It appears you and I will sleep in the cottage instead of in the warriors' hut. At least we'll have the fire."

＊＊＊＊＊

Richard and Leesha had a fire of their own going in the loft. Though lost in Leesha's needs and favors, Richard heard the intruders come in. He cautioned her to silence and slipped into his clothes. She dressed too, cursing under her breath for having no weapons with her.

Peering into the gloom, Richard counted four men studying the weapons on the wall. He thought they planned to steal them until one of them roared with grief.

"Leg-Biter! My brother would never surrender you unless he was dead!"

Richard flew down the ladder. He side-kicked the nearest Viking to the ground and seized a battle-axe from Leesha's collection. Leesha landed behind him and hefted Leg-Biter from the wall.

The man Richard had downed leapt to his feet. "I am Snorri the Black. I will avenge my brother's death!"

Leesha brandished Leg-Biter with both hands and forced him back.

Snorri drew his sword and challenged her. "You flaunt my brother's sword, vile woman? You will join him in death!"

＊＊＊＊＊

Gayth ordered Carney to stay where he was. Swords drawn, he and Marcan raced from the cottage. Talty followed, tanto knife in hand.

While Gayth and Marcan engaged two men in the courtyard, Talty rushed to the warriors' hut and threw open the door.

Moonlight flooded the scene. Two intruders had fallen. Richard had a third pinned against the rear wall. Unable to wield his sword against Richard's battle-axe in the tight space, the Viking dropped his sword and drew a dagger from his belt.

"Oh no, not a second time!" Richard dropped the axe. His left fist bashed the Viking's gut. His right walloped the man's head. The Viking fell.

Leesha seemed to be holding her own until her opponent knocked her

138

against the wall. The tip of his blade pierced her side. Her outraged shriek filled the hut.

The man whirled and bolted for the door, thrusting his sword at Talty. "No woman can stop Snorri the Black!"

She stumbled back, regaining her balance straightaway and scrambling after him. Gayth and Marcan came running, their bloodied blades affirming the fate of the other intruders.

"Marcan," Talty called as she ran. "Leesha's hurt!"

Marcan ran to the barn. "Get him, Gayth! Hunt the devil down!"

* * * * *

Talty and Gayth homed in on Snorri's desperate thrashing through the woods. They were closing in on him when the racket stopped.

Gayth pulled Talty behind a tree. "We are near the pond. He is trapped. Stay here, lady. You have only a small knife."

"I don't even need that." Ignoring his objections, she sheathed the knife in her boot and slipped into the shadows.

A moment later, an eerie wail echoed through the woods. "I've come for ye, Danmarker! You have killed me, but my spirit has come for ye!"

Talty would've traded the unorthodox hunting technique for a pair of night vision goggles in a minute. Still, her trick worked. Snorri ran straight at Gayth to escape Leesha's "ghost." When Gayth's sword whacked the blade from his hand, he screamed and fell whimpering to the ground.

Talty came running and kicked his sword away. She knew that the Vikings believed they couldn't enter Valhalla if they died without their swords. From Snorri's reaction, he shared this belief.

Gayth dragged him to the pond and drowned him.

* * * * *

The ordeal of cauterizing and dressing Leesha's wound ended at dawn. Talty helped Marcan put the herbs away while Richard packed the provisions they'd take on their journey.

Carney returned from the abbey helping several friars pull a wooden wagon. Talty laid blankets in the cart while Gayth sat in the cottage with his mother. And then he and Richard were easing Leesha into the wagon.

She stroked Gayth's cheek. "Take my love with you, my fine man son. I pray I'll see you soon."

Gayth kissed her forehead. "If not in this world, then in the next."

"Richard, take Leg-Biter. Christy, take the Viking bow. I swear it claimed you the first day you saw it."

Talty squeezed her hand. "You're strong, Leesha. You'll be whacking those straw men again in no time."

"Thank you, friend. And thank you, Richard, for reminding me there are more than straw men in the world. Guard my son."

Richard kissed her. "We'll guard each other. Good-bye, lovely lady."

Carney hugged his brother. "Come back to us, Gayth." He ran off to push and pull with the men from the abbey. The wagon rolled away.

* * * * *

For three rainy days, the Dalcassians rode two hundred strong. They made cold camps and ate what food they carried with them.

The men had balked at bringing a woman along until Gayth described the holy woman's warrior skills. Still, Talty sensed their disapproving glares. She and Richard kept to themselves.

On the third day, Gayth called a stop to rest and forage for fresh provisions. Talty and Richard tethered their horses and made their separate camp. While Richard prepared a fire pit, Talty rummaged beneath the shrubbery to find dry wood.

"Can't we cheat and use matches, Richard? I'm tired of being cold and wet."

"So am I. Nick is missing a fine old time, isn't he?" Richard poked through his toolkit until he found the waterproof matchbox. When the fire was burning well, he invited the others to come and light their torches from the holy woman's fire. The exhausted men came, muttered vague thanks, and returned to the main camp.

The rain stopped at twilight. Snug beside their crackling fire, Talty and Richard finished the last of their oatcakes and ale.

"So here I am, the protector of a holy woman. Who knew?"

Talty winced. She regretted agreeing to the deception. Gayth had told the men her presence would protect them. "I wish Leesha hadn't started this. I'm not some saint who can heal battle wounds with a touch."

"They don't know that, darling. We have an edge as long as they think you're no ordinary woman. Why did she say that, anyway?"

"She was afraid I'd spirit Gayth away to fairyland. She needn't have worried, though. He seems able to resist me just fine."

"Perhaps you married too young to learn how devious men can be. Our friend Gayth isn't finished with you, holy woman."

Gayth's reaction to the scars on her chest said otherwise. Talty sighed and brought their bags near the fire to dry. She fretted over the leather sack Brother Marcan had entrusted to her.

See that one of the healers gets the bag, Christy. It contains all I could spare from my

140

physic garden and my drying shed.

Marcan had described the contents of the various pouches: yarrow, sorrel, St. Patrick's leaf, comfrey root, and even fungus dust to keep wounds from festering. Cobwebs to staunch bleeding and prevent inflammation, hare pelts for dressings, linen strips and cobblers' wax to hold them in place. Jars of honey and salt for infection, bees' wax and mutton fat for burns.

The clay jars would be fine in the dampest weather. The herbs worried Talty, though when she checked them she found that the leather bag had protected them well.

Gayth stepped from the darkness. Both pleased and annoyed, Talty tied the bag up tight.

"Hello, Gayth," Richard said with an irritating smile. "All's well, I trust."

"Yes. My kinsmen are grateful for your fire. The furze is too wet to burn. They invite you to join them in a game of spear fishing, Richard. There's salmon nearby, and we need the food as well as the sport."

"I'm reluctant to leave Christy alone."

Talty bristled at Richard's protectiveness. "You should get to know the men. I'll be safe enough at my prayers."

Gayth's chocolate eyes sparkled in the firelight. "I will stay and protect you while you pray."

Still smiling, Richard found a spear and went off to fish. Though Talty had encouraged him to go, his abandonment annoyed her. "I'm going to pray beside the pond. It could be a watering hole for game."

"You hunt game, holy woman?"

"Even holy women must eat." She left him by the fire and was soon scanning the ground at the edge of the pond. The twilight's glow revealed animal tracks in the rain-damp soil. She walked toward a dense stand of trees, not quite sorry that Gayth and his sparkling eyes had caught up.

"Did you see any tracks?" he asked.

"Yes. Deer, I think. Smaller game as well, and I'm sure I heard waterfowl a while ago."

"I like roast goose. Can you pray for some?"

Silently groaning, she studied the sky. "Do we have time to roast meat?"

"The men must eat. Once we've rested and refilled our food sacks, we'll ride again. We should reach Dublin in three, maybe four days' time."

"What day is this?"

"Monday of Holy Week. What holy woman wouldn't know that?"

Barely aware of his teasing tone, she supposed they could reach Dublin by Good Friday, though that would be cutting it close. Yet in this world, the Battle of Clontarf might not take place on Good Friday. Perhaps no battle would occur at all. Perplexed, she stole into the trees.

Gayth followed her.

"This will make a fine blind." She spoke more to herself than to Gayth.

"You intend to wait here for deer? Praying?"

Ignoring him, she returned to the fire to bank the embers and fetch the Viking bow.

Gayth was right beside her.

She slung the quiver and arrows over her shoulder. Her hooded cloak went on next to protect both her and the bow from the weather.

Her preparations seemed to mystify Gayth. "Why don't you simply rush the herd and cast a spear when they bolt?"

"This way I'll get the deer I want, not one who falls behind because it's old or sick."

"I'll come with you."

"I need silence."

"Yes, I know. To pray. I promise to be quiet."

They stood in the natural blind together and watched the water's edge. She didn't resist when he pulled her against him.

"Lean on me, lady," he whispered. "Rest a little."

He wrapped his cloak around her. She leaned against him, breathing in smoke and sweat, banishing all thought until a small herd of deer appeared to investigate the clearing. Though tempted to forget them, she broke away from Gayth and uncovered her bow. Silence was critical now.

He caught her face in his hands and kissed her well. After the briefest pause, she kissed him back, grateful for the fading light that hid her burning cheeks. Then she nudged him away. The deer wouldn't tarry long.

Kiyoshi's words flowed back to her: *See the target as a reflection of your mind, as a mirror. Your mind will find the target.*

Gayth stepped back. Talty fixed on the biggest doe in the herd. She drew without breathing, released, and held her position until the arrow pierced the doe's side.

Shot clean through, the doe hovered over the ground for the briefest moment before collapsing in a motion so natural, the other deer failed to notice. The arrow's strange whoosh had alarmed them, however. They scattered into the forest.

Pleased with her success, Talty lowered her bow. The kiss that lingered on her lips unexpectedly angered her. "Why are you here, Gayth? You ran from me before."

"I ran from a holy woman. Your warrior skills bestir most unholy thoughts in me." He ran a knuckle over her breast.

142

She slapped his hand away. "Help me get the meat back to camp."

She left him smiling in the trees.

*****

By Holy Thursday the Dalcassians had crossed into Leinster, the province ruled by the disaffected petty king who waited in Dublin with his Viking allies to challenge King Brian. Smoke from burning crops and cottages blackened the skies. The surviving livestock roamed freely. The people remained in hiding. Talty still wondered if she were in her own past.

Richard rode grim-faced beside her. "Could the battle have reached this far south? We're nowhere near Dublin, let alone Clontarf."

"I don't know. I do know that King Brian sent his son Donough to pillage Leinster so reinforcements couldn't reach Dublin. Anyway, we aren't going to get to Clontarf by Friday."

Richard's attention was on the burning fields. "We have more immediate concerns than Clontarf, darling. Keep your eyes skinned and your weapons handy."

The intense vigilance had everyone skittish. The men had eaten the last of the venison—they'd cheered Talty when Gayth lugged the doe to the fire pit—but no one would hunt tonight.

A scout reported that a nearby stream teemed with trout and salmon. Talty shared in the sport this time, spearing as many fish as the men. Before long, her razor-sharp tanto knife was slicing out gills and excising intestines. Soon the aroma of roasting fish scented the air. For the first time, the Dalcassians invited Talty and Richard to eat at their fire.

In the dwindling twilight, the weary men settled down to rest. As they tidied their gear, the sudden thunder of hooves sounded in the distance.

"We are attacked!" the sentries cried.

Gayth told the men to form a shield wall. "Christy, get behind them."

Talty objected, but Richard insisted. He winked as he unsheathed Leg-Biter. "You'll be our secret weapon."

In moments, hundreds of snorting horses had closed around the camp. When the din subsided, Gayth emerged from the serried Dalcassians. "Who comes?"

A mud-splattered black stallion pranced forward. The equally filthy rider dismounted and limped bowlegged toward Gayth. "Donough Boru and his brave men come. Is that you, Gayth MacDunlan?"

A collective sigh rose from the Dalcassian ranks. Their own kinsmen surrounded them.

Gayth sheathed his sword and embraced his cousin. "Donough! Praise

God we've found you. Where is Brian?"

"In Dublin, two days hence. We ride at dawn to join him. You'll come with us. My father will rejoice to see the sorry lot of you. Now, we eat!"

The men responded with volleys of cheers. The meat and ale Donough's troops had looted from Leinster's homesteads provided a welcome feast.

Donough washed the grime from his hands and face and sat by the fire to tell how he'd led a battalion south into Leinster. Brian believed the tactic would force Leinster's fighting men to stay and guard their homes rather than join their petty king and his Viking allies in Dublin. The ploy had worked. The Leinstermen wouldn't leave their homes and families defenseless now.

Donough's account matched Talty's understanding of the pre-battle events. As for the other factual inconsistencies she'd encountered, she considered the very real possibility that the chronicles of future historians weren't entirely accurate. She hadn't abandoned the idea that this place was her ancestral homeland. Staring in awe at Donough's handsome face and dark red hair, she thought he resembled a young Kieran.

Bellies grew full as the storytelling progressed. Talty noticed Donough staring at her from across the fire. Her presence seemed to disturb him.

"A woman, Gayth? Have you brought camp followers with you?"

Talty stood and addressed the young prince. "I am Christy McKenna, sir. This is Richard Gale, my friend and protector. We are honored to meet you. Even in our homeland, we have heard of King Brian and his deeds."

After Gayth told the holy woman story again, Donough studied Talty as she had him. "A holy woman," he murmured. "You and your protector will ride with us. We leave at dawn."

That night, raging fires lit the northeast skies. In Talty's Ireland, Brian Boru had burned Dublin's outlying districts the day before the Battle of Clontarf to goad the Vikings from their stronghold. It seemed this Battle of Clontarf would take place on Good Friday after all—and Clontarf was still two days away.

* * * * *

The Dalcassians reached Dublin on Easter Sunday. The sweep of the holocaust stunned them. Fires burned everywhere. Water ran red with blood. Screeching ravens blackened the skies, circling thousands of corpses in greedy anticipation of a feast. Rats competed with other vermin for the pieces of men strewn over the battleground.

Talty touched Marcan's little herb pouches and wept.

Donough hailed a healer who toiled among the survivors. "You! What of the battle?"

The exhausted man peered up from wrapping a bloody arm. "The battle is won. The Danes fled to their vile black ships. Most drowned."

"Where is King Brian?" Donough asked. "I see not his blue and gold standard."

"You will find the king's camp in the Wood of Tomar." The healer turned his head and returned to his grisly task. "King Brian is there."

The men guarding Tomar's Wood shouted when Donough cantered in at the head of his troops. Talty rode behind him, between Gayth and Richard. She couldn't tell if the shouts were warnings or greetings. Inside the camp, bedraggled men turned to see who'd come. Their eyes were dull, their movements labored. Many were wounded. All had been weeping.

Donough dismounted and addressed a bloodstained warrior. "Kean of Desmond! Where is my father? Where is my brother Murrough?"

Kean of Desmond pointed to a circle of flaming torches. In its center stood a yew tree. Beneath the tree lay a mound of woolen cloaks. "Brian lies there. Murrough lies beside him. We have sent for the clerics to carry them to Armagh for burial."

Staring as if he didn't understand—or didn't want to—Donough licked his lips. "The rest of my brothers? Murrough's young son?"

Kean slowly shook his head. "We found the boy drowned, each hand clutching the hair of a Dane he took with him to death."

Grief darkened Donough's face. He stepped toward the bloody cloaks and stopped.

Morbidly curious, and heartsick for Donough, Talty touched his arm. "Come, Donough. We'll go together."

With Gayth and Richard beside them, she and Donough approached the yew tree. The prince fell to his knees. He pulled back the nearest cloak to reveal the remains of Murrough Boru. The gray, lifeless face bore a resemblance not only to Donough, but to Talty's own kinsmen as well.

"We are lost without you, brave brother!" Donough wrenched the second cloak aside and wailed in outraged agony. The king's head had been split from the top of his skull to his chin.

Talty squeezed her eyes shut. So old, she thought. What coward would slay such an old, old man?

Gayth replaced the makeshift shrouds. He led his sobbing cousin to the shade of a nearby tree and called for a skin of ale. Donough drank and asked for Laiten, his father's attendant.

A man emerged from the crowd. His hair was white, his eyes swollen. Dried blood covered his clothing. "I'm here, Donough."

"Where in battle did my father fall?"

"He did not fall in battle," Laiten said in a sorrowful voice "Due to his great age, his chiefs and his sons implored him to let Murrough lead. He agreed at last and went to his tent to pray for victory."

Laiten described how Brian had asked for reports of the battle's progress. Twice he'd asked if Murrough's standard still stood. Twice Laiten answered that it did. The third time he'd had to say that Murrough's banner had fallen. Making no reply, the king returned to his prayers.

"A band of fleeing Danes came then. The king's guards challenged them. They fought bravely, yet the Dane called Brodir the Sorcerer drew his sword and slew the king. Brodir fled. The surviving guards gave chase and captured him. Never have I seen such horrible vengeance."

For uncounted moments, no one moved, until Donough straightened his shoulders and trudged into the woods alone.

* * * * *

The grieving victors buried their dead. They burned the Vikings. While Richard and Gayth joined in the grim chore, Talty helped the healers care for the wounded.

Gayth stopped to see her. "Bless you for tending my kinsmen. The stench of blood and burning flesh sickens strong men, yet you toil without rest." He stepped close enough to whisper in her ear. "Return to Killaloe with me. We'll make fine sons to replace those lost here."

"You would wed a holy woman covered with scars?"

"After what I've seen here, I am grateful you survived whatever befell you. And I know you are no holy woman. My mother confessed her deception before we left. She thought she was dying and wanted no sin to mark her soul."

Talty smiled at Leesha's mischief, and then she gazed sadly at Gayth. "I can't stay," she said, though she wished for a moment she could. "When the time comes, Richard and I must travel on."

Sighing with resignation, he touched her hand. "Then comfort my heart and soul. Lie with me in my tent at moonrise. I'll ask no more of you."

He turned and left before she could answer.

* * * * *

The Archbishop of Armagh came at noon for the mortal remains of Brian Boru and his son. Clerics washed and oiled the bodies, dressed them in burial clothes, and laid them on biers packed with holly boughs and funeral herbs. A circle of torches protected their souls from evil spirits. St. Patrick's religion hadn't completely replaced the old ways.

Donough asked Talty and Richard to accompany the funeral procession to Armagh. The setting sun found her organizing her gear into the leather satchel Leesha had given her. The Viking bow would ride on her shoulder.

In the stream behind her tent, she scrubbed away blood and vomit until her teeth chattered. Peeled to the ivory, she sat on a boulder to dry. A review of the lessons she'd learned in Imi's marriage class warmed her. Soon she was in her tent brushing her hair and slipping into her cleanest clothing.

Gayth's tent was a short walk through Tomar's Wood. He waited beneath a hawthorn tree and greeted her with needy arms, putting his mouth to hers for the first of many kisses.

"My heart leapt the day you softened your eye to me, lady," he whispered. "Lie with me. The gentle breeze stroking the leaves in the moonlit wood will be our lullaby."

Spellbound, Talty clasped his waist, trusting his nudging thighs to back her into the tent and draw her down to his blankets. His gentle caresses and squeezes led her through the ages-old ritual so new to her. He probed and nuzzled and coaxed, piercing her at last with a merciful thrust, riding her until she thought she'd burst.

They slept entwined. When she woke at daybreak, she gently disentangled herself from his arms. The nascent light revealed the most peaceful expression she'd seen on his face in days. Leaving him sleeping, she stole back through the woods.

Richard waited by her tent. His saddlebag lay at his feet. He had to know where she'd been, yet his eyes held no judgment.

"Is it time to go?" she asked.

"Yes. The procession is forming."

She slipped her tanto knife into her boot, clipped her toolkit around her waist, and slung the Viking bow over her shoulder.

"Richard!" Gayth called from the rise in the woods. "Christy! Donough awaits us."

Talty raised her hand to wave. She cried out at the pain that sliced her forehead. Holding his head, Richard fell to his knees beside her.

"Stay away!" he shouted when Gayth came running toward them.

Gayth froze in confusion. He crossed himself as they vanished.

CHAPTER FIFTEEN

Hidden Positions

Talty woke in a Fort Pinard hospital bed exhausted, hungry, and expecting Vikings to burst through the door any minute. The return trip through the Peregrine Portal was a blur, though she remembered where she'd been and what had happened there.

Once Samantha and Creek had completed their annoying tests and declared both Peregrine travelers fit, Creek demanded detailed accounts of the mission. Talty's summary excluded her brief affair with Gayth MacDunlan. That was her secret, one that left her aching.

Once Creek reviewed the reports, he rejected the possibility of the Peregrine Portal being a time machine. He'd already diagnosed and repaired the problem that had stranded Richard and Talty in a parallel world, leaving Nick behind.

"I felt about as useful as a milk bucket under a bull," Nick said when he drove Richard and Talty home from the medical wing. "You kids really had me worried. You still do. Looks like you both lost weight. Good thing I've been cooking. Come to dinner tonight, Major Lady."

Talty happily agreed and asked Nick to drop her at the PX. Soon she was back in her Spartan quarters, a palace compared to her tent in Tomar's Wood, putting away groceries and browsing through mail.

An envelope bearing Aidan's flowing handwriting caught her eye. Thrilled that he'd written, she opened it and sat at the kitchen table anticipating an enjoyable read.

Dear Christy,
Hello from the desert. This place couldn't be more different

from Ireland. It rarely rains, and we've all gotten such bronzies our own mothers wouldn't know us. My father says it sounds like his days in Africa.

As you know, peacekeeping duties are quite different from army duties. Most of the time I'm in the command center tackling stacks of paper, though it's not all work. The lads have organized football matches and road races, and we attend games or shows almost every night.

Few women serve with the battalion. Since colloguing with the local girls is out of the question, many of us are lonely. Not our Neil, though. He's going strong with a journalist who's here doing interviews for a magazine back home. Don't say I let on, but he intends to ask her the big question after we return home.

I hope you're well and settled in California. Please write when you can. I'd love to hear from you.

Your broiled friend,

Aidan

The letter shook in Talty's hands. She knew that Aidan had omitted the more hazardous aspects of peacekeeping duties, yet worry for her cousins' safety hadn't caused her sudden distress. Her brief affair with Gayth MacDunlan had stirred vague emotions that had long haunted her. Aidan's letter had pinpointed those emotions: Her aching wasn't for Gayth.

* * * * *

Funds from Eric's generous bequest, which included the substantial trust her father had given him to take care of her, allowed Talty to buy a sporty new car. Savoring freedom she'd never known, she explored the California coast, stopping where she pleased and staying out as long as she liked.

When Richard announced his upcoming trip to London, she drove him to San Francisco International Airport. Proud that she'd negotiated the airport traffic so well, she pulled into a drop-off spot.

Richard retrieved his overnight bag from the back seat. "You seem to be finding your way around Mendocino well enough."

"I am. Do you know your way around London well enough to find a tea shop on St. Peter's Street called Todd & Upton?"

"For a good cup of tea, I'll find it. What do you want?"

"A pound or two of their Mokalree Estate Black Assam, please."

He wrote it down. "I'll see you in a week. Do you have plans for the rest of our break from work? Something to keep you out of trouble, I hope."

She couldn't help grinning. "In exchange for enjoying Nick's cooking, I'm going to save your gardens. Big trouble there. Have a safe trip."

*****

Satisfied that his financial affairs were in order, Richard left the bank and opened his umbrella. Catching a taxi in the pelting London rain would be a challenge, but he intended to try. His favorite tailor expected him for a rare session of fittings for new clothing.

The tailor finished by teatime and promised to have the apparel ready by week's end. Richard left the shop looking forward to a decent supper, a hot shower, and bed. Another taxi delivered him to the apartment he kept in London's Mayfair section.

The reek of cigarette smoke hit him the instant he unlocked and opened the door. A lamp glowed in the living room, though he hadn't left the lights on. Prepared for trouble, he hit the wall switch. The flat lit up.

Fortunately for the man sitting on the sofa, Richard recognized him. "What the bloody hell are you doing here, Bert?"

MI6 Chief Bert Benson squashed his cigarette in an overflowing ashtray. "Sampling your excellent whiskey for one thing. Care for some?" Bert poured a hefty shot into a tumbler and handed it to Richard.

Annoyed but curious, Richard tossed his raincoat over a chair and sat. He left the drink untouched. "How did you get in?"

"The doorman let me in. I want to bounce a few things off that analytical mind of yours."

"I don't work for you anymore."

"Exactly. You're removed from it now. I need your objectivity." He set his glass on the table and tapped a cigarette from the pack. "I'll tell you, some days I wish I'd taken my mother's advice and become an accountant."

"It's not too late. And don't smoke in my flat. Now what the bloody hell is going on?"

The cellophane-wrapped pack fell from Bert's hand to the table. "There's an ugly movement afoot, Richard. A few bad eggs are plotting to remove King John from the throne."

"What? Who would dare?"

"Roger Wessex. He's always been an overblown peacock, and a nasty one at that. He's gaining support, though I don't fancy his chances."

"So arrest him and be done with it. The Wessex name can't protect him from treason."

"It's not that simple. As I mentioned, there's a movement. Hundreds of men and women report to me. I'm not sure where their sympathies lie."

"Where do *your* sympathies lie?"

"Where yours do, I believe. With our rightful king. John isn't the idiot Thomas was, nor is he the cretin Geoffrey says he is. He's understood everything I've discussed with him perfectly. I rather like the fellow."

Richard wondered where all this was going. "This sounds like Home Office business. Why are you involved?"

"We believe Roger is planning to commandeer English naval vessels, courtesy of Staff Admiral Andrew Mayne, for some sort of foreign invasion. We're not sure where yet, though Ireland is the most likely target. The oil wells and all."

"Andrew Mayne? Aren't he and Geoffrey the best of friends?"

"They were. They might still be. However, Andrew is also Roger's godfather. I don't know what's going on there. Not yet. As for Geoffrey, they're waiting to talk to you."

"Are they indeed?" Too angry to sit still, Richard bounded to the window. "And who the bloody hell are *they*, Bert?"

"Prince Geoffrey and one of my best field agents. Catherine Dolliver. Top of the tree. Geoffrey thinks she's watching Roger for him. Roger thinks she's watching Geoffrey for him. In fact, Catherine is watching them both for me. Do be careful not to give her away, won't you?"

"Sounds like an imperial balls-up in the making."

"Not if I can help it. As for what they want with you, you've recently had dealings with members of the Irish royal family. You have a new officer in your Research and Development program, and some of the Irish royals attended her husband's funeral in Tokyo."

"You can't be serious."

Bert picked up his cigarettes. The cellophane crinkled as he tossed the pack from hand to hand. "I'm very serious. Geoffrey is keen on keeping tabs on the Borus. As of now I don't know why, other than they seem eager to get their hands on Roger."

"What would the Irish want with Roger Wessex?"

"Again, I'm not sure, though I'll find out. Have you thought about coming home? I could use you here."

"You and your superiors sacked me, as I recall."

"No, Richard. We asked you to resign, which you did. The Foreign Office has always been grateful for your sacrifice."

Richard saw it all again. He'd been shooting his camera from a hidden position when shooting of a different nature left two friends dead and a double-dealing diplomat in possession of sensitive documents. Claims of diplomatic immunity had undermined every attempt to convict the diplomat for murder and espionage. The man's embassy had leveled harassment charges against Richard and his deceased partners. Though guilty of no wrongdoing, Richard resigned to spare the Foreign Office the embarrassment of yet another international scandal.

Slipping his cigarettes into his pocket, Bert downed the rest of his whiskey. "Be a good fellow and say nothing of what we've discussed here. I'm on the wire as it is."

Thinking that the Vikings had been less trouble, Richard picked up his raincoat.

* * * * *

Bert drove to an exclusive London club and brought Richard upstairs to a private dining room. The muscle men guarding the door nodded and stepped aside to let them pass. Inside, an attractive blonde sat at a table set for dinner, a glass of white wine in her hand. A file folder lay open on the table before her.

All business now, Bert approached the table. "Hello, Catherine. Catherine Dolliver, Richard Gale."

Catherine closed the folder. She made no move to shake Richard's hand. "Delighted, Colonel Gale. Please, gentlemen. Sit."

Richard complied. Adopting an air of boredom, he poured himself a glass of wine, which he raised to her in mock salute.

"ISF keeps you busy, Colonel? Research and Development, isn't it? You must find it quite different from the work you did at MI6."

"You're well informed. Well enough to know that an ISF officer can't interfere with the way any nation runs its internal affairs. I can't imagine what you want with me. Surely you have enough help right here at home."

Catherine set the folder on the cabinet behind her. "Sometimes one needs special help. ISF will allow its officers to help if such help is requested, especially if an officer's own nation makes the request. You are loyal to your own nation, aren't you?"

"I'm loyal to my lawful king, and no one will ever question that."

Richard listened as Catherine detailed Roger Wessex's treasonous plans. He pretended to be hearing them for the first time, though even hearing it for a second time worried him. *The man has to be barking mad.* "I still don't understand what you and Bert want with me, Miss Dolliver."

A nearby door opened. Geoffrey Wessex entered the room looking many pounds heavier than Richard remembered. His different-colored eyes observed Richard with aristocratic distaste. "Allow me to explain it to you, Colonel Gale. Since my nephew John has been king, England has experienced great stability. I want to maintain that stability. I also want England to enjoy the economic prosperity she's entitled to, through proper treaties and honest business arrangements. What I don't want is civil war, or further trouble with Ireland. We need their good will, and perhaps some of their fuel. If Roger is planning some sort of attack against Ireland or the Irish royals, we must stop him."

"Why would Roger attack Ireland, sir?"

His attention on Richard, Geoffrey accepted the wineglass Catherine filled for him. "Our legal issues with Ireland over the oil wells we're entitled to are difficult to resolve. Each time the World Court sets a hearing date, King Brian requests a continuance."

"I see. And Lord Roger is impatient."

"An understatement, Colonel. Roger doesn't believe in the legal process. At times, I must say I despair of it myself. He thinks if he attacks and simply takes what he wants, the people will gladly declare him king."

"How does all this concern me, sir?"

"You recently met with members of the Boru family in Japan."

"They weren't visiting me."

"No, they were visiting your new officer. However, you met them, didn't you?"

"Yes."

"What is their interest in the young lady?" Geoffrey's tone changed to that of a man addressing a dimwitted person—one he was ready to crush like an insect.

Richard slipped his clenched fists under the table and fought to suppress his growing rage. "Major McKenna became friends with Kieran Dacey's son while both were teaching at one of Ireland's military schools. His family was kind enough to send representatives to her husband's funeral."

"Kind, indeed." Geoffrey sniffed. "Commander Dacey himself and the Crown Prince of Ireland flew halfway around the world. Why? What has she to do with them?"

"No more than I've said, sir. Nothing about the visit was inappropriate."

"No? The Boru men marry beautiful, intelligent women. Your Major McKenna is both. I suspect one of the young Borus is considering her as a possible bride. I'd guess Prince Liam or Aidan Dacey, since Neil Boru's family has just announced his engagement."

The news surprised Richard. He'd have bet that Neil was the one with his eye on Christy. "I'm sure I have no idea. Anyway, what of it?"

"If we're to stop Roger, we must watch everything he does. That means watching his intended targets as well. Is your first officer the sort to look after herself?"

The implied threat drew Richard to his feet. "My first officer is still recovering from her husband's death. The Borus have shown her kindness. If any of them are courting her, I've seen no sign of it."

"Jealous?" Catherine asked.

Richard glanced icily at her before addressing Geoffrey. "You will not involve Major McKenna in any of this, sir."

Geoffrey's eyes grew round as saucers. His face turned scarlet.

Bert jumped in to referee. "We'll use any means we can to monitor the Irish royals if it will help us keep tabs on Roger's activities. If your officer is getting cozy with one of them, just let us know. It's not a big thing. It might even keep the young lady from harm."

"If Lord Roger even thinks about harming her, I'll personally sort him out." His velvet threat delivered, Richard calmly left the room.

* * * * *

While Richard was away, Talty kept busy spading, weeding, and fertilizing. Besides rescuing a unique array of perennials from a jungle of weeds, she'd planted a few accent shrubs, leaving more than enough room for the fairies to dance. The terraced beds would never be Takumi-san's gardens, but they were on the road to respectability.

Satisfied with her day's work, she retreated to the guest room to shower. On her way she stirred the fragrant tomato sauce Nick had left simmering on the stove before he drove to San Francisco to meet Richard's flight.

She'd just set the table for dinner when they came in. "Welcome home, Richard. You're just in time for tea."

Nick went straight to the stove. Richard looked weary. He set down his bag. His head turned to the sliding glass doors that opened to the gardens. "That sounds wonderful, darling. I could murder a good brew up. By the way"—he reached into his bag—"here's your Mokalree Estate Black Assam. I see you've been busy in the yard. Looks like we have the beginnings of a botanical masterpiece."

"Not quite." She smiled her thanks for the tea. "How was London?"

While Nick busied himself sizzling garlic in a sauté pan, Richard and Talty chatted about England's miserable weather and California's sunshine. Soon wineglasses replaced the teacups. Talty brought out the salad she'd made, and dinner was underway.

Richard unfolded his napkin and reached for the garlic bread. "I hear you and Nick have been cooking up a storm while I've been gone."

Nick finished setting plates laden with linguini and chicken Parmesan on the table and took his seat. "Christy's a great cook. She's been teaching me stuff I never knew."

The compliment delighted Talty. "It's great having a roomy kitchen. I don't think I can last in that little flat much longer. I'm going to find a place of my own."

A blind man couldn't miss the anxious look that passed between Richard and Nick. Wondering what she'd said, Talty dipped a chunk of bread in a shallow bowl of rosemary oil and waited.

Richard salted his salad. "Nick and I were discussing this house on the ride back from the airport. Our property taxes have increased again. We'll probably have to sell it if we don't get a roommate."

"Yeah. I was gonna have veal tonight, but I could only afford chicken, and the wine is domestic. I don't know if I can continue living in such uncouth circumstances. Maybe you should move in with us, Major Lady."

Richard agreed. "You're already spending more time here than at you're flat, and there's plenty of room. We can have an architect knock down a few walls and make a private suite for you."

Talty's stomach lurched. "I don't know, guys."

Nick grated cheese over his pasta. His usual nonchalance seemed forced. "Real estate's a good investment. You can be our partner."

Though certain Richard and Nick weren't the same sort of friends Eric and Kiyoshi had been, Talty had no wish to disrupt their bachelor lifestyle— nor did she wish to surrender her newfound freedom. She also had a gut feeling they weren't telling her everything. "You guys are settled here. I'd shake up the mix."

Nick shrugged his shoulders and handed the grater to Talty. "No more than an earthquake would. We get lots of little earthquakes here. They don't bother us."

Talty dusted her meal with cheese and set the grater down. "They should. This house stands on a complex, triple-junction geological area, at risk from both offshore and onshore earthquakes, not to mention tsunamis."

Her recital had Richard chuckling. He began twirling pasta around his fork. "An engineer looked the place over before we bought it. It's as earthquake-proof as any dwelling in the area can be. After dinner I'll show you the quarters we think you should have."

While Nick cleared the table, Richard brought Talty to a room obviously used for storage. A swollen wooden door opened to the gardens. Another door at the back of the room led to a private ensuite bedroom in need of modernization.

She glanced around, determined to find fault with the place. "It has no whirlpool."

"A detail easily remedied. Picture your things here, darling. It can be your home from home too."

Home. The familiar longing took the fight out of her. It didn't matter where she lived in California. Ireland was home. "Do you ever miss England, Richard?"

"At times I do. Rain, bubble and squeak, London traffic, politics, and royal intrigue."

Talty tugged the door to the gardens open. Wondering what Richard knew about the Wessex family, she breathed in the clean ocean air. "Were you involved with royal intrigue when you were with MI6?"

"I was aware of it. Too much skullduggery for my taste."

"Really? I heard things were better since John became king."

"To a degree. His uncle still calls the shots."

"Doesn't he have a shady cousin too?" She shivered at the understatement.

"Roger, yes. A popinjay who fancies himself a conquering hero."

That sounded odd. "Conquering what?"

"I meant he's one of those spoiled chaps who wants what isn't his. Listen, darling. You can rent if you don't want to buy in with us. Do give it some thought. Your tea is better than any I had the whole time I was in London, and you'd be much safer here than on your own."

Irritated that he'd changed the subject, she agreed to think it over. As they strolled back to the kitchen, Richard mentioned he'd spoken to Samantha earlier. "We're getting a new member for the team. Came to ISF from Mossad, Israel's intelligence agency."

"Great," Nick said from the sink. "You two ex-spies can talk over old times."

"Not if I can help it." Richard stretched. "All right, friends, I'm off to bed. I'm arse over tip with the time change, and I need some sleep."

Talty thanked Nick for dinner and said good-night. While she drove home, she thought about her tiny apartment. Creek had promised to return her Viking bow once his experts finished studying it, yet she had no space to display it properly. The kitchen was cramped, and her cot barely fit in the bedroom. The bookshelves screwed into the living room wall had already cracked the plaster. One more book would bring them crashing down.

And she had no garden.

* * * * *

Recovered from his jet lag, Richard spent several hours reviewing the file for

Peregrine candidate Zev Eisen. It seemed the factional violence endemic to Zev's native Israel had claimed his wife and infant son. Zev had left Mossad for an ISF post in Brussels, where he put his training as a mechanical engineer to work developing non-lethal weapons.

When the sad-eyed man arrived in Mendocino, Richard ushered him into Creek's office and introduced him to the team. Christy shook his hand and told him she'd come to Fort Pinard to learn about non-lethal weapons. In her gracious way, she said she hoped that might still happen. Zev's dark eyes brightened. He promised to discuss his research with her.

Richard's opinion that the man didn't belong with the Peregrine Team was one he'd keep to himself. As he knew too well, his doubts would not sway Creek.

CHAPTER SIXTEEN

The *Kincora*

Neil Boru thought he should spend time with his fiancée before he left for two weeks of rescue training with the King's Rangers. He invited her to a choice Dublin restaurant. They spoke, as usual, of superficial matters, while he admired her long, golden hair and ivory skin. Allison Lyons would make him a suitable wife.

After dinner, Allison asked him to drive to a quiet place. He parked his Jaguar in a secluded area of Phoenix Park and prepared for another trivial conversation.

"I'm canceling the wedding, Neil."

Panic grew as her words sank in. "What are you talking about? Everything is all set. This isn't right."

"Going on this way isn't right. I'm wondering why you ever wanted this marriage."

"I want it because I love you." He reached for her arm.

She pulled it away. "I'm sorry, Neil. I don't believe you don't love me at all. You're good to me, yes, but you act like you're going through a drill, doing and saying the things you think you should."

"That doesn't mean I don't love you. I'll always treat you well. I always have, haven't I? I'm in love with you!"

"You're in love with someone, I think, but it isn't me. When we're alone together, you're off somewhere else." She stroked his fingers. For a moment, her eyes squeezed shut. "It's no good. I want you to be happy. You won't be happy with me. You'd resent me after a while, and I couldn't bear that." She removed the diamond ring from her finger.

His hands covered hers. "No. We can talk it out. We can fix it."

"I shouldn't have let it get this far." She pressed the ring into his hand. "Please take me home."

He slumped in the seat. He'd sought her out with honorable intentions, ready to share his life and all he had with her, yet those honorable intentions were born of deceit. He'd lived the lie so long he almost believed it himself.

His guilt suddenly gave way to tremendous relief. Straightening up, he slipped the ring into his pocket. He would have it reset with a different stone, something for friendship, and send it to her.

* * * * *

Peggy's emotional call to the King's Residence interrupted Liam's study session. He told her not to worry. He would find Neil. A half hour later, he slipped out the kitchen door to Aidan's waiting car.

Aidan seemed torn between amusement and worry. "Did Allison really ditch him?"

Glancing behind him to be sure he'd escaped the house undetected, Liam fastened his seat belt. "Apparently so. Peggy said he shouted at her."

"Neil shouted? At his mother? We'd better find him before Uncle Peadar does."

"I've been calling around. He's down at Glensheelin."

Tucked away in the Wicklow hills, Glensheelin, the "glen of the fairy pool," was the royal family's largest country residence, a sprawling place where they raised Irish wolfhounds, horses, and Connemara ponies. For generations, Glensheelin's rolling hills and glades had provided a quiet retreat for the Boru clan. That Neil would go there now seemed natural.

The scenery blurred as the cousins sped south in the summer twilight. An hour later they reached the estate and found Neil's Jaguar parked askew near the carriage house.

Aidan whistled. "It's worse than we thought. He'd never park his fancy car so careless."

Old Robbie Buckley shuffled from the caretaker's cottage and squinted at them. "Oh, it's you, young sirs. God bless you, Your Highness. You fellas havin' a party here tonight?"

"No," Aidan said. "Just looking for Neil. Where is he?"

"He was in the house for a bit. Then he went to the pond."

Liam and Aidan found him sitting against a tree, staring at nothing. An open bottle of liquor rested between his knees.

The unprecedented sight astonished Liam. He hurried over to Neil. "Howya, Neily. We've been looking for you."

Neil gawked up, his blue eyes unfocused. "Go away, Liam."

"Well, that's just fine! I come all the way down here to see are you all right, and what do I get? 'Go away, Liam.'"

Aidan stepped closer. "Holy Maloney. He's polluted, Li! What the devil are you drinking, Neily?"

Neil swigged the liquor. "Lay off."

Aidan snatched the bottle and flung it into the pond. Liam's backward step to escape the scuffle he expected proved unnecessary. Neil couldn't move.

Liam sat on the grass beside him. "What happened with Allison?"

Drunk as he was, it took Neil a moment to answer. "Have you ever tried not to love a girl, Li? I tried not to love her, but I can't."

"You tried not to love Allison?"

"No. Not Allison. I tried to love Allison, but I don't."

"You aren't making sense, Neily."

Neil slapped the tree. "Here's sense! Depraved and degenerate! That's what you said!"

Liam winced at the words. He slowly realized that Neil's affliction had nothing to do with Allison Lyons. "Who is it that you do love?"

"I don't love anyone! Leave me alone! I'm dying here." Neil wobbled to his feet and fell retching to his knees.

Aidan held him until the heaving stopped. "A great waste of fine whiskey. Give us a hand, Li."

They dragged Neil to the edge of the pond. Aidan pushed his head into the water. Neil came up sputtering and cursing, and his cousins guided him back to the house.

Aidan helped Neil into a shower and found him a change of clothes. Liam called Peggy to say all was well. At Liam's request, Robbie's wife brought a tray of tea and a bottle of aspirin. Shaking her head, she took Neil's filthy clothing away.

Liam handed him two aspirins. "I don't know who's in bigger trouble, Neil. You for taking the whiskey, or Aidan for tossing it into the pond."

A cautious swallow of tea washed the pills down. "I'm in worse trouble than that. Did you call my mother? My father will murder me for speaking to her so."

Concern had displaced Aidan's usual cheer. "That bad, was it? What happened, Neil? Why did Allison change her mind? You said you didn't love her. Did you mean that?"

Neil sighed. "I thought I loved her. She said I didn't, and I expect she knows what she's talking about."

Aidan shook his head. "How could you not know you don't love a girl?"

Liam leaned on his elbows, seeing the whole picture now. "He knew. He figured if he couldn't have the girl he really loves, he might as well marry one who's nice enough and get on with it."

Aidan stared in confusion. His eyes slowly widened. "Talty? No, Li. You're wrong."

"Am I wrong, Neil?"

Neil, the oldest, the leader, the one they all looked up to, stared into his tea looking utterly miserable.

No sickness worse than secret love. "There are ways," Liam said with gentle affection. "There are dispensations."

Neil banged his mug down. Tea sloshed over the table. "Let it go, Liam. I won't hurt her, and that's the end of it."

Not for Liam. "How could you hurt her? You're already good friends."

"Yes, and I want to keep it that way, not have her think I'm some depraved, what did you call it? Degenerate? Pervert?"

"We were horsing around," Aidan said. "Anyway, you aren't blood cousins."

"We're legal cousins, and that's all that matters. I won't have whispers about incest, because that's what it would be. I won't cause a scandal in the family, and I won't hurt Talty."

Liam tried again. "The Law of Consanguinity says—"

"I know about the Law of Consanguinity. It's about a bunch of fuckin' cows, and I don't want to hear it!"

Biting back a smile, Liam glared through his gold-rimmed glasses. "My sister is not a cow."

Neil sank his forehead onto his hands. "I'm sorry, Li. I never meant for anyone to know how I feel about Talty. I'll look after her as I'm meant to, but that's all I'll do."

At last, the cousins settled on their story. The breakup with Allison had caused Neil's abnormal behavior. They wouldn't mention Talty to anyone. Talty herself would never know.

* * * * *

Three days later, Neil flew the Air Corps' newest Sea King over the North Atlantic. He and the three King's Rangers with him were off for search and rescue training on the *Kincora*, the drill ship that had been exploring the Fargan Trough for weeks now.

Neil glanced through the helicopter's windshield. The ocean glittered beneath him, the morning sun rose behind him, and the blue skies ahead beckoned him. Dan Joyce—a natural pilot like Neil, and in Neil's opinion, his only contemporary whose flying instincts were better than his—sat beside him in the copilot's seat.

Lieutenant Barry Malone and Flight Sergeant Rory Doherty lounged in the cabin behind them. Platinum-haired Barry had served as winchman/paramedic on countless search and rescue missions, usually with Neil and Dan piloting. Barry always flew with winch operator/flight engineer Rory, a wiry young man whose nose was a tad too big for his face. All four Rangers had received letters of praise for their courageous rescue efforts, though superstitious Rory credited the luck penny he kept in his pocket rather than skill.

"I can't imagine a boat big enough for two helidecks," Dan said into his microphone.

Neil nodded at a speck on the horizon. "Look down there."

"Is that Fargan?" Barry asked.

Dan glanced at the radar screen. "No. It's the wee ship."

Fifteen minutes later, supply boats and other support vessels came into view, providing sharper perspective. The Rangers gawked at *Kincora*'s size. Her length could swallow a major sports arena. The steel derrick that loomed midship had to be twenty stories high.

Neil pushed his radio and requested permission to land. Static crackled, and then the cheerful voice of the Helicopter Landing Officer cleared the chopper to land on Helideck One.

The helideck crew scurried to set the chocks and tie-down straps. After a final check of the cockpit, Neil followed the others onto the windblown helipad. Stretching stiff muscles, he breathed in the tangy mix of salt air and diesel fuel.

The grinning HLO welcomed them aboard and led them down a flight of metal stairs, where he turned them over to Operations Manager Denis Heard. Heard familiarized them with the ship's working parts. After a review of emergency procedures, he showed them the escape pods and assigned muster areas in case of an abandon ship order.

Early the next morning, the exercises began. Neil and Dan took turns keeping the helicopter hovering while Barry and Rory assumed their respective roles as winchman and winch operator. Working with the *Kincora*'s crew, they practiced retrieving victims—man-sized inflated rubber sections—from the icy sea.

In the evening, the Rangers mingled with the off-duty officers and drill crews in the recreation areas. Neil and Dan passed time playing billiards and cards. Barry and Rory made friends with the women on board. Neil silently wished them luck. He himself had no intention of becoming involved with any female in any way for a very long time.

* * * * *

After three days of simulated rescues from the decks of hypothetically sinking vessels, Neil and his friends joined off-duty officers and crew in the packed recreation room for an impromptu farewell party. Though beer accompanied the party fare, the Rangers limited themselves to one brew apiece, since they'd be conducting one last drill the next morning.

Neil didn't drink at all. He and Dan played a round of billiards with Denis Heard and Thady O'Connor, the *Kincora*'s captain. Barry and Rory sat enjoying female company.

From a corner of the room, a hulking roustabout glared at the Rangers. When the lights flashed to send everyone "home," the big man left with the maintenance workers.

Barry and Rory departed with the ship's geologists, two lovely ladies named Astrid and Holly. Neil and Dan followed at a discreet distance. The party approached the staircase to the living quarters.

A voice grumbled from the dark: "You pretty fellas do all right with our girls, don't yez?"

A huge young man stepped into the light. His muscles swelled from years of working oil rigs. The stench of alcohol intensified his menacing air.

Holly's nose wrinkled. "Who let you out of your cage, Bernie Sheehan?"

Bernie moved closer. Barry and Rory stepped in front of the women. Neil tapped his friends' arms and nodded toward Dan. Both refused with subtle shakes of their heads.

And then Neil stunned them with an astonishing "That's an order." Blinking in disbelief, they nudged the women back and obeyed.

Two quick strides put Neil face to face with Bernie. "You're outnumbered here, friend. Go off and leave these boys alone."

"Oh, are you their mother, then?"

"I'm not their mother at all. You're the only mother here." Neil shifted sideways and balanced his weight on both feet.

Barry groaned. "Don't, Neil."

Instead of defusing the situation as all Fianna were trained to do, Neil shoved Bernie's chest. Bernie charged, and Neil let loose the frustrations of the last week. His left fist hit Bernie's stomach. His right smashed the roustabout's jaw. Bernie lost his footing, but he regained his balance and swung. Neil grabbed Bernie's wrist with both hands and twisted it over his shoulder. Bernie went flying.

The sound of running feet clattered above them. The surveillance cameras must have alerted security to the brawl. Rory yelled at Neil to stop.

Neil was too focused on Bernie to respond. "Getting a little old for it, big fella?"

Gasping for breath, Bernie pulled himself to his feet. "You put on a good show, pretty boy. One good punch and you'll hide behind those Ranger patches and cry like a baby."

Neil stripped off his jacket and flung it down. "No patches, Bernie. Just you and me. Come on."

Bernie lunged. Neil twisted and drove an elbow down to trap Bernie's arm. Bernie heaved to free it, a move that catapulted Neil's arm up to whack the side of the roustabout's head. Bernie stumbled and swore.

Another elbow strike spun Bernie sideways. Neil clasped his fists and landed a kidney punch. Bernie went down, and he didn't get up.

Barry scooped Neil's jacket from the floor. "Get it on fast."

Neil was straightening his collar when Denis Heard and two safety officers rushed through a fire door. Heard's head swiveled over the scene. "What happened here?"

"This fella tripped and fell," Barry said.

Dan agreed. "Yes, sir. He fell."

No one contradicted them. Heard scowled and turned to his men. "Get him to medical."

✳ ✳ ✳ ✳ ✳

Over breakfast in the captain's office the next morning, Captain O'Connor and Denis Heard viewed the security recording of the scuffle between Neil Boru and Bernie Sheehan.

Heard grinned and switched off the player. "Bernie never had a chance."

"Tell those boys they're welcome back anytime," the captain said, calling "Come" when a knock sounded on the door.

Holly entered the room. "Good morning, sir. Mr. Heard. Sorry for the interruption. I thought you should know. It's the drill stem tests."

The captain spun his chair toward her. "Good news, I hope."

"I wish it were, sir. Astrid and I have been over them several times. The microorganisms in the sediment here are eating right through the drills and the pipes. They're destroying everything. We've never seen anything like it."

"Can you identify them?" asked Heard.

"No. We've sent pictures to several labs. No one knows what they are."

The captain drummed his fingers on the table. "The king will be unhappy. He had great hopes for this site."

"He'll be more than unhappy," said Holly. "The site is doomed."

Another knock. The radio operator burst in. "Coast Guard Marine Rescue has a Mayday, sir. There's a trawler sinking off Killybegs. Fire in the engine room. They can't reach her in time. They're requesting that the Sea King deploy immediately."

* * * * *

Keeping an eye on the storm clouds barreling up from the south, the Rangers and a two-man medical team set out over the choppy ocean. Neil offered silent thanks that they were going out by day. He pushed the Sea King to 160 knots, the best he could do against 70-knot winds.

Five minutes after the helicopter reached the trawler's last known coordinates, the Sea King's antenna picked up a signal from a floating distress beacon. Neil descended to eighty feet, close enough to glimpse oil slicks and floating wreckage.

"What have you got, Dan?"

"Infrared shows survivors. The boat's gone for its tea, though."

The Sea King flew in ever-expanding squares above the growing swells until Rory's voice crackled through the headsets. "There they are. Three o'clock."

Neil's position in the cockpit blinded him to the drama below. "What do you see, Dan?"

"A raft tossing about like a gnat in a hurricane. Three men holding the safety straps for dear life. No life jackets."

Neil turned the Sea King into the snarling wind. With no fixed reference point to help maintain a stable hover, he needed Rory's eyes. "Go, Rory."

Rory's steady patter guided the helicopter into position over the pitching raft and conveyed what was happening in the cabin. The medic was helping him and Barry into their safety harnesses. Barry was ready to go. They were timing the rise and fall of the swells. Now! Rory was lowering Barry on the winch cable. Barry was in the water, swimming to the raft.

Then Rory was winching Barry and the first survivor up. The medic helped pull them in and unbuckled the fisherman's rescue harness. Barry shouted that the other two were badly burned and nearly drowned. Twice more he dropped back into the sea, delivering a shivering man to the medical team each time he returned.

He'd just brought the last man through the door when a blast of wind slammed him against the helicopter. The bang had Neil scanning his instruments for trouble.

Rory shouted that Barry was hurt. Neil unhooked his straps. "Take her, Dan. I'm going back."

The cabin reeked of diesel, brine, and vomit. Barry lay in a saltwater puddle laboring to breathe, yet his limbs moved, and he knew his surroundings. The doctor gave him an injection that soon had him past caring about his situation.

Neil worried that his flying had somehow caused the accident. "What happened?"

Rory continued cutting away the remnants of the fishermen's sodden clothing. "I thought maybe I'd lost my luck penny, but I still have it." He peered up at Neil in understanding. "The wind did it, Neil. I've never seen better flying. We couldn't have got these fellas out if anyone but you and Danny were in the cockpit."

Neil half-smiled and knelt beside Barry. "How bad, doctor?"

The doctor slid an oxygen mask over Barry's face. "He might have broken ribs. We have to him quiet. One of the fishermen said six others were on that boat when it blew. Do we have enough fuel to keep looking?"

"We can last another twenty minutes if the weather holds."

The futile search continued until dwindling fuel reserves compelled the Sea King to deliver the injured to Sligo Hospital.

✳ ✳ ✳ ✳ ✳

Barry had suffered a few cracked ribs. Leaving Rory behind to keep him company, Neil and Dan flew back to Baldonnel Aerodrome, southwest of Dublin. They signed off the duty roster and stopped at Dolly O'Brien's Alehouse for a hard-earned brew.

The next morning, Neil woke in his parents' Dublin townhouse. His muscles ached. A hot shower provided some relief. Nora's breakfast worked wonders, and as always, the old cook doted on him.

"Where are Kevin and my parents?" he asked after telling her she'd just prepared the best meal he'd eaten in days.

Nora looked up from whatever she was chopping. "Young Kevin's gone off to his law school. Your parents are out front. I'm getting their lunch ready now."

He strolled down the hall. A lively discussion resounded from the small sitting room. Hoping it didn't concern him, he rapped the doorframe and went in to find his parents sitting together before the fire.

Peadar turned his head toward the door. A jovial smile lit his face. "Neil! Come in, lad. Come in! We were just speaking of you."

Oh no. Neil crossed the room and kissed his mother's cheek.

She patted his face as if he were a child. "Yes, darlin'. We're planning a party for your twenty-fifth birthday."

Oh no! "It's nearly noon. I guess I slept in."

"You needed the rest," she said. "Come tell us all about it."

Neil sat in a nearby chair and, omitting his run-in with Bernie Sheehan, described his adventures from his arrival on the gargantuan *Kincora* to the rescue of the fishermen. Though he downplayed his part in the effort, the pride in his parents' eyes pleased him.

Peggy beamed. "We're proud of you, darlin'. I have to go. I'm late for my meeting, but I wouldn't have missed your story for the world."

She bustled out, and Peadar sat back. "We haven't seen you smile much lately, Neil. Everyone is worried about you. I wouldn't be much of a father if I didn't ask about Allison."

"Tell them not to worry. I'm fine. The marriage would've been a mistake. She figured it out first, is all."

"The thought crossed my mind. I wasn't sure you really loved her. Still, we need to learn some things for ourselves."

"Please don't ever hesitate to tell me I'm an idiot, Dad. You'd save me a lot of time."

Rising easily from the couch, Peadar laughed and slapped Neil's shoulder. A few short steps brought him to the sideboard, where he poured two whiskeys. Neil felt he'd graduated to some new level when their glasses touched. Mindful of his recent fall from grace at Glensheelin, he barely sipped the heady liquor.

"You'll be done with active service soon, Neil. My brother wants you at Tara Hall, if you've a mind to come. Think about it, will you?"

Neil heard the unspoken command in his father's words. As a rule, all members of the Boru family worked at Tara Hall in some capacity. Neil had always expected to do the same. His father worked to protect Ireland. Kieran worked to protect the family. Both wanted Neil to work with them. If he did, perhaps he could help bring Talty home.

Talty. He missed her little pout, missed tugging her hair. The familiar longing flared from its secret place in his heart. He downed the whiskey in one quick gulp.

* * * * *

Peadar and Peggy moved the household to Garrymuir for Neil's birthday party. Nora soon had the kitchen bustling. The ovens roasted and baked. The freezers brimmed with dips and desserts. Crystal and silver glittered on counters, ready for the catering crew.

No stranger to the pre-party pandemonium that upended his home, Peadar retreated to his gardens. While he snipped faded roses, Peggy walked beside him, catching the spent blooms in a basket. They reached the rosebush he'd planted for her, and he kissed her.

The head steward's cough interrupted them. "A solicitor is here, sir. She wants to see Neil." The steward produced a business card.

Peadar scanned it and frowned. "Thank you, Owen. Bring Mrs. Mulvey to the study. I'll let you know if we need Neil."

"Yes, sir." Owen returned to the house.

Peggy's voice quivered. "Do you suppose Allison—"

"I don't know, darlin'. Let's go see what the lady wants."

* * * * *

Two lazy wolfhounds lolling by the fire woofed when Peadar and Peggy entered the study. A woman he assumed to be Eleanora Mulvey waited by the window.

The crisp, fortyish solicitor stated that she'd come concerning Mr. Francis Christopher, the natural father of Neil Boru. Mrs. Mulvey worked for the same Dublin law firm that had drawn up Mr. Christopher's will twenty-six years before, shortly after Mr. Christopher learned he'd have an heir. If Mr. Christopher predeceased his heir, that heir would inherit the bulk of his estate on his or her twenty-fifth birthday. As today was that heir's twenty-fifth birthday, Mrs. Mulvey wanted to speak to Neil.

Peadar let out a relieved breath and touched a button on his desk.

Soon Neil was shaking hands with the solicitor. He listened in stunned silence while she repeated the purpose of her visit. Then he asked, "What do you need from me, Mrs. Mulvey?"

"For today, a signature to show I've informed you of your inheritance. You must come to our offices next week to execute some additional paperwork."

Mrs. Mulvey removed a sheet of paper from her briefcase and handed it to Neil. "This summarizes the current worth of the investments Mr. Christopher bequeathed to you."

Neil's face grew pale as he skimmed the document. "Is this some sort of joke?" He handed the paper to Peadar.

Peadar eyed the balance. Even for a Boru, the figure was astounding.

"It's no joke, sir. I have another copy here. If you'll sign both, I'll leave one with you and be on my way. We'll need two witnesses."

Again, Peadar touched the button on his desk. A moment later, Owen and the head housekeeper came in and signed the papers after Neil. Formalities completed, Mrs. Mulvey thanked everyone and departed.

Struggling for words, Neil gaped at Peggy.

She shook her head and smiled. "I knew nothing about it, Neily. It would've been like him, though. Happy Birthday, darlin'."

* * * * *

Long after his staff had left Tara Hall for the day, King Brian sat at his desk tossing an ugly blob of gray-green rock from hand to hand. The geologists had no name for it, or for the mysterious bacteria that had produced it. Brian only knew that the bacteria fed on metal, metabolizing it into a slimy substance that clogged the *Kincora's* pipelines and corroded the well casings. At his request, Captain O'Connor had sent him a sample of the stuff as a keepsake, a souvenir to remind him of his bumble-arsed folly—as if he needed a reminder.

At least Peadar and Kieran hadn't been foolish enough to risk more than they could afford to lose. Still, he dreaded telling them their investments were gone.

He set the rock beside Jack's note, a handwritten message that had given Brian his only smile of the day: *Everything is in order. See you tonight at the party.*

Jack was telling him that, though Neil wasn't Peadar Boru's natural son, the adoption was well founded and held Neil to be the son of a born prince. Under Irish law, the child of a born prince or princess could become a duke or duchess by the king's command. Tonight, in honor of Neil's twenty-fifth birthday, Brian intended to grant him the title of Duke of Leinster. He thought about what he'd say and imagined how the nephew so dear to him would react.

Pleased with his plan, Brian went home to dress for the party.

* * * * *

The women had congregated in a cozy corner of Garrymuir's great room. The men and the wolfhounds sat near the blazing hearth enjoying beer, gossip, and an occasional hors d'oeuvre from a passing tray.

From the sitting area he occupied with Aidan and Kevin, Neil watched the musicians set up their gear. He turned toward the door when Liam came in with a red-haired lady on his arm.

Neil eyed the ivory-skinned young woman with approval, and for more than the generous curves beneath her casual attire. Intelligence sparked in her pretty green eyes. Any makeup she wore was invisible. "So that's Maura Donovan. Now I understand why Liam's been grinning like an idiot lately. Where'd he find her?"

"In that dusty old mausoleum at Trinity," Kevin said. "She caught him with a piece of ancient pornography and called him a filthy pervert. Now they're in the same class, brushing cobwebs off old manuscripts together."

Aidan chuckled. "If that isn't love, I don't know what is." He stared off wistfully. "One of these days, I'm going to bring Jill around."

"You should have brought her tonight," said Neil. "You might think you're keeping her a secret, but everyone knows about her."

A fiddle riff announced that the musicians were ready. The men led their ladies to the floor. Liam delighted everyone when he and Maura joined them: he'd chosen a girl who could dance.

Watching from their seats, the partnerless boys drummed fingers on capering knees. The first dance had just ended when Dan Joyce, Rory Doherty, and a slow-moving Barry Malone came in to join the celebration.

Shouts greeted the Rangers, and then some subtle signal caused the musicians to shift their lively tunes to slow airs. The caterers opened the doors to the adjoining dining room. Tantalizing aromas lured the partygoers to a splendid dinner.

At long last, the head caterer rolled in the candlelit birthday cake: a single-propeller chocolate-frosted airplane emblazoned with letters that spelled "Flying High." Neil loathed being the focal point of the party, yet he accepted the silly hoots and toasts with grace and humor.

Then Brian rose from his chair, and the room calmed. "This birthday is a mark of passing time for us," he said. "It seems we old fellas were just twenty-five ourselves. My father told me once, 'There are three things on which everyone should think: where they came from, where they are, and where they're going.' Birthdays are a fine time for such reflection. I'm sure you've given it thought, Neil. Your schooling's done and your military service will soon be over. However, things are beginning for you as well."

Brian adopted his formal stance. "Neil Ryan Christopher Boru, as you are my beloved brother's son and the nephew of my own heart, I'm asking you to favor your king and country by accepting the fine old title of Duke of Leinster. It's yours to the end of your days, if you so wish."

After a moment of open-mouthed gawking, Neil stood. "You honor me, Uncle. If it's your pleasure, it's certainly mine, though I'm not sure what you'd require of me."

The king's stately mask melted to an avuncular smile. "We'll talk, Neily."

Congratulations filled the room yet again. The caterers served tea. The women chatted. The men cornered the Rangers to hear about their recent adventures. Soon Liam and Maura said good-night, as did Aidan, off to meet the secret girlfriend everyone knew about.

Neil basked in the glow of affection bestowed upon him that evening. The party would have been perfect if Talty had come. He wondered where she was.

CHAPTER SEVENTEEN

Sandstorm

Talty rolled when she hit the ground. The pain in her head faded quickly this time. She suffered no nausea at all. Senses alert, she rose from the tall grass and scanned the sweltering, barren wilderness before her. Behind her the shade of a thick forest beckoned. Wondering where the men were, she turned her back on the desert and stole into the trees.

Birdsong and rustling leaves were the only sounds in the pine-scented air. Suddenly the birdsong changed to warning calls. A man's scream pierced the air. Talty slipped behind a tree and drew her tanto knife from her boot. Following the sound, she maneuvered through the trees to a rocky outcrop. A stream ran beside it. She ran to a boulder and peeked around it.

Zev lay thrashing on the ground. Nick and Richard knelt beside him. "Hey, Zev," Nick was saying. "Take it easy. It's your first time. It's okay."

Talty sheathed her knife. "Guys?"

Richard and Nick jerked their heads toward her. They should have relaxed when they recognized her, but they didn't. They were worried about Zev, she thought, and she scrambled down to help. She knew at once she could do nothing. The fields of Clontarf had shown her mortal injury.

Zev stared up unseeing. Trembling now, he rolled on his side and vomited. The trembling turned to convulsions. Blood flowed from his nose and ears, and then from his eyes, as if his brain had burst in his skull.

His death throes horrified Talty. Even at Clontarf, she'd never seen such suffering. Too shocked to cry, she squatted helplessly next to Nick, listening as he murmured a soothing mixture of English and Italian. At last he set Zev's arms over his chest.

"I'll find a good place," was all he said. He pulled a folding shovel from his toolkit and stomped away.

"What happened, Richard? Zev was fine after the test run."

"I don't know. He had the right numbers, the right scans. There must be some other factor they don't know about."

Or Creek doesn't know what he's doing. "Go and help Nick," she said.

Richard went off. Talty wept, emptying her canteen to clean Zev's face. She sat in the fading light guarding his corpse.

Dusk fell before the men returned to the clearing. They carried Zev's corpse to the grave and eased it inside. True to his word, Nick had found a good place, a peaceful, pleasant patch beside a flowering shrub.

"I don't know a lot about funerals," he said, "but we should do something."

Richard studied the sky. "We can't do much. It's getting dark. We have to find shelter."

Talty plucked white blooms from the shrub and scattered them over Zev. Richard and Nick filled the grave and smoothed the soil. They were bidding Zev a final farewell when the sound of frenzied shouts in the distance startled them.

Nick stared toward the racket. "I suggest we depart quickly, folks."

Talty stared as well. "Maybe we should check it out. Someone could be in trouble."

"I agree," Richard said. "The dark will provide cover."

Nick shook his head. "Aw, man. I hate when this happens!"

The trio prowled through the darkening forest until they reached a knoll. Below them, a large fire burned in the center of the torch-lit camp. No women laughed, no children cried. A hunting camp, Talty thought—or a war camp.

"Aw, man!" Nick whispered. "We gotta help that guy!"

Talty watched in horror as two dozen bronze-skinned men dressed in doeskin garments and moccasins tortured a man whose arms were bound to branches above his head. His clothing was in shreds, and it appeared the rest of him would soon follow suit.

Richard let the branch he'd been holding fall back into place. "He might deserve his fate, but I don't care for the odds against him."

"We need a diversion," Talty said. "A fire would do."

Richard nodded. "I'll go down and prepare to cut him loose. We'll have a better chance if you two can find their weapons and destroy them."

One by one, they crept to the camp. No one challenged them. The impending execution—Talty had no doubt of the mob's intentions—preoccupied the natives.

She and Nick rifled through piles of camp provisions until they found a disorganized heap of spears, bows, and arrows. Talty pointed to the fire, then to the weapons. Nick in turn indicated a pile of clothing and blankets.

Before they could scheme further, a new undercurrent rippled through the crowd. A man wearing a bear claw necklace snatched a flaming branch and thrust it toward the captive.

Talty drew a bow and a quiver of arrows from the pile of weapons. After a few test pulls, she nocked an arrow and raised the bow. Kiyoshi's voice guided her: *The target is in your mind. Your mind will find the target.*

Bear Claws lowered the burning branch to the captive's face. Sensing rather than aiming, Talty released the arrow. It pierced Bear Claws' wrist. He screamed and dropped the branch.

"Nice shooting, Major Lady." Nick scrambled to the fire and grabbed two pieces of burning wood. He tossed one on the clothing, the other on the weapons. Erupting flames lit up the camp.

In the chaos that followed, Talty fired a barrage of arrows to cover Richard as he slipped behind the captive and sliced through his bonds. The man fell at first, but jumped up and bolted into the woods with Richard.

Talty tossed the bow on the fire and ran with Nick. When they reached the trees, Nick put two fingers to his lips and whistled.

"Over here!" Richard called. They ran to join him.

The bedraggled man spoke in a jumble at first, and then his words grew crisp and clear: "We must leave at once. If they catch us, our deaths will not be pleasant."

"Which way?" Nick asked.

The man took a moment to orient himself. "Follow me."

They tore through the underbrush, racing as fast as the darkness allowed. Soon they were running down a slope to a wide, shallow stream.

"Come," the man said. "If we travel in the water, they will have no trail to follow."

For an hour the fugitives trudged in and out of streams. Even after the sounds of pursuit died away, the man insisted they cover as much ground as possible before sunrise. Taking only the briefest breaks, they trudged on until the first light of dawn sparkled over a roaring waterfall. Beckoning them, the man disappeared behind the cascade. The travelers followed, emerging soaked and cold on a rocky ledge.

The man barely paused. "A camp lies ahead. We will rest there."

By sunrise they'd reached a scraggly, shrub-lined clearing. A squat stone hut stood near a jagged rock formation. A pile of dry wood sat beside a fire pit containing a metal tripod. The man knelt near the edge of the camp and moved three large stones to uncover a well. Richard brought the canteens. While he and the man refilled them, Talty set the wood in the fire pit.

Nick found his matches and lit a fire. Once he had the flames going well, he sank to the ground and removed his sodden pullover.

The man sat beside him and removed the remnants of his shirt, revealing clusters of angry welts and bruises. "You saved my life. I am grateful. I was not sure how brave I would be when they burned my eyes. Who spared me from finding out? I have never seen such shooting."

Nick and Richard both nodded at Talty, who had no intention of removing her own dripping shirt. "My name is Christy. These are my friends, Richard and Nick."

The man's eyes widened at the female timbre of her voice. "I am Joseph ibn Basim. You must be from a far off land. No woman I know has such white skin."

"Far enough." Richard shook out the shirt he'd just removed. Blood oozed from a gash on his forearm, though he didn't seem to notice. "Why were those men so brassed off, Joseph?"

Joseph didn't answer. His eyes were on Talty, who was shivering. "Come, Christy. We will find a blanket in the hut so you can remove your wet things."

Talty thanked him and asked who had built the hut.

"My ancestors," he said. "It is one of many shelters against inclement weather."

"You mean it rains here sometimes?" Nick asked.

"Not often. The hut is for Al-Khamasin."

"Who's he?"

"Al-Khamasin is not a man, Nick. It is the sandstorm. If we see Al-Khamasin on the horizon, we must find shelter at once."

Joseph rose and held out his hand. Ignoring the winks Nick and Richard exchanged, Talty reached up, allowed him to pull her to her feet, and walked to the hut with him.

Inside, the hut was cool and dry. Joseph uncovered one of several chests hewn from stone. The receptacle held more than blankets. Bows, spears, a stash of clothing, even first aid supplies waited to serve needy travelers.

Careful of the weapons, Joseph rummaged through the clothing. "My cousins have been here. They left shirts. Perhaps you would prefer one to a blanket." He lifted a colorful, rough-woven garment. "This is the right size, I think."

Talty agreed with a shivering nod. "Give me the shirt and turn around."

He grinned and obeyed. She removed her sopping shirt and slipped into the dry one, giving the garment a good shake first to dislodge any creepy-crawly inhabitants. The fit was decent, the shirt was warm, and it covered her to her neck.

"What's in there to treat bruises, Joseph?"

"Herbs that can make poultices and teas to counter swelling or draw out poison. We will leave them for those who need them."

"You certainly need them, and Richard's arm is hurt."

Joseph sighed and sifted through the herbs. Kneeling beside him, though not too close, Talty chose strips of cloth and small metal pans. She also selected shirts for the men.

Back at the fire, she inspected Richard's arm. "Not bad, but we don't want it to get infected. We'll fix you some tea to help."

Joseph squatted by the flickering flames steeping herbs. Richard's eyes widened in alarm. "That's not all-heal, is it?"

"I do not know this all-heal," Joseph said. "This is harjal and willow bark. It might not cure our injuries, but we will no longer care about them."

"Interesting," Richard said after he'd tasted the tea. "What does willow bark do?"

"It relieves pain," Talty said. "I don't know about harjal. What is it?"

Joseph's dark eyes reflected the firelight like a pair of lustrous mirrors. "You did ask for the herbs, pretty bow woman. I promise we will not become wild men. Is your shirt comfortable?"

Annoyed that her cheeks were burning, she nodded. "You said your cousins left them. How did you know?"

"From the designs on the cloth. Each clan has its own pattern. All who use our camps must leave something behind for those who come next."

"We have nothing to leave." Richard sounded lazy. And happy.

"We will gather firewood. Others may need a ready fire, as we did."

"Others?" Talty asked. "Your tribe?"

"The Nejdoul, yes. When the sun sets, I will return to them. I should reach them by sunrise." Joseph sipped his tea.

Staring curiously at Richard, Nick raised the pan of steeping herbs and sniffed. He grimaced in revulsion. "Who were those guys chasing us?"

A frigid smile prefaced Joseph's response. "Rasignards. They claim they own the forestlands. We believe they belong to everyone. I was crossing the forest from the desert and was not as furtive as I should have been."

Richard's eyes began to droop. "How do your people survive in the desert, Joseph?"

"The Nejdoul move from place to place, as our sheikh and tribal elders decree. Each move allows the grazing lands to renew themselves and the dates to grow again. My clan camps at H'raybay Oasis now. They will break camp soon. I must get back."

"We'll get you back." The tiniest slur had crept into Richard's voice. "Let's rest for a few hours. We'll keep an eye open for trouble."

"You may close both eyes." Joseph sounded as if he'd like to close his own eyes. "The Rasignards will not enter the desert. They fear the spirits who live here, and the desert has no respect for fools."

"Hey, you guys are drinking on an empty stomach." Nick opened his toolkit and offered dehydrated food all around.

While Talty ate, she caught herself wondering how her hair looked. Scolding herself, she assessed Joseph with more objectivity. He was tall, lean, and in his late twenties. His skin was deeply tanned, his bruised face evenly proportioned. The black hair he'd untied to dry fell in waves to his sturdy shoulders. And he smiled a lot—especially at her.

Abruptly she set her food aside and stood. "This stuff tastes awful. I'm going out for groceries. Nick, why don't you make a shelter for our giddy friends? The sun will be hot soon."

She returned with several small animals, skinned, gutted, and dangling from a leather strap. Too tired to roast them now, she hung them in the hut, where the cool air would keep them till suppertime.

Nick had draped sheets of canvas-like material from their toolkits over the rocks: a large open shelter for the men, a smaller one for her. "I put some blankets in there for you, Major Lady. Get some sleep. Richard and Joseph are already gone. Now that you're back, I'll grab a few zees myself."

Talty thanked him and retired, settling onto the Nejdoul blankets. Quiet male voices drifted toward her. From Nick's apologetic tone, he had inadvertently woken Joseph.

Soon all grew silent again. Talty closed her eyes, but then she sensed someone watching her. She glanced at the men's shelter.

Joseph was smiling at her.

* * * * *

Late in the afternoon, Richard refilled the canteens. Nick took down the shelters, while Joseph returned the blankets and other supplies to the hut.

Talty busied herself stoking the fire. In high spirits, she skewered and roasted the anonymous tidbits she'd snared that morning.

When they were done, she called the men for supper. "It's not much, but hunger makes a good sauce."

Nick sat cross-legged by the fire and sampled a mysterious morsel. "Not bad. It could use a little garlic. With a salad, some Scali bread, and a good

Pinot Grigio, it would be perfect."

Joseph smiled as he ate, clearly enjoying the banter. "I do not know this Scali and Grigio, but I promise we will eat well when we reach my clan."

They broke camp beneath the dramatic desert sunset and set out across the bleak terrain. The temperature dropped as night fell, though the brisk pace Joseph set kept everyone warm. A scattering of stars lit their way until the full moon rose and brightened the odd bones and partial skeletons littering the ground.

More than once, the eerie landscape sent shivers down Talty's spine. No wonder the Rasignards feared the desert, she thought.

At the first glint of daylight, Joseph announced that they were near H'raybay Oasis. "It is just over those cliffs."

Talty scanned the dawn skies to orient herself. The sight of a bird of prey floating on air currents evoked unpleasant memories of her hospital stay in Scotland. Suddenly, the bird dove behind the rocks.

"Looks like someone found breakfast," Nick said.

Joseph repeated his promise that they would soon eat well. He led them through a pass in the rocks. From the other side, they looked down on a large pool of shimmering water surrounded by palm trees. Men, women, and children traipsed between pegged tents and penned livestock. Smoke rose in orderly columns from cook fires. Even from such a distance, succulent aromas reached the travelers.

"Quite a camp, Joseph," Richard said. "It appears well run. Who's in charge?"

"Sheikh Basim. A great man, and my father."

Their descent set stones flying and dogs barking. Several young boys ran ahead, shouting, "Joseph has returned!" The people called joyful greetings to the sheikh's son and scrutinized the strangers with fearless curiosity.

A cadaverous man in a simple white headdress stood apart from the crowd. His beady gaze bored into Talty, and then he seemed to vanish.

Joseph went to the largest tent, where a tall man of noble bearing stood with a falcon perched on his forearm. A circlet of braided black cord held his long white headdress in place over his graying hair. Middle age lined his bearded, sun-darkened face. His eyes glowed with affection. "Welcome home, my son. We worried when you did not return by the full moon."

"I was delayed, Father." Joseph held out his arm. The falcon hopped over. "Hello, Najla. My friends admired your hunting skill this morning." Joseph set the bird on a carved wooden perch and hugged his father. "I would not be here at all if not for these people."

Joseph's father calmly observed the Peregrine travelers, and then he bowed his head. "I am Sheikh Basim ibn Gabir. You are welcome in our camp, and welcome to travel with us."

"Thank you," Richard said. "My friends and I would be honored to journey with you. My name is Richard. This is Nick, and Christy."

"Sabiha will bring your woman to the *maharama*," Basim said. "Then I will hear how you rescued my son."

Talty stiffened but knew she must follow the native customs. Graciously, she dipped her head and prepared to visit the *maharama*.

"No, Father. This woman saved my life. We will welcome her to our side of the tent, at least this first time."

Basim's eyebrows jumped, but he nodded. "Come," he said, and he turned and strode into the tent.

Torches lit the interior of the *mag'ad*, the men's side of the tent. Mosaic rugs and plush cushions surrounded a low wooden table laden with food. Flames fueled by camel dung crackled in a pit in the center of the dirt floor.

Everyone settled around the table, and Basim clapped his hands. Two boys of about eight entered the tent. One carried a stone jug and a soft cloth, the other a large wooden bowl.

Basim introduced them as Karif and Ghalib, his youngest sons. "They will free your hands of the desert's dust."

Talty thought they must be twins. One held the bowl beneath Richard's hands. The other poured water and offered the cloth. The boys repeated the process with Nick. Their eyes bugged when they saw Talty, though they lowered their heads and continued their hospitable dousing.

Once the ablutions were completed, Basim clapped his hands again. A smiling young woman produced a silver urn filled with cardamom-scented coffee. Another set a tray of matching cups on the table. Both women wore multicolored clothing embroidered with the clan's distinctive pattern.

"My daughter Zahrah, and my wife Kaleela." Basim hefted the coffee urn and poured five cups to the brim, raised the nearest to his lips, and watched Richard expectantly.

Richard chose a cup and sipped. It had been the right thing to do.

"And now," Basim declared, "you are under my protection."

Without warning, the cadaverous man Talty had seen earlier emerged from the shadows in a swirl of colored robes.

Basim scowled. "What do you want here, Fugara?"

Fugara inched forward. A hooked nose dominated his face. His tiny black eyes burned with passion. He rattled a large bone marked with strange carvings. Lightning-fast, he pointed the bone at Talty. "Many times have I seen that warrior's soul in my dreams. We need not fear the evil Jinn." He whirled and disappeared into the tent's darkest nook.

"Fugara is our healer," Joseph said. "He eats little to strengthen his soul, and sees things only he can see. His magic is powerful. The spirits whisper remedies for illness to him."

Talty hoped she and her friends remained healthy.

* * * * *

At dusk Basim ordered the tents taken down. He asked Joseph and Richard to walk by the water with him.

"Joseph told me how you and your friends saved him from the Rasignards," he said. "I regret we cannot honor you with a proper feast now. The clan has consumed most of the herbs and onions that grow here, and grazing for the livestock is nearly gone. When we reach our next camp, I will have the women prepare a celebration."

Richard had thought the meal in the tent a feast. In his opinion, an even bigger feast would prove an unnecessary burden to the tribe's resources. He knew better than to insult Basim, however. "Thank you. Where will you make your next camp?"

"Across the desert, at Zitoon Oasis. Joseph and Zahrah will marry their betrothed mates in the village there. On our way, we will stop at Wadi Bakhoor to trade our goods and race our camels."

Fugara burst from the palm trees. "No, Basim! Evil Jinn have claimed Wadi Bakhoor. They live in the rocks. Bad spirits serve them. I have seen this in my dreams!"

"We have always stopped at Wadi Bakhoor," Joseph said. "We are not afraid. You can protect us from any Jinn, Fugara. Your power is great."

Fugara paused, as if considering Joseph's words. "In my dreams tonight, I will meet the evil Jinn master and challenge him. I will make amulets for you." He slunk away through the trees.

* * * * *

The clan would trek for two weeks over parched wasteland. Talty wanted one last bath. Wearing the Nejdoul robe Basim's daughter Zahrah had given her, she ambled to the women's bathing place, undressed, and soaked for as long as she dared.

Clean and content, she slipped back into the embroidered robe. She treasured the generous gift. Even without its lovely colors and intricate designs, the loose-fitting garment would protect her from both the chill of the night and the heat of the day. Feeling refreshed, she stepped onto the secluded path that led to the camp.

Joseph met her along the way. "I saw you walking here, sweet warrior."

"Hello, Joseph." She was surprised though not sorry to see him. The light in his eyes was one she recognized, one she'd seen in Gayth MacDunlan's eyes. Yet the memory of her first and only sexual encounter wasn't what set her cheeks ablaze now.

Since she'd lain with Gayth, she'd often dared to imagine sleeping with Neil. While the illicit fantasy excited her, it also disturbed her. Perhaps Joseph could put an end to her forbidden dreams. Perhaps the time had come to dust off Imi's marriage lessons again.

Joseph's fingers traced the line of her chin and slid along her neck to the back of her head. He drew her close and kissed her. "You are my white desert flower. My pearl. Stay with me when your friends move on. Our tribe is wealthy and powerful. Our clan alone has fifty camels. You will be my second wife. My father has had four. My tent is large enough for three."

Confused, Talty pulled away from him. "Your second wife? You're married, Joseph?"

"Not yet. I will marry my cousin Taroob when we reach Zitoon Oasis. Our fathers betrothed us when we were infants. The Nejdoul must wed one wife for duty. The others we can marry for love. I love you, Christy."

Fugara came crashing through the reeds. "She is not for you, Joseph. She is a king's daughter and a great warrior. She is not for you!" Shaking his bone rattle at them, he stared through wild, unblinking eyes.

Talty suspected the shaman used hallucinogens to dream his dreams. Still, how could he know she was a king's daughter? Suddenly afraid of the skinny man, she stepped back.

"You are scaring her, Fugara. Go away."

Fugara drew a small silver amulet from his robe. Beaded cords adorned it on either side. He thrust it at Talty. "Wear this necklace, woman. I have put great magic in it. I have written charms on the bones of the desert wolf and prayers on the skin of the python. These I have ground to powder and placed in this amulet to protect you, so that you may protect us."

He vanished into the reeds. Talty gawked at the amulet in her hand.

"Do not be afraid of Fugara."

"I'm not. It's just that… You'd marry your own cousin, Joseph?"

The question seemed to amuse him. "Of course. I am a sheikh's son. Taroob is a sheikh's daughter. We must keep the dowry in the tribe to keep the tribe strong."

Disappointed and angry—and a tad jealous—Talty clutched the necklace to her chest. "Fugara is right. I'm not for you." Still tasting Joseph's kiss, she hurried back to camp.

* * * * *

For two nights Talty walked with the women while the Nejdoul clan drove their bleating livestock over the desert. On the third night, the travelers found that Al-Khamasin had blocked the familiar route to Zitoon Oasis. Basim declared they would circumvent the massive sand dunes.

Fugara objected. "That way will bring us to the home of the evil Jinn."

"We can neither turn back nor go another way." The sheikh pointed to Talty, Richard, and Nick. "You yourself said these warriors would protect us. We will go on."

The Nejdoul procession detoured around the mountains of sand. By the next sunrise, a large outcrop loomed before them.

Talty marveled at the rainbow of rocks gleaming on the desert floor. They glistened pink, orange, green, blue, and a host of shades between. Only the clan elders recalled having seen such rocks before.

Fugara proclaimed the rocks evil Jinn. Despite his protests, Basim decreed a stop for a few days' rest. While the clan set up camp, the shaman shook his bone talisman and beat his drum to frighten the evil Jinn away.

Talty wanted to see the rocks up close. Richard went along. "I'm curious," he said, "and I suspect there's something in that encyclopedic head of yours that knows what they are."

"Not evil Jinn. Lichens, I think, though they'd have to have been here for centuries to produce this much color."

"How can such delicate things live under these extreme conditions?"

"If there's any moisture around at all, lichens can survive."

"They might not survive Fugara's mumbo jumbo."

Talty touched the amulet at her neck. Most of the women wore similar jewelry, and she'd decided to wear hers to keep from offending the shaman. "He isn't hurting anything. When we move on and no one comes to harm, he'll say his magic protected the clan."

Richard peered at the horizon. "The sun is rising. Let's get back before things heat up."

Just then, the roar of a wild animal rumbled over the desert.

Talty listened for a second roar, but the desert remained silent. "That was a lion, I think. I hope it's as far away as it sounds."

"I'm sure it is. Still, we'll alert Basim. No one should be out here alone."

"Should we tell Fugara to come in?"

"Don't worry about Fugara, darling. A lion would take one bite and spit him right out."

* * * * *

Others had heard the big cat. Fugara declared it an evil omen. Basim asked

Richard and Nick to attend a conference of elders in the *mag'ad*.

"The men will keep their weapons ready to protect our livestock," the sheikh declared.

The voice of Sabiha, his chief wife, rang from the *maharama*. "Have them practice with their bows while they stand around doing nothing, Basim. Their aim will be more accurate."

Basim sighed. "We will set up targets, Sabiha. They will practice."

"Tell the men to protect us while we gather plants. No one has camped here for ages. There is much to harvest. We have even found arnebia to make Zahrah's cheeks pretty for her wedding."

"Zahrah is pretty enough."

Sabiha continued as if he hadn't spoken. "We will gather milkweed to cure the mange on the camels."

"My camels have no mange, woman!" Basim sighed again. "Gather your plants, Sabiha. We will protect you."

* * * * *

Basim refused Talty's request for a bow. "Do you object to foraging with the women, Christy?"

She replied with respectful insistence. "No. I enjoy working with the women, but I want some means of defense."

Raising his eyes in the manner of men bedeviled by women, Basim sent Joseph to the camp's store of weapons.

Joseph returned with a small bow, a composite of wood and antelope horn strung with camel gut. The accompanying quiver of arrows made a colorful addition to Talty's Nejdoul costume. Offering Joseph a cool nod of thanks, she slung both bow and quiver over her shoulder and went off to join his sister.

Zahrah was already rummaging for the herbal treasures the women would boil for dye. For over an hour, Talty helped collect the tiny plants, though she inspected the ground for more than flowers. Still, the tracks unnerved her when she found them. The paw prints were fresh and depicted a bad limp and huge, hairy feet, the spoor of an old, injured lion.

She called Richard. He came at once.

"What is wrong, Christy?" Zahrah asked.

"Gather the women. Go back to camp. Tell your father the lion is here."

Zahrah gasped. As she and hurried off with the women, the men wandered over to see what was wrong. They grew brave and animated when Richard showed them the lion tracks.

Joseph and Nick came running with swords and knives. Basim followed.

He frowned at Talty. "Return to camp, please. This will be dangerous."

"If you want this lion," Richard said, "Christy comes with us."

Talty shot him a silent thank you. Basim raised his eyes and sighed, and then he called for the hunt to begin.

* * * * *

The tracks showed that the lion had wandered in circles. The men, armed with spears and bows, split into groups. Basim assigned each to a cluster of paw prints. Nick went with one group. Richard and Talty joined Joseph and Basim and followed the tracks Talty had found to a spot of flattened grass.

Basim knelt and studied the ground. Then he pointed. "The lion rested here. See the imprint of the mane, and how he drags his hind leg? It might be broken. If he cannot hunt, he will be hungry—and very dangerous."

"He'll seek shelter from the heat," Richard said. "Those stands of scrub ahead would provide suitable cover."

Basim's silent hand signals spread the foursome out. Each covered a quadrant of ground. Richard and Basim readied their spears. Joseph and Talty nocked arrows to their bowstrings. They prowled, alternately studying the scrub and the tall grass.

An ominous growl froze them all. Joseph raised his bow to cover the scrub—but the cat wasn't in the scrub.

He was in the grass. With a thundering roar, he mowed Joseph down, though the beast's useless hind leg bungled his jump. He toppled over before his deadly jaws could tear Joseph's throat away. Snapping at empty air, he landed on his tawny side.

Joseph rolled in a desperate attempt to escape. Just as desperate, the maddened lion hauled himself forward and clamped Joseph's arm in his powerful jaws.

Joseph screamed. Richard shouted. He tore off his shirt and threw it behind the beast. Like a kitten chasing a new toy, the lion released Joseph and slashed the shirt to pieces.

While Richard dragged Joseph from the animal's range, Talty's arrows flew. The lion bellowed with every thwack to his side. He hefted himself up on his three good legs and turned to charge.

Richard raised his spear. "Christy! Your knife!"

Talty dropped the bow and pulled the tanto from her boot. Richard's spear pierced the lion's heart at the same instant the knife punctured his throat. For a few unsettling moments, the beast rocked on his three good legs. Then, with a final shudder, he collapsed in a shaggy heap.

Talty and Richard ran to Joseph. Basim was already kneeling beside him.

The commotion had brought the men running. Some retrieved weapons from the lion's carcass. Others helped bring Joseph back to camp.

Turning to Richard and Talty, Basim placed his right hand on his chest, closed his eyes, and bowed his head. He cast one last look at the lion and walked away.

* * * * *

Fugara chanted outside Basim's tent. Inside, Richard and Nick found Joseph fevered and dosed with harjal and willow bark. Sabiha and a female healer sat with him. The healer shook her head and prepared to bind his mangled arm.

Richard nudged the woman aside. "We must set the bones first," he said, wishing Samantha was there. He drew an invisible diagram in the air. "We need something strong and narrow."

Sabiha ran to the *maharama* and returned with the metal poles from her loom. Richard and Nick set to work. They did their best, but Richard suspected Joseph's arm would never heal properly.

* * * * *

Talty went to the tent at dawn. Joseph gazed at her, his fevered eyes aglow in his pain-wracked face. She moved quietly to keep from waking Zahrah, who slept beside the bed.

"How are you, Joseph? What can I get for you?"

He pressed his dry lips together. "Water, please."

She filled a metal cup. Joseph raised himself on his good elbow and drank until he emptied it. Breathing hard, he lay back down.

The movement woke Zahrah. She touched Joseph's forehead and frowned. "I will prepare more harjal. Do not worry, brother. We will soon have you ready for your wedding."

Joseph shook his head. "There will be no wedding for me. A cripple cannot provide for a wife. I am a burden to the tribe now."

Talty touched his uninjured arm. "You don't know that. Your arm will heal and be strong again."

He looked up at her. "Will you marry me if it becomes strong again? I would take no other wife."

"Even if I wanted to, I can't. When the time comes, I must travel on with Richard and Nick."

"Then leave me, Christy. No lion could tear at me as you do." He closed his eyes and turned away.

* * * * *

At daybreak, the children frolicked with baby goats on the rocks overlooking the camp. When the sun grew hot, the youngsters left the goats to graze and retired to their tents to sleep, along with most of the camp.

A mother goat wandered among the tents, bleating nonstop for her kids. Unable to sleep, Talty decided to play shepherdess and herd the baby goats down from the rocks. She slipped on her robe and passed the livestock pens, where Karif and Ghalib were feeding the animals. She welcomed their offer to help.

At the bottom of the overlook, they split up. Talty took the middle ground. She soon heard bleating from the rocks up ahead.

One down.

Currents of air blew at her robe. Dust swirled at her feet. Out of nowhere, sand and stones whipped her face. Turning away from the gritty blast, she squinted in alarm at the monstrous brown cloud headed straight toward the camp.

"Christy! Christy! Al-Khamasin! Christy!"

The air had darkened so fast, she couldn't see the boys. A sudden gust of wind knocked her down. Inch by inch, she fumbled toward the rocks. She shrieked when her hand hit the furry corpse of a baby goat.

Her groping hands found the rocks. Heartened, she rolled behind them to a flat ledge big enough to hold her. The whipping wind eased. She pulled the robe over her head and settled down to wait out the storm.

Suddenly the ledge collapsed. She screamed into the wind. Clutching for something to stem her fall, she slipped and screamed again when a sharp rock sliced her thigh. Somehow she hooked her arms around a boulder jutting over a dark abyss.

I'm going to die here!

The boulder lurched and gave way.

* * * * *

Such a lazy morning. Wake up a little, doze back off. The dreaming was pleasant until a sandstorm swirled around Glensheelin and buried the crying wolfhound pups.

Talty shot up like a jack-in-the-box and raised an arm to ward off the stinging grit. The pounding in her chest eased as the nightmare receded. She was in a warm bed, tucked beneath a blue sheet that slid down when she sat up. Pulling the sheet over her bare chest, she glanced around at the cavernous room and wondered if this was heaven.

Bright lights blazed on the other side of the cool, concrete chamber. Shiny machinery hummed, its silver parts being poked and pulled by a strange, elderly man who tapped his chin and bobbed his bald head as he made notes and turned dials. The flowing metallic robe he wore hid his feet, and so he appeared to float when he walked.

Talty tried calling to him. The drone of the machines overpowered her parched croak. She looked for her clothes, but only saw Fugara's amulet beside a stone beaker and cup on a nearby table. She poured a clear liquid into the cup. Then she dipped her finger in and tasted it.

"It's water."

She jumped and pulled the sheet to her shoulders. She hadn't seen or heard the man approach. He stood at the foot of the bed, studying her through owlish round eyes. His wizened face was beardless. He hopped back and forth from one foot to another, as if his shoes were on fire.

"Water," he repeated in a cracking, high-pitched voice. "Best thing for you. Have it. Then have more."

Though he seemed odd, his concern for her welfare eased her anxiety. She sipped the water and tried a brief, "Hello."

"Hello? Not, 'Where am I? What is this place?' Those are the usual questions, but you are not a usual visitor. So you would not ask the usual questions." He cackled with delight at his observation. "Please tell me your name, visitor."

"Christy. Christy McKenna. Who are you?"

"I am Lutano. How are you feeling, Christy McKenna? I think the repairs went well."

Repairs. She had fallen, sliced her leg, hit her head, and cracked her ribs. She put the cup down and slid her hand beneath the sheet. Her thigh was undamaged.

"All is well, Christy McKenna. I have fixed everything for you, though I couldn't fix those scars on your chest. Too old. Your people might be advanced enough to send travelers out, but they're still barbarians with medical care." He turned and floated across the room.

He knew about travelers? "Wait! Where are my clothes?"

Lutano stopped and put his finger on his chin. "Clothes? Gone. In tatters. Ruined. Nothing left. Torn to pieces. Useless."

"So I'm to wear a sheet?"

"Ah! You want new clothes! I'll send for some." He turned his back to her and continued working.

She sipped the water until the container was empty. Then she propped herself up on the bed, recalling the vicious sandstorm. Surely the Nejdoul tents had sheltered the clan and her friends. When Richard and Nick looked for her, however, they'd think she'd perished.

In tatters. Ruined. Nothing left.
She had to get back.

* * * * *

The Nejdoul camp was digging out from the sandstorm when Karif raced to Basim's tent, gasping for breath. "Christy is missing!"

Richard followed the boy up the sand-covered outcrop. Nick and Basim came behind them. Ghalib showed them the bloodstained robe and the black void far beneath the collapsed ledge. Shreds of cloth hung on the blood-streaked rocks.

Hands shaking, Nick drew a compact infrared detector from his toolkit and aimed it into the abyss. "I wish I could tell you different. There's nothing alive down there."

Richard gathered the fragments of the robe and tossed them into the chasm. Losing Zev had saddened him. Losing Christy broke his heart. "Good-bye, darling," he whispered.

Basim cursed the stones and proclaimed that the tribe would leave the evil place as soon as they could pack their gear.

* * * * *

Every room in Lutano's stark facility hummed with the machinery he operated with the help of a staff of silent androids. According to Lutano, the desert tribes' customary routes circumvented this part of the wilderness. Hence, they weren't aware of his presence. Even if they had been, Talty suspected the superstitious clans would find the building's geodesic shape unearthly and sinister—the home of evil Jinn—and avoid it.

Talty had seen solar panels before, but she wondered how Lutano harnessed enough solar power to maintain his machines and provide enough air conditioning to combat the sweltering desert heat. He still hadn't explained how he'd healed her injuries so quickly. She not only meant to find out, she also intended to ask if he could mend Joseph's arm.

After she described the lion attack, Lutano spent several minutes tapping his chin until she grew impatient. She asked again: "Can your machines repair such an injury?"

"Of course, of course. A simple matter if we don't wait too long. But where is this injured arm? I can't bioaccelerate an arm unless I have an arm to bioaccelerate!"

"They're somewhere in the desert. You said your instruments could find them, remember? Do you have transportation?"

"We have air trams, though we use them to travel underground. You'll have to hike."

"You travel underground?"

"My goodness, yes. The desert here is honeycombed with subterranean caverns. We were out in them when the sandstorm struck. That's how I found you. Good thing, good thing."

Talty agreed. "Why, Lutano? Why are you here?"

"This area is rich in ancient microbes. The colors on the rocks above the ground tell me where to find what I need below the ground. That's why I'm here."

"The colors on the rocks are lichens."

"Yes, yes, and microbes too, but I'm not after those. I look for a special microbe that only grows underground. I'm after the substance it metabolizes from the rocks."

"I'm lost, Lutano. The microbes eat the rocks?"

"Some do, yes. They metabolize rock into gases or minerals just as humans use oxygen."

"It sounds like the microbes they put in the ocean to clean up oil spills."

"Yes, yes. That's one example. When some common microbes ingest dissolved metals, they transfer electrons to the metals and remove the nonmetallic element. This leaves behind solid metal. A simple explanation, but accurate enough."

Talty smiled. "Simple for you, perhaps."

"Of course, I'm not looking for common microbes. The microbes I'm looking for metabolize rock into a fuel called xenoterrahexolicalurium."

Talty's stammering attempt to repeat it ended in laughter. "What do you do with this…"

"Xenoterrahexolicalurium runs all the machines in this building. I mine it here and transport it back to my home dimension."

"Home dimension. You're a traveler too, aren't you?"

His owlish smile crinkled his face. "How I have missed intelligent conversation! Yes, Christy McKenna, I am a traveler. Many of us mine xenoterrahexolicalurium. It's hard to find. However, we've found a great deal of it here. I can spare enough for you to take back to your scientists. They can produce more bioaccelerators, but once you use up the xenoterrahexolicalurium, you'll have to find your own source. I'll give you special detectors. If your scientists can send travelers, they should be able to process xenoterrahexolicalurium into the necessary fuel."

And find a different name for it. "That would be wonderful, Lutano. Now, how can we find my friends?"

"Hmm. Let's go to the communications center."

✷ ✷ ✷ ✷ ✷

The clan broke camp at sundown. Richard and Nick lifted Joseph onto the litter the men had prepared. Sabiha and Zahrah packed blankets around him. They were about to set out when Fugara appeared outside Basim's rolled-up tent to report his latest dream.

"The new route will take us past the home of the evil Jinn master, Basim. We must find him. Only he can save Joseph."

Basim closed his eyes. "Let us hope Joseph lives until we get there."

***** * * * *

Lutano tapped his chin. "The camscan shows they've camped on that hill above us. Too bad I don't have a portable bioacceleration unit. I could come with you, Christy McKenna, and see to the young man in his tent. I never get out, never."

"Please, Lutano. I'd like to go before the sun gets too hot."

"Walk carefully when you go outside. There are snakes, scorpions, and many hungry animals. Small, but dangerous. I remember now. That's why I never go out!" He squawked with glee at his cleverness. "But they *are* dangerous. Perhaps I should take you after all."

He hurried to a door that led to a dimly lit cavern and pointed to a row of sleek mining trams. "Come, come. No time to dally."

Talty hopped into the first tram. Expecting the vehicle's motion to thrust her backward, she clung to a guardrail. When Lutano started the engine, however, the tram rose and drifted down a stone passage, ascending then through a vertical shaft hewn from a natural cleft in the rocks.

Lutano shrieked with joy and donned a pair of bug-eyed goggles. "Pull your collar over your face, Christy McKenna. We'll be kicking up dust when we reach the surface. This is great fun. I must get out more!"

***** * * * *

From his vantage on a rocky hilltop, Richard gazed over the brightening wilderness. Basim stood beside him, petting the falcon on his arm.

"Where are we, Basim?"

The sheikh nodded toward a line of moonlit hills. "Wadi Bakhoor lies over that ridge. If Fugara is right, we should be near the home of the Jinn master." He sent the bird soaring for her breakfast.

Richard's trained eye gauged the ridge to be five miles away. He doubted Joseph could survive such a long trip. Wondering what to do, he watched the falcon glide. The rising sun rose behind the bird and lit the rocks below.

Not rocks, Richard thought, but a strange abode that didn't belong in the desert. The building's curious geometric patterns set his pulse racing. Beside him, Basim gasped. Both men stood speechless at the sight.

Fugara seemed to appear from nowhere. "He is a powerful Jinn. He will help Joseph."

Jinn or not, Richard meant to find whoever lived in the dwelling. "Let's get Joseph and see if we can find the doorbell."

Accompanied by Basim, Fugara, and two armed guards, Richard and Nick carried Joseph to the hilltop. Suddenly one of the guards shouted and pointed to the desert floor. A small cloud of dust barreled toward them. The guards drew their swords. Richard and Nick set the litter down and drew their own weapons.

The dust cloud neared the hill. At its head flew a small metal craft carrying a driver and a passenger. The driver brought the vehicle to the hilltop and set it to hover over the ground.

The driver shook his head and lifted his goggles. "Bring the injured man here! Hurry!"

Fugara pointed his bone rattle. "Are you the evil Jinn master?"

Indignant, the driver stood straight. "What nonsense! I'm neither evil nor one of your naughty Jinn. I am Lutano. Now please, hurry!"

Lutano's passenger pulled her hood away. "Come on, guys. The sun's coming up!"

Already astonished by the appearance of the floating craft and its futuristic driver, Richard stood gawking at Christy until Nick's joyous "Aw, man!" moved both men to action. Exchanging jubilant grins, they carried Joseph to the tram and helped Basim and Fugara board the vehicle.

Lutano changed gears and left the flabbergasted guards behind. Twenty minutes later, he and two androids were guiding a gurney carrying Joseph down a long, bright hall.

Arms open, Nick started toward Christy. Richard beat him to her. He caught her in a tight hug and kissed her forehead. "How did you survive that rock fall, darling?"

"How could I not, between Lutano and this?" She pulled Fugara's amulet from inside her robe. "Let's find something to wash the sand from our throats and I'll tell you all about it."

✳ ✳ ✳ ✳ ✳

From the doorway of the small "recovery" room in which she'd first awakened, Talty stood between Basim and Fugara. They were all watching Joseph, who couldn't stop staring at his arm.

He looked up at them. "What magic is this?"

"It is as Fugara dreamed." Basim beamed at Talty. "Twice you and your friends have saved my son. *Shukran.*"

She hugged him, clearly surprising him. "You're welcome."

Smiling, Basim left the room. Joseph started after him, but stopped when Talty said, "Looks like you'll have that wedding after all, Joseph."

"My wedding for duty." He squeezed her hands. "I would still wed for love. Please stay, pretty bow woman."

"I can't. I must go with the others."

"When the white desert flower blooms, I will think of you." He kissed her and left.

Fugara raised his bone rattle. "Each time I see your spirit, another spirit stands beside you. A powerful spirit with sky-colored eyes. He has always watched over you. He always will." The shaman whirled out the door.

Talty smiled sadly. Joseph's kiss still lingered on her lips, but the spirit with sky-colored eyes had just tugged her hair.

* * * * *

Twisting knobs and checking dials, Lutano scurried from machine to machine. "We must hurry. My trajection instrumentation predicts you'll return to your home port soon. Where is Christy McKenna?"

"Saying good-bye to her friends," Richard answered. "How can we bring this knowledge back with us, Lutano? We aren't scientists."

"I've prepared photoinstructive language packs and converted them to whatever it is you call your language." He placed a package in Nick's arms. "Here's a sample bioaccelerator. You only need to find a source of xenoterrahexolicalurium. When you do, all will be well."

Nick eyed the parcel with suspicion. "This stuff really works?"

"Oh my, yes. It works quite well if the injuries aren't too old, like those on Christy McKenna's chest." He tsked. "Terrible things. I'd like to speak to whoever did that to her. Why, I'd bop him for sure!"

"Scars?" Richard frowned. "On Christy?"

"Yes, very nasty, very bad. It's unfortunate we couldn't get this knowledge to you sooner. We could have spared her a great deal of suffering."

"Any chance we'll see you again?" Nick asked.

Lutano brought a bony finger to his lips. "Not likely, unless I come and visit you. Your navigation is haphazard right now. You must learn to steer better. I could give you that knowledge as well, but you can only transport so much. I think the bioaccelerator is more important."

Christy came in then. Lutano had a parting gift for her. "This doesn't contain desiccated animal components, but it will pick up any sign of xenoterrahexolicalurium. Search your deserts. We've had our greatest success there." He slipped the device around her neck to hang beside Fugara's amulet. "Good-bye, Christy McKenna. Good-bye, everyone!"

The headache came on fast. The last thing Richard saw before he passed through the portal was Lutano, smiling, waving, and bobbing his owlish head.

CHAPTER EIGHTEEN

New Digs

Roger Wessex barely glanced at the servant pushing the tea cart into the sitting room. While the woman served tea for three, Roger waved a teaspoon in time to an operatic duet trilling from ceiling speakers. His eyes closed as the singers reached the crescendo. The spoon in his hand chopped down, right, left, and up until the voices faded and the servant left.

Philip poured the tea. "Why did your uncle send for you this time?"

"He's in a dither over Hoy's Neck. I managed to calm him down."

"How does he know about Hoy's Neck?" Andrew asked.

"Catherine Dolliver. She's wonderful at letting him know just enough."

Andrew huffed. "I'd written her down as Geoffrey's floozy."

"It doesn't matter what she is," Roger said. "I only tell her what I want her to know. She slips it to Geoffrey, and he thinks he's up-to-date. Don't worry, Andrew. We're quite safe."

Annoyance etched Andrew's face. "Are we? Geoffrey is coming undone. He told me some ridiculous rumor that you, not Thomas murdered those Boru women. Where would he get such an idea?"

Philip's hooded eyes widened with worry. They had never told Andrew the truth about Thomas's wedding night. Roger smiled to reassure Philip.

Then he sought to placate Andrew. "Who can believe Geoffrey? I personally think he *is* coming undone."

"Indeed," Andrew said. "Has he told you the fairytale about Princess Taillte being alive?"

"What?" The color drained from Philip's face. He stiffened in his chair. "Why on earth would he think that?"

Squeezing lemon into his tea, Andrew told them about the rumors

Geoffrey had heard a few years back. "He asked me to look into it."

Roger fought to sound unconcerned. "What did you do?"

"I humored him and sent two chaps to Ireland. The police found them shot to death in a crime-ridden section of Dublin. They'd been taken for wealthy tourists and robbed. So unfortunate. Of course, there never was any trace of Princess Taillte."

Disturbed, Roger shifted in his chair. "You didn't think their deaths odd, Andrew?"

"No. I saw the police reports, and I doubt the Borus have the girl hidden away in a convent somewhere. What would be the point? Your uncle is having you on. I believe a few of his shingles have popped off."

Fingers drumming the table, Roger nodded in agreement. "Still, we've come too far to have any loose ends. I want the Borus watched. Send Havelock and Poulton over, Philip. They're good at sniffing out such things. If Princess Taillte is alive, she won't be for long."

* * * * *

The portal stopped crackling. Talty wondered why no one was helping her up from the floor of Creek's lab. Too queasy to stand herself, she knelt beside Richard, leaning against him when he reached to steady her.

Across the room, Nick lurched to his feet and waved his arms at Samantha and Creek. "You killed Zev! You and your damned portal. You have no business sending anyone through that thing!"

Creek answered as if he were trying to calm a violent dog. "I'd never allow anyone who lacked the proper neural baseline frequencies to go through the portal, Nick. If they didn't, they'd die the way Zev did."

"What are you talking about? You let him go, and he died anyway!"

Unusually serious, Samantha stepped between Creek and Nick. "Zev had the proper frequencies. He was fine on the pre-mission test. What happened was—"

"Murder!" Nick spat.

Creek wagged his head. "No, Nick. Zev deliberately modified his neural baseline pattern by pharmaceutical means."

Talty brought her hand to her mouth. "Oh, no!"

Nick's head swiveled toward her. The movement sent him wobbling like a drunken man. "What the hell does that mean?"

"It means he committed suicide." Samantha's voice trembled. "We found a letter in his quarters. The nightmares of his dead wife blaming him for not saving her and their baby were too much. But I don't think he realized his death would be so painful."

"As for the Peregrine Project," Creek said, "the research will continue." The tiniest twitch appeared in his shoulder. "Now, what's all this stuff you people brought back?"

* * * * *

Richard's initial report about the bioacceleration process had Creek's shoulder twitching out of control. The scientist wasted no time analyzing Lutano's photoinstructive language packs. He quickly sent a team of geologists to comb America's deserts for xenoterrahexolicalurium, which he'd blessedly renamed "lutanium."

The day after Creek released his travelers from the medical wing, Richard convinced Christy to move into the house. Though he'd never tell her, he rested easier having her in more secure quarters. He hadn't forgotten the implied threats Prince Geoffrey had made in London—and she made a damn good cup of tea.

The contractors he and Nick had hired still had some detail work to finish, but they'd already expanded the bedroom suite, adding a whirlpool bath and sliding-glass doors that offered a view of the gardens and ocean.

"I thought you'd like to pick out the color schemes and things," Richard said, enjoying Christy's amazement at the renovations. He'd seldom seen her in awe of anything.

"Geez, Richard. For someone who's worried about paying his property taxes, you've gone all out here. I want you to give me the bill for this."

"We'll sort it out when we rewrite the deed to the house."

She tugged the sliders open. A salty breeze freshened the room. Outside, masons had repaired the stairs leading to a private beach. Landscapers had finished clearing the rest of the gardens.

Moving her in didn't take long. She hadn't had enough room in the Officers' Quarters to unpack most of the boxes she'd brought from Japan. Dressed in jeans and sneakers, she worked hard. Soon she was setting the last of her innumerable books into a tall bookcase.

Across the room, Richard screwed a hook into the wall for her Viking bow. "Do you want to hang your amulets too?"

"No. I'm going to wear them." Mischief shone on her face. "They're so unique. No other girl has a lutanium detector or a necklace containing pulverized animal parts to ward off trouble."

"Perfect jewelry for you. I'm amazed Creek allowed you to take them."

"He was too excited about the bioaccelerator to care about jewelry. Wouldn't it be something if he could get it to work? He really is a mad scientist, isn't he?"

"Completely 'round the bend. I suspect our trips will gear down while he's analyzing the thing, and that wouldn't bother me a bit."

"Me neither. I'd like to pop over to Japan to visit Imi, if that's all right."

"Why not? But do take your amulets."

"Get out." She smiled and set down an armload of books. "How about you? Will you go to London again?"

"Why? Are you out of tea already?"

"No. It's that intrigue thing you mentioned." She fanned the pages of a hardcover book. "This is a text I used to teach a history class. Hannibal, Caesar, Napoleon. Seeing them reminded me how you said Roger Wessex fancied himself a conquering hero. I'm curious. Why did you say that?"

After one last twist, Richard set the screwdriver down and hung the Viking bow on the wall. It wouldn't matter if he told her. Roger had too many followers for his intentions to remain secret much longer. "It seems Lord Roger is looking to topple his cousin John from the throne. Have you heard about the dispute over the oil wells in the Irish Sea?"

She tucked the book onto a shelf. "I heard something about it."

"MI6 suspects that Roger is planning to seize those wells."

"What?" Her hand froze on the book; her voice softened to a near-whisper. "Why?"

"To gain support for his cause. Show he's a better leader than both John and Geoffrey."

"Are the Irish aware of his plans?"

"I expect so." Richard set the screwdriver down. "Anyway, he can't succeed. He has support, but not enough to start a war."

"I'm glad to hear it." Standing back, she viewed the Viking bow with an introspective smile. "The right tool for the job, eh?"

"That bow certainly kept us from going hungry. Speaking of which, I could use a cup of tea, and whatever Nick is cooking smells wonderful. Let's take a break, shall we?"

They strolled to the kitchen. Nick was speaking into a wall phone. He put his hand over the mouthpiece when they approached. "It's for you, Christy. A guy named Sasaki's been trying to reach you."

*****

The familiar sight of Ron Chambeau's offices eased Talty's distress. Ron kissed her cheek and scolded her for not telling him she was coming.

"I didn't know I was coming myself." She settled into the chair beside his desk. "I only learned of Imi's death two days ago."

"From what I hear, you're her main beneficiary."

"You probably know more about it than I do. She not only left me her house, she left me some fairly substantial funds. And you're going to help me spend them."

"Yeah? What's this all about, Major Princess?"

Affecting a snobbish air, Talty crossed her legs. "I've grown accustomed to traveling in my husband's private helicopter. I'd like one at my disposal, and I want the best. Soundproofing, a gourmet galley, leather seats, air conditioning, night-flying, retractable weapons. You know."

Ron's eyes slowly narrowed. "The Bellwether Sachem?"

"The Bellwether Sachem."

"You're full of beeswax, little girl! You might be a princess, but you're the farthest thing from muckity executive accommodations I've ever seen. If you don't tell me what you're up to, you can take your cute little butt right out of here. If fact, I ought to smack it and boot you out!"

Talty had missed Ron. "You told me once, 'You can't keep peace without teeth.' In Ireland we say, 'Don't show your teeth until you can bite.' I'm hungry, Ron."

"What the hell are you thinking of doing with a gunship?"

"Keep peace, I hope. I heard a rumor about a threat to Irish oil wells."

"Shouldn't you let Kieran and your uncle deal with the Wessex gang?"

So he'd heard it too. "Maybe, but I'm a Fian warrior. It's my duty to help protect Ireland—with the right tool for the job, of course."

"Yeah? If ISF catches you supplying arms to a sovereign nation, they'll not only court-martial you, they'll take your CO down with you. Maybe it's a good thing you don't work for me anymore."

He looked so comically ferocious, she almost laughed. He tapped his fingers on the desk. His eyes bored into her until the tapping stopped. "All right, Major Princess. I'll get you the bird. We can bill it as executive transport. As for the rest, you better never say where it came from."

"Never."

"These things are expensive."

"As you noted, I now have an abundance of disposable income. How long will it take to negotiate purchase and delivery?"

"About six weeks."

"Who do I talk to?"

Plainly enjoying himself now, Ron leaned back and set his feet on his desk. "Don't you know? Bellwether was one of Eric Yamada's subsidiaries. That's how we got connected with Ryota Sasaki for the weapons. His brother Kiyoshi? Your good buddy who taught you all that ninja stuff? He owns most of Bellwether now."

Talty's jaw dropped. "I knew Eric had different companies. He seldom discussed them, though. This is incredible! And it's not ninja stuff."

"Yeah, right. Kiyoshi is your man, but you'll need me to get the peripherals transported and delivered if you're doing it on the QT."

"I'll speak to Kiyoshi. After I settle Imi's estate, I'm leaving for Ireland."

"How do I reach you?"

"I'll have to contact you. I'll be staying at Eric's house in Malahide. It's mine now. I don't know the number, or even if there is a number. Maybe I'll pick up a cell phone." She waited while Ron made notes on a pad of paper.

"I always did like a challenge," he said at last. "Did I ever tell you Kieran said you were a pretty sharp kid?"

She smiled. He had.

* * * * *

For three days Talty met with estate appraisers and distributed the mementos Imi had bequeathed to friends and museums. She still marveled that most of the treasures, including the house and grounds, were now hers.

Late on the third day, she fixed a light supper for herself and Kiyoshi. "I've been thinking, Ki," she said while they ate in the kitchen. "I want you to have this place. You could develop your own dojo here."

Kiyoshi's chopsticks froze in midair. "Hime-san, I cannot accept this."

"Neither can I. I don't belong here."

"Imi-san's death has upset you. You cannot mean such a thing."

"It wouldn't come without a price. I need your help. I spoke to Ron Chambeau about obtaining a Sachem. He said I should talk to you, since you own the company now. I'm going to need you and your brother to deliver the chopper and the armament for it."

Kiyoshi set his chopsticks down. "Deliver...armament? Here?"

"No. To Ireland. The helicopter won't be a problem, but the weapons should come piecemeal, so no one will know. Lethally armed helicopters aren't exactly standard issue in the Irish Defense Forces."

"Hime-san. Whatever you have in mind, I will help you. I will always help you. I would be offended if you did not request my help. There is no price. However, may I be bold enough to ask what you are thinking?"

Talty let out a relieved breath and repeated her conversation with Richard about Roger Wessex. She then detailed her arrangement with Ron.

A deadly glint lit Kiyoshi's eyes. "Wessex. He is the man who hurt you?"

"Yes."

"I will call Ryota. He will know what to do."

"*Domo arigato, Sensei-san.* Let's look at the dojo after dinner. How should we advertise it? As a retreat for rich folks who want to perfect their souls and refresh their combat skills?"

Kiyoshi answered with one of his happier grunts.

* * * * *

Talty couldn't sleep during the long flight to Dublin. Due to the illicit nature of her scheme, Ryota Sasaki had refused to deliver his merchandise to anyone but her. How could that happen if she was in California or away on a mission? And what would her father think about having a missile-firing gunship in the kingdom's arsenal?

At last, invisible fingers tugged her hair and soothed her aching head. Images of Neil's brilliant smile and vigilant blue eyes stoked the private embers she no longer tried to dampen. She fell asleep wondering what he'd been doing since she'd last seen him.

* * * * *

Neil drove through Malahide's four-corner village and turned onto a series of streets that brought him to an old manor house. The black security gates were open. He slipped into the circular drive just as a taxi pulled out. Frowning at how easily he'd gotten in, he parked his Jaguar beside the carriage house. As he walked up the path to the front door, he admired the dwelling's round tower, bow windows, and granite and brick facades.

Despite the splendor he saw, the property was tired. Weeds invaded the gardens. Dead and broken wood hung from the branches of ornamental trees. Somehow he had to convince Talty she couldn't stay here. As for why he was here, he'd tell her he'd been driving by and saw the taxi drop her off. That should work.

Eager to see her, he rang the bell.

The door opened. She scowled at him. "What are you doing here? Ooh, that Richard Gale!" She whirled back into the house.

At least she hadn't slammed the door in his face. "It's nice to see you too!" Her appearance bothered him, though he couldn't say why. Her face was tanned, her hair streaked with russet and bronze. She reminded him of a lion he'd once seen pacing inside a cage at the Dublin Zoo.

He followed her to the kitchen. "Why didn't you tell us you were coming, Tal?"

"I would've soon enough. The flight was long. I need some sleep."

"All right, but you can't stay here."

She spun on him. "Why not?"

He wanted to hold her and calm her. Instead, he opened the refrigerator. As he suspected, it was empty. "There's no food in the house, and everything is dusty. Come home with me, at least for tonight."

"I'm not up for socializing with your parents."

"No, not there. I have my own place now. It has a private guest suite. Ted comes in to help. Did you ever meet Ted? My old Air Corps aide?"

"No. You told me about him. Sorry, Neil. I didn't mean to eat your head off." She reached over and squeezed his hand. "I'd love to see your place."

"And I'd love to show it to you. And, Tal? When you speak to Richard, will you tell him I was wonderful and you never suspected a thing?"

✳ ✳ ✳ ✳ ✳

Security gates guarded the entrance to Rowan Court, an exclusive apartment complex in Dublin's Ballsbridge section. Neil pulled up to the main entrance and lifted Talty's bag from the back seat. He left his car with the valet and held the gilded glass door open for her, greeting neighbors as he led her across the sumptuous lobby.

Talty watched everyone and everything, including a bevy of glaring, gray-haired women. After the elevator door closed, she said, "What nasty old hens. I don't believe they think you're safe with me, Neily."

"Don't mind any of them. They're all used to seeing me bring girls here." He knew at once he'd made a serious mistake.

"I see." She bit her lip but couldn't keep from smiling. "I'm just another in a long line of women of dubious morals."

"I'm delighted to see you smiling. I'd undergo any trial and tribulation to see you smile."

"Trial and tribulation, is it? In California they call it shacking up."

They were both laughing when the elevator stopped. A moment later, Neil punched in the security code and opened the door to his living room. "Welcome to my home, Tal."

Neil's aide, former Air Corps Sergeant Ted Geary, came hurrying down from the second floor. An even-tempered, pleasant man, Ted wasn't much older than Neil, though several tours of peacekeeping duty in the Middle East had left his face lined and leathery.

Ted picked up Talty's bag. "Good afternoon, sir. I'll put this upstairs."

"Wait, Ted. I want you to meet my cousin Talty."

Talty held out her hand. "Hello, Ted. It's fine to meet you at last."

Ted dropped the bag and stood gawking. He seemed to be wondering if he was allowed to touch a princess. After a moment's hesitation, he smiled and shook her hand. "A pleasure, ma'am."

Careful to hide his amusement, Neil asked his aide to put the bag in the guest room. A great grin appeared on Ted's face. Toting the bag, he marched down the hall.

Neil laughed. "I think he's as happy to have you here as I am. Almost. Come on, I'll show you around."

While Talty oohed over each room, Neil told her about Frank Christopher's bequest, and how a small portion of it had gone toward the purchase of the penthouse, a two-story apartment with wraparound balconies and panoramic views. The first floor included a library and formal dining room, both with antique marble fireplaces. The butler's pantry included a service elevator for the house staff, which presently consisted of Ted. Double French doors in the kitchen led to a private terrace.

When they reached the kitchen, Neil pulled tea things and a bag of crackers from the shelves. Talty filled the kettle and set it on the stove.

She giggled when she opened the refrigerator. "I see why you wanted me to stay here. Your fridge is much better stocked than mine."

Catching a whiff of her musky perfume, Neil peeked over her shoulder at a container of milk and an old bag of take-away. "We'll eat out tonight. In fact, the fellas are having a party. Do you remember Packy Hewitt?"

"Vaguely. Wasn't he in Fianna training with us early on?"

"Yes. He has his pin. He's an Air Corps man, Communications and Information. Today's his birthday. Would you like to go?"

"No, thanks. I just want to go to bed. You go."

"It's at a pub. Barry Malone will be there. There'll be music, and we'll get you fed."

Talty surrendered. "I'm sure I can find proper pub attire in my bag."

* * * * *

Dolly O'Brien's Alehouse, a centuries-old former inn near the aerodrome, was a regular Air Corps haunt. As the king's own nephew frequented the establishment, the pub had become a routine stop for the two men Roger Wessex had sent to observe the Irish royals.

For weeks Havelock and Poulton had been popping in to nurse a few beers and view the sports programs playing over the bar. Tonight, when Neil Boru arrived with an attractive young woman, they ordered more beer and settled down to watch.

* * * * *

Holding Talty's elbow, Neil approached the table. "Looks like we'll have to catch up to join the fun. Happy Birthday, Packy."

Packy Hewitt raised his brawny frame from his chair and shook Neil's hand. "You came, Neil! And brought a lady friend. That's grand."

"Say hi to Christy." Neil introduced her to Barry, Rory, and the young women with them. Only Barry knew who Talty really was, as he'd attended her pinning ceremony. He played along splendidly and introduced the young women at the table.

Talty sat beside him and patted his arm. "I heard about your accident," she said in her clipped American accent. "How are you?"

She knew the Malones well. Barry's sister had been a classmate. But when she asked about his family—with her hand still on his arm—Neil bristled, until Packy distracted him.

Ignoring groans from Barry and Rory, Packy drew a leather case from his jacket. "Wait till I show you what my ol' da gave me for my birthday, Neil. It's un-fuckin'-believable!" He grasped the handle of a double-edged commando knife and playfully sliced the air.

In seconds he was on the floor, his head against the wall, his brown eyes twitching and bulging. Talty's knee pinned his chest. She held the knife against his throat.

As the frightened young women scurried to the powder room, Neil rose cautiously. He'd never seen Talty move so fast. "Talty, let him go. There's no harm here." He reached for her arm, but thought better of it.

She released the terrified young man but held onto the knife. "Where's the sheath, Packy?"

"I, it's, I dropped it. I don't know. It's here somewhere."

Barry found the case and gingerly handed it to her. She slid the knife away. "You're too little a boy to be playing with such a fine weapon, Packy Hewitt. It's mine now."

Neil stepped toward her. "Come on, Tal. He was only showing it. Give it back to him."

Again, Neil reached for her, though something savage in her eyes stopped him. She slipped the case in her pocket and left the pub.

Rory and Barry helped their shaken friend from the floor. Rory gawked at Neil. "Talty? She's really Talty, Neil?"

Oh, no! He'd called her by her name. The pub was noisy, however. No one at the other tables could have heard him.

Barry righted the chairs. "Of all the people to pull a knife on, you eejit! You're lucky she didn't kill you."

Packy was shaking. "I'm sorry, Neil. I didn't know."

"It's all right, Pack. Sorry, but I have to go." Neil slapped a wad of cash on the table and went after Talty.

* * * * *

Neil clicked on the fireplace in the den. Talty sat on the sofa, staring into the flames. Wondering what had happened to her in California, he sat beside her. "Tal—"

"Don't ask about the knife again. Packy's lucky he isn't in jail for flashing it about so. It'll be a while before he gets it back, if he ever does."

"It's more than Packy, I think. What's bothering you?"

She looked down at her hands the way she did when she was trying not to cry. "I can't do it anymore, Neil. I can't keep pretending to be someone else. I want to come home, but you've all forgotten me."

"No, we haven't. Everyone misses you. I certainly do." He pulled her to him and hugged her.

At first she allowed it. Then she nudged him away.

He shouldn't have done it. He must be more careful. "If the weather is good tomorrow, I'll take you walking in the hills."

Her eyes brightened at the idea. "You're good to me, Neily. Thank you."

"As it happens, I'm a bit fond of you." He kissed her mouth, a quick cousin kiss. She didn't seem to mind. He nearly kissed her again, and in a less cousinly manner, though she saved him by saying good-night.

He stared after her. Somehow he had to find out what she was doing in California.

CHAPTER NINETEEN

Trapped

Once, John Wessex would've requested permission before visiting his uncle's chambers. Today he'd followed Cousin Claudia's suggestion and dropped in unannounced.

Geoffrey greeted him amiably. "You're just in time for lunch, John. Sit. Have something to eat."

The slovenly table curbed John's appetite, though he poured himself some tea. "Claudia says we've received invitations to Liam Boru's engagement party."

Geoffrey's beef-laden fork hung in midair. "That Brian is sly. He thinks inviting us will make him look good."

"An engagement party is a family affair, not a political maneuver."

"Political maneuver?" The fork continued on to Geoffrey's mouth. "Where did you learn such big words, boy? Painting pictures? Hah."

John's stomach hurt. He'd promised Claudia—and himself—that he'd ignore his uncle's sarcasm. He drew in a silent breath. "I'd like to attend, to wish Prince Liam well."

Geoffrey didn't quite smile. "I should allow it. Just the sight of you would reassure the Irish they have nothing to fear from us."

The knot in John's stomach tightened. He could think of no response to the biting words. "The invitation says I may bring a guest."

"Really, John? Who would go with you?"

"I'm the king, Uncle. Many young ladies have shown an interest in my company." He didn't add that he was too nervous to converse beyond polite pleasantries with them.

"Have they? It doesn't matter. We aren't going. Our ambassador in

Dublin will attend the party to keep things tidy."

John let it go. Perhaps Geoffrey knew best. "Will Cousin Roger go?"

Geoffrey laughed so hard he nearly choked. Failing to understand what was so funny, John left his uncle to his lunch.

* * * * *

Rain hammered the penthouse windows. Kieran shook his dripping raincoat and tossed it over a kitchen chair. Thoroughly irritated, he sat and waited while Neil made tea. "This had better be important, Neily. Stealing me from my Breege on a fine, rainy, stay-in-bed Saturday morning is a capital offense."

Neil set a steaming mug before Kieran and pulled the milk from the refrigerator. "Talty's here. She stayed the night."

"How nice for you."

The refrigerator door slammed shut. "What the hell does that mean?"

The outburst startled Kieran. Neil usually parried his teasing with quick-witted barbs of his own. "Sorry, lad. I meant no offense. Now, what's up?"

Neil told him the whole story. Each word worried Kieran more. "Did the people at the other tables hear you call her by name?"

"Not likely. The music was too loud."

"And she won't tell you what she's doing with ISF?"

"No, but from the way she acted, I'm thinking it's hazardous duty. We sent her away to keep her safe. What are we going to do?"

Thoughts racing, Kieran sipped his tea. "We're going to find out what she's doing for ISF. I'll speak to Brian and your father. For now, you'll look after her, protector that you are. Will she be in town long enough to attend Liam's engagement party?"

"I don't know."

"Talk her into going with you."

"Me?"

"You're her Shivail. She'll be safe with you, and Liam would love it." Kieran stood and slipped back into his raincoat. "You were right to call me. We'll get to the bottom of it. And next time you call, have some scones or something. A fella gets hungry getting up at dawn."

* * * * *

With Neil at her side, Talty strolled through Glensheelin's orchard and into the fragrant woods. Moss and holly tugged at her homesick heart. Deer tracks she'd explored as a child beckoned. She promised herself she'd rediscover them soon.

"I'd love to go to Liam's engagement party," she said when Neil asked,

205

"but I'm not sure I'll still be here. Speaking of engagements, I heard about Allison. I'm sorry. She sounded like a great girl."

"She is, but that's all done and dusted. Everything's fine."

"I'm glad. Been busy with your Ranger training?"

"Yes. I also have a new title." He told her about his birthday party.

"A duke? My, my, Your Grace! I wish I'd been there to see your face." She stood on her toes to kiss his cheek, delighted that he seemed flustered.

They continued on. A brook bubbled beside a path that led to Glensheelin's main waterfall. Craving the soothing effect of the verdant glen she knew so well, Talty walked faster, but she slackened her step when she entered the clearing.

"What's wrong, Tal?"

"Nothing." How could she tell him she half-expected Vikings or strange tribesmen to attack from behind the trees?

He waited for a bird to finish its glorious trilling before he spoke. "Talty, it's me, Neil. Is it such a secret that you can't tell me? Who do you think is going to ambush us here?"

Despite her uneasiness, she smiled. Neil knew her too well, and she trusted him with her life. "Promise you'll repeat this to no one?"

"Whatever you say will stay between us. I promise."

His blue eyes beguiled her. How could she not believe the spirit with sky-colored eyes who had always watched over her and always would? "Remember the tales of the Otherworld?"

"Yes. In mythology. The old gods and fairies lived there, among others."

"Well, there really are other worlds. We've found them."

Skepticism clouded his blue eyes now. She couldn't blame him. She'd been skeptical herself when Richard first told her.

Leaving him to ponder her words, she walked on until the waterfall's cool spray dampened her cheeks. The gentle cascade trickled and splashed, its music supplanting all thought. She sat on a boulder and watched little rainbows dance in the mist.

Neil sat beside her. "You and Richard? You go to these places?"

She heard the worry in his voice. "And Nick, yes. To gather scientific data. But the places are strange. It takes a while to get used to being back."

"I see. And poor Packy got the brunt of it this time, did he?"

"I shouldn't have let you talk me into going." She stood and started toward the path.

He reached for her elbow and stopped her. "Listen to me, Tal. I called you by your own name last night. The fellas heard me."

She jerked her arm from his hand. Anger burned her cheeks. "What of it?

Plenty of people know who I am and nothing happens. No one cares anymore. Why can't I come home?"

He had no answer. His arm fell over her shoulder, imparting his gently soothing strength. Needing comfort—Neil's comfort—Talty hugged him as she might a lover. "You're good to me, Neily. I love you for it."

He pecked her forehead and broke away. His affection for her was considerable, but they were cousins. He would never feel more than cousinly affection for her.

She turned away to hide her embarrassment. "Let's get back to the house. They'll have supper waiting."

* * * * *

"Come on, Jillie. Let's get it going."

Aidan's whisper was just indecent enough to kindle the amorous activity on her couch, but Jill Scanlon couldn't let his nuzzling crumble her resolve. "I need to speak to you, Aidan."

"Are we not already speaking our own special language, darlin'?"

The first time Aidan had spoken to Jill, she'd been upgrading security for Tara Hall's computers with Jimmy Gallagher, Commander Dacey's second-in-command. Aidan had come by to see his father and stopped to express his appreciation for the fine job she was doing.

Jill knew he had no idea what she was doing. She'd heard her share of silver-tongued tactics and recognized Aidan as a master of the craft. When he invited her to dinner, she refused. She wouldn't have gossipmongers crediting any career advancement she might achieve to her friendship with a member of the royal family.

Aidan, however, had radiated the confident demeanor of one who'd have his way in the end. His persistence paid off. They became lovers, discussing dreams between kisses. Yet Jill had insisted they avoid popular places until her career was on track.

Now she had an opportunity to advance. Jimmy needed her help with a special project.

"It could mean a promotion, Aidan. If it does, we can stop caring who knows about us."

"I've never cared who knows about us, and well you know it. What's the old fella got you doing?"

"All he said was it was something your father wants. He tried for hours this afternoon, but he needs help. He said I was the one for the job."

Aidan swooped in and kissed her. "Jimmy's a smart fella if he said that. Get that promotion, and we'll get married."

"What am I going to do with you?" She smiled at him and locked her arms around his neck. "All right, we'll talk about it. For now—"

"For now, you're my girl, and I love you." His lip-nibbling kiss ended the discussion.

* * * * *

Roger Wessex pounded his desk. Though Havelock and Poulton hadn't seen the dark-haired young woman clearly in the pub's dim light, they insisted they'd heard Neil Boru address her as "Talty."

Roger's other watchers had observed Aidan Dacey escorting a dark-haired young woman around the Irish capital, and being quite furtive about it. Could Princess Taillte really be alive? Roger ordered his agents to concentrate their surveillance on both Boru and Dacey.

* * * * *

Tara Hall was quiet so early on a Sunday morning. Over tea and scones, Jimmy told Jill what he'd already tried to hack into the invincible ISF database. Jill set up different decryption programs and began. By noon they'd found files code-named "Peregrine" that referenced both Richard Gale and Christy McKenna, the key names Kieran had given them. By late afternoon, they'd downloaded the files onto Kieran's computer.

He arrived soon after they let him know. "Well done, you two. Have the kitchen send me some tea and go home."

He went to his office and printed the reports. His tea arrived in time for the first reading. A tumbler of whiskey accompanied the second.

* * * * *

Aidan brought Jill to an out-of-the-way Italian restaurant to celebrate her success. Secure in their private world of red-checkered tablecloths and commercial Italian music, they gave no thought to the two men sitting on the other side of the artificial trees beside them.

While they waited for their dinner, Aidan caressed Jill's fingers, soft and warm beneath his. "My father said you did a good job?"

"Yes. Whatever he needed, we got it." Her lovely smile grew. Joy sparkled in her eyes. "Jimmy said I'm to have a promotion."

"That's great, love. Now I can tell the world about you." Aidan imagined introducing her at the next family gathering. He'd take her to the royal jeweler soon, and they'd pick out wedding rings.

Jill bit her lip. "I'm still nervous about what people will think, y'know?"

"No, I don't know. We agreed that after this, we wouldn't need to hide you away anymore."

"Oh, Aidan, are you sure?"

"I've never been more sure." He brought her hand to his lips. "You're my very own princess, and I intend to see that you're treated so."

The waiter brought their food, and they dined in contented silence.

＊＊＊＊＊

"You'll wear a hole in the rug, Brian."

Brian glared at his brother and continued pacing. His outrage grew with each glance at the misappropriated reports in Peadar's hands.

Peadar, however, sat chuckling at the table in Brian's conference room. Talty's ISF adventures obviously delighted him. "This is the most fantastic stuff I've ever read!"

Kieran stood by the fire, deep in thought. "It amuses you, does it?"

"It does. The girl has a way about her. I'd like to think her Fian training helps her get the job done." He slapped the table. "And maybe I envy her! It all sounds like great fun."

"Fun?" Brian shouted. "She's living like a barbarian. I want her home! Learning new technology in California indeed. We need to get rid of those Wessex gobshites!"

"Speak to Talty," Peadar said. "I'll bet she'll have an idea how to do it." Chuckling away, he returned to his reading.

Brian told Kieran to get Talty to the Hall that afternoon. "We'll see about these ISF shenanigans."

Kieran suggested that Neil should read the reports too, since he had alerted them to all this.

Brian agreed. "Have him come up. Jack too. It's time we settled this business."

＊＊＊＊＊

The fourth time Roger heard the recorded conversation between Aidan Dacey and the dark-haired young woman, he cursed and hurled the recorder against the wall.

Philip jumped. "Calm down, Roger!"

"I knew it! I knew something would come along to spoil my plans."

"No one can spoil your plans. You're far too clever. You said if she were alive, she wouldn't be for long. What are you going to do?"

Philip's calm demeanor settled Roger. He brushed an imaginary speck of lint from his sleeve. "Get Gordon on it, Philip."

"See how clever you are, Roger? Gordon will fix it. He always does."

＊＊＊＊＊

From behind his desk, Brian watched Peadar enter the conference room and close the glass door. Neil was already in there. He'd just finished reading the reports and was mumbling angrily to himself.

Eyes on Neil, Brian lifted the ugly, gray-green rock from his desk and ran his thumbs over its scratchy surface. Perhaps he couldn't hear what Neil was saying, but he remembered all too well his gentle nephew's blistering condemnation years before: *What kind of king are you if you can't take care of your own family?*

"Neil might not have the Boru temper," Jack said from his nearby seat, "but if Talty is involved, he can bite with the best of you. Whatever are you fiddling with, Brian?"

"A substance from the bottom of the ocean. A reminder that I'm not the smartest king who ever sat on Ireland's figurative throne."

"Fargan?"

Brian nodded. "My liquidity is gone. I haven't told Leenie yet. Things will be different from now on. Liam's engagement party? I'll have to borrow from restricted funds to pay for it. As for the wedding..."

"Kieran told me about the investments. So you gambled and lost. Adversity is the source of strength. However high the tide, it ebbs away."

"Blarney, Jack, and not very helpful."

"Is that why you called this meeting? To tell everyone about Fargan?"

"No. I'm calling the meeting to find a way to bring Talty home. Maybe I can't manage my financial affairs responsibly, but I'll be damned if I can't take care of my family." He set the ugly gray-green blob on his desk. "And my kingdom."

Jack crossed his legs. "I read those reports. Very impressive. ISF is giving Talty a rare opportunity, and she's eating it up."

"What she's doing is dangerous, Jack."

"My thought exactly when Kieran went off to Africa, but I wouldn't think of stopping him. He was a grown man, intelligent and capable, and doing his duty. Would you have Talty shirk her duty?"

"Talty's duty is here. She belongs in Ireland."

"You married her off twice and sent her away, and she's not the Crown Princess anymore. What would you have her do?"

Brian's intercom chimed. His assistant's crisp voice announced the arrival of Commander Dacey and Christy McKenna.

"Send them in, Violet." Brian glanced into the conference room. Peadar was smiling, blast him, but at least he seemed to have placated Neil. Brian's gaze shifted to the opening door.

Talty swept in wearing a simple green dress. Her cheeks were flushed, her eyes intense. Kieran came in behind her, moving like a cat and peering about like a bird of prey.

Greetings exchanged, they stepped inside the conference room with Brian and Jack. The chairs around the table whispered over the rug as everyone took their seats and filled their glasses from a crystal water pitcher.

Brian rested his elbows on the table. "All right, let's get straight to it. As you all know, Geoffrey Wessex wants the oil wells that were part of Talty's dowry. He's challenged the validity of the annulment in the World Court. Talty's reappearance will void his lawsuit. He'll never touch those oil wells.

"As for Roger, we can't charge him for his crimes unless he's on Irish soil. Even if we could, we'd need Talty's testimony to convict him. If he knew that she's alive… Talty, we want you home, but until we've eradicated all threats to you, you'll continue to visit us as Christy McKenna."

"Yes, sir. May I ask what you're doing to eradicate these threats?"

"Roger will be out of the way soon," said Peadar. "Once he is, we'll deal with Geoffrey."

Neil looked surprised. "Out of the way? How?"

Brian asked Kieran to summarize Roger's invasion plans. He expected the request to surprise Talty, but she didn't flinch. Neil, however, grew pale.

Steepling his fingers, Kieran succinctly described Roger's plot to seize the oil wells Geoffrey was trying to obtain lawfully. "His idea is, why sue for oil wells when you can simply take them?"

"What are we doing about it?" Neil sounded more businesslike than worried.

"We might not have to do anything," Peadar said. "Our military is strong enough to stop the little gobaloon if he gets this far, which he won't. His own people will arrest him for treason soon enough."

Talty asked what they were waiting for.

"They don't want just Roger," Kieran said. "They want his entire gang of traitors. We'll let Roger get far enough to hang himself, so to speak. He's a Wessex. The worst he'd get is life in an English prison."

"For treason! What about Grannie Deirdre?" Talty slid her chair back and stood. "You can't charge Roger with murder unless he's on Irish soil. The English won't extradite anyone facing a possible death penalty, not to mention Roger is King John's cousin."

A tiny smile played at Peadar's lips. "What are you thinking, Tal?"

"Let him invade. He'll be on Irish soil, and we'll be waiting with open arms."

The sight of the gawking faces around him prompted Brian to close his own mouth. Amazed, he listened while Talty pulled her threads together.

"Between our own intelligence and Kieran's English friends, we'll have plenty of warning. But we'll want extra defense in place just in case. We already have the latest radar to aid the maritime industries."

Peadar nodded. "We'll know if Roger sends a fly our way."

"And your fly swatters, Uncle? Our navy boats are equipped with machine guns and small cannon. The Air Corps choppers have two general purpose machine guns apiece. Fine for practice, but you're depending on MI6 to alert you to this invasion activity. What if their intelligence is flawed, or deliberately misleading? What if Roger is more powerful than everyone thinks? Can our artillery ward off a real attack?"

Impressed, Brian swallowed a mouthful of water to steal a moment to think. How much should he reveal? *There is no strength without unity.* He decided to tell it all.

"Your concerns are valid, Talty. When I first heard of Roger's invasion scheme, I asked Peadar to take extra measures. Asking for Exchequer funding would raise too many questions, so we opted to avoid public scrutiny and the government approval process by using our personal funds to build and equip a special arsenal behind Clontarf Castle. We said we were building dry storage for the *Lady Grania* and the family's smaller boats."

Talty flashed him an admiring smile. "And here I thought you were just sitting about."

Would she still be smiling when she learned what a dolt her father was? "We barely had the framework up when we ran into some financial problems. A year or so ago, I convinced Peadar and Kieran to invest in an offshore oil project with me. The project failed. We don't have the funding we thought we'd have to finish building our fortress, let alone arm it."

"How serious are the losses, Uncle Brian?"

Brian eyed Neil fondly. He suspected his chivalrous nephew would offer the entire inheritance he'd received from his natural father to help. "We aren't going begging just yet, Neil. I'm sure we'll see most of the money returned in time. Still and all, we simply don't have the funds for the defense you're discussing, Tal. The Exchequer would never approve it. Even if they did, the ministers would bog down in debate over it for years."

"You don't need their approval," said Jack. "You can issue a royal mandate to protect your kingdom."

"I could, but we agreed with MI6 not to tip our hand."

Talty gripped the back of her chair. "We don't need the Exchequer, Dad. As you know, Imi Yamada recently passed away. For some reason I can't fathom, she left nearly everything she had to me. I have ample funds at my disposal to do with as I choose, and I choose to complete your storage facility at Clontarf Castle. However, I suggest that instead of a dry dock, we make it a hangar for a gunship."

Neil blinked up at her. "A gunship? Are you talking about an attack helicopter, Talty?"

"We don't have one," Peadar said, "much as I wish we did."

Cunning frosted Talty's eyes. "Oh, but we do. I wondered where we'd keep it. Now I know. I'd like to see the facility tomorrow, if I may."

The room crackled. Uncle Jack pulled his pipe from his pocket and twiddled it in his hands. "Talty, you took an oath as an ISF officer. You can't become involved in the internal affairs of a sovereign nation. There are penalties."

"I took the oath of the Fianna too, Uncle Jack. To be faithful to Ireland. To defend the kingdom against invaders."

Jack waved his pipe at her. "If ISF catches you, they'll not only court-martial you, they'll court-martial your commanding officer, whether he knows about this or not."

"I'm sure they'd exonerate Richard once the facts came out. I'm more concerned that the English could charge him with treason if they think he's working against them. As Kieran said, they hang traitors in England. Richard mustn't know about any of this."

Kieran's hawk-like eyes narrowed. "He'll know something. Richard Gale isn't stupid. We might have to do the job without you."

"You can't. My friends in Japan are bending the rules. They'll only deliver the helicopter and its components to me. I'll have to be here to accept each delivery."

Leaning back, Kieran folded his arms. "You're bending a few rules yourself, girl. How do you intend to get back and forth from California to accept these deliveries without ISF wondering what you're up to?"

"I'm selling Eric's house. It needs work. I'd have to visit often for that."

"Not good enough," countered Kieran. "Anyone could sell that house for you, whether you fix it up or not."

"What do you suggest?"

Kieran's lazy grin chilled Brian. Sure his crafty cousin had caught Talty in some sort of trap, he closed his eyes in gratitude that Kieran was a loyal Irishman and not an enemy.

"Here's what I'm thinking," Kieran said. "Our Neil is a young, wealthy bachelor. Everyone knows he's interested in pretty girls. Christy McKenna is such a girl, isn't she?"

No one answered.

"Well, isn't she? Here it is: Neil, you find the beautiful young widow intriguing. You court her. You visit her. She visits you. Love is a grand thing. No one would ever question her motivation for coming to Ireland so often. It's good, isn't it?"

Neil glanced at Talty. She stared at her hands. Both were clearly uncomfortable with the idea.

Kieran, however, seemed quite pleased with himself. "It's great! Talty, you want to come home, don't you?"

"I…yes, but Neil just got his own place. I don't want to be in his way."

"You're staying with him now. It's not so bad, is it? You'd have a perfect excuse to come home anytime, since everyone will think the two of you are in love."

Talty seemed frozen. So did Neil, though he recovered and found his voice. "I'll do whatever you want, Kieran. If it's all right with Talty."

"Good lad. Talty?"

"All right, if it's the only way. I want to come home, and not just now and then. I want to come home for good."

"And we want you home," Brian said. "I'm not at all happy with this interdimensional traveling you're doing for ISF."

The one-two punch stunned her. She turned disbelieving eyes on Neil, who appeared ready to crawl beneath the table.

"It wasn't Neil," Brian said gently. "Did you think I wouldn't want to know what you've been doing all this time? We know all of it, from your first trip with Richard Gale."

Peadar slapped the table. "I would've loved to go on that one with you!"

"How could you know?" she demanded. "What have you done?"

"We'll let you wonder about that for now." Brian stood, a signal that the meeting was over. "Kieran is right, darlin'. Just think! You could attend your brother's engagement party without anyone suspecting who you are."

The idea brought a smile to her face. "Yes, I could. I'll call Richard. I'm sure he won't mind if I stay a little longer."

Neil rose and smiled half-heartedly. "It'll be our first date. Come on, Tal. I'll drive you home."

Talty kissed Brian's cheek. Neil shook his hand. They left together.

Jack returned his pipe to his pocket. "You're playing with fire here, Kieran. They aren't children anymore. Someone will get hurt."

"I doubt it, Dad. Neil would never hurt Talty. Anyway, they won't be doing this long enough for anyone to get hurt. Once Roger's out of the way, that letter from Jerome's niece will bring Geoffrey tumbling down like Humpty Dumpty. It will work. You'll see."

Brian hoped so.

* * * * *

Jill found she couldn't sleep without Aidan's arm around her. She dressed and crossed St. Stephen's Green. Her favorite Dublin bookstore would be open till midnight, and she often haunted the place late at night.

Just after midnight, she carried her purchases back across the park. The only other person on the path, an elderly man, hobbled along with the aid of a metal cane. She called good evening and hurried past him.

Rain spit down and wet her cheeks. She quickened her step.

So did the old man, though she didn't hear him. His right hand swung the cane around her neck. His left hand grabbed the other end. One savage jerk, and the cane crushed her throat.

The bag of books fell. Jill's instinctive clutching ceased when the man wrenched the cane again and jammed his knee into her back to snap her spine. He let her fall to the ground like a broken marionette.

For a moment, he stood in the rain and listened. No one was around. He retrieved the bag he'd hidden earlier behind a shrub and dumped three dozen Princess Taillte roses over the lifeless girl, as Lord Roger had ordered.

CHAPTER TWENTY

Raising the Stakes

Late the next morning, Talty stood in the shadow of Clontarf Castle's round tower remembering the blood-soaked battleground she'd visited with Richard. A sea breeze blew wisps of hair over her face. She brushed them away and wondered how she'd gotten herself in such a fix.

Neil stood nearby scanning the castle's landscaped grounds. How could she pretend to be in love with him when she *was* in love with him? Despite his assurances at the meeting, he seemed irritated over the arrangement. He had, however, been eager to hear about the gunship. Although he'd never flown a Bellwether Sachem, his knowledge of the aircraft impressed her.

His hand shaded his eyes from the sun. "Here comes my father."

Peadar's car rolled through the security gate. Aidan drove in behind him. Together, the four warriors trekked behind the castle to the skeleton of the boathouse that stood on the bank of a saltwater inlet. A private access road approached the area from the other side of the castle.

They walked around the scene. "We can put a small scale heliport here," Talty said. "The hangar should include a command center with computers and an area for the pilots to study the Sachem's simulation programs. We'll need communications and navigation equipment, weather instrumentation, and firefighting and fuel supplies. What else, Neil?"

"Lockers and fold up cots. A maintenance area. A decent sized runway and a parking area for personnel."

"Of course," added Aidan, "we'll paint it all a lovely pastel color."

Peadar smiled and swatted the air beside Aidan's head. "I have a friend who's a civil engineer with the Defense Department. If anyone can turn this thing into a hangar, he can. Meet with him, Neil."

Talty's heart soared. They were really doing it! "What do you need from me, Neil?"

"The span of your Sachem, love. Does it have skids or wheels? That sort of thing."

Beeping cut the conversation short. Peadar spoke briefly into his cell phone and snapped it shut. "That was Kieran. Brian wants us back at the Hall right away."

* * * * *

The atmosphere in Brian's conference room hovered like still air before a violent storm. From the expressions her father and Kieran wore, Talty knew something awful had happened.

Brian's words confirmed her fear. "A Garda Inspector came by a while ago. Early this morning, a woman walking her dog in St. Stephen's Green found Jill Scanlon."

Aidan blinked stupidly. His mouth opened several times before he could speak. "What do you mean, found her?"

"I'm sorry, Aidan. Jill is dead."

The color drained from Aidan's face. His chest heaved, as if he couldn't catch his breath. "You're wrong, Uncle Brian. I was with her last night. We're going to be married. It's a mistake!"

Kieran's voice trembled. "It was a mistake all right. Whoever did this threw Princess Taillte roses over her. For some reason, they thought she was Talty."

Talty couldn't breathe.

"She was murdered?" Peadar closed his eyes when Brian nodded.

Aidan jumped up. His chair tumbled over. "I did this! I told her she was my princess. Someone heard me." He lifted the chair and hurled it against the wall. The crash shook the room. "I killed her!"

Kieran clutched Aidan's arms. "You couldn't have known, lad."

Aidan shoved him away. "What's the matter with you? You're all a bunch of sniveling cowards. You let them butcher your women and you do nothing about it. I'm done with the lot of you." He bolted from the room.

Cheeks pale, Neil hurried after him. "He didn't mean it. He's lost his head, is all." And he was gone.

Peadar's stern gaze snapped from Brian to Kieran. "Who did this? How did he do it?"

"Strangled her," Kieran said. "We don't know who did it, not yet." He drew an envelope from his pocket. "The inspector left these with me. They aren't pretty."

Peadar took the envelope and slid the photographs from it. Talty changed chairs to sit beside him. No one stopped her.

Each image burned itself into her memory: a once pretty face, dark and twisted in agony; a neck horribly bruised and bent at an unnatural angle; and, the roses.

Shocked that the Englishmen were still after her, Talty cried for the girl—Aidan's girl—who was dead because of her. "Aidan is right. This never should've happened."

Brian looked away when he answered. "We do what we can."

Talty punched the table. "I know what you're doing! You're playing games! Do you never get tired of it? Why don't you challenge them, deal with them like men?"

She ran weeping from the room.

* * * * *

Neil arrived home near midnight. He found Talty reading on the couch before the fire.

She set a leather bookmark in place and closed her book. "Why aren't you staying with Aidan?"

"Because Aidan said, 'Why aren't you staying with Talty?' and threw me out. I'm sorry I left you alone. It's just that he was in such a state. His heart is broken." Longing for sleep, Neil sat beside her. "Kieran said you gave them all a good larruping before you left. Are you all right with them?"

"Yes. I called them all and apologized. I know we have to leave it to them." She gave him a lopsided smile. "You're lucky you don't have the famous Boru temper. Come on, I'll fix you a cup of tea."

While Talty filled the kettle, Neil described the funeral arrangements. "It's the day after tomorrow. Everyone in the family wants to go. Kieran wasn't going to allow it, but he changed his mind when my father said the murderer would be expecting them if he'd really gotten you this time."

Her face fell at that, and he regretted saying it. She rallied right away, however. "What about Aidan's classes?"

"Someone will cover them for a few weeks. He's going to stay with his parents for a while. I'm going to Curragh Camp with him after the funeral to help close up his house."

"I'll come with you if you like."

Neil tugged her hair. "I was hoping you would."

* * * * *

The investigators traced the purchase of the roses found on Jill's body to three separate flower shops. After interviewing the florists, the Chief

218

Inspector concluded that one man had made all three purchases, paying in cash each time, signing nothing.

Despite the man's precautions, the florists identified him from photographs. The Chief Inspector told Kieran the rose buyer was a man named Gordon Randolph, a well-known associate of Lord Roger Wessex.

✳ ✳ ✳ ✳ ✳

Richard slid the patio doors open to let in the cool Pacific breeze. As he drank in the heady mix of salt air and breakfast aromas, something struck him as odd. "I don't see a single seagull."

"I thought it was quiet this morning." Nick was shaking so many frying pans he seemed to be juggling them. "Not that I'm complaining. Those guys can make a racket."

Samantha sat sipping coffee while she read the newspaper. As she often did, she'd come by for breakfast. "I hear them from inside my apartment at all hours. Come to think of it, I didn't hear them this morning, either."

Wondering at the unusual silence, Richard ambled toward the table. "Perhaps there are fishing boats offshore. Better pickings for them."

The telephone rang. Reaching for the handset, Richard eyed the clock and made a quick calculation: just past teatime in Ireland. "Hello?"

"Hi, Richard. I hope you were up."

"Yes, darling. Samantha's here too. We're just about to have breakfast."

Concentrating on every word, he listened to the troubling account of Jill Scanlon's murder. Christy wanted to stay not only for the funeral, but also for Prince Liam's engagement party. Neil had invited her as his guest.

"If you can spare me, that is," she said.

"Be glad you're away. Creek is all over the shop testing the bioaccelerator—with most impressive results, I might add. His shoulder hasn't stopped twitching for days. I must say, this murder has me concerned, darling. Where are you staying?"

Nick and Samantha stopped what they were doing and stared.

"In Ballsbridge." Christy paused before adding, "with Neil."

She'd be safe enough with him, thought Richard. "Do you have your amulets?"

She chuckled in his ear. "Yes, in my suitcase."

"All right. Do be careful. Check in with us now and again." He ended the call wondering if she'd fallen in love with the soft-spoken aristocrat.

Behind him, Nick announced breakfast and set a plate of muffins on the table. "So who's she staying with?"

"Neil Boru."

"Man, he works fast." Scraping his chair on the floor, Nick settled into his seat. "It's only been a few days since you asked him to check on her."

Richard took his seat more quietly. Apparently Neil had done more than check on her. Between bites of pancakes, Richard relayed the news about the murder.

Samantha cringed as she listened. "Poor Aidan. I hope they get whoever did this."

So did Richard. "The police are investigating. It is sad. The Boru family has certainly had their share of tragedy."

"I read about that." Nick poured maple syrup over his plate. "The king's daughter died."

"Yes." Richard recalled the headlines, saw the newscasts again. "His daughter and mother both died under strange circumstances the night the princess married King Thomas. Taillte Boru was a lovely girl, an aspiring naval officer. Perhaps Christy reminds Neil of her."

"Christy must like him if she's staying with him," said Samantha.

Nick shrugged. "What's not to like? A good-looking rich guy. A duke, no less. Y'know, he could take her away from us for good."

"I think you're jumping the gun," said Richard. "It's only been a year since her husband died, and Neil just got over a broken engagement. They're probably just having fun."

As if disagreeing, the house shook. Samantha jumped up and shrieked. Dishes crashed from the table. Pictures flew from the walls. The tremors toppled the chairs and knocked everyone to the floor, where they cringed and waited for the earthquake to end.

CHAPTER TWENTY-ONE

A Memorable Party

The royal jeweler's shop was a short, misty walk to the end of Wicklow Street. Neil slipped in the door beneath the sign marked "DeWitt & Sons" and took the steps two at a time to the shop on the next floor.

The jeweler lowered his lens and stood. "Good morning, Your Grace."

Neil shook the damp from his raincoat and hung it on a hook. "It could be worse, Adam. I need some things for a yellow gown. The lady's aide says topaz, amber, or garnet."

"All fine choices, sir. I have plenty to show you, of varying quality."

"This lady will have your best." Neil sat at the client's table, prepared by prior visits for an educational show.

After unlocking a cabinet filled with narrow drawers, Adam removed the fourth drawer and set it before Neil. "Topaz, sir. A hard silicate mineral, though not as hard as diamond."

Neil inspected rings, bracelets, necklaces, and earrings. Several would match Talty's gown. He committed his selections to memory and waited for the next round.

Adam presented trays of amber and garnet. None of the specimens impressed Neil. "You recommend the topaz, do you?"

"No, sir. I'd recommend sapphires for a lady who will have the best."

"But sapphires are blue."

"Sapphires are blue when clear corundum is contaminated with iron and titanium. However, different combinations of minerals result in different colors. The orange-yellow sapphire is very rare. Consequently, I don't have many, but I'll show you what I do have."

The stones in the third tray had a brilliance akin to that of diamonds.

Neil saw the difference right away. Talty would wear sapphires tonight.

As Adam said, he didn't have many. The tray was only partially-filled with the rare gems. Neil noticed several unusual pieces sharing the tray with the sapphires.

A gold ring drew his attention. The brilliant-cut diamond in the setting was fine enough, but the pattern on the ring itself was what had caught his eye. Tiny roses adorned the band. This ring was meant for Talty's hand. Perhaps it would be an engagement ring, if he found the courage to speak to her. Even if she refused him, he'd give it to her in friendship.

Jenna had told Neil that Talty's high-necked gown would require no necklace. "Let's have that yellow sapphire ring, and the matching bracelet and earrings." He tapped the gold ring. "And this, Adam. Set your best diamond in it and keep it until I send for it."

Neil left DeWitt & Sons with yellow sapphires in his pocket. His thoughts, however, were on the band of roses.

* * * * *

Richard opened the door to Christy's rooms. He and Nick stepped inside.

"Like I told you," Nick said. "It isn't so bad in here."

They'd spent over a week cleaning up after the earthquake. The house itself had suffered no damage, though two barrels full of broken glass and pottery were on their way to the recycling center.

Since Christy's rooms were vacant, they'd left those for last. The quake had toppled her dresser and scattered her books. Remnants of hanging plants lay scattered over the floor.

While Nick swept up the debris, Richard returned the books to their shelves. Together they heaved the dresser upright. Then Richard knelt to retrieve the contents of the jewelry box.

Nick picked up a gold case that lay open on the floor. "What's this?"

"I'll be damned." Richard took the case and stared at the pin inside. "It's a Fianna pin. Why would she have it?"

"Neil must have given it to her. Like a fraternity pin, or a pre-engagement present."

"If so, they've been close friends a lot longer than we thought." Even if that were true, would a Fian warrior really give a girlfriend his priceless pin? To a lady he cherished, he might.

Believing now that Neil Boru meant to marry Christy, Richard returned the case to the jewelry box.

* * * * *

"Ow! Whatever are you putting in my hair, Jen?"

"Sit still till I get your eyes done."

"Not too much. I don't want to look like a Geisha."

When Talty's appearance finally received Jenna's approval, the aide slipped a tube of lipstick and a comb into a satin evening bag. "I'll get your shawl," she said.

While Jenna was in the closet, Talty added her amulets to the purse. She was Irish after all, just superstitious enough to think the things might ward off disaster.

* * * * *

Upstairs in the master bedroom, Neil held out his arms. Ted helped him into his dinner jacket. Already dressed to go, Aidan relaxed in a nearby chair. Neil had persuaded him to attend the party; Talty had practically ordered him to come. He'd lost weight since Jill's death and tended to stay home and brood. Around others, however, he tried his best to be cheerful, as he was doing now.

"It sounds like there's a bunch of geese in Talty's room. How many of them are down there, Neil? I thought just old Jenna was coming."

"There's only the two of them. It's been a while since Talty went to a party at Tara Hall, and she's having fun. All right, I'm ready. Thanks, Ted."

Aidan stood and straightened his jacket. "You look good, Neily. So do I. Thanks for having me along. I couldn't have gone on my own."

"You're never on your own. Don't ever forget it." Neil tucked two black velvet boxes into his pocket and followed his cousin downstairs.

They entered the living room just as Talty and Jenna did. Aidan covered his eyes. "I'm blinded, Beauty! I'll need to find a new name for you. Beauty can't touch such splendor. Look at you, every inch a Celtic goddess!"

"What codology, Aidan Dacey. Do you never stop?"

He kissed her hand. "What do you think, Neil? Am I overstating the case?"

Aidan was trying hard. Neil smiled. He'd missed his cousin and good friend. "Not at all. You're surely easy on the eyes, love. Something's not quite right, though."

Talty looked down at herself and frowned. "Don't you like the dress?"

"The dress is perfect. It's the pearls. They're a shade off, and I won't be seen with a girl in off-shade pearls." He produced one of the velvet boxes and handed it to Jenna.

Talty's frown turned to a smile. "Neil! What have you done?"

"I got a few baubles to go with your dress."

Jenna opened the box and nodded. "Good choice, sir. A perfect match."

Aidan went over to peek. "What are they?"

"Sapphires," said Neil

Aidan and Jenna both cast doubtful looks Neil's way. Aidan's eyebrow arched the same way Kieran's did. "I didn't ride up the river on a bicycle, Neily. Even I know sapphires are blue."

Talty traded her pearl bracelet and earrings for sapphires. "Not all of them, Aid. The basic mineral that forms sapphires is clear. Different combinations of impurities make them different colors, though blue is the most common."

For the first time in ages, Aidan laughed. "Knew that off the top, did you? Beautiful *and* smart!"

A blush crept over Talty's cheeks. "I read it in a book."

Neil opened the second box. Talty gasped and reached for the shimmering sapphire ring. Jenna warned her not to spoil her nails.

"Here, let me." Neil slipped the ring on her finger and kissed her hand.

"Oh, Neil. You've got me all in a dither!"

Aidan grinned. "That's our Neily. The quiet ones cause all the trouble."

That his surprise had succeeded so well encouraged Neil. He took the shawl from Jenna and draped it over Talty's shoulders, inhaling her perfume as he did. "The limo is waiting. Shall we go?"

✳ ✳ ✳ ✳ ✳

Splendid in their formal attire, Liam and Maura stepped onto Tara Hall's ballroom floor and danced the evening's first dance. The lilting waltz had family members and distinguished guests applauding the handsome young prince and his red-haired, emerald-eyed princess-to-be.

Others joined them. Soon Kieran was whirling his nimble mother among a throng of graceful dancers.

"Liam's a handsome boy," Nuala said without missing a step. "And Maura's a pretty thing. They'll have lovely children. Talty looks fine tonight too. Why, she's almost as beautiful as I was at her age."

"You're still beautiful, Mum," Kieran said dutifully. All night he'd been hearing admiring comments about "the lovely girl with Duke Neil." He'd also overheard a few crude remarks regarding her lodging with Neil. Although Kieran had devised the arrangement himself, the perceived stain on Talty's reputation troubled him.

"Look at them," Nuala chuckled. "If I didn't know better, I'd say those two are getting cozy. Are you sure they're pretending?"

When Kieran was Neil's age, he'd have pursued a girl as pretty as Talty in a minute with no thought for the consequences.

They aren't children anymore.

He decided to have a word with Neil.

✱ ✱ ✱ ✱ ✱

A traditional band played the evening's first lively reel. It was time to *dance*. Shouts filled the air. Feet stomped the floor. Talty joined in, spinning from brother to cousin to uncle.

After the end of the first set, Kieran pulled her from the dance floor. An American wouldn't know the Irish dances so well, he said. Disappointed, she wandered to the bar and ordered a soft drink.

Kevin came by, handsome in his formal attire. "Have you seen your father? It's time to start the Siege of Dublin."

"I don't know where he is. Have you checked upstairs?"

"No. If you'll check upstairs, I'll check the men's lav."

Happy to have something to do, Talty rode the private elevator to the fourth floor. A light glowed beneath the door to her father's office. She knocked and found him sitting at his desk, turning a rock in his hands.

"What are you doing up here, Dad? It's time to start the Siege."

Sighing heavily, Brian set the rock down. "I'm coming, darlin'. Just having a moment of peace."

"What have you got there?" Curious, she approached the desk. Her evening bag began to vibrate. Startled, she moved closer to the desk.

The vibrating increased.

She snatched the gray-green blob from his desk. Her bag was humming now.

Brian scowled up at her. "What the devil is going on?"

"Oh! Oh, no! Give me your phone, Dad!"

CHAPTER TWENTY-TWO

Out of Line

Dressed in an army sweat suit, Aidan sat on the couch in Neil's living room with a mug of tea. As he sipped, he relived the conversations he'd enjoyed with friends and relatives the night before. His Scottish cousins had dragged him to the dance floor and made him dance. So had Talty. The dark cloud that had trapped him for weeks had brightened a little.

Talty and Neil came in from the den. Talty's ISF friends were on their way, something about the Fargan Trough. Aidan watched her pace, so like her father.

"I need to get some groceries," she said.

"All right," Neil said. "I'll take you."

She didn't seem to hear him. "Malahide's not far. They can get in and out of the city easily enough. The cleaners are at the house now. I have to go and see that everything's ready."

"If the house isn't ready, they can stay with my parents."

"All right." She put on her raincoat, picked up her purse, and left.

Neil shook his head. "She didn't hear a word I said."

"The girl's in a state, Neily. What's going on? Why aren't her friends staying here?"

"A state? She's going right over the edge." Neil sat opposite Aidan. "They're all coming because of a rock on Uncle Brian's desk."

"A what? Oh, I've seen that thing. What is it, anyway?"

"He got it from the captain of the *Kincora* to remind him what a disaster the whole Fargan thing was. But Talty knew it for something her research people have been hunting for. They're coming to take a look. And they aren't staying here because they aren't supposed to know that Talty and I keep separate quarters."

Aidan slapped his forehead. "That's right, I forgot. You're only *pretending* to be a rascal. We can't have them finding out you're really a saint." His tone turned serious then. "Have you thought about talking to her?"

"It's crossed my mind. Sometimes I wake up thinking she's sleeping beside me. I put my arm out, and she's not there. I'd tell her—I really want to—but I can't stop imagining the awful things she'd say."

"Talty wouldn't say awful things to you. Talk to her. Talk to my grandfather. Find out what can be done."

The phone rang, the doorman calling to say that Commander Dacey was on his way up. Neil thanked him and relayed the news to Aidan.

"My ol' da is probably looking for me," Aidan said. "I'd better get dressed." Tea in hand, he headed toward his room. He paused at the door. "I'm sorry, Neil. I should mind my own business. It's just that you have a girl you love sleeping all alone in your guest room every night. My girl is gone. I'd give anything…" The dark cloud returned.

"Are you all right, Aid?"

He smiled for Neil and started down the hall. "Right as radishes. Don't mind me."

Behind him the front door opened and closed. Mumbled greetings followed. Kieran asked where Talty was.

"On an errand," Neil answered. "What's up?"

"You two were acting cozy last night."

Aidan stopped. He knew that tone. He didn't like it.

"We were dancing," Neil said.

Aidan didn't care for Neil's defensive tone, either. He set his tea on a hall table and rushed back into the room.

His father was glaring at Neil. "So you say. You're taking the pretending a little too far, I think."

"You'd better be joking." Neil took a challenging step toward Kieran.

Aidan moved between them. "Let's calm down here, fellas."

Kieran nudged Aidan aside and puffed up like a cobra about to strike. "Joking? It would be a sad day if you took advantage of the girl while she's in your care, and her your own cousin."

Neil stood open-mouthed. "It was your idea to have her stay here so I could look after her!"

"You're looking after her very well from what I can see."

Neil took another step toward Kieran. "I've never done anything but look after her, and you have no cause to say otherwise. What exactly are you accusing me of?"

Aidan's heart battered his ribs.

"Are you bedding the girl?"

Neil swung. Aidan lunged and grabbed his arm. Neil shoved Aidan aside, knocking him into an end table, sending a lamp crashing to the floor.

Kieran trampled the shards of porcelain and went at Neil. Aidan regained his footing and pushed him back. "Are you crazy, Dad?"

"You think I'm bedding Talty?" Neil shouted over Aidan's head. "Why? Is it something you'd think of yourself, you filthy-minded bastard?" He lunged at Kieran.

Aidan shoved Neil back. "Cool off, Neil. And you're out of line, Dad."

"So I'm wrong about it, am I? I saw the two of you dancing last night."

Neil backed away from Kieran. His furious eyes never left the older man's face. "And I saw you take her off the dance floor. If it were up to you, she wouldn't have danced with anyone. We were dancing last night, Kieran. That's poles apart from what you're suggesting."

"Enough!" Aidan roared. "What's the matter with the two of you?"

Kieran looked from Aidan to Neil as if seeing them for the first time. His temper seemed to fizzle. "Look, Neil—"

"Get out of here, Kieran. Just go!" Neil bounded up the stairs.

He would never speak to Talty now. Aidan wanted to hit his father. "You've done more damage here than you know, Dad. What the hell were you thinking?"

Without another word, Kieran left the apartment. Moments later, Neil raced down the stairs and flew out the door.

Aidan stared at the broken lamp and sighed. The day had started so well.

✳ ✳ ✳ ✳ ✳

Aidan was still picking bits of the lamp from the rug when Talty returned, her arms filled with sacks of groceries. What would he tell her? Maybe she'd still be as distracted as she was earlier and wouldn't notice the mess.

"What on earth happened here, Aidan?"

"Um, a little accident. Clumsy, that's all." He took her bags.

She followed him into the kitchen. "The doorman said your father was here. Where is he? Where's Neil?"

"My father's gone, and Neil, he went out."

"He's supposed to take me to Malahide."

"I can take you." He returned to his cleanup task in the living room.

Talty followed him. She folded her arms. "Aidan, where's Neil? I suppose he left because he was upset that you broke the lamp?"

"Don't be silly. It was an accident."

She stomped her foot. "Aidan! What's going on?"

If he refused to tell her what happened, she'd be angry, though not as angry as she'd be if he told her what did happen. Deciding to tell her as little as possible, he slid broken glass into a paper bag. "Neil and my father had a few words."

"Neil and Kieran? I don't believe it. Over what?"

"I disremember, Tal."

"You're lying."

He gulped and stood to face her. "Yes, I am. Let it go."

"Why would they argue? What happened?"

Aidan clutched her arms. "Please let it go. Be a good girl and help me clean up this stuff so we can go to Malahide."

Between Aidan's desire to escape the scene and Talty's angry energy, they had the rug spotless in minutes. While they were putting on their coats, the telephone rang.

Talty answered, spoke a few words, and hung up. "That was Uncle Peadar. My father wants us at the Hall. Neil will meet us. I'm really starting to dread going there, Aidan."

* * * * *

Brian was pacing, not a good sign. Wondering what had upset him, Talty sat between Aidan and his father. Kieran had little to say. Equally tight-lipped, Neil sat opposite the Daceys, next to Peadar.

The pacing stopped. Brian leaned his wrists on the back of his chair. "I've asked you here to review this ISF mission. Peadar and Kieran and I have been discussing it for some time." He glowered at Kieran. "Among other things. Talty, how important is this mission?"

An image of Joseph's mangled arm prompted her immediate response. "More important than anything."

"More important than what we've been doing to get you home?"

"Yes, sir."

Brian pulled out the chair and sat. He drank from his water glass and continued. "Talty, you've asked us to make the *Kincora* available to your research people. It's an expensive request. We can offer *Kincora* for a short time, but the financial difficulties we've experienced preclude any long term exploration."

"ISF will lease *Kincora* on your terms, Dad."

"For how long? What will they be doing? We must let Captain O'Connor know."

"I can't answer either question exactly. I only know they want to conduct tests. You know from the reports you've read what this stuff can do, if it really is the right stuff."

"I believe I do. I'll back your mission for as long as I can. Every resource available will be at the disposal of ISF."

"They can stay at Garrymuir until the house in Malahide is ready," Peadar said.

"Thank you, Uncle." Talty glanced uneasily at Neil. "Perhaps I should stay with them. Richard is the only one who's ever been to Ireland before."

Brian forbade it. "You'll stay with Neil. First, your gunship will arrive soon—see if you can find out exactly when—and you must be free to come and go without having to explain your activities to your friends." His scowl and the anger in his voice grew more ferocious by the minute. "Second, it will hide trouble. I won't have anyone thinking there's a rift in this family. And third, there will be no rift in this family! You will make peace! I don't give many orders, but that is a definite, direct one, and you will obey it!"

Had the argument between Neil and Kieran been that bad? Talty had never seen such a mortified expression on her godfather's face.

"I'm sorry, Neil," Kieran said. "It isn't the first time I've been wrong, and I don't expect it will be the last."

Neil looked ready to run out the door. "I'm sorry too. We'll have a beer later and forget it." To Brian he said, "I can stay at my parents' place with Talty if she wants to be with her friends. It'd be more hospitable than leaving them on their own. We'll help them settle in. I've already made reservations to take them to Antonio's for dinner."

Aidan appeared eager to gloss over the rift between Neil and Kieran. "If Neil is buying, I'll go too. I can act as driver, or whatever else they need."

Brian nodded. "Good idea, Aidan. You're the only one here who hasn't read those reports Talty mentioned. You'll read them now. All right, let's get to work. And don't any of you ever forget: 'There is no strength without unity!'"

✳ ✳ ✳ ✳ ✳

Neil and Talty returned to Rowan Court in awkward silence. Neil yearned to pull the car over and kiss away the hurt he sensed in her, but he could never do that now. Damn Kieran.

He hung her jacket in the closet, holding his breath to avoid inhaling the subtle scent of her delicious perfume on its collar. "We'll be out late to meet your friends. Why don't you rest?"

"All right." She started toward her suite and stopped. "Why won't you tell me what happened today? Is it because your argument with Kieran concerned me? I think maybe... I think it would be better if I left. I can't bear that you're angry with me."

"I'm not angry with you, and I don't want you to leave." He raised her hands to his lips and kissed each hand. "I love having you here. My quarrel with Kieran was no fault of yours. Now go and rest."

And she was gone. He wanted to go after her and comfort her, yet he didn't dare.

It would be a sad day if you took advantage of the girl... Damn Kieran.

* * * * *

The sight of Richard sitting at Uncle Peadar's kitchen table lifted Talty's mood. She sensed they were in awe of each other, though she knew neither would ever admit it.

At the other end of the table, Samantha chatted with Peggy. Nick was trading recipes with Nora, who'd prepared a spectacular midnight buffet.

Creek had no interest in food. At the first opportunity, he and his twitching shoulder cornered Talty. "Where's that rock, Major?"

"In a safe place. We'll see it tomorrow. Eat something and go to bed."

Soon everyone retired for the night. Neil escorted Talty to her room. His sudden formality confused her. His refusal to reveal the cause of his argument with Kieran annoyed her.

When they reached her door, the sound of Richard and Nick coming down the hall behind them provoked her to retaliate by throwing her arms around Neil's neck and pressing her mouth to his. He tightened up, and she thought he'd break away from her. Then he was kissing her back, the taste of him warming its way down her throat like the burn of fine brandy. The close male scent of him nearly overwhelmed her.

Nick coughed politely. Richard said, "Pardon us."

Neil released her and moved to let them pass. Richard kept his face carefully neutral. Nick, however, was smirking.

After he and Richard continued down the hall, Neil surprised her by bending his head for another kiss.

She pushed him away. "That's enough illusion for now."

His arm shot to the doorframe and blocked her way. "You're a bad girl, y'know?" He pecked her mouth and left her with a curt "Good-night."

She closed the door, miffed that he could be so casual about kissing her when her knees threatened to crumble. Her galloping heartbeat had just returned to normal when Kiyoshi called from Japan.

"Your package shipped today in one of our air transports, Hime-san."

"That was fast. I thought it would take longer."

231

"I rearranged several orders for you. The additional components will arrive separately, as we agreed."

Talty thanked him and set the phone down, grateful to have a distraction from Neil's uncousinly kiss, a kiss that replayed itself in her mind for hours. She didn't sleep well.

* * * * *

Neil tossed and turned all night. The turbulence roiling in Talty's eyes when she closed her door haunted him. The game had gotten out of hand. What had possessed him to kiss her like that? What should he do now?

Nothing. Another man would claim her and kiss her, another more deserving of her, like Richard Gale or Barry Malone.

He punched his pillow. What would an ancient Fian warrior have done if someone told him he couldn't have the woman he loved? The Fian motto pulsed in time to his pounding heart:

Truth in our Hearts, Strength in our Arms, Dedication to our Promise.

The words chanted through his frenzied thoughts until he knew what he must do. At long last, he fell asleep.

* * * * *

Talty was in the kitchen at daybreak. Comfortable in her uncle's home, she brewed a pot of tea and brought it to the table, choosing the seat that afforded the best view of Peadar's gardens. The roses would be in full bloom when Liam married Maura Donovan.

While the tea steeped, she thought about Liam. And Liam's party. And dancing with Neil. And Neil. And now?

"Got enough in the pot for me?"

Relieved that he'd sought her out, she smiled. "Always, Neily."

He filled their cups. "Will you walk in the gardens with me? It might be the last peace we have before we start searching for funny little rocks."

"Those funny little rocks are serious stuff. The bioaccelerator will heal burn victims and shorten the recovery time for wounds, and—"

"I read about it, remember? Come on, let's have that walk."

Tea forgotten, they strolled in the gardens. When Neil turned down a side path, Talty tried to remember where it went, though it didn't matter. She'd go anywhere with Neil.

He stopped before a pair of newly pruned rosebushes. She knew where they were now. The smaller bush was Kevin's apricot Derry Rose. Neil's deep red Ace of Hearts had already started to bloom.

"That's Kevin and me." Neil nodded toward the Ace of Hearts. "My father planted that one because he called me his son. That makes me your

232

cousin, Tal. I had no right to kiss you like that last night, though I'm not sorry for it. I'd have to be dead not to want to kiss a girl as pretty as you, but I don't want it to happen again."

"I'm sorry too. I behaved like a brat last night."

"That doesn't matter. What does matter is that I have a duty to look after you. When you come home, and it will be soon, I don't want anyone to have the slightest suspicion that we've done anything wrong. We can't play games that can cause misunderstandings. There's the invasion to deal with, and now we have this mission with your friends. We have to concentrate on those."

She took his hands. "I'll concentrate better if I know we're friends."

"We're the best of friends. We always will be. I promise you that. But don't ever forget who you are." He raised her hand and kissed it. "You are the heart of this kingdom." He kissed her hand again. "You are my own heart." Then he kissed her mouth, though his lips barely touched hers. "You have my everlasting love and devotion, beloved Princess of Ireland."

Resigned that his duty to protect her always had and always would come before anything else, she accepted his homage with grace and returned to the house with him.

CHAPTER TWENTY-THREE

Storytellers

Sunbeams danced over the remnants of breakfast on Prince Geoffrey's desk. Bert Benson shifted his feet to dodge not only the blinding rays, but Geoffrey's tirade as well. Bert's agents had reported Richard Gale's arrival in Dublin soon after the ISF jet landed. Bert had made a mistake by not telling Geoffrey straightaway. He must be more careful.

"Your people aren't on top of things, Benson," Geoffrey said through a half-chewed sausage. "My man in Dublin tells me Gale and his people are staying at Peadar Boru's townhouse. What are they doing there?"

Bert resolved not to report to Geoffrey at mealtime again, though that might be difficult. Geoffrey's meals seemed unending these days. "Unknown at this time, sir. We only know they came in by military air transport late last night. We'll monitor their activities."

"See that you do. What's the latest on Roger?"

"As you know, Lord Roger converted a former sports facility on Hoy's Neck into a command center of sorts. We suspect that the captains of some of our smaller naval vessels will answer his call when it comes." Bert longingly patted the pocket that held his cigarettes.

"So Catherine tells me. Each and every one a traitor, eh?"

Most of the "traitors" were either Bert's agents or military people he knew to be loyal to King John. If all went as planned, Roger's activities would land him in the hands of the Irish.

"From Hoy's Neck," Geoffrey said, "Roger could easily take Dublin by surprise. We'll let him amuse himself with his fantasy for now, but before I decide what to do about him, I want to know what the ISF people are doing with the Borus. Get Catherine on it."

Geoffrey's attention locked on a plate of scones. Bert had been dismissed. After a quick cigarette, he'd give Catherine a call.

*****

Catherine eyed the clouds blowing in over Hoy's Neck and silently cursed Bert. She'd be flying straight into the storm tearing toward England's west coast from the Irish Sea.

Roger sat in a chair watching her pack. "I don't want you to go, Cat."

"It's a short job, darling. I won't be long. Bert wants me to speak to some people."

"Will you sleep with them too?"

She contrived a smile, a task that required increasing effort these days. "Not if I can avoid it. I'd rather be with you."

"Yes, I know. What do you suppose those ISF people are doing in Dublin? When you find out, let me know. Before you speak to Geoffrey."

Catherine closed her suitcase. All the duplicity had her head spinning. She'd have a drink on the plane and try to relax.

*****

A crystal chandelier cast its glittering light over one of Tara Hall's vintage conference rooms. The flames in the marble fireplace kept the gloomy weather at bay. Talty stood beside the hearth keeping a nervous eye on both her families.

Some conversed near the tea cart. Others laughed across the room. Shoulder twitching, Creek hovered near the small cardboard box on the burlwood table. Richard gossiped with Liam, though he excused himself to greet Brian and Eileen when they entered the room.

A few more pleasantries and the meeting came to order. Brian opened the box. Shoulder jerking like the top of a boiling coffee percolator, Creek selected an instrument from his bag and scanned the rock inside.

After several tense moments, he looked up with the biggest grin Talty had ever seen on his weathered face. "It's lutanium, all right."

Eyebrows raised, Eileen folded her hands and smiled. "Isn't that lovely. What is it? What does it do?"

"What it is, madam, is a substance that will revolutionize medical science. What it does is fuel bioaccelerators."

"Bio what?"

"A bioaccelerator, madam, speeds up the healing process. Cuts recovery time for surgery to next to nothing. Wounds and burns are gone in a matter of days, even hours, depending on the severity of the injury. But bioaccelerators need a special fuel only lutanium can provide. Lutanium is rare, but it's in this little rock."

"The rock from the Fargan Trough?"

"Yes, ma'am." Creek slapped the table. "We need to get to Fargan!"

Unaffected by Creek's ebullience, Brian peered at the faces around him. "*Kincora* is on loan now, but we can interrupt the assignment. She'll be ready in two days."

Richard nodded. "Thank you, sir. We'll arrange transportation to Donegal right away."

"My Rangers will transport you. Is everything set, Neil?"

"Yes, sir. We'll take the Gulfstream to Donegal Airport Wednesday morning. A Sea King will be waiting for us."

"Excellent," Brian said. "I believe we're done here."

Talty returned to Peadar's town house with Neil to help the ISF team prepare for the move to Malahide.

* * * * *

After touring her friends through her Malahide home, Talty showed Samantha to the master bedroom suite. Creek claimed a room with a small side office. Leaving Nick to explore the kitchen, she brought Richard to the guest suite.

He glanced around the room. "Very nice, darling. Please come in and close the door."

They settled in chairs near the window. Relaxed as he might appear, Richard was at work. "I don't want to get on anyone's wick, but I have to ask. How well do you know Neil's family? Are they attempting to control our activities, or are they just being friendly?"

Talty had to smile. "I know them well enough. We aren't under house arrest. I believe they really want to help. Even if they weren't nice people, they stand to gain a potential fortune from this venture."

"I agree. Let's face it. We need their help. The Irish Crown owns the Fargan Trough, unless England wants to reopen that can of worms."

She should've known he'd be abreast of the matter. "It's my understanding that England signed a treaty relinquishing its claim to Fargan. Are you worried they'll rethink the situation?"

"They might if they learn what's down there. No doubt they already know we're here. I'd rather they didn't know why, if possible."

"We'll be careful." She checked her watch. "We should get ready for dinner."

* * * * *

Amused, Richard watched while Aidan slipped to Antonio's maitre d' that the Duke of Leinster was dining with friends. The resulting service and fine food made the night a treat for all—even for Creek, who'd tried his best to have pizza and root beer delivered to the house so he could stay in and study the *Kincora's* drill stem reports.

Hours later, as the contented diners departed the restaurant, Richard spotted Catherine Dolliver sitting at a table near the door. She was reading and didn't seem to notice him. He told Neil he'd be right along.

Neil's sharp eyes hunted the room. He must have seen the attractive blonde. His expression remained neutral, however. He went outside.

Richard approached the table. Catherine looked up and smiled. "Richard Gale. What a delightful surprise."

"Codswallop! What the bloody hell are you doing here? And don't say having dinner."

"But I *am* having dinner. I'm attached to the English Embassy now. I come up here to shop. Antonio's is one of my favorite places."

"Then I'll be on my way and let you enjoy it."

She snagged his arm as he turned. "Can't you stay and chat? What are *you* doing here?"

"Visiting. How long have you been with the embassy?"

"Oh, a while now. I like it. Easy duty, lots of parties."

"You're lying through your teeth, Catherine." He ran a knuckle over her cheek. "Don't involve my people in the games you're playing, or I'll personally wring your beautiful neck."

He left her to her dinner.

* * * * *

Back at the house, Talty herded everyone—minus Creek, who'd disappeared to review reports—into the den for after-dinner drinks. She'd just switched on the fireplace when Liam and Maura stopped by. Kevin came with them, holding hands with a honey-haired pixie he introduced as Nancy. They settled on various sofas and chairs.

Nick sat beside Samantha. "Hey, you guys are okay. I have to admit, I was nervous about meeting royalty."

"Reports of our regality are greatly overstated," Liam said with a genial shrug. "We'll go anywhere there's beer."

Aidan sat alone. "That fire is casting a spell. Tell us a story, Li."

Samantha sat back, ready for entertainment. "You tell stories, Liam?"

Neil caught Talty's hand and pulled her beside him on the loveseat. Supposedly playacting, Talty snuggled against him, enjoying the press of his thigh against hers.

He bent his head and pecked her mouth. "Liam visits the schools and tells the old stories to the children. If I were there, I'd sit with them and listen."

Talty knew the look of delight on her brother's face well: he had an audience and would give them his best.

"All right," Liam said. "Since you're all military folk here... Front to front twelve warriors stood before me ready to fight. Not one remains of the lot of them that I did not leave slaughtered. The Morrigan flings her long red hair over her back and urges us into battle. Terrible are the wounds on the corpses she washes in the river."

Liam told mesmerizing tales of the shape-changing Morrigan, the battle goddess who appeared to warriors in the guise of a raven, a young woman, an old hag, or a cow.

"Her heart flamed with love for the warriors. She helped them in their battles if they returned her love, but if they spurned her, she hindered them through enchantment, stealing their power by drinking blood from their very hearts. And woe unto those who fled the battle. The Morrigan would hunt the cowards down—and she always caught what she hunted.

"She swooped over the battlefield as a huge black raven, spurring the warriors on beneath a rain of fire and blood that fell from blazing clouds created by her sorcery. They saw her perched on the shields of those who would die, and heard her battle cry, a cry louder than the screams of a thousand men."

Like children around a midnight campfire, Liam's audience—even those who'd heard the tale before—sat transfixed.

Talty closed her eyes and imagined a gleaming black gunship swooping down, raining fire and blood.

CHAPTER TWENTY-FOUR

Little Bugs

In his role as Ard Laoch, Peadar worked out a live-fire practice schedule with the Defense Forces and the Department of Marine Resources. Once the rest of the helicopter's weaponry arrived, he would isolate the Air Corps' usual training area, a three-mile radius of uninhabited islands off the north coast, for air-to-ground firing exercises. Naval vessels would enforce the exclusion zone to keep unwanted eyes from observing the gunship's capabilities.

Neil and Dan spent the morning familiarizing themselves with the glistening black gunship. That afternoon they were taking her up. Peadar and Talty were going along to observe. They waited in the cabin.

Savoring the rich scent of leather, Peadar admired the galley and the entertainment consoles beside the divans. "So much stuff, Tal. The kingdom will think your father frivolous, treating himself to such a toy. I can't picture weapons on her, she's so elegant. The Morrigan. A fine name for the poor thing."

"It fits. When the rest of her gear arrives, she'll be able to change into battle mode"—Talty snapped her fingers—"just like that."

Admiring his beloved niece, Peadar sat back and wondered how he might ease the hardship of what he was about to do. He could think of nothing but to plunge into it and trust in her inner strength.

"Roger is ready to move. We old fellas are at odds over it."

"At odds? Why? Don't we want him to move?"

"Kieran is worried that the missiles aren't here yet. Your father is just plain worried."

"I was about to tell you. Ryota called today. Those Akuma missiles will be here soon. I'll tell Kieran if you like. Now, what's worrying my father?" She sounded confident enough to solve all the world's problems, this Banfian who'd trounced Vikings and wild lions.

"He and Kieran are debating whether to put a nail in Roger's tires or let him come. I presented a third option, but Brian has forbidden it. I still think it's a good idea. I'd like your advice before I decide to press harder for it."

"Advice from me?" Humor shone in her eyes. "All right, let's hear it."

Peadar kissed her hand. "I'm sorry for this, Tal, but if I'm going to gamble with the security of Ireland, I must know the odds. I need more insight into Roger's character. You looked into his eyes when he hurt you. I want to know what you saw. You once told me he was cold and business-like about…what he was doing, until you tried to fight him off."

The color faded from her cheeks. Her hand slid from his. "Yes. He was detached. Bored, almost, until I hit him. It was hard. I was hurt and I couldn't move, but I tried." She looked up at Peadar. A haunted look replaced the humor in her eyes. "I tried hard, Uncle Peadar," she whispered, childlike.

"I know you did, darlin'. And he changed when you hit him, didn't he?"

Her eyes closed. Her lips pressed into a thin pink line. She was back there, reliving it. Peadar squeezed her trembling hands.

Blinking back tears, she nodded. "It wasn't a gradual change. When I tried to fight him, it was like someone flipped a switch. He turned into a frenzied maniac." She shook her head. "That's all I remember."

"It's all I need. You moithered the little gobshite, and he couldn't deal with it. It's one of his better character flaws, one we can exploit."

"How?"

"What if we were to hit Roger's weapons cache, not to stop him, but to spur him on? Would he attack sooner? Or would he run and hide until he could rebuild his stores?"

She answered with a smile. "He'd attack as fast as a fiddler's elbow. And if we wiped out his munitions stores and damaged his ships, he'd have that much less power. We could control the invasion better."

Peadar approved of her reasoning. "My thought exactly. If I'm right, we'll only need one of your Akuma missiles. I'll lobby for it, and we'll have you home before you know it."

Her grin faded. "I'm concerned about Richard and the others getting caught in all of this. I think I should resign from ISF."

Peadar considered that. "It might be a good idea. Talk to Uncle Jack or Liam. Have them put some legalese in writing for you."

The arrival of Neil and Dan put an end to the planning session. The eager pilots said hello and slipped into the cockpit to start their checklists.

Aidan, who would monitor the aircraft's progress from the newly completed hangar, jumped aboard to see them off. "We should have special Morrigan flight suits. Something with appropriate insignia on the shoulder patches, like ravens with gore hanging from their beaks."

Aidan's clowning had Peadar chuckling, not for what Aidan had said, but for his obvious effort to fraternize. Still, Peadar liked the idea of the suits, if not the insignia. "Call Supply and Services at Curragh Camp, Aidan. Get flight suits for the crew. Black, if they have them."

"For me too," Talty said. "A medium size will do."

Aidan grinned. "My pleasure, Lady Cousin. They'll surely have the gory raven patches in stock."

Soon the chopper lifted off and headed south over Dublin Bay. Peadar eyed the familiar Irish coastline and silently reaffirmed his Fian vow that no one would steal it from the people of Ireland. "It's so quiet in here. I can hardly believe I'm in a helicopter."

Talty handed him a bottle of mineral water. "The cabin is soundproofed. We have noise suppression as well, to impede acoustical detection systems."

"And turret-mounted cannons." He twisted the top from the bottle. "I've often wished for one of those in Dublin traffic. This is great fun."

Her eyes turned hard. "The fun will end when Roger Wessex comes."

Peadar patted her hand. "No, darlin'. That's when the fun will begin."

* * * * *

Aidan drove down to Curragh Camp the next day. Impeccably attired in his day uniform, he entered the Supply and Services Depot as the garrison's church bell rang noon. A young woman whose nametag read "Lt. Bevin Quinlan" offered a curt "good afternoon, sir" that stirred some vague recollection in him of having met her before.

"Hello, Lieutenant. Major Aidan Dacey. I'm here for the flight suits."

"They're ready, sir. The smaller one is a sleeveless body suit with a jacket rather than a one-piece like the others. We didn't have a one-piece in that size. I can order it, if you like."

Her voice pinpointed her. She had taken over his classes after Jill died, and he'd met with her about it. "The body suit will be fine. You're a talented lady. You can teach *and* run this place."

Bevin lowered her eyes. "I wasn't sure you'd remember me, sir."

"I remember you. In fact, I'd like to discuss those classes some time."

"How about now?" She smiled shyly at him. "It's time for lunch."

He nearly refused, though he saw no reason to hurt her feelings. Besides, he was hungry. "Who could resist the prospect of an elegant meal in our gourmet cafeteria?"

She unhooked a jingling key ring from the wall and locked the door when they left.

* * * * *

Having determined what she could safely tell Bert, Catherine called him from her Dublin flat. "Our watcher at Donegal Airport reports that King Brian's private jet arrived this morning. The entire party, including the ISF people and the king, took a helicopter out to sea almost immediately."

"King Brian went with them?" Bert whistled. "Where were they going?"

"I don't know."

"Find out, Catherine. Have you spoken to Roger and Geoffrey yet?"

"No. I'll call them next."

"Be vague, as always. Call me if anything comes up." He ended the call.

Catherine poured herself a drink. She was juggling too many things.

* * * * *

While in Tokyo, Talty had flown with many helicopter pilots. Neil's flying and his smooth landing on the *Kincora*'s helideck in the pitching North Atlantic impressed her.

So did the *Kincora*. She remembered her father's first descriptions of the big drill ships and his determination to use them to meet the kingdom's energy needs. Now he owned one.

Brushing her wind-whipped ponytail from her face, she descended the stairs with Brian and her ISF friends to a conference room. Brian pumped Captain O'Connor's hand and greeted the senior crewmembers and geologists assembled for the rapidly convened meeting.

One of the geologists who'd first discovered the bizarre bacteria, a no-nonsense lady named Holly, took notes while Creek explained the drill stem tests he required. She set her pen down when he finished. "What are you looking for? You have our reports. The site failed because of some unknown bacteria in the oil reservoirs. Every hydrocarbon sample tested was loaded with them, and they were immune to all the standard treatments. They literally ate up the pipes and left behind a residue worse than any contaminant."

Creek slapped his knee and whooped. "And that residue is exactly what we're looking for. Bless those little bugs! They're metabolizing lutanium. Now, how soon can we get that drill down there?"

* * * * *

After a long and lavish shipboard dinner, Neil catnapped in the cabin he shared with Aidan. At twenty-two hundred hours the alarms on their watches woke them.

"I'm off to shoot some snooker," Aidan said as he tied his shoes. "Have you spent any time with Talty since we've been aboard, or are you too busy being a Ranger?"

Neil took his jacket from the metal locker. "If your father's opinion is any indication what the rest of the family will think... Forget it, Aidan."

"My father thought you were taking advantage of the girl. He'll change his mind fast once he knows you're thinking marriage." Aidan slapped his hand over his chest. "'Lady, you have aimed the dart that rankles in my ruined heart.' You can't escape, Neil. I'm going to dance at your wedding. Now be a man and speak to Talty."

Swallowing the lump in his throat, Neil zipped up his jacket. "I don't even know where she is on this behemoth."

"She said she was going to that fancy observation deck. Maybe she thought I'd tell you."

"I doubt that."

"All right. Do what you like. Will you come up to watch the playoffs?"

"Yes. I have to stop by the radio room first and report to my father."

Aidan went off to his snooker game. Steeling himself, Neil ventured up to the observation deck.

* * * * *

So high above the ocean, Talty felt as if she were floating in the darkened observation deck. The full moon lit the ocean for miles. She half expected mystical creatures to burst through the surface of the sparkling sea.

Behind her, the glass door opened. Despite her understanding with Neil, she prayed he'd come to see her. He must know she was here. She'd told enough people where she was going.

Yellow-white hair glowed in a patch of moonlight. The newcomer wasn't Neil.

Though disappointed, she put a smile in her greeting. "Howya, Barry. Not watching the game?"

Barry Malone stiffened, but relaxed when he recognized her. "Hey there, Talty. I didn't think anyone was here. Sorry if I'm intruding."

"Not at all. Did you come up to see the moon?"

"Not really. I had other plans, but the lady preferred Colonel Martin's company. Rory says it's my own fault for not keeping a sprig of mint in my left-hand pocket."

Talty laughed. "Well, it's a lovely night anyway."

Barry moved closer. "Are you waiting for someone?"

"No. Just stealing a quiet moment, like yourself."

"I'll leave you to it, then."

"I was just leaving," she fibbed. "I've been up here a while."

"You're a good girl to tell a lie so's a poor, suffering soul can enjoy the moonlight." He brought her hand to his lips.

"See you later, Barry." She kissed his cheek and left.

* * * * *

Miffed that Neil was ignoring her, Talty sat with her father in a quiet corner of the rec room sipping white wine. Beside them, the pool table sat idle. No cards shuffled, no darts flew. Riveted to the big screen television, the Rangers and off-duty crewmen cheered and taunted and heckled the teams playing the hurling finals.

Brian enjoyed a rare second glass of ale. "How do you like our *Kincora?*" he asked with one eye on the hurling match.

"It's a floating city, Dad. I found my way to the lab and talked to the geologists. They're brilliant—and one of them has a crush on Creek."

Across the room, Creek and Holly chatted over their beer. At the table behind them, a group of roustabouts gestured and shouted at the television.

The biggest of them was scowling at Neil.

CHAPTER TWENTY-FIVE

Turning Up the Heat

The sun had set by the time Neil dropped the bags on the hall rug. The lights were on, yet the place seemed deserted. Tomorrow he'd drive Talty to Malahide so she could help her ISF friends locate a suitable research facility. He missed her already.

She hung their jackets in the closet. "You did a fine job these last few days, Neil. I'm proud of you."

"We had precious cargo to look after."

She smiled at that. "I enjoyed talking with my father. Neither of us had much else to do, with you and your lads looking after things."

"I hope you don't think I was avoiding you. I wasn't."

"Of course not."

She didn't sound convinced. He traipsed into the kitchen after her, watching while she filled the kettle and set it on the stove to boil.

"I wasn't avoiding you," he repeated. "In fact, I went looking for you last night up on that glass deck. For the illusion of the romance and all."

"I must have left before you got there."

"No, you were there, but you were... Barry was with you. I didn't want to intrude, so I left." Seething at the image of her kissing Barry's cheek, he slipped his hands in his pockets and looked away.

"Neil Boru, you're a big dope! Barry is a fine fella, but he's only a friend. He didn't even know I was there when he came in." She folded her arms beneath her breasts, unaware she'd framed a picture for him to admire.

"You don't think Barry found out you were there and went after you? We fellas can be devious, y'know."

"It wouldn't matter. I like Barry, but not like that."

The kettle came to a boil. Neil reached behind her and shut off the gas. His arm brushed her waist. He couldn't bear anymore.

...be a man and speak to Talty...

"Is there someone you'd rather be with than me? You don't have to stay here if you don't want to."

Angry color suffused her cheeks. "What are you saying, Neil? Is this a diplomatic way of asking me to leave? I'm starting to suspect I've worn out my welcome here."

"What have I done or said to make you think that?"

"It's what you *don't* say. I can't help wondering how you really feel about my being here. I think sometimes it's hard for you."

He wanted to shove her, spar with her, anything but this maddening nonsense. Recalling again how she'd kissed Barry's cheek, he moved in on her, pleased by the puzzled look in her eyes. "Then maybe it's time to tell you how I really feel. You think it's hard for me? You're right, it is. Sometimes I don't think I can stand it anymore."

"What? I'm leaving, Neil. Now."

"No, you're not. Not yet." He stepped even closer. "I don't mind you being here. It's no hardship to hold hands with you, or to pretend to kiss you. The hardship is not being able to kiss you the way I really want."

A well-aimed thigh press pinned her safely against the stove. He swooped and slid his lips over hers, kissing her well, creating little kisses within his kiss, telling her everything words couldn't say. Before he released her, she'd have no doubt that he loved her in a most uncousinly way. Damn Kieran anyway. It was none of his business.

When he finally released her, her beautiful Boru eyes looked up at him as they never had before. He braced himself for a slap.

"Don't expect me to apologize for kissing you so," he said.

"Apologize? Oh, Neily. I've dreamed of you kissing me so."

Was he really hearing this? Understanding rushed over him. He caught her in a hug and squeezed her tight. "You're as big an idiot as I am, aren't you?" He squeezed again. "Aren't you?"

She laughed and flung her arms around his neck. He kissed her again, and then again, until at last she snuggled against his chest.

"Neil. Neil. I love saying your name." Suddenly she pushed him away. "What are we doing? This isn't right, Neil. You said so yourself."

And there it was. The familiar jumble of voices droned in his head:

Talk to the girl, Neil.

It would be a sad day if you took advantage of the girl.

Truth in our Hearts, Strength in our Arms, Dedication to our Promise.

One haunting chant overcame the others: *Truth in our Hearts.*

He took her hand and brought her to the living room. They sat on the couch, she looking dazed, he staring at the flameless fireplace, unsure how to start and dreading the outcome.

"I love you, Tal. More than I ever thought I could love anyone. Somewhere in there"—he ran his fingers over her heart—"I think you've always known it. When you finally came home for good, I was going to speak to you, but I don't think I can wait until then."

"Speak about what? What—"

His fingers pressed her lips. "I think we can obtain a dispensation to be married. If we decide it's something we want, I'll speak to Uncle Jack."

"You want to marry...me?"

He smiled. "What do you think I've been talking about?"

"But...but you can have any girl you want!"

He tapped her chin. "Can I?"

"What will the family say? I can't think, Neil!"

He glanced at the end table, bare since the lamp had broken during his scuffle with Kieran. "Could you at least pretend you've thought it over before you say no, so you won't kill me?"

"I'm not saying no. I'm not saying anything. I'm so confused. I thought you didn't want me here anymore. And now—"

"You're wrong about that. I've said so."

"Am I? One day you were giving me jewels, and we were dancing and happy. The next you were hardly speaking to me. Why? What did I do? Was it because of what happened between you and Kieran? You'd better tell me, Neil Boru!"

Her fierce glare nearly made him laugh. "If we're to clear things up, I suppose I'll have to. Kieran had an idea in his head that I was bedding you, and I got angry about it."

"Why on earth would he think that?"

"Because we were dancing and happy, I suppose. He got me wondering if the rest of the family might be thinking the same thing. I was afraid to touch you after that."

"I see."

"Now *that* was wrong, and I'm sorry for it. But Tal, I could court you for real. They've given us a perfect excuse to be together. Think how much fun it would be to pretend we're pretending. We can talk all we like."

"Oh." She tugged the front of his shirt. "Talk."

"Don't think I wouldn't like to take you upstairs right now, girl."

She gasped at the lusty suggestion. He kissed her for a few delicious moments. "I can't think if you're going to kiss me like that," she said.

Neither could Neil. Wary of the pulsing in his jeans, he stood. "There's time enough. Before we start any serious cuddling, you're going to be mine, right and proper."

"I've always been yours, Neil. Didn't you know?"

The intoxicating words stunned him. He smiled and shook his head. "I don't think we should wait till tomorrow. I think I'd better take you to Malahide tonight."

* * * * *

St. Stephen's Green seemed deserted at such an early hour. From behind a rhododendron, Kieran watched Bert Benson curse the threatening sky and plant his lanky frame on a park bench.

Tipping his Donegal cap, Kieran crossed the path to the bench. "How's things at Hoy's Neck, Bert?"

Bert moved his umbrella so Kieran could sit. "Lord Roger has arms and vessels enough to carry out his invasion. Are you sure you really want this, Commander?"

"As long as we can keep Roger's plans on hold until after Prince Liam's wedding. The people Roger thinks are his followers will help us knock him flat on his duff, and we'll have him. We'll put him away for a long time. That should make Geoffrey happy, and your lads won't have so many simmering pots to watch."

The reluctance in Bert's demeanor contradicted his nodding assent. "I know we've agreed to this, but it's my job to prevent things like insurrections. I should pull the plug now. I'm starting to suspect that Geoffrey has his own reasons for allowing Roger his treason."

A soft rain began to fall. Bert glanced at his umbrella, though he didn't touch it.

"What agenda, Bert?"

"If Geoffrey claims no knowledge of Roger's plans, he'll come up trumps and have the oil wells that were part of Princess Taillte's dowry sooner than the World Court could adjudicate the matter. If he rids himself of Roger in the process, all the better."

"What does John think of it?"

"That's another pair of shoes. As far as we know, John knows nothing about it. He's a simple man, you know. Wouldn't say boo to a goose. There's something else. We've learned that ISF has chartered the *Kincora*. They've gone out to the Fargan Trough. Geoffrey wants to know why."

Kieran had to offer something in return. That was how it worked, though he had no intention of revealing the lutanium expedition. "Some science thing. Ocean biology. It has nothing to do with Geoffrey. I'm sure your people are watching it for you."

"They are. Well, I expect we've done all we can for today."

The men rose and shook hands. Bert turned down the path. He hadn't taken two steps when the rain fell in torrents. Cursing loudly, he opened his umbrella and trotted away.

Kieran turned up his collar and smiled. After his time in Africa, he'd never minded the rain.

* * * * *

A pharmaceutical company had recently vacated the brick building Creek selected for his new lab. Located in Swords, a town north of Dublin, the building was near both Malahide and the Dublin Airport. Its parking area was large enough to land the helicopters that were soon delivering the staff and equipment Creek had ordered from Fort Pinard.

Stopping by in the midst of the move-in frenzy to take Samantha shopping for things for her new office, Talty parked well away from the bustling movers. She strolled through the front door, straight into a forest of pallets and crates. With fumes from paint and cleaning fluid stinging her eyes, she tried to decide how to get around the maze of boxed equipment.

Angry shouts resounded from a nearby room. "What's that thing doing here? It's probably ruined, and we don't even need it. Who brought the damned thing here?"

Recognizing Creek's voice, she hurried into a small office and found the grumpy scientist cursing before a tall, half-opened crate. The Peregrine Portal was inside.

Its presence in Ireland alarmed her. "Why did they send that?"

Creek wheeled toward her and smiled. "Don't worry, little lady. I'll fix it up as good as new and send it right back."

Talty didn't care if he ever fixed the thing. She left him shouting for his staff and took the elevator to Samantha's office.

* * * * *

Later that evening, Neil treated Talty to dinner at an exclusive restaurant. Their hands touched often, and they didn't care who saw. A blessedness akin to magic protected them.

Afterwards, they strolled through St. Stephen's Green. Neil's arm slipped around Talty's shoulder. They came to a stand of rhododendrons, and he drew her in and kissed her.

She pulled his hips against hers. "Let's go home and do it right."

The familiar warning whispered in his ear. "We're supposed to be talking things over, darlin'. We haven't done much talking"—his finger brushed her lip—"y'know?"

"We don't need to talk. I understand you well."

"And I love you well. I don't want it spoiled by talk of incest."

"When does it turn to incest? Aren't we already guilty just by holding hands? Some fella giving us a piece of paper will make it all right?"

Her logic joined forces with his yearning, weakening his resolve. If they were careful, who'd know? They left the rhododendrons to find a taxi. As Neil raised a branch to let Talty pass, he gawked in disbelief.

Talty gasped. She'd seen Kieran too.

Seen *them*. Transfixed, they watched their kinsman embrace a woman who wasn't Breege. He kissed her cheek, and when she turned and left him, Neil recognized the woman he'd seen at Antonio's the night he'd taken Talty's friends to dinner.

"That woman was in Antonio's," Talty whispered.

"You're an observant girl, love. Richard stopped to speak to her."

"Get out! What's going on, Neil? Who is she?"

He lowered the branch. "I don't know, but we're going to find out."

They caught Kieran at the taxi stand. "Hey, Kieran," Neil called. "We're about to grab a cab ourselves. Come back to my place for a nightcap."

He seemed surprised to see them. "Thanks, but I have to get home."

Talty seized his arm. "We insist." She pulled him to the nearest cab.

He offered no resistance.

✳ ✳ ✳ ✳ ✳

Neil hung the coats in the hall closet. Talty wore her public mask, though he guessed she felt as he did: both relieved and disappointed that their tryst had been foiled.

The half-smile on Kieran's face betrayed not guilt, but knowledge that a time of reckoning was at hand. "I don't suppose you kidnappers have any food. I was on my way home to dinner when you shanghaied me off the very streets of Dublin, and I'm hungry."

"Come out to the kitchen," Talty said. "I'll see what we have."

While she rustled through the refrigerator and cupboards, Neil poured Kieran a glass of wine. "I'm not sure we can deal with a tarnished image of you, old fella."

Kieran accepted the wine and took a hefty swallow. "It's a grave responsibility we old fellas have, leading exemplary lives for our progeny."

Talty served him a reheated dinner of tarragon chicken, scalloped potatoes, and casseroled vegetables. "Eat before you disappear before our eyes from starvation." Her tone held no humor.

He grunted and picked up his fork. "So we're down to it."

"Yes." She pulled her chair closer. "We're down to it. Who was she, Kieran? How is she connected to both you and Richard?"

"Her name is Catherine Dolliver. She's with MI6, but she's been in my back pocket for years."

Somehow, Neil wasn't surprised. "Even so," he said, "you were a little tender with her, don't you think?"

"What would you do, Casanova? The woman is coming undone. All I did was offer a little encouragement. You want to condemn me for it?"

"No. Go on."

Kieran swallowed a piece of chicken before he continued. "Her uncle was Jerome Dolliver, the reason I got the Medal for Gallantry."

"He was in North Africa with you?"

"Yes, Tal. His unit was there when mine was. We were helping oversee a cease-fire and monitor POW exchanges. Not bad duty. The worst of it was the heat."

Another swallow. Kieran refilled his wineglass. He seemed relieved to be telling the story. "We were stationed near a village called Oulad Qalil. My good friend Joe Rafferty, who was—still is—a crackerjack cook, infiltrated the kitchen and managed to fix us some proper meals. When word got round about Joe's cooking, the officers of all the English-speaking troops would come by for dinner now and again. We passed our off-duty time playing cards and such.

"One night we were playing cribbage with some English lads who came for Joe's tea. We heard gunshots in the desert. The cease-fire had been broken. Then, out of nowhere, rounds of mortar fire starting hitting our post like the devil. We never did find out if we were deliberate targets or just got caught in accidental crossfire, but it didn't matter when everything began to blow apart. We scrambled for our lives. Before we got far, a wall came down on three of our boys. An English lad helped Joe and me pull them out. We got them down to the bunkers. I'll tell you, we were shaking."

"You never talked about it much," Neil said.

"No." Kieran sampled the potatoes and reached for the salt grinder. "We hero types don't like anyone to know how terrified we can be. Anyway, we joked with Joe that someone didn't like his cooking. Then it got quiet. I thought we were all right, and I said I was going to take one last look around. I went back up, and that's when I heard Jerome.

"He was trapped, and hurt, and then those rounds started pelting us

251

again. I was scared to death, but I managed to kick away a concrete block or two and pull him out. I got him to the door. A shell hit the spot where we'd been only seconds before. The place exploded. That's when I got this." He rubbed the scar on his cheek. "I threw him over my shoulder, and we got the hell out of there."

"And he was grateful," Talty said. "You kept in touch?"

"We did, for a few months. Then years went by before I heard from him again." He peered into his wineglass, as if the whole tale were replaying itself in its contents. "Jerome's brother Evan was the gunnery officer on the HMS *Coulter*. You've heard about the *Coulter*?"

"The English vessel that claimed Fargan." Neil flinched at Kieran's sudden fury.

"Call it what it was, Neil! They stole the fuckin' thing! Evan Dolliver witnessed—actually participated in—the massacre of the crew of the *Fancy Annie*, the fishing trawler that disappeared a day or so before."

"Massacre?"

"Yes, Talty. Evan was with the boarding party that detained the *Fancy Annie*. He told Jerome it wasn't supposed to happen. Things got out of hand. Someone panicked, and shots were fired. Evan couldn't live with the guilt that he'd killed innocent men. He wrote it all down in a letter and gave it to Jerome before he hanged himself."

Shock contorted Talty's face. "How awful!"

Kieran nodded. "Evan asked Jerome to give me the letter, but Jerome thought that might be treason. He didn't want trouble on his family. But he called and asked me to meet him. He was sick and couldn't travel himself. I went to Cornwall to see him, and he told me the story. Gave me a copy of the letter. He died soon after."

Neil asked who had the original.

"Evan's daughter, Catherine. She was working for MI6 by then. Jerome told her everything Evan told him and made her promise to contact me. For her part, Catherine vowed to bring Geoffrey down for causing her father's death, as she saw it."

"She set herself an impossible task," said Neil.

Kieran's head shook in disagreement. "She didn't think so. Jerome and Catherine were among those who thought Geoffrey was abusing his position as regent."

"Do Catherine's superiors knew about her dealings with you?"

"No, Tal. Even my good friend Bert Benson, who's helping us with Roger's invasion scheme, has no idea Catherine and I know each other."

"Who does know?"

"Besides myself, only Brian and Peadar. It's the treason thing again. The English could charge Catherine with treason if they learn she's been feeding us information all this time. But if I have my way, the only ones charged with treason will be Roger and his cronies."

"So you were the one who told her we'd be at Antonio's."

"I did, Neily. A blind nudge on my part. Catherine was supposed to find out what ISF is doing here, and I wanted to see how Richard reacted."

"That was stupid," Talty said. "People like Richard nudge back."

"It seems that's exactly what Geoffrey was counting on." Kieran drained his glass. "Catherine told me tonight that Geoffrey once asked Richard if his new officer could look after herself. That's you, love. My guess is, Richard tries as hard we do to keep you out of harm's way. Probably why he asked you to move in with him and this Nick fella." Kieran's smile was double-edged. "And I'm sure he finds, just as we do, that no one can keep you out of trouble."

Red-faced now, Talty snatched the empty wineglass from his hand and carried it to the sink. "What does Geoffrey care about Christy McKenna? Isn't it bad enough I have to be careful because of who I really am?"

Neil wouldn't let her out of his sight now. "Does Geoffrey know about Roger's invasion plans?"

"He does. He's happy to let Roger plot and scheme. At least he knows what the gobshite is up to."

Talty returned to the table and reached for the salt and pepper grinders. "But does he know about our part in it?"

Neatly pouncing, Kieran grabbed her wrists. "Stop worrying, Tal. Geoffrey knows nothing about us. Some of the MI6 people, like Bert, know. They want their rightful king on the throne. They'd just as soon get rid of Roger and Geoffrey both."

"Leaving John," said Neil.

Kieran nodded. "John might not be the brightest of fellows, but from what I hear, he has good intentions." He stood and stretched. "May I please go home now? Be a good lad and call my driver."

"I'll take you home. I'm bringing Talty back to Malahide anyway. We're going out on the *Lady Grania* tomorrow. Liam and Maura want to escape the wedding frenzy for a while, and they've invited Talty's friends."

"Should be a fine day for a cruise," Kieran said. "Thanks for the dinner, Talty. You're a damn fine cook. Even better than Joe." He settled his tweed cap on his head and turned to Neil. "And now you know I'm no more guilty of improper behavior than you are, Neily."

Kieran turned toward the door. Neil tugged Talty's hair and smiled.

CHAPTER TWENTY-SIX

Trouble Brewing

Prince Geoffrey brooded over Fargan all morning. That the troublesome rock might have some worth after all rankled him. If it were true, he meant to reclaim it—and he knew just how to do it.

He invited Roger to lunch. "A pity you couldn't attend Prince Liam's wedding," he said, plucking a roll from a basket. "I had a lovely time."

Roger's manicured fingers picked at the salad. "Why would I attend such a vulgar affair? Look at them, marrying their Crown Prince to the daughter of a common librarian."

"Professor Donovan is chief curator of rare books at Trinity College. Not a member of the nobility, but distinguished enough. Still, the Borus do like consorting with commoners."

"The Borus are an unpedigreed clan of farmers who sprang from a pile of cow manure. I'm sure their tawdry party would have bored me to death."

Geoffrey nearly said that Roger had found ample entertainment at their last tawdry party, but he didn't want to irritate his nephew too much. He needed Roger's help. "Prince Liam's wedding wasn't the gala affair his sister's was, but King Brian put on an elaborate show for someone reported to be experiencing financial difficulties."

"Then your reports are flawed," Roger said, sounding bored.

"No. Something's turned his fortunes around, and I think I know what."

"Is that why you've sent for me?"

Smiling at the kinsman he so disliked, Geoffrey ripped the roll in half. "No, Roger. It's been a while. I've missed you. I thought it would be good for the family image if we dined together. And I want to reassure you that I wholeheartedly support your plan to invade Ireland."

"You're still deluding yourself with that fairy tale?"

"Dearest Roger. I know all about your storage buildings full of weapons, and I want to help." Geoffrey neglected to add that once Roger's plan succeeded, he'd denounce him as a traitor and reveal his part in the murders of Deirdre and Taillte Boru. Roger would be out of the way, and Geoffrey would have both Fargan and the oil wells.

A contemptuous smile crept over Roger's face. He raised his wineglass to his lips. "Your wanting to help wouldn't have anything to do with King Brian's financial recovery, would it?"

"They cheated us out of those oil wells, Roger. They made us give Fargan back." He pounded the table. "I want Fargan! It's mine!"

"Their test wells turned up nothing. Fargan is worthless."

"That's what they led us to believe, but Brian himself went to reopen the well. They're actively mining it, and ISF is involved."

Roger's glass seemed to hang in the air. He set it down. "Why would ISF be interested in mining?"

"ISF is interested in many things. They're up to something, and that something is rightfully ours. We need each other, Roger. I'll gladly back your invasion. What do you require? Funds? More weapons? Attack vessels? Here"—he refilled their wineglasses—"let's drink to our success."

Roger left his wine untouched. "What about John?"

"I'll convince him to abdicate. No need to tear England apart with civil war. We can have the penny and the bun if we unite our endeavors."

Scowling, Roger kicked back his chair. "I don't need an overstuffed slobberchops telling me what to do. And I have no intention of creating a civil war. England will only have one side when I'm done. Mine." Elbowing past a servant who'd entered the room, he huffed out.

Geoffrey pounded the table again. He'd been willing to let Roger live—rotting in prison, of course—after his futile invasion failed. Now he wanted his nephew gone for good.

He decided to play his trump card: an attack on the McKenna girl. Such a move would surely outrage the Irish royals, if not Richard Gale. He'd seen her with Neil Boru at Prince Liam's wedding and noticed the affection the Irish royals bore toward her. Gale—or Neil Boru, it didn't matter which— would surely deal with Roger.

He reached for the telephone.

* * * * *

While Nick scrambled eggs in the kitchen in Malahide, Samantha set the table for three. Brooding over Liam's wedding, Richard stirred sugar into his tea. His guard had gone up when Geoffrey Wessex walked into the wedding reception, and it wouldn't come down.

"That was one heck of a party," Nick said, "and they said they toned it down. Man, I'd like to see how they do it all out. Hey, what's up, Richard? Couldn't sleep in that creepy castle last night?"

"Not at all. I'm delighted the Borus invited us to stay. Clontarf Castle is quite historic." Richard paused to taste his tea. "Neil and Aidan were wearing Fianna pins. I'm wondering how Neil got his back. Did you get it on one of your runs to Mendocino, Nick?"

"No. He probably borrowed someone else's."

"Yes. I'm sure you're right." Forgetting that he'd already done so, Richard stirred more sugar into his tea.

Samantha touched his forehead. "Are you okay?"

"Are you ticked off that Christy stayed at the castle?" Nick asked.

"I must say, it's been some time since anyone fussed over me like this, and Christy's a big girl. She's coming back today isn't she?"

Samantha nodded. "We're going shopping again."

Once breakfast was on the table, the conversation changed to more trivial topics. The Fianna pin still bothered Richard, though. The timing was all wrong. If Neil had given Christy his pin as a pre-engagement gift, they must have been involved while Eric Yamada was alive. Yet Christy had too much integrity to cheat on her husband, Richard would bet on that.

Still, if Neil had been wearing his own Fianna pin at Liam's wedding, where had the pin in Christy's jewelry box come from?

* * * * *

After an enjoyable afternoon of exploring the shops in Swords, Talty and Samantha carried their packages to the car park. As they turned down a side street, a man in a black leather jacket emerged from an alley. Eyeing his buzz cut, unblinking eyes, and beefy hands, Talty instinctively reached for the tanto knife she didn't have.

"Cross the street, Samantha."

Samantha frowned in confusion. "Isn't the car over here?"

Her question delayed the women long enough for the man to block their way. "Hand your purses over, luvvies."

His English accent clinched it. Talty assessed his height, weight, age, and stance. "Get your own purse, mate."

Robbery seemed to have slipped his mind. He flicked a switchblade from a wrist sheath. "Lord Roger sends his regards."

Purse and parcels fell to the ground. Talty lunged. She grabbed his forearm and drove her knee into his back. Spinning the opposite way, she snapped his arm over her thigh. The knife clattered into the gutter.

The man's face twisted in pain. "You broke my arm, you bitch!"

Another man rushed from the alley, hefting a billy club. Samantha screamed a warning. Talty ducked and rolled. The second man tossed the weapon away and bolted down the alley.

Neil's Jaguar screeched to a stop in the parking lot. Neil and Aidan burst from the front doors, Richard and Nick from the back. Neil tore down the alley after the second man. Aidan ran to Talty. Once she assured him she was all right, he ran after Neil. So did Nick.

A gunshot pierced the air. Richard dropped to the ground and dragged Talty behind a parked car. Samantha scooted in beside them.

Talty glanced from behind the car. The first man lay unmoving on the ground heap, a dark red halo flooding the concrete beneath his head.

✳ ✳ ✳ ✳ ✳

Sensing that the second man was somewhere in the alley, Neil approached a metal dumpster and an old chest of drawers. A *thunk* sounded across the alley. Someone had tossed something, though Neil didn't look. His peripheral vision had caught a flash of metal arcing toward him.

He wrenched the second man from his hiding place and smashed him against the dumpster. A knife fell. The man shoved him and ran for the fence. Neil grabbed his collar and had just pulled him down when Aidan and Nick came running.

"Leave off," Neil shouted. "He's mine!"

Neil deflected a vicious blow and landed one of his own. Turning sideways to reduce his exposure, he never stopped moving. His elbows and knees blocked and jabbed. His left fist smashed the man's jaw and slammed him into a trashcan.

Covered with garbage, the second man lay groaning on the ground.

CHAPTER TWENTY-SEVEN

Blurred Lines

A passionate soprano-tenor duet resounded through the gym in the Hoy's Neck command center. Such passages focused Roger when he kickboxed.

When the workout ended, Philip draped a towel over Roger's shoulders and switched the music to an orchestral march. Timing his movements to the beat, Roger puffed his bare-chested physique before the full-length mirror. "I do relish being a catalyst in world events."

Philip opened a bottle of mineral water and set it in Roger's hand. "The idea of invading Ireland is a bit daunting."

"Not for me." Roger swallowed a cool mouthful of water. "Different scenarios for success continually play through my mind. Strategic moves of my own creation. My favorite is to seize the oil wells right off. Meanwhile, half our attack boats will position themselves in the northern part of Dublin Harbor, the other half in the south. We'll have a pincer move that will effectively take the harbor. Our friends in Dublin—I'm thinking you'll lead them, Philip—will already have captured key positions. I'll sail straight in with a fitting escort."

"It sounds simple enough."

"The simplest plans are always best." Roger sank into a chair. "Still, we'll need a diversion. Something to occupy the attention of the Irish while we're maneuvering into position. A funeral would do the trick. It's been years since they've sponsored one."

"Whose?" Philip's eyes widened. "Neil Boru?"

"Yes, Neil Boru." Roger had never forgotten the night Boru attacked him in the hospital lobby. "He'll be the first to go. I'm still working on an accident to eradicate the rest of them."

"You'll want Gordon, I expect."

"No. Gordon was careless when he dispatched that girl. The Irish police suspect him of her murder. We'll hire an independent contractor. There's a nasty scrote in my uncle's employ who owes me a favor. If anything goes wrong, the authorities will trace him back to Geoffrey. For now, we need someone to keep tabs on our friend Neil so we can plan accordingly. Havelock and Poulton are in Killybegs watching the crew of that drill ship. Call them, Philip."

* * * * *

Inside the Fiddler's Dock, a waterfront pub in the port of Killybegs, Havelock and Poulton sat at the table farthest from the blaring jukebox. All afternoon they'd observed members of the *Kincora*'s crew tossing darts and shooting billiards with hard-drinking fishermen. The two Englishmen had spoken to some of them, trying without success to learn why the drill ship had returned to the Fargan Trough—and to ask how often the king's nephew returned to the ship.

They were about to call it a day when a big roustabout came in and sat at the bar. Moody and mean, he called for a pint. Havelock and Poulton sat on either side of him.

"Looks like you need a holiday," Havelock said. "Rough time out?"

The man downed a mouthful of ale and ignored him.

Poulton signaled the barkeep and ordered three pints. "That bad, is it? Lots of activity out there these days, I hear. Helicopters going back and forth all the time. They must keep you hopping, eh?"

When the barkeeper set the glass before him, the roustabout grunted his thanks. "Those muck Rangers keep coming. Them and the Americans."

"We heard about the King's Rangers," Havelock said. "Must be important doings to lure them away from their cozy digs in Dublin."

The man scowled. "They get the prettiest girls, the best quarters."

"We're journalists," Poulton said. "We're writing about offshore oil. Perhaps you could help us. What's your name?"

After a long moment, the man said, "Bernie. Bernie Sheehan. I don't know anything."

Havelock smiled. "Maybe you do. "We hear King Brian's nephew comes to the ship now and then. That he even brought the king once. Maybe you could tell us when he comes again, and when he leaves."

"That Boru muck? Pretty boy. Flies the chopper. Is he in trouble?"

"No. Does he fly out often, Bernie?"

"About once a week."

"The next time he comes, let us know." Havelock handed him a card. "We'll pay you."

Bernie tucked the card away. "How much?"

Poulton drew a wad of bills from his pocket and passed them to the roustabout. "A down payment, Bernie. There'll be more."

Havelock and Poulton left Bernie to his ale.

* * * * *

Richard had no trouble finding Catherine Dolliver's Merrion Square address. He climbed the stairs to the second floor and knocked.

"Who's there?" her nervous voice called from inside the flat.

"Richard Gale."

A crack of light appeared beside the door. Richard heaved it open. Catherine pulled her robe closed and squinted at him. Her hair was a slovenly mess. She reeked of stale whiskey.

Richard clicked the door shut. "You're ruining my image of you, Catherine."

"I'm relaxing."

"After a busy day in Swords with Geoffrey's goons?"

"What do you mean? I've been here all day." She staggered to the kitchen table and collapsed onto a chair. An empty glass and an open bottle rested near her hand.

"Two men tried to hurt one of my officers today. One said Lord Roger sent his regards. What do you know about it?"

Catherine reached for the whiskey. "Nothing. What does it matter? You won't believe anything I tell you."

Richard snatched the bottle and emptied it down the drain. He then yanked Catherine to her feet. "Was it Geoffrey? Does it have anything to do with our meeting in London?" He shook her. "Does it?"

"Stop it! You're hurting me!"

Disgusted, Richard released her. "Am I supposed to become furious now and go after Roger?" He lowered his voice. "Do you really think I'm that stupid?"

"I don't think anything," she whimpered, rubbing her arms. "I just do what they tell me."

Three short knocks sounded from the hall. Catherine bit her lip. "Go into the den and close the door."

Richard had no intention of hiding. Still, he could protect them both better from a concealed position. He drew his pistol and slipped into the adjoining room, leaving the door ajar.

Catherine wiped her eyes and opened the door. Kieran Dacey stepped into the apartment and looked her up and down. "You did well to warn us about the attack on the McKenna girl. She's fine. I wish I could say the same for you, Catherine."

Richard's surprise at seeing Dacey turned to shock. Catherine had warned the Irishman about the attack on Christy? What was going on? Should he come out? Not yet.

"I'm sorry," Catherine said. "I'm so tired."

Kieran sat her down in the living room. "All right, love, it's over. You've done enough. I'm getting you out of it."

"It won't work," she muttered. "They'll find me. And Richard—"

"Richard, is it? Let's go. You wouldn't want him to see you like this, would you?"

"It's too late for that," Richard said from the doorway.

Kieran whirled. He cut short his hair-trigger reach for his gun when he recognized Richard. "Since you're here, be a good lad and help. Find some paper. We need a suicide note."

Catherine's head jerked. "What?"

"A little extreme, don't you think?" Yet Richard obeyed and scanned the room for a notepad. "They'd be looking for a body."

"Not if she jumped from a bridge. The Liffey goes straight to sea. Get dressed, Catherine. Leave everything behind, even your passport. We'll get you another, and anything else you need. Hurry, now."

Hope brightened Catherine's eyes. She bustled to her bedroom.

* * * * *

Despite the early morning hour, the house in Malahide buzzed preparing to spirit Catherine out of Ireland. Neil and his Rangers would fly her to the *Kincora* to await the next ISF run to California. When all was ready, he stole into Talty's room to say good-bye.

"I should come with you," she said.

Loving her tiny pout, he slipped his arms around her waist and kissed her. "Three women would draw attention. We won't have your fierce protection, but I think we'll be all right."

Tomorrow he'd see Uncle Jack about the dispensation. If he found he and Talty could obtain one, he'd lay her down and claim her properly. He kissed her again.

A quick rap at the door and Aidan burst in. "Practicing. That's good. You'll have them all fooled."

"Get out," said Neil.

"All right, I'm leaving, but don't be long, Neily. We're ready to go."

The door closed. One last kiss and Neil followed Aidan downstairs.

* * * * *

Richard helped Catherine into a borrowed raincoat. A few hours of sleep and a shower had done wonders for her. A suitcase, overflowing with cosmetics, clothing, and magazines, sat on the bed.

"Your ladies are most generous to donate their things for me," she said.

"My ladies are the best." He zipped up the suitcase. "How did you get yourself into such a mess?"

"It's a long story. I'll tell you about it on the plane."

"I'm not coming. Christy and I don't usually go on these runs, and we don't want this one to appear unusual. Nick is going, though, and you'll be quite safe with Neil and his men."

"Oh. I see."

Her sad face compelled him to hug her. The kiss that followed had to happen.

Then he said, "We should get downstairs."

* * * * *

Windshield wipers clicking, the Jaguar coasted to the kitchen door. Neil prepared himself for Aidan's inevitable teasing.

Aidan jumped into the passenger seat and wasted no time. "So how long have you and Talty been at it?"

"We're not *at it,* Aidan. We're talking things over."

"Ah, the state of chastitution. Talking but celibate. Talking's good. I've been doing some celibate talking myself lately."

"Talking with who?"

"With *whom.* A girl named Bevin. She taught my classes at the Curragh."

Before Aidan could elaborate, Kieran opened the back door. Neil jumped out to help him settle Catherine and Samantha into the car.

"Richard and Nick will drive with me," Kieran said. "Richard and I will bring the cars back. Who's going with you besides Aidan and Nick?"

"Dan Joyce and Packy Hewitt are meeting us at Baldonnel."

"That should be enough." Kieran lowered his voice. "Straight out and straight back, Neil. Talty's missiles will be here soon."

Talty had told Neil about the plan to attack Hoy's Neck. Worried now about more than Aidan's teasing, Neil put the car in gear and drove away.

* * * * *

Just past sunrise, Richard called Bert about the attack on Christy, omitting

Catherine's part in thwarting it. "Do you know anything about it, Bert?"

Bert's raspy voice sounded distant in Richard's ear. "No. Best guess would be Geoffrey. The two thugs you're describing sound like his. The one that got himself offed probably got it from one of his own chaps to keep him from talking. As for the one they caught, he'll talk when he's ready, I expect."

"That won't be for some time. Neil Boru put him in the hospital."

The click of a cigarette lighter broke the flow of the conversation. "Glad your girl's all right," Bert said. "Appears to be quite a serious affair she's having with Duke Neil. I think they're more than lovers, though."

"What do you mean?"

"We've been wondering why she's been participating in the King's Rangers' training exercises. I suspect they're tapping the knowledge of helicopter weaponry she gained during her time with ISF in Japan."

What? "Well, you're wrong, since conspiring to advance the weaponry of a sovereign nation would be a breach of conduct for an ISF officer."

Bert snickered in his ear. "She couldn't possibly be bamboozling you, could she? Great chatting with you, Richard. Keep in touch, and do try to keep that major of yours out of trouble."

Richard set the phone down. As far as he was concerned, Christy McKenna was already in big trouble.

CHAPTER TWENTY-EIGHT
Boiling Kettles

Later that morning, Talty found Richard sitting at Creek's computer. She asked what he was doing. He reached for his teacup and answered that he was running background checks on Catherine Dolliver and Kieran Dacey to see what they had in common.

"Some sort of professional association, I'm sure." Talty hoped she sounded casual.

"I don't believe MI6 knows of any professional association between them. What would make her ally herself with Kieran Dacey?"

Talty detected an unprofessional concern in Richard's question. Although she sympathized, conflicting loyalties prohibited her from revealing what she knew about Catherine. "Who is she, Richard? How well do you know her?"

"Hardly at all. She works for MI6, and through them, for Prince Geoffrey and his nephew Roger. Apparently she works for Kieran, as well."

"Why are you looking into it? It's not an ISF matter, is it?"

"No, but I'm curious. All this undercover work has shattered her. I want to know what's so important. I also want to know about the clandestine help you've been giving the Boru family with their military exercises."

She grabbed the back of Richard's chair. "What are you talking about?"

"I suspect you know exactly what I'm talking about. You've broken a critical rule, darling, one that could have us both up on charges. What are you doing?"

Too stunned to speak, she said nothing.

Richard, however, had plenty to say. "How do you know Neil Boru isn't playing you for a fool? Or do you offer your professional expertise to any man who smiles at you?"

"That's not fair. Neil's a gentleman. He's good to me."

"Is he? He and his family call the shots, and you jump. I don't understand how a woman of your caliber could let them use you like this. Anyway, it's over. We're returning to California tomorrow. Creek's staff is in place. He doesn't need us anymore."

No! She couldn't leave now. The Akuma missiles were on their way.

"I'm sorry to be such a disappointment to you, Colonel. I'll resign, of course. Effective immediately. You'll have it in writing by this afternoon."

If he answered, she didn't hear him. She was out the door and on her way to Dublin.

*****

At times, Bernie Sheehan hated the drill ship. Except for one or two roustabouts, he had no friends aboard the *Kincora*. The women avoided him. The rest of the crew ignored him.

He enjoyed cleaning the glassed-in drill shack. High above the rest of the ship, he could work alone and pretend he was the driller.

He'd just run his polishing cloth over the glass walls for the fourth time when the helicopter landed. When he saw the King's Ranger jackets, he smiled and gathered his cleaning supplies.

*****

While Neil and Nick checked in with Captain O'Connor, Denis Heard and Rory Doherty escorted the women to *Kincora's* VIP quarters. Heard unlocked the door and returned to his duties; Rory stood guard while Samantha helped Catherine settle in.

"Stay in your room," Samantha told her. "They'll bring your meals. The next time Nick makes a run to California, he'll take you with him."

Catherine smiled and thanked her.

*****

The Rangers always waited in the dining hall for the ISF people. Bernie found them there having lunch. He filled a tray and sat at a corner table. The two redheaded Rangers sitting across the room had come before. Their nametags read Aidan Dacey and Patrick Hewitt. Two black-haired men came in and joined them.

One was Neil Boru. "We're refueled," he said to his pals. "Let's go."

Abandoning his food, Bernie slipped his hand into his pocket and rattled the coins there. He had to walk by the Rangers to leave the room.

Boru looked right at him. "Why, hello, Bernie."

Bernie stomped out. The nearest satellite pay phone was down the hall. He inserted his coins and dialed the number the Englishmen had given him.

*****

As she raced toward Dublin, Talty called her brother at Tara Hall. "I'm glad you're back, Liam. I need your help. I need a letter of resignation delivered to Richard Gale this afternoon."

"It takes months to resign from military service, Tal."

"Not with special circumstances." She recited the wording she wanted.

Two hours later, she'd signed the letter. Liam's assistant dispatched a courier to deliver it into Richard's hands. Feeling pounds lighter, Talty enjoyed a quiet lunch with her brother in his office. For over an hour, they discussed his honeymoon tour of France. He described the house where he and Maura would live and the roses he'd plant for the children they'd have.

At last Talty stood. "I want to tell Uncle Peadar about the resignation letter. Thanks for helping, Li."

She hugged him and went down the hall to Peadar's office. She found her uncle in a heated argument with her father.

"We are *not* going to attack Hoy's Neck!" Brian shouted.

"A well-controlled jab would give us the upper hand," Peadar shouted back.

Brian shouted louder. "It'd be an act of war!"

Talty took a deep breath. "Hi, fellas."

A grin lit Peadar's face. "Talty! Come in. Your father and I are having a friendly chat about those missiles. Do you know when they'll arrive?"

"They should be here tomorrow."

Brian glared. "And we'll keep them for defensive purposes."

Peadar was clearly prepared to dig in his heels. "We'd only need one. No one would ever know where it came from."

"*I'd* know where it came from! No, Peadar. I forbid it."

Peadar's intercom buzzed. His secretary announced a call from Kieran. Peadar took the call. As he listened, he raised his hand over his eyes.

Talty and her father exchanged worried glances.

Then Peadar set the phone down. "A gunman attacked our lads when the helicopter landed at Baldonnel. Neil and Packy Hewitt have been shot."

*****

Richard set the unopened envelope on the kitchen table and cursed. No mark betrayed its origin, yet he suspected that Liam or Kevin, or perhaps even Jack Dacey had helped her with it.

When Nick called about the shootings, Richard forgot the letter and sped to St. Brigit's Hospital. He found a somber scene. Most of the royal family, including King Brian, waited in a sitting area, though Peadar and Kieran were missing. An elderly couple—Packy Hewitt's parents, Richard guessed—sat together, distraught and confused.

Nick drew Richard aside and described how a stranger had stopped Neil and Packy on their way to sign off the duty roster. Neil had managed to tell how Packy saw the gun and pushed him aside, suffering a serious gunshot wound in the process. The gunman squeezed off another shot as Neil smashed his jaw. While Nick and Dan flew Samantha and the injured men to the hospital, Aidan and Kieran seized the gunman.

Richard suspected the interrogation would not be a polite affair. "How bad is Neil?"

"Samantha said the bullet ripped his waist and hit his ribs. He should be okay. Packy might not be so lucky."

"They both need blood," Brian said when Richard asked how he and Nick could help. "Packy and Neil are both A-positive. Our negative Boru blood isn't much good to them."

The statement sounded odd, though before Richard could think why, Christy came in with Aidan. She'd been crying, and Aidan exhibited none of his trademark clowning.

Richard crossed the room to meet them. "Could I have a word with you, Christy? Somewhere private?"

She told Aidan she'd be right back and followed Richard to a vacant room. He closed the door. Mindful of her anguish over Neil, he toned down his intended scolding. "I'm sorry for the argument, darling. I can't and won't accept your resignation."

"I'm sorry too, but it really would be best if you did."

"Not until you tell me why you're involved in Irish military exercises."

"Please, Richard. Let it go."

"You might as well tell me. What are you trying to protect me from?" Her eyes widened. He'd hit on it. "I'll find out, and when I do, I'm going to put you over my knee and give you the spanking you deserve. Until then, you're still a member of the Peregrine Team. I've torn up your letter."

Her cheeks flamed. "I'll write another. I'll write as many as I have to."

"And I'll find some airy-fairy excuse every time. I'll say you didn't enclose the required number of copies or attach the proper questionnaire. I'll find some stop-loss rule to keep you in service for months. You've had your chips, darling. See you at tea time."

Cheered by her withering glare, he left the room.

*****

"What the hell did you say to make her resign?"

Glumly watching Nick bang around the kitchen, Richard sat stirring his tea, cringing each time a cabinet door slammed. Though tempted to confide in Nick, he wouldn't reveal Christy's illegal activities. "I'm really not sure."

"She can't just resign, can she?"

"Anyone can resign, though I've refused her resignation."

"Yeah?" Nick stood lost in thought. "Well, that's good, I guess. Hey, all this strife is making me hungry. How about I fix us some steak and salad for dinner?" He started pulling food from the refrigerator.

"That sounds fine," Richard said, though he wasn't really hungry.

The cork popped from a bottle of burgundy. A frying pan plunked onto the stove. Dishes appeared on the table, salad and vegetables on the counter. Richard didn't care. As he pondered the events of the last two days, his thoughts ricocheted from one piece of the puzzle to another. He sensed they were related somehow, but he couldn't find the thread.

"If she resigned to marry Neil," he said, "I'd agree in a minute."

Nick stood at the sink rinsing a tomato. "I'm not sure Neil's looking to marry her. He's a terrific guy, but he's real proper with her. Maybe they're just friends. Or maybe it's like you said before. Christy reminds him of that cousin who died."

The puzzle fell into place. Richard smacked the table. "I can't believe I've been so blind! Why wouldn't she remind him of his cousin? She *is* his cousin. Christy is Talty Boru!"

Dishtowel in hand, Nick turned from his salad. Worry etched his forehead. "Talty Boru is dead, Richard."

"No, Nick. If I'm right, and I know I am, she's very much alive."

Nick flung the towel down. "Christy's no princess. All the stuff I've seen her do? No way."

"Think about it. It would explain why she married Eric Yamada, a man nearly twice her age. To protect her while she recovered."

"From what?"

"Lutano said she had terrible scars. Whoever did it probably cut her face as well. Now she looks just different enough."

Nick pitched two steaks into the hot skillet. The meat sizzled instantly. "Christy's American, Richard."

"You've heard her speak Japanese, and she picked up some Italian easily enough when you taught her. Learning American English wouldn't take more than a speech coach and some practice."

Richard vaguely heard the doorbell. "The Fianna pin we found after the earthquake? Neil didn't give it to her. It's hers. She's a Fian warrior too. That would explain how she knows the knife throwing and other things she knows. It explains all the hand kissing. It explains everything!"

"This is pretty farfetched, Richard. You're talking about highflying spy stuff with secret identities and everything. How could she do that?"

"Kieran Dacey just did it for Catherine Dolliver. He'd surely do it for the Crown Princess of Ireland."

"And he did," Liam said from the doorway. "The front door was open. I hope you don't mind. Whatever you're cooking smells wonderful, Nick. Got enough for a fella who's had a bad day?"

"Hey, Liam. You bet. Are Neil and Packy okay?" Nick drew three wineglasses from a shelf as he spoke.

"They're doing well enough. Thanks to you lads, they've got more than enough blood. Packy will be there for days, but Neil should be ready to come home tomorrow if they can treat him with that bioaccelerator thing."

For the first time, Richard noticed Liam's hair was the same chestnut brown as Christy's. "Did Christy send you here?"

"No. My father did. If my sister knew what I was about to do, I'd be in hiding forever."

"Your sister."

"Yes, Richard. Your analysis of the situation is quite correct, at least what I heard of it. We thought you'd have figured it out by now. It's a credit to Talty, and to Neil, that you didn't."

Nick shook his head. "Aw, man."

CHAPTER TWENTY-NINE

Unforgiving Strikes

Drugged and angry, Neil sat in his hospital room glaring out at the rain. Why hadn't Talty come to see him?

Peadar sat with him now, fussing over him one minute, offering encouragement the next. "That lutanium is grand stuff. I can't believe the change in you from this morning. Samantha said she'd be by later for one last treatment."

Neil rubbed his side. "Kieran said Roger Wessex did this to create a diversion for his invasion. What are you doing about it?"

"Sending the Morrigan to take out his key storehouse."

Neil's medicated mind slowly processed the statement. "Uncle Brian will allow it?"

"Brian ordered it, right after he heard you and Packy were hurt."

Packy. He'd saved Neil's life, and now the doctors were fighting to save his. It was like Talty all over again. "Will Talty come by?"

Peadar said she had, and Neil had been sleeping. She couldn't stay. She had to help Dan and the others prepare for the strike. Each time Neil thought of Dan, Rory, and Barry flying off on a mission without him—and of Talty abandoning him to be with them—his rage grew.

"She'll come by when she can." Peadar stood and mussed Neil's hair. "I should be getting back to the Hall."

Needing someone to hold onto, Neil clutched his father's hand and squeezed tight. He wondered how Talty had dealt with months of living in a hospital when he'd lost all patience by the end of two days.

Talty. Gone off.

With Barry Malone.

Brian still disapproved of the plan. If they were found out, Ireland would be guilty of aggression against a sovereign nation. He studied the warriors in Peadar's conference room: Peadar and Kieran, Dan, Rory, and Barry, and his precious daughter, whose fingers danced over the keys of Peadar's laptop computer. None of them would betray the attack.

Enlarged aerial photographs of Hoy's Neck hung on the wall. Peadar had drawn a red mark across the entrance to the cove where Roger's attack vessels anchored. Calm as a fine June day, he swallowed a mouthful of water and continued his presentation.

"Catherine Dolliver gave us extensive information about the layout of the place. Our target"—he pointed to an outbuilding—"houses explosives and ammunition. We already know our timing, fuel consumption, and stealth capability from our previous flyovers, all of which went undetected. We should have no trouble trapping the boats in the cove. Talty?"

Earlier she'd impressed Brian by explaining the objectives, distance, aircraft capabilities, weather, and time frames she'd entered into a mission planning program. The computer would calculate different scenarios, including possible glitches, for the planned sortie.

She looked up from the laptop now. "If we hit the outbuilding from the north, the debris will block the entrance to the cove. Roger will lose most of his firepower, and his gunboats will be stranded."

Rory sat tossing his luck penny from hand to hand. "Won't they know it was us?"

"Good military investigators could put the pieces together," Peadar answered, "though that would take time. Most likely, Roger will think some sort of accident set off his explosives. Even if he suspects us, he'll never prove it."

"Neil will be sorry to miss the party," said Dan. "How is he?"

Peadar replied that he'd seen Neil an hour before. "He's better, though nowhere near able to join you. You'll manage all right without him. I have great confidence in you lads."

Talty glanced up from the laptop. "The lads and me. I'm going too."

Kieran's right eyebrow shot up. "You can't. You're an ISF officer."

"Haven't you heard? I resigned. I'm free and clear to go."

"There's no need for you to come," Barry said.

"Thank you for your concern, gentlemen, but I see no warnings on this laptop that say we're attempting anything that might exceed the Morrigan's capabilities. And it recommends that an observer go along to corroborate what the video equipment records. I'm coming. I won't interfere."

Brian assented by changing the subject. "What about backup? Where is *Alastrina?*"

"Off Galway," Peadar said. "On fishery patrol. She'd never get here in time. I have two search and rescue helicopters standing by, though I doubt we'll need them. We'll be in and out, and our invaders will have that much less firepower when they finally decide to come."

Talty snapped the computer shut. "As long as Roger Wessex comes with them when they do."

* * * * *

Ted had delivered fresh apparel to Neil's hospital room to replace the clothes the trauma team had cut away. The garments hung in the tiny closet, ready to aid Neil's escape.

Furious at the insult of the attack, sick from the pain medication, and worried about Packy, Neil paced his hospital room like a caged tiger. His side hurt worse than any pain he'd ever known.

When Samantha failed to come by with the bioaccelerator on time, he dressed, slipped out of the hospital, and took a taxi to Clontarf. Driven by anger and adrenaline, he stalked up the path to the helipad. The Morrigan's rotors were already spinning.

Barry stepped from the shadows. His yellow-white hair glowed in the twilight. "Hey, Neil. What are you doing here? Everyone's looking for you."

"I'm coming with you."

"You can't. You're hurt."

"I'm fine."

"I'm glad, but your father says you're to stay behind."

Neil turned toward the helipad. Barry blocked the path.

"All right, Barry. You've done your duty, now get out of my way."

"No, Neil. I can't let you go. You aren't fit—"

A savage punch to Barry's ribs forced him to his knees.

"Now you can tell my father it wasn't your fault." Neil wanted to be sorry for hitting his friend, but he wasn't. He started again for the Morrigan.

Aidan stood in his way. "Here you are, Neil. You've got everyone in an uproar. What happened to Barry?"

Gasping for breath, Barry struggled to his feet. "Nothing happened. I fell, is all. Neil came by to see us off and wish us luck. You'll see he gets back to the hospital, won't you?"

Aidan turned furious eyes on Neil. "I will, Barry."

"Wish us luck, Neil?" When Neil didn't answer, Barry hobbled toward the helicopter.

Neil had to say it: "Good luck, Barry."

Barry waved and boarded the Morrigan. The gunship lifted off, leaving Neil glowering after it and Aidan glowering at Neil.

"Come on, Neil. Let's get you back before anyone finds out what an eejit you are."

"I should be going with them. I trained for it!"

"What would happen if you passed out flying? You'd kill them all. And what were you thinking, hitting Barry? Are you gone in the head as well? Ah, look at you. Eejit!"

Blood soaked through Neil's jacket. His swing at Barry had torn open his side. At first, he hadn't noticed. Now the pain made him dizzy.

Firmly gripping Neil's arm, Aidan guided him down the path. "It's back to the hospital for you. And please try not to bleed all over my car!"

* * * * *

After Aidan delivered Neil to St. Brigit's, he checked his messages. He returned Bevin Quinlan's call first, and was soon on his way to Curragh Camp to see her.

Bevin kept sparse quarters. Still, something Aidan couldn't put his finger on made them distinctly feminine. When she made tea for him, he cupped the hot mug in his hands, grasping at the tiny comfort.

"Tell me about yourself, Bevin. What brought you to Curragh Camp?"

"It's not a big thing. My people are fishermen. I wanted something different."

Her creamy voice mesmerized him. He set his tea down, wanting nothing more than to listen. "Nothing wrong with fishermen. Fishing is one of our biggest industries."

"No, nothing wrong, except I couldn't bear to be one of those women who waits for her menfolk to come home from sea. I watched a broken heart kill my grandmother, and my mother's eyes were haunted all the time, wondering if my father would come back each time he went out. He always has, but her own father's death affected her like that."

"I'm sorry. Your grandfather died at sea?"

"Yes. He owned a trawler called the *Fancy Annie*. He and his crew disappeared one Christmas. We never learned what happened to them."

The small peace Aidan had found disappeared. He reached across the table and stroked Bevin's hand. Incongruous thoughts of how their children might look drifted through his mind. Would they have her dark hair or his gingertop?

Her soft flesh stirred him. Her blue eyes ambushed him, and he fell willingly into the trap. He drew her from her chair, and when he kissed her, his intended gentleness gave way to voracious need, as if he could hide from his troubling memories by burying himself in her.

She led him to her bedroom. For a precious while, he forgot about Jill. He brushed aside the image of Neil lying hurt on the ground at Baldonnel. He gave no thought at all to the Morrigan's impending mission.

* * * * *

From her leather swivel chair in the cabin, Talty watched flight engineer Rory patrol the Morrigan up and down. Twice he assured her that his luck penny sat snug in his pocket, a much more important factor than having the infrared suppression and radar jammers in working order.

Just beyond the cabin in the helicopter's nose, Barry occupied the gunner's seat and monitored his instrument panel. Colorful images danced on the radar screen.

"Target detected," he reported.

"Get us a lock," Dan said from the pilot's seat behind him.

"Locked on target."

Thrilled to be aboard the aircraft she'd worked so hard to obtain, Talty sat quietly, as she'd promised. The men with her were trained professionals, and she felt secure in their hands.

Then Dan flabbergasted her. "We fire on your order, Your Highness."

The grin in his voice made her smile. She wondered if anyone was in the building. Then the phantoms of Grannie Deirdre and Jill Scanlon flashed before her eyes.

She gripped the arms of her seat. "Fire!"

Barry's hand moved. A missile burst from the Morrigan's firing rail. Dan's expert touch reduced the recoil from the launch. "Less than two minutes. Buckle in, ma'am. You too, Rory."

Talty obeyed. Rory sat opposite her and clicked his seat belt around his waist. A moment later, the skies lit up. The roar of the initial blast came next. A series of secondary explosions followed as the outbuilding's combustive contents caught fire.

"Game ball!" Rory shouted. "This is a lot more fun than the simulator."

"It is," agreed Barry. "Do you think the wee bang went unbeknownst?"

Dan skillfully countered the rocking. "Someone will surely notice."

"Ah, they'll just think it's the fuckin' Aurora Borealis," said Rory, who then gasped and cast a horrified look at Talty. "Oh, excuse me, ma'am!"

Smiling fondly at him, she relaxed her grip on the chair. "Good job, lads. Let's take some pictures and go home."

CHAPTER THIRTY

Owning Up

Even in the dim light of Dolly O'Brien's Alehouse, Barry Malone's yellow-white hair was easy to spot. Burning with shame for hitting his friend, Neil ran his tongue over dry lips and crossed the room. "Hey, Barry. Thanks for meeting me."

Barry clasped Neil's hand. "Howya, Neil. Sit and I'll buy you a jar." He signaled the waitress, who quickly returned with two pints of dark ale.

Feeling unworthy, Neil touched his glass to Barry's. Both men tasted the foamy brew.

"I can't look you in the eye, Barry. I'm sorry for what happened. I don't know what was wrong with me."

"Wrong? You'd only been shot and drugged, and maybe a little agitated at not being able to help us rattle those scuts. I knew you weren't yourself, Neil. Don't give it a thought. We can tolerate a little aberrant behavior from you now and then."

"It's no excuse. I'm sorry. Maybe you'd want to hit me back."

"That'd make everything fine, would it? I'll tell you what. Instead of hitting you, I'll ask you something that's better than a good punch. Did it have anything to do with Talty?"

Better than a good punch, indeed. Neil thought he had been more discreet with his green-eyed guarding of Talty.

Barry downed more beer and licked a dollop of foam from his upper lip. "When I heard she was going to marry King Thomas, I realized what an eejit I was to think I could court a princess. Still, it had crossed my mind."

"I thought it had. So what's stopping you now?"

"As it turns out, the girl doesn't return my affection. I've been waiting to

275

see if you'd claim her yourself, cousin or no. If you don't do something about it soon, I might give you a good run for all that money of yours."

Neil toyed with his glass. "I have talked with her a little."

"A little? Don't wait too long, Neil. If I really put my mind to it, she won't be able to resist me. And if I don't get her, someone else will."

Neil grinned. "You might be right. After tonight, Packy might start courting her."

Barry laughed. "Isn't that the gospel truth? What a sight! I wish I'd had a camera. She got him good, didn't she?"

Earlier that evening, Neil brought Talty to the hospital to visit Packy. They found Dan, Barry, and Rory in his room. Seeing them had surprised her, though it hadn't stopped her.

"I hope you don't mind my stopping by, Packy. I wanted to thank you. I can't think what would've happened to Neil if you hadn't...well, I have no cause to keep this anymore." She retrieved the case containing Packy's knife from her purse and handed it to him. "You're a fine warrior in my mind, Packy Hewitt."

Packy opened the case. "Thank you, ma'am. It's thoughtful of you, surely." He stared at the knife as if it were a well-loved girl. "Un-fuckin'-believable!"

Sudden shouts brought Neil back to the pub. Rory and Dan had come in. They pulled up chairs. The good-natured bang of Barry's empty glass on the table summoned the waitress. In the company of good friends, Neil relaxed and heard all about Hoy's Neck.

First thing in the morning, he would visit Uncle Jack.

✶ ✶ ✶ ✶ ✶

Roger kicked a blackened chunk of debris and cursed the fingers of smoke rising from the smoldering rubble. "Who would have the audacity to attack me, Philip? Who would dare to undermine my efforts? Geoffrey? That miserable sycophant, Bert Benson? Who?"

"Calm down, Roger. You're going to blow a fuse. MI6 wouldn't attack us. They'd simply monitor our activities. What about the Irish?"

"How could they have known about it? Even if they had, what could they have done? No, Philip. They don't have the capability—or the nerve—to launch such an attack."

"What about Catherine? We haven't heard from her for days."

Roger considered and quickly dismissed Catherine's possible involvement. "No. She knows better than to cross me. It had to be Geoffrey. I'm amazed he'd divert his attention from a leg of mutton long enough, but this would be his way of repaying me for refusing to help him uncover Ireland's activities in the Fargan Trough." He turned his back on the ruins and tramped toward the outbuilding that had just become his new command center.

Philip followed. "We'll find out about Fargan soon ourselves. Havelock and Poulton signed on with the catering company that services the *Kincora*."

"Have them take care of that roustabout. I don't want any loose ends."

"It's all arranged."

"Excellent. Despite this setback, we'll move forward with our plans. I'll show Geoffrey what real power is. When we're done, we'll control all of Ireland, including Fargan."

Philip opened the door to the building, stepping aside so Roger could enter. "But all this debris has our attack boats trapped."

"As we speak, Andrew is compiling a list of available vessels sufficient for our purposes. We'll take the oil wells first. Then we'll capture the Irish royals and arrange that accident we discussed. They'll disappear, just like the Romanovs."

"What do you need me to do?"

Roger inspected the cramped, crude building. It would suffice for now. He reminded himself he wouldn't be in it long. Soon enough he'd move into John's apartments at Southwick Castle.

"Killing Neil Boru failed as a diversion. We must try again. Get into Tara Hall, Philip. Find a Boru—any Boru—and kill him."

* * * * *

Neil knocked on the door of Uncle Jack's study. Jack's voice boomed from inside: "Is that you, Neil? Come in, lad. Come in!"

Swallowing the lump in his throat, Neil entered the book-lined room and shook hands with his granduncle. "Thanks for seeing me, Uncle Jack."

Affection glowed in Jack's eyes, so dark beneath his snowy brows. His smile set a web of wrinkles dancing over his face. "Why wouldn't I see you, lad? How's the side? Does the rain bother it?"

"Not a bit. It's all healed."

"That's what I wanted to hear." Jack caught him in a tight hug. "You put the heart crosswise in us, getting yourself hurt like that."

They sat in red armchairs between the hearth and a tea cart laden with pastries. Lazy fingers of steam wafted from the spout of a silver teapot.

Jack settled into his seat. "How can I help you, Neily?"

"I need some advice. I'm thinking of marrying."

"Ah. We can update the antenuptial agreement we drew up for you the last time."

"I wish it were that simple. I don't know if I can marry the girl. We're...related."

Jack rubbed his chin. "I see. Talty, is it?"

Counting his drumming heartbeats, Neil paused before blurting it out: "I love her, Uncle Jack. I don't mean to cause trouble, but I have to know if I can marry her."

Jack pulled out his briar pipe and turned it in his hands. His thoughts had gone off somewhere, not unusual for the pensive man. Still, Neil wished he'd stop fiddling with the old jaw-warmer and give him an answer.

"Have you spoken to her about it, Neily?"

"I—yes. We've been talking it over."

Jack stared hard at him. "Have you done more than talk?"

Neil pulled his collar from his neck. "I haven't bedded her, if that's what you mean."

"That's exactly what I mean." Still rolling the pipe in his hands, Jack walked to the window and gazed outside. It seemed an eternity before he turned around. "All right, here it is. Ireland's Law of Consanguinity states that marriage between first cousins is incestuous and void. The law defines incest as the willful cohabitation with, intermarriage with, or engaging in sexual intercourse with any relative within the prohibited degrees of kinship. You and Talty are first cousins. Not blood cousins, but adoptive cousins, which is just as binding, and puts your relationship within the prohibited degrees of kinship."

Neil shrank into the chair. What had he been thinking?

Jack slid the pipe away and strolled to the tea cart. The recitation continued. "Irish law treats an adopted person as if he or she were born the natural child of the adoptive parents. In your case, we only need to refer to your adoptive father, since Peggy is your natural mother. The legal and familial status conferred on you by the adoption is the same as if you'd been born Peadar's natural son. Any relative of any degree under an adoptive relationship is considered a blood relative."

It all sounded so perverted. What must Jack think of him?

"Don't despair, Neily. The Law of Consanguinity allows three exemptions for marriage between first cousins. One of them might suit you. Tea?"

Neil shook his head. "What are they?"

"Scones. Very good. Have one."

"Not scones! Exemptions! What are the exemptions?"

Jack chuckled gently. Despite Neil's refusal, he poured two mugs of tea and set one in Neil's trembling hand. "The first allows marriage between first cousins to consolidate herds of cattle for the strength and prosperity of the clan."

"I see," Neil said, though he really didn't.

"The second allowance is to close the ranks of the family for the protection of the clan, or for the defense of the very kingdom itself. That comes down from the times when various peoples attempted to invade Ireland. It must have some use, though it isn't helping us today."

Jack's use of the word "us" encouraged Neil.

"The third permits marriage between first cousins in a case of incurable love."

"That's it? Just that?"

"Just that. You shouldn't have any trouble convincing a panel of Brehons. I suspect we can find several witnesses who can attest to this incurable love. A few of us have noticed."

Neil let out a sigh of relief. "Then we can do it?"

Jack's right eyebrow shot up the same way Kieran's did. "Do what? You aren't going to get a dispensation to have an affair. Still, a girl needs to know a fella can take care of her. Especially a Boru girl. The women who marry into the family call the Boru men rascals. They don't know about the female of the species." He chuckled again. "I do. I'm not telling you to keep your hands off the girl, but for heaven's sake, be discreet. Incest would be a monstrous charge to level at the king's daughter. Discretion, Neil."

Neil reached for a scone and rejoiced.

* * * * *

While Neil visited Jack, Talty returned to Malahide. She found Richard and Samantha in the kitchen devouring Nick's bacon and eggs. Her arrival caused an awkward silence at first.

Then Samantha spoke. "Hey, Christy. How's Neil?"

"Much better, thanks to you."

Nick pointed to the table. "Have some breakfast, Major Lady."

"Thanks, but I'm not staying. And I'm not a major anymore."

Richard poured tea for her anyway. "Once a major, always a major." His amused tone annoyed her. "I haven't accepted your resignation, and so you were still an ISF officer when you and your friends blew up Hoy's Neck."

Talty fought to keep her public face in place. She wished Neil had come with her. "I heard about that. Some sort of accident."

"Codswallop! What's going on?"

"You can't get involved, Richard."

"We already are. We're involved with the lutanium processing. You're involved with the Borus. The Borus are involved with the lutanium processing. Do you see?" He pushed the teacup toward her. "We've been in sticky situations before. If we work together, we can help. No one has to know a thing."

"Yeah," Nick said. "We're a team. We take care of each other."

"Exactly." Richard stood and took her hands. "After all we've been through together, you have no business excluding us, Your Highness."

Astounded, Talty staggered to the nearest chair and plopped down.

Nick reached into his shirt pocket and handed her the small gold box that held her Fianna pin. "We sent to California for this. We thought you'd like to have it here."

As her fingers closed around the box, tears of tremendous relief filled her eyes. When she spoke again, her American accent was gone. "I worked so hard for this, but I've only worn it once. At the pinning ceremony. Someday I'll wear it again."

"Listen to you talk Irish, girl!" Samantha produced a tissue from somewhere.

Talty smiled her thanks. Sniffling and dabbing at her eyes, she gazed at her friends. "How did you know?"

"Richard figured it out," said Nick. "He's a smart guy."

"Oh? If he's so smart, then he knows the English authorities can charge him with treason if he gets involved."

"Your accent is delightful, darling. Your father sent an emissary to explain how you've been helping your family lure Roger Wessex into a trap. We know all about your marriage to Eric Yamada, and your staged romance with Neil."

"Hey, Neil is a terrific actor." Nick set an overflowing plate before her. "If anyone ever asked me to fake being in love with my cousin, I could never pull it off."

For now, Talty's relationship with Neil would remain private. "Neil would do anything for me. He's my Shivail."

"Is that Irish for cousin?"

"No, Samantha. A Shivail is a protector, part of a circle of Shivaillta. The king is in the center of the circle. Each Shivail protects someone closer to the king than he or she is. My Uncle Peadar is my father's Shivail, and Kieran is his. Well, Kieran is everyone's, I suppose. He's the Ard Shivail, after all."

"That's Irish for High Protector?"

She nodded at Richard. "The idea is, if the king doesn't have to worry about protecting himself, he's free to look after the kingdom."

"We'll protect you too," said Nick. "Stay with us. Neil must want his place to himself."

Not since we've been kissing so deadly. "Maybe. I'll talk to him."

Richard said that Nick would leave soon to fly Creek to California for a conference. "Catherine will go with them. I'm seeing her off. When I return, we'll discuss your resignation. All right?"

Talty beamed at her new circle of Shivaillta. "All right."

* * * * *

After leaving Uncle Jack, Neil drove to Garrymuir. He went straight to the gardens, correctly suspecting his father would be outside on such a fine morning. Peadar stood near the roses, squinting out over the sea. He smiled when he saw Neil. Neil hoped the smile would still be there when he left. He knew, had always known, of Peadar's deep affection for Talty.

"Neil! How are you feeling?"

"I'm fine. No need to worry. Could we walk a bit, Dad?"

They strolled through rows of perfect roses. Neil inhaled the heady, perfumed air and began before he lost his nerve. "I spoke to Uncle Jack this morning. We discussed my adoptive status."

"Did you? Thinking of changing it?"

"No, Dad. I'm thinking about having another go at marriage."

Peadar cast a sideways glance at Neil. "Do I know the young lady?"

This was it. Peadar would be the touchstone for the way the rest of the family would react. If he didn't approve, Neil could never have Talty. He wouldn't do that to her.

"Yes. Talty."

Peadar stopped like a man trapped in the path of a train. "Talty?"

Neil swallowed. "Yes, sir."

"Talty your cousin?"

"Yes."

"Talty my niece?"

When Neil nodded, his bear of a father grabbed him beneath his arms and lifted him off the ground. "By God, boy, it took you long enough. I thought you'd never get the rocks out of your head!"

Neil laughed, first with relief, and then at the absurdity of Peadar lifting him as if he were a child. "Put me down, Dad. For a minute, I thought you were going to throw me over the wall."

"You didn't really think I'd be angry, did you? By God, Talty!" Peadar's grin turned sly. "You'll never have a dull moment with that one, Neily. What

281

does she think about it?"

"I only spoke to her recently. As you said before, I'm a little slow."

They started walking again. "Jack said you could obtain a proper dispensation?"

"He thinks so. I hope Uncle Brian will agree. I already know what Kieran thinks."

"Don't worry about Kieran. These things have a way of working out." Peadar stopped at a stone bench and asked Neil to sit with him. "You know that I married your mother after your father died. Did you know that I courted her before she ever met Frank Christopher?"

"No, I didn't. You were—"

"Lovers, Neily. It's no secret. When I told my father I wanted to marry Peggy, he said he'd arranged for me to marry Claudia Wessex. I wasn't happy, but I believed it was my duty to do as my father asked. I told your mother it was over between us. I made light of my feelings for her. Why hurt her, I thought. It seems I didn't turn up the day they distributed sense. Later, I learned I'd hurt her more than I knew by letting her think she meant nothing to me.

"My father's death postponed the marriage to Claudia Wessex. Then Peggy and Frank announced they were expecting you. As you know, Frank died in a car accident soon after. I asked Brian's advice. He said, 'Do you still love her?' When I said yes, he said, 'Then go and get the girl, and don't come home without her.' I did, though it took some doing to convince her to marry me. Since then, I've done all I can to make it up to her."

"I had no idea, Dad. What happened with Lady Claudia?"

"Brian had Uncle Jack smooth things over. Geoffrey married her to some other fella."

"It's a great story."

Peadar clapped Neil's back. "You and Talty have your own story. And I'm telling you now, lad: go and get the girl, and don't come home without her!"

CHAPTER THIRTY-ONE

Truth In Our Hearts

The constant clang of the *Kincora*'s big drill drowned out Richard's knock. He wondered if Catherine had heard it. Then the lock clicked. The door opened.

He stepped into the cabin and closed it behind him. "Hello, Catherine."

She looked rested and beautiful, more like she had when he'd first met her. "Richard! Am I to leave this rolling monster at last?"

"Yes. An ISF jet is waiting at Donegal Airport. Do you have much to pack?"

"No. Two minutes to toss my mink coat into a bag should do it."

He smiled, pleased to find her in better spirits. "You should eat something before leaving on such a long flight. I'll take you to the cafeteria for a proper meal."

"I'm really not hungry right now," she said. "Let's stay here for a while."

Having no objection to working up an appetite, he locked the cabin door.

* * * * *

Talty's reach to hang her jacket in the closet accentuated her tantalizing backside. The sight aroused Neil, as it always did, but today he didn't tear his gaze away. He kissed her when she turned.

She didn't kiss him back. "Richard and the others know who I am."

"I suppose they had to find out sooner or later. Who told them?"

"It seems my father had a hand in it. He could have warned me."

A worrisome thought crossed Neil's mind. "Do they know about the Morrigan?"

"Richard guessed I was involved with the Hoy's Neck incident, though I

283

didn't admit to anything." She sighed and smiled wearily. "It's all right. They aren't angry. In fact, they were more upset that I didn't tell them what was going on. Then they said that I should live in Malahide from now on and stay out of your way."

"That's funny, Tal." He stepped closer and kissed her again, enticed by her perfume, loving the feel of her arms snaking around his neck. "Mmm. Pretending to pretend to pretend." He kissed her yet again, but broke away when she pressed against him. "Easy, girl. Remember, we're supposed to be talking things over."

"What?" She bulldozed past him. "You big dope! I'm tired of talking! And I'm done with your teasing. If this is your idea of love, I want no part of it. Go away, Talty. Come home, Talty. Not now, Talty. I'm tired of your codology, and I'm sick of stupid rules!"

Suppressing a smile, he reached for her.

She backed away. "I know why you don't want to bed me. You don't know how! All bluster is what you are, Neil Boru. I'm going back to Malahide." She reached for the closet door.

He spun her around and forced her against the wall, savoring the intimacy of each small collision. "You think I don't know how? We can't have that now, can we?"

A string of well-timed pecks smothered her retort. He locked his lips on hers, and then her arms were back around his neck. "Don't tease me, Neil. I can't bear it anymore."

"Let's see what you *can* bear." He ran his thumb over her lips and squeezed them into the pout he loved so well, peppering her mouth with quick little kisses that left her panting. Breathing hard himself, he pulled her to the living room. A click of the remote control infused the room with firelight. He tossed some sofa pillows on the rug and held out his hand. "Come here to me."

She sank beside him. He kissed her again, kneading her breasts as he did. When she whimpered, he eased her onto the pillows. The trust in her beautiful Boru eyes stirred a rumble of doubt in him.

It would be a sad day if you took advantage of the girl...

I'm not telling you to keep your hands off the girl...

Truth in our Hearts...

He lay beside her and pressed his lips to the hollow of her throat. Such small touches were tiny sins, yet committing them with Talty aroused him more than the most wanton spree of sin he'd ever known. Settling himself over her, he wedged his knee between her thighs. She moaned, and he thrust her thighs apart, wriggling onto her until he found the right fit. He dug his elbows into the rug and rocked her against the floor in a gentle rhythm that left them both breathless.

He rolled off her and pulled her to her feet. Arms hopelessly entwined, they made their dreamy way upstairs. The ritual of undressing began.

Talty's fingers shook as she undid the buttons on her blouse. She paused before removing it. "I wish I could be prettier for you, Neil."

His shirt landed on a chair. "Because you have scars?" His fingers brushed the welts on her chest. "These are reminders that we nearly lost you. I, for one, am glad you're here." He patted his newly healed side. "Would you not want me if I had scars?"

She smiled and shook her head. He eased her out of her blouse and camisole and tossed them on the chair. His fingers sank into her bare breasts, and he squeezed her doubts away.

"I'm not looking at scars now," he whispered. "I'm looking at a half-dressed woman. I want the rest of her."

"And I want the rest of you."

In seconds, the chair overflowed with their clothing. He nudged her onto the bed and barraged her with kisses from brow to breast. "I'm going to claim you, babe. Are you sure this is what you want?"

"I've always been sure"—she nipped his lower lip—"and didn't I tell you I'm tired of talking?"

Neil ventured the sweetest claim he'd ever known. At times, he rode Talty hard, and then he cuddled her tenderly. He loved her again and again, until they collapsed in a contented tangle.

When their hearts finally stopped pounding, he tugged her hair. "What do you think, Tal? Do I know how?"

She snuggled against him. "I never doubted you, Neil. I never could."

He stretched his arm over her, guarding her and needing her. "I love you, Tal."

* * * * *

Havelock and Poulton's weeklong stint as part of the catering staff had revealed nothing about the *Kincora*'s mission. They'd only learned that the drills were active and the scientists were happy with whatever they'd reaped from the ocean bed.

Though ship's rules prohibited the catering staff from roaming the *Kincora*, Lord Roger's agents moved about freely, hiding their features beneath the hard hats and safety glasses they'd stolen from the permanent crew. This job had been so easy.

They'd learned that Operations Manager Denis Heard monitored the channels of the ship's security cameras from his office. He locked his door when he left, and no one else viewed the monitor screens while he was gone.

Bernie Sheehan's habits were just as predictable as Heard's. Starting tomorrow, Bernie would be on shore leave for a week. It had to be now.

* * * * *

Richard considered dallying in Catherine's cabin until departure time. Already exhausted from their stateroom sport, he decided it would be best if they went out. "We have an hour, darling. How about a walk? I don't know my way around the ship well, but I do know how to get to the observation deck."

"I'd love it."

They climbed a flight of metal stairs to the glassed-in deck. Nearly as high as the drill shack, the enclosure provided a panoramic view of the surrounding ocean. Tiny ships speckled the western horizon. Black clouds roiled in the sky to the south.

Catherine leaned against him. He nuzzled her soft blond hair. "You'll be safe in Mendocino. I'll visit you when I can."

Movement above him caught his eye. Someone was leaving the drill shack.

* * * * *

Bernie Sheehan had been polishing windows in the drill shack. Soon it would be time for lunch. Utility pail in hand, he closed the door and crossed the rocking, windblown bridge that spanned a quarter of the ship.

He didn't know the two men waiting at the end of the bridge. It was too early for the next driller, and Bernie was in no trouble that he could think of—unless someone had found out about his deal with the Englishmen.

When he approached the men, one of them removed his hard hat and safety glasses. "Hey there, Bernie. We wanted to thank you for your help."

Bernie smiled. Then he saw the gun. "What do you mucks think—"

The gunshot blew his throat away. The blast was lost in the clang of the drills. Havelock heaved the roustabout over the railing. Poulton tossed the pistol and utility pail after him. They scrambled down the metal stairs to cut through the observation deck.

* * * * *

Richard drew his gun and stepped in front of Catherine.

"Richard, what's wrong?"

The door burst open. Richard recognized the two men in the doorway.

Havelock flashed an ugly grin. "Why, it's former Agent Gale. We hear you're working for them royal bogtrotters now. Too bad. You'll be out of work when Lord Roger offs them all. And Miss Dolliver. We've been looking for you."

Richard raised his pistol. "Go downstairs, Catherine."

Havelock jerked out his gun. Richard muscled Catherine against the wall and dove sideways. Havelock dropped to his knees. Both men fired.

Screaming, Havelock dropped to the deck. Poulton swung his pistol toward Richard. Richard's bullet ripped through Poulton's heart.

Gut shot, Havelock spat through bloody teeth. "It doesn't matter. Lord Roger will wipe out those mick friends of yours, and you can't get there in time to stop it."

Catherine snatched Havelock's gun from the floor and shot him.

CHAPTER THIRTY-TWO

Strength In Our Arms

By dawn, the veil of fog in the Irish Sea had swirled away to Scotland. Southeast of the Isle of Man, HMS *Cecilia*, a Verburg class patrol vessel with missile capability, drew eight small craft to her like a maritime magnet.

From *Cecilia's* bridge, Staff Admiral Andrew Mayne monitored the congregating boats on the radar screen. Roger swaggered nearby in his olive-green dress uniform. Competent, brilliant even, he was Andrew's ideal of a conquering hero.

Roger caught his reflection in a sunny window and smoothed his hair. "Whoever destroyed our setup at Hoy's Neck did us a tremendous favor. The training boats joining us this morning can deploy faster and maneuver into areas inaccessible to larger ships. They'll snare the oil wells quite effectively. Well done, Andrew."

The ease of it had astounded Andrew. He attributed his success to the clout of seniority and a certain amount of skill. They didn't have as much firepower as he would have liked, but the plan was solid. "When the boats from Bristol arrive, we'll be ready. Philip should be in Dublin by now."

Roger glanced at his watch. "He'll be there soon. Our men will get him into Tara Hall. The Irish royals congregate in that mausoleum every day. Once we have them, we have Ireland. No one can stop us now."

Roger would gather the Borus and somehow annihilate them. Nothing personal. The triumphant lion must eliminate the cubs to establish dominion over his new pride.

Andrew himself would seize the Irish oil wells. He'd taken care to man the support vessels with commanders and crews he believed were loyal to Roger. Soon he'd join the small flotilla and lead his training boats south.

Before he left for Claudia's charity auction, John intended to question his uncle about Hoy's Neck. John had heard rumors that the incident was no accident, as the press reported, but an attack on his kingdom. Geoffrey wouldn't brush him aside this time.

John raised his hand to knock on Geoffrey's door. Two familiar voices inside stopped him. His uncle sounded furious, though Chief Benson seemed quite calm.

"What's going on, Benson?" Geoffrey shouted. "Where is Catherine? She's been out of touch for a week."

"I don't know where Catherine is, sir. We found a handwritten note at her Dublin flat. I fear she might have taken her own life."

"Well, that's inconsiderate of her, I must say. She was my best pipeline to Roger. What happened at Hoy's Neck?"

John strained to listen.

"Most likely an accident," Benson said. "Something must have set off the munitions Lord Roger amassed there. A rogue environmental group or some other left wingers could be responsible, though I know of no organization in this part of the world outside of our own military that commands such firepower."

"Roger's boats might be sitting useless at Hoy's Neck, but it seems he's obtained others. Who ordered our university training vessels to gather in the Irish Sea for a naval exercise?"

"Admiral Mayne, sir, and it's no exercise. The *Cecilia* is escorting the training vessels to Dublin. Mayne has no idea that *Cecilia*'s captain and first officer both report to me."

Benson's words shocked John. How could a man he'd trusted and confided in be helping Geoffrey and Roger invade Ireland?

"Get out, Benson," Geoffrey bellowed. "See that Roger gets whatever he needs. I'll be damned if I'll give up those wells a second time."

Benson left the room and closed the door. He jumped when John barred his way, and then he relaxed. "Good morning, Your Majesty."

"Is it? I'm appalled, Mr. Benson. How can you be a party to such a horrific action?"

"If we can go somewhere private, sir, I'll explain."

Back at John's apartments, Benson revealed that he'd already warned King Brian about the pending invasion, and that few officers and crewmembers aboard the pseudo attack vessels were devoted to Roger's cause. "There are those who believe in Roger. However, over time we've created the illusion of much larger numbers to give him the confidence to go forward with the attack."

"But why? And where have all these men come from?"

"From your own loyal military, sir. There's no danger of a real invasion, though when Roger arrives in Dublin, King Brian intends to have a word with him about the deaths of his mother and daughter."

John sighed. "I suspected he was involved. What will they do to him?"

"They'll charge him with murder, sir. Something they can only do on Irish soil."

As the words sank in, John slowly grinned. "They *want* Roger to invade! You've been conspiring with the Irish all along! Very naughty, Mr. Benson. I'm impressed. I shouldn't have doubted you, though from now on, you'll let me know what you're up to."

"My pleasure, sir. As for Lord Roger, he's your cousin. We can stop it, if you wish."

"So he can return to depose me? No, Mr. Benson. I might try to keep the Irish from executing Roger, but an extended prison stay should make him rethink his nasty ambitions."

"Many of us have been working hard to preserve the integrity of your throne, sir."

The declaration pleased John. "Will you be joining Roger's bash?"

"Yes, right after I leave Southwick Castle. I'm to join Commander Dacey on the Irish flagship, though for the sake of all the English men and women who've worked to support you, it must appear that the Irish acted alone to foil the invasion."

John held out his hand. "Good luck, Bert. And thank you."

✳ ✳ ✳ ✳ ✳

Long before Prince Geoffrey or Bert Benson knew that Roger had launched his invasion, LÉ *Alastrina*'s long-range radar detected the tiny armada gathering in the Irish Sea. Her captain alerted Peadar, who'd wasted no time summoning Brian and Kieran to his conference room at Tara Hall.

Chuckles interspersed his rundown. "We moithered the little cockalorum all right. For a while I was worried he'd sit back and lick his wounds after we blocked the entrance to Hoy's Neck. He's on his way though, and with a much weaker force than if we hadn't."

"When will he get here?" Brian asked.

"Just in time for tea. Benson reports he's headed straight for Tara Hall. He also said that Roger has men in Dublin preparing to take the family hostage. I want everyone to go to Clontarf Castle. They'll be safe there. We'll say you want them at a special dinner. It wouldn't be the first time you

290

ordered a spur-of-the-moment event."

Brian agreed. "What about the oil wells? Will Roger try for them?"

"Yes," Kieran said. "He's targeting the four named in Talty's dowry."

Peadar pointed to one of several maps on the wall. "Those wells are here in Quad 42, a hundred miles off the coast between Wicklow and Arklow. 42/19-1, 6, 12 and 22. I have a contingent of Rangers on each well. To all appearances, they're conducting search and rescue exercises, but anyone who attacks those wells will receive a nasty surprise."

Nodding, Brian rubbed his beard. "Where is *Alastrina* now?"

"On her way from Belfast," Peadar said. "I've ordered her converted to combat mode. She'll easily counter any hostility, and Kieran will be there to keep an eye on things."

Kieran rose. "I should be going. How am I getting to the ship, Peadar?"

"Drive up to Clontarf. The Morrigan will get you to the *Alastrina* just as she rounds Howth Head."

"Find Neil for me. I don't like flying with anyone but him, but don't tell him I said so."

Kieran's smile sent a shudder through Peadar. The English attack vessels were under the command of Staff Admiral Andrew Mayne—the same Andrew Mayne who'd been in command of the HMS *Coulter* when the *Fancy Annie* vanished.

Peadar almost felt sorry for Admiral Mayne.

* * * * *

Kevin never expected such balmy weather when he obtained permission to take the *Lady Grania* for an afternoon cruise. Nancy was with him, and Maura had come along to enjoy the rare sunshine. They planned to meet Liam, who was telling stories at a local school, at the Clontarf Yacht Club for dinner. They had just passed Lambay Island when Peadar's call directing them to get to Clontarf Castle right away cut the outing short.

* * * * *

Wearing only a silk kimono, Talty stood in Neil's living room watching the sunrise over the Wicklow Mountains. The promise of the blossoming summer day touched her soul even as the pleasant chafing Neil's loving had left behind had her pondering his wonderfully demanding intimacies.

She thought of Gayth MacDunlan, whose passion for her had been dampened by terrible grief. He had gently gone through the motions, but he hadn't really made love to her—and she'd never known it until last night.

Neil had been masterful. Despite Imi's marriage lessons, Talty had been the one who hadn't known what to do. Someday she'd confess her lack of experience. Neil wouldn't mind teaching her, she thought with a smile. When she felt more confident, she'd tell him about the marriage lessons and teach him some tricks of her own. They were training partners after all.

And then he was hugging her from behind, nuzzling her ear. "I had a beautiful girl under me last night who told me she was loving it. I'm wondering how she feels in the light of day."

She melted in his arms. They were on their way back upstairs when the telephone rang.

By the end of the brief call, Neil was frowning. "My father needs us at Clontarf. Roger Wessex is on his way."

"What, now?" Both irritated and alarmed, Talty sought strength in the mundane. "What will I wear? I have no Ranger gear, and I can't wear my ISF uniform."

"You girls never have anything to wear. What does a well-dressed princess wear to an invasion, anyway? Your black flight suit is still at the hangar. Put on some jeans and change when we get there."

The air had grown hot by the time Neil parked behind Clontarf Castle. The Morrigan shimmered on the sun-baked helipad. Rory poked through it, checking things. Neil and Talty waved and hurried to the hangar.

Talty powered up the command center and radioed Peadar on a secure channel. "Hangar C to Gabriel Two. We are on station."

Peadar's voice crackled in the receiver. "Kieran should be there soon, Hangar C. The Morrigan will take him to the *Alastrina*. When Neil and Rory get back, I want you all down here. We're moving the rest of the family to Clontarf for safety. Gabriel Two over and out."

Talty placed the handset in its cradle. When she looked up, Neil was leaning against the doorframe, arms crossed. "Did you tell him you can't come because you have nothing to wear?"

His lazy smile made her already thumping heart beat like an Irish drum. She went to the changing room to escape his bewitching gaze.

He followed her. "I want you to stay here with the rest of the family."

Undressing in front of her locker, she spoke to Neil's image in the mirror. "You heard your father. He wants all of us down there. *All* of us!" She stepped into the sleeveless black body suit and slipped the straps over her bare shoulders. "I'm Fianna as well as you are, Neil Boru. It's our duty to guard the kingdom, so don't be looking at me like that!"

His reverse image grinned. "I'm not looking 'like that' at all. I'm enjoying the show. You forgot your shirt, love."

"It's too hot for the shirt. The jacket is light, and it will hide the scars."

"I wasn't thinking of the scars, darlin'. Keep that jacket on. We don't want your female shape distracting the lads." He stepped over and kissed her. "You'll wait here for me, won't you? No going off on your own, right?"

She kissed him back long enough to get a good taste of him. "Right. Go help Rory. Kieran will be here soon."

He arrived as she spoke. "Let's go, Neily. Talty, get Peadar on the radio. He'll fill you in. And wait here for Neil. Don't even think about going off on your own."

Neil and Kieran sprinted to the helipad. Shaking her head, Talty unlocked the miniature armory and selected a gun belt and matching accessories to complete her Morrigan-black outfit.

* * * * *

Dressed as tourists, Philip Leverington and the two men who left the ferry with him wore sunglasses, T-shirts, jeans, sneakers, and caps with rugby logos. Cameras hung from their necks. Their shoulder packs contained cosmetic items, cell phones, and weapons.

Philip knew the stocky man waiting for them, though he couldn't recall his name. "How close can we get to Tara Hall?"

"Them guards won't let us drive past the gate, but there's an old hut in the woods a mile behind the fence with a bricked-up tunnel in the cellar."

Philip huffed his annoyance. "Well, what good is that?"

"It ain't bricked up no more, and it goes straight inside Tara Hall's grounds. I done it twice and no one caught me. I don't know how to get in the building, though."

No longer annoyed, Philip set a brisk pace toward the waiting car. "I'll take care of that."

CHAPTER THIRTY-THREE
Dedication To Our Promise

When Nick learned of the shootings on the *Kincora*, he found another pilot to fly Creek and Catherine to California. His presence bolstered Richard now, though it didn't ease his concern. They followed Dan and Barry from the helipad to Tara Hall's fourth floor, where Aidan admitted the four anxious men to Prince Peadar's conference room.

King Brian greeted them with a ready smile. "I'm glad you're all here. I wanted to speak to you before I leave. Did Miss Dolliver get off all right, Richard? We heard what happened on the *Kincora*."

Brian's composure worried Richard. Didn't the man realize that a hostile gunboat was racing toward Dublin? "She's on her way to Mendocino. Sir, I'm strongly suggesting you contact the Security Council in Brussels. ISF can intervene in a situation that threatens world peace if one of the involved parties requests that intervention."

"It's only a little raid, not a coordinated assault force."

"Perhaps, but Lord Roger can cause serious damage if no one stops him. We want to help, but we can't unless you make a formal request."

The serene expression on Brian's bearded face reminded Richard of a lion in total control of his territory. "Relax, lad. I already have. I hear you refused my daughter's resignation. Since we don't want either of you court-martialed, I had Jack contact the Security Council. You'll be receiving permission shortly to, how do they say it? 'Make official recommendations for the resolution of this latest threat to international peace.'"

Nick was looking over Peadar's maps. "First recommendation, sir: counterattack. That ship can fire missiles."

"No, Nick." Peadar sounded as congenial as Brian. "We can defend ourselves well enough if we must. Right now we're happy to monitor the *Cecilia*'s progress. We're looking forward to Roger's visit."

"Yes," Brian said. "I plan to welcome him personally."

"We both will." Peadar chuckled. "Geoffrey wants Roger to leave England. We Irish are a hospitable people. We'll let him stay with us."

Richard gawked at them. "You've been working with Prince Geoffrey over this?"

"Certainly not," said Peadar. "Geoffrey thinks Roger's invasion is real. We've been working with MI6."

Bert. And Catherine. Richard saw it all now. "Does MI6 know that Christy—Talty is alive?"

"Not yet," said Brian. "When we charge Roger with my mother's murder, Talty will be our witness against him."

Talty. She'd been in the thick of it from the beginning. Richard couldn't be angry with her. Roger had turned her life upside down and was about to do so again. "All right, Nick and I are officially here. How can we help?"

Brian nodded his thanks. "Liam's been telling stories in a local school. He's on his way here now. I'd take it as a personal favor if you could escort him to Clontarf Castle as soon as he arrives."

Peadar tapped Brian's shoulder. "The helicopter is waiting. Dan will fly you up. Barry will stay here and take charge of the men until Neil arrives. I'll call you when it's over."

Brian sighed wearily. "Let's go, lads. I'll not only have to calm the family, I'll have to address the kingdom soon to prevent panic."

Ten minutes later, the Sea King lifted off. Just as it did, Peadar's telephone rang. He spoke for a moment and hung up. "That was the front gate. Liam is here. Bad timing. He could have gone with Brian. Richard, would you and Nick be kind enough to bring him up?"

* * * * *

Binoculars raised, Philip followed the black limousine until it stopped at the royal family's private entrance. The chauffeur jumped out and opened the door for Prince Liam, who entered a security code on a keypad. He opened the door and let himself into Tara Hall, and the limousine rolled on.

Philip's binoculars had zoomed in on the keypad as the prince hit each number. "Let's go, mates."

Wielding a noise-suppressed pistol, the man nearest Philip dashed to the limousine and shot the astonished chauffeur. The henchman jostled the corpse aside and drove the intended getaway car into some nearby bushes.

Philip raced to the entrance and tapped the numbers on the keypad. The door clicked open. The intruders slipped into Tara Hall.

* * * * *

"I must be in trouble again," Liam said when Richard and Nick met him on the ground floor. Their tense expressions set his skin prickling.

"Nah." Nick waved his hand. "Your uncle wants us to take you to Clontarf Castle until the crisis is over. Your family's there."

"What crisis now? It seems there's one after another these days."

"We'll tell you about it on the way," said Richard.

Liam wanted to stop by his office first. He rummaged and packed some papers into his briefcase. "I was to meet Maura in Clontarf anyway. She's sailing with Kevin and Nancy today. Do they know about this?"

Richard said they did, and they were on their way there now. The loud *bat-bat* of an approaching helicopter drew his attention to the window.

"What the heck is that?" Nick shouted over the noise. "Sounds like a combat chopper."

"That," Liam said, "is my sister's pet helicopter, a gunship she named the Morrigan." In his scariest story voice, he added, "And she always catches what she hunts." He clicked the briefcase shut. "I'm all set. We should be in Clontarf long before Wessex gets to Dublin."

The door opened. Three men in tourist attire stepped into the room, though Liam doubted they were tourists. They were pointing guns at him and Nick and Richard.

The gunman in the middle stepped forward. "Actually, Your Highness," he said in a cultured English accent, "we've alerted Lord Roger that your family is now gathering at Clontarf Castle. He's on his way there. He'll catch your family on the hop."

Liam had seen the man before. He tried but failed to place the hooded eyes and prematurely gray hair. "Who the hell are you?"

"Such language, Your Highness. I'm Philip Leverington, friend and devoted follower of Lord Roger. We'll be escorting you to Clontarf Castle to join your family—for the last time."

"You were with Wessex the night he attacked my sister!" Liam hurled the briefcase.

Leverington ducked. The briefcase smashed against the wall. Papers scattered over the floor.

Richard and Nick sprang. They froze when the henchmen trained their guns on them.

Liam and Leverington glared at each other. Leverington swung his gun at Liam's head.

Again Richard sprang, this time grabbing Leverington's arm. One of the henchmen shouted and thrust his gun against Richard's chest.

Liam held his breath.

The man reached inside Richard's jacket and plucked out his pistol. The second man repeated the process with Nick.

Crimson with fury, Leverington brushed his sleeve. "You're Gale, aren't you? Working with the Irish now. A traitor."

Richard didn't answer.

"Colonel Gale's presence has inspired me to change our initial plan. We'll have the rest of our party in the basement." Leverington waved his gun. "Nip along, gentlemen."

✶ ✶ ✶ ✶ ✶

"Nice flying, Neil," Talty said when the Morrigan landed behind Tara Hall.

Rory sounded indignant. "It wasn't his flying at all, ma'am. I spit three times for luck before we left."

Talty chuckled and jumped from the gunship. Neil and Rory sprinted after her.

Halfway to the Hall's private entrance, Neil stopped beside a stand of bushes. "What's that limousine doing there?" He trotted over to the car.

Talty and Rory followed. Talty spun in horror from the sight of the corpse in the bloodied front seat. Rory crossed himself and drew his gun.

Neil opened the door and touched the man's neck. "Still warm." He snapped his handheld radio from his belt. "Aidan. Who's with you?"

Aidan answered at once. "Your father and a few of the lads. Liam just arrived. Richard and Nick went down to meet him."

"We have a limo with a body down here. The man's been shot. Seal the exits. We're coming up the back stairs."

✶ ✶ ✶ ✶ ✶

Arms bound behind him, Liam squirmed between Richard and Nick on the basement floor. He had no illusions about Leverington's intentions. "Whatever you're going to do, get it over with. Or can't you do anything without Roger the Eejit telling you how?"

Leverington sat gloating on a crate beneath a dusty ceiling light. The basement behind him was dark. "This was my own idea."

"Was what happened to Princess Taillte your idea too?" Nick asked.

"No. That was Roger's brainchild. I think you'll agree he did a fine job on the bitch. The old woman too." Leverington laughed at Liam's efforts to loosen the tape around his arms.

"Gordon Randolph killed that girl in the park," Richard said. "Why?"

297

"You remember Gordon? Then you'll appreciate how much he enjoyed that little job. We heard a ridiculous rumor that she might be Princess Taillte. Dumping those roses over her was a stroke of genius on Roger's part." Leverington shifted on the crate. "All Roger's plans are brilliant. Soon John will have an unfortunate accident, and Roger will assume the throne."

"You're going to murder your own king?" Enraged, Liam renewed his futile efforts to burst his bonds. "You won't get away with it!"

"Oh, but we will." Leverington stood, hefting a pistol in each hand. "We'll start by creating the appearance of an argument to explain your unfortunate death, Your Highness. The ballistics reports will show that Colonel Gale's gun shot you and Major Tomasi, and that Tomasi's gun shot Colonel Gale."

"And whose gun will shoot you, Philip?"

Leverington whirled and raised the guns toward the disembodied voice. A shot blazed from the dark. A small black hole appeared above his right eye. He collapsed in a graceless jumble of limbs.

Talty ran into the light and kicked the guns from his hands. His corpse received a second, harder kick. The overhead lights came on. Leverington's flabbergasted henchmen offered no resistance to the King's Rangers who surrounded and disarmed them.

Aidan's Swiss army knife quickly sliced through the tape on the prisoners' arms. Nick seized Talty and kissed her.

Richard shook his hands to restore the circulation. "That was a tad close, darling. I had every confidence, however."

Liam staggered to his feet. "Not me. I thought I was going home to Maura in a box. I've never been so happy to see you, Talty."

The Rangers who knew her as the American Major McKenna stared. Liam didn't care. Feeling roguish after his brush with death, he dropped to one knee and snatched her right hand.

"I will kiss your hand as you are the heart of this kingdom." He did so and wobbled up again. "I will kiss your hand as you are my own heart. And I will kiss your mouth to show my everlasting love and devotion, beloved Princess of Ireland." Liam completed the Obeisance to the Lady Princess and stood back relishing his sister's scarlet cheeks.

She glanced at the startled Rangers. "This isn't exactly how I planned to come home," she said to no one in particular.

"Have your homecoming party later," said Richard. "Roger Wessex is on his way to Clontarf Castle."

Aidan alerted Peadar. Neil ran, shouting that he'd start up the Morrigan.

CHAPTER THIRTY-FOUR

Taking Out the Trash

On HMS *Cecilia's* bridge, First Officer Bradley checked the compass while Lord Roger and the thug called Gordon Randolph chatted with the captain.

Roger suddenly pointed east. "What boat is that? She seems to be on course for Clontarf."

Randolph raised his binoculars. "The *Lady Grania*, King Brian's yacht."

Roger's lips stretched into the alligator smile that turned Bradley's stomach. "Captain, can *Cecilia* overtake that yacht?"

"We can easily outrun her, Your Grace."

"Let's prevail upon them to give us a lift. We can approach Clontarf Castle with more stealth on King Brian's own yacht, and still arrive in time for dinner." Roger laughed. "I'm just in the mood for cabbage pie. Gordon, fetch our specialists. They're about to earn their keep."

Hiding his revulsion, Bradley returned to his instruments. Soon it would be over. Chief Benson must have arrested Admiral Mayne by now.

★ ★ ★ ★ ★

In one of *Alastrina's* sparsely furnished cabins, Kieran flipped a chair backward and straddled the seat. "I've been waiting a long time to talk to you, Andrew."

Andrew sat at the table. His eyes darted everywhere but at Kieran. "I have nothing to say."

Kieran kept his tone friendly. "You'll help yourself if you talk to me."

"You seem to know what happened well enough. Roger got tired of waiting for Geoffrey to act. I agreed with him."

"Not Roger." Steel crept into Kieran's voice. "The *Fancy Annie*. You remember the *Fancy Annie*, don't you, Andrew? You were there. You murdered those fishermen."

Beads of perspiration sprouted on Andrew's forehead. His hands trembled. "They…they pulled guns on us. We had no choice."

Kieran stretched his fingers to keep them from curling. "What did they pull on you? Uzis? Bazookas? Rockets? Is that why you slaughtered them?"

"They were only fishermen! What do you care about fishermen?"

Years of restrained fury exploded from Kieran's fists. Andrew and the table toppled to the floor. Kieran yanked him up by the collar of his uniform. "One of your officers left a letter detailing everything that happened. We have the letter and we have you. Tell me about Geoffrey's part in it, and we might go easier on you."

Andrew wiped his bloodied mouth and squinted through the eye he could open. "Please. No more. I'll tell you whatever you want to know."

Kieran opened the door. Bert came in and eyed Andrew's bedraggled state. His face remained inscrutable. "Trouble, Commander?"

"Not at all. He fell."

Bert nodded and set the table on its legs. "That's it for you then, Admiral. And for Roger. He'll have a surprise waiting for him at Tara Hall."

"No," Andrew said between gasps. "He's not going to Tara Hall. He's going to Clontarf Castle."

Kieran cursed and flew to the ship's communication center.

✱ ✱ ✱ ✱ ✱

Kieran's warning that the *Cecilia* was past Bull Island and fast approaching Clontarf had Peadar beside himself. Would his Fianna be the first in Ireland's history to fall to invaders? During the Morrigan's short flight from Tara Hall, he huddled with Talty and Aidan.

When they landed behind Clontarf Castle, Peadar was his chuckling, confident self again. He sent fifteen Rangers to the marina with Aidan, and another dozen into the castle. He and Talty waited for Neil, who left the helicopter last.

Peadar called him over. "Keep Liam with you, Neil. Richard and Nick too. If anyone hears Richard's English accent, they'll think he's one of Roger's men."

Neil glanced at Talty. "What about the one I'm supposed to protect?"

"She'll stay with me. Get the men into the tunnels. We can cover the great hall from every angle that way, and no one will know we're there. Be ready to pop out when I need you." Peadar slapped his son's back. "You'll be my ace in the hole, Neily."

300

"Yes, sir." Smiling now, Neil jogged into the castle.

Peadar's radio vibrated. Aidan was calling from the knoll above the marina. "Wessex and three armed men are heading up the front walk, sir."

Incredulous, Peadar stared at the radio. "Three? That's his invasion? Why the devil didn't you take them?"

"They have hostages. They captured the *Lady Grania*."

"Kevin?"

"Yes, sir. And Maura and Nancy. The *Cecilia* is coming in now."

"We'll deal with Wessex. Secure the *Cecilia*."

Talty gestured for the radio. Peadar handed it to her.

She held it close to her mouth and spoke softly. "Show our English friends some Irish hospitality, Aidan. The weather is warm, and their uniforms are heavy. Tell them we're more casual here in Ireland. They can take off their jackets. Trousers too. About ten uniforms should do."

"Is it a masquerade ball we're having, Beauty?"

Chuckling away, Peadar reclaimed the radio. "For a privileged few," he said and signed off. "You have a devious mind, Lady Princess."

"It's a lesson you taught me well, Uncle: 'All warfare is founded on deception.' I'll tell you more on the way in."

* * * * *

Despite the warm weather, a fire roared in the great hall's hearth to counter the castle's dank chill. Brian took little comfort in the flames. He didn't relax until he heard the helicopter that should be delivering Liam. Once Kevin arrived, he would tell the family what was happening.

The double doors to the great hall burst open. Roger Wessex swaggered into the room, a semi-automatic pistol in his hand. He strutted to the center of the room and bowed. "Good evening, Your Majesty. I hereby inform you that I claim this wretched island."

Brian leapt from his chair. "You claim nothing here. Where is my son?"

Three men tramped in behind Roger. One wielded a submachine gun. The second nudged Kevin before him, while the third pulled Nancy and Maura by their hair.

"Do sit down, Your Majesty," Roger said. "Clontarf Castle has seen no bloodshed yet, though I'm afraid we can't say the same for Tara Hall. By now your son is dead."

Maura shrieked. Brian lurched. Could it be true? Had the plan failed? Where were his Rangers? He struggled to remain calm. "You wouldn't dare harm my son. Stop this nonsense now, or my Rangers—"

"Your Rangers? Those at Tara Hall are dead. So are those who guarded

301

your oil wells. My oil wells now." He inspected the hall as he spoke. "Very nice. It will do for my more provincial holidays. I can already hear Rigoletto reverberating from the walls."

"You won't get away with this!"

Roger laughed. "But I already have! Raise the *Cecilia*, Gordon. Have her crew join us."

While the man called Gordon spoke into a hand radio, another of Roger's men thrust Maura and Nancy toward the table. The third shoved Kevin after them. Moments later, ten armed English naval officers and sailors trotted into the room. They spread out behind Roger and his men and surrounded the dumbstruck family.

Reeling with rage, Brian wondered what to do. A sudden movement in a doorway behind the invaders caught his attention.

Talty! She waved and disappeared.

"It seems that you and your clan are now homeless," said Roger. "We'll soon escort you to your yacht. You can sail wherever you like, as long as it's away from Ireland."

"This is outrageous!" Brian roared. "I want to speak to the Ard Laoch."

"Your High Warrior, I believe that means." Roger smirked. "You'll have trouble doing that, since he and your Fianna are captured or dead."

Hoping he displayed more dignity than he felt, Brian straightened his shoulders. "Summon the Ard Laoch!"

Ostensibly oblivious to the guns whipping toward her, Talty pranced into the hall, smoothing her tied-back hair. "The Ard Laoch is in Dublin, sir. Oh, excuse me. I didn't know you had company."

Roger eyed her up and down and sneered. "Who in ruddy hell are you?"

"Why, I'm the Deputy Ard Laoch, Your Lordity."

"You? No wonder we had no trouble taking over."

"Is that what you've done? Oh, my! I don't see how you could have."

"Look around you, you stupid little—"

"Do you mind if I check?" She pulled a radio from her belt.

Gordon snatched it away. "What do you think you're doing?"

"Just calling the lads on the wells. It'll be a right lemoner for me if they aren't there."

Roger's laughter echoed through the hall. "Give her the radio, Gordon."

Talty took it and pushed the transmit button. "Unit One, report."

A man's voice overrode a crackle of static. "We've come under attack, but our position is secure, ma'am. We have taken no prisoners."

Roger's sudden confusion tickled Brian. He began to enjoy the show.

Pacing now, Talty pressed the button again. "Unit Two, report."

"Our position is secure, ma'am. We have taken no prisoners."

"What does this mean?" Roger cried.

"That's what we're finding out, Your Gloriousness." Winking at Brian, Talty thumbed the button again. "Unit Three, report."

"We are secure from attack, ma'am. We have taken no prisoners."

"How many oil wells did you say you had, Your Worship?"

Roger's face darkened. "Four! The four we're entitled to! Your information is flawed!"

"Is it? Unit Four, report."

"We are secure from attack, ma'am. We have taken no prisoners."

A volatile silence descended over the hall. Talty clipped the radio to her belt and stared straight at Roger. "Unit Five, report."

Behind him, a familiar voice shouted, "We are secure from attack, ma'am. We have taken four prisoners."

Guns clicked and pointed. Feet scrambled. "Get your hands in the air, the lot of you!" Aidan shouted as he and the disguised Rangers with him disarmed Roger and his gang.

Brian noted the ill-fitting uniforms and familiar faces on the men surrounding the intruders. The image of English seamen detained in their underwear delighted him. He roared with joy when Peadar and his men burst from behind tapestries and through indiscernible doors in the walls.

One side of the hearth swung open. Neil bounded into the hall, followed by Liam, Richard and Nick. Maura rushed across the room and threw her arms around Liam.

Talty approached Brian. "We are secure from attack, Your Majesty. Commander Dacey has captured the English training attack vessels. Roger Wessex is in your custody, as you requested."

"This is impossible!" Roger screamed. "Who are you to do this, you miserable Irish—"

Aidan's fist doubled Roger over. "Speak respectfully to the king!"

Brian stepped to the center of the room. "Roger Wessex, as you now stand on Irish soil, the Kingdom of Ireland accuses you of grave crimes. I call on the Ard Brehon to recite the charges against you."

Jack left his seat and stood at Brian's side. His white hair and calm deportment cast an air of integrity over the room. "Roger Wessex, the Kingdom of Ireland charges you with the murder of Deirdre Boru."

"How dare you, sir! You know very well my cousin Thomas was responsible for that. Even if he wasn't, you have no proof."

"We have a witness who saw you strike her down," Jack said.

"You lie. No one else was there."

Talty stepped forward. Hatred burned in her eyes. "I was there."

Roger stared. "Liar! Imposter! No one could have survived that—"

Talty unzipped her jacket and wrenched it off. Her black shoulder straps framed the hideous scars. The sight smothered every sound in the room.

Brian coaxed the jacket from her clenched fingers and helped her slip back into it. "The Ard Brehon will continue."

Jack obliged. "Roger Wessex, the Kingdom of Ireland charges you with assaulting Princess Taillte. The Kingdom of Ireland charges you with complicity in the assaults on the Duke of Leinster and Lieutenant Patrick Hewitt. And, the Kingdom of Ireland charges you with complicity in the murder of Jill Scanlon. We hereby detain you at the king's pleasure."

Roger glared at Brian. "My uncle will have something to say about this."

"Your uncle helped us, you jackass! You'll stand trial and, if I have my way, you'll hang. Now get this garbage out of my sight!"

Peadar supervised the removal of the invaders. When he led them out, he turned to Brian with a great grin and shook his fist in the air.

Arms around his weeping daughter, Brian grinned back.

CHAPTER THIRTY-FIVE
Slithering Snakes

From Donegal to Wexford, Princess Taillte's fantastic return from the dead rocked the Kingdom of Ireland. The media covered no other story. Calls flooded Tara Hall. King Brian and Talty appeared at the Irish Parliament for an entire day to address the kingdom's concerns.

Brian detailed the entire scheme, from the horror of Talty's wedding night to the arrest of Roger Wessex and his followers. Talty herself parried all questions with candid replies that ranged from humorous to biting, depending on the relevancy—or idiocy—of the questions.

A few miffed politicians and citizens vented their outrage at the deception, though most expressed their approval of Brian's handling of the tangled affair. Talty's story had captured the imagination of the legend-loving people of Ireland.

* * * * *

Geoffrey Wessex snickered over his seafood bisque. Not only did the Borus have Roger in custody, their elaborate charade had painted them into a corner. Brian Boru had signed a treaty stating his daughter would marry the King of England. That a different king sat on the English throne now made no difference. Geoffrey had them, pure and simple.

He called his aide. "Get me our Ambassador in Dublin."

The spoon in Geoffrey's hand blurred. He must remember to have his eyes examined.

* * * * *

The police had pegged Gordon Randolph as the man who'd purchased the roses found on Jill Scanlon's body. That didn't prove that the purchaser and the murderer were the same man. Kieran sat in his study now, trying to make Aidan understand this.

"That Leverington bastard bragged about it before Talty put out his lights, Dad. I heard him myself. He said Randolph enjoyed doing it. Isn't that enough?"

"It's hearsay, Aidan. Leverington is dead. We can't question him. When we get the facts together, we'll charge Randolph with murder, if we have enough evidence."

"If I'd known that was him in the castle, I'd have killed him right there!"

Kieran recalled Andrew Mayne lying smashed and bleeding on the *Alastrina*. He couldn't begrudge the boy his anger. "Once we learn which men are Roger's and which are King John's, we'll make individual charges. Be patient, Aidan."

"I hope Uncle Brian hangs them all." Aidan stomped from the study.

＊ ＊ ＊ ＊ ＊

Richard had left Malahide early to fetch Creek at the airport, and he was hungry. Aromas of Irish bacon and French toast sizzling on the stove set his stomach growling.

Creek plopped down at the table and laid his napkin on his lap. "Our bioacceleration process stunned the scientific world. A whole herd of scientists is chomping at the bit to visit Fargan. I'll have plenty of company after you kids leave."

"We aren't going just yet," Richard said. "Brussels is sending inspectors to monitor the English prisoners. We'll fill in until they arrive. Then Talty can have her house back."

Nick clicked off the gas and filled plates, which he passed to the table. "I bet it's a big relief for her to stop playacting. Neil too."

"I don't know." Samantha handed a plate to Creek. "Sometimes I wonder how much they were pretending."

Nick kept doling out dishes. "You can't fool around with your cousin. It gives the babies birth defects."

Grinning at the feast before him, Creek drizzled maple syrup over his plate. "Cousin marriages don't cause genetic defects, Nick. Mutant genes do. Even unrelated couples can produce offspring with genetic diseases like heterochromia iridium if both partners carry a mutant gene."

Nick shook his finger at the eccentric scientist. "I told you before, Creek. No big words before breakfast."

"He means different-colored eyes," Samantha said. "Like Prince Geoffrey's."

"See?" said Nick. "Everyone in that family's a little weird."

"If a particular group inbreeds for generations with mutant genes present, the defective genes will become concentrated, with obvious results." Creek reached for a bowl of fresh blueberries. "If no mutant genes are present, everyone is fine. Responsible genetic counseling is the key."

"But—"

"That boy Joseph, whose hand was bitten by the lion? If I remember correctly, he was on his way to marry his cousin. Did you see any defects in their tribe?"

"No, but—"

Samantha blessedly derailed the debate. "It might not even be an issue here. I could be completely wrong about Neil and Talty."

Movement outside the window caught Richard's eye. Car doors slammed shut. "Speak of the devil. They just pulled in."

Talty came in the back door, dressed in denim and looking weary. Her pleasant greeting lacked her usual smile. Laden with luggage, Neil came in behind her.

Nick helped him set the bags on the floor. "You're just in time for breakfast. Sit down. I'll make more tea."

"I'll do it." Talty hung her jacket on a peg and filled the kettle.

Reaching over the counter, Nick opened a tea tin. "What, a princess-slash-TV star making tea? Hey, you're gorgeous on TV. Why so many suitcases?"

"Only one is mine," Neil said right away.

"I'll put it in the spare room. What's with the luggage, Major Lady?"

"If you watched the hearings, you heard those cretins who questioned my lodging with my disreputable bachelor cousin."

"So you've abandoned the den of iniquity," Creek said, pointing his fork at the bags.

Talty glanced around the kitchen. "Actually, we're just changing its location. You can put Neil's bag in my room, Nick. If you wouldn't mind."

Samantha smiled. So did Richard, but Nick's mouth dropped open. "Aw, man! You mean you weren't pretending?"

Neil crossed the kitchen and slipped an arm around Talty. "We were at first. This is a fairly recent development."

"My parents wanted me to come home and live with them," she said. "I convinced them I'd be safe here, and that I should stay and keep you company until you return to California."

"And Neil can visit you on the QT," Samantha said matter-of-factly.

"Aren't you worried about kids?" asked Nick.

"I love kids," said Neil. "I want lots, especially if Talty is their mother."

"But—"

"But what if they have six toes?" Neil explained how Peadar Boru had adopted him at birth. He described the legalities of the situation, and the need for discretion until he and Talty could announce their intentions. "We have to talk, but we aren't going to get much privacy with everyone in Ireland looking to meet their reinstated princess. Her mother is already planning grand receptions."

The timer for the tea buzzed. Talty shut it off and set the steeping teapot on the table. "We were hoping to hide out here now and then, but we don't want anyone to feel uncomfortable. We can find another way."

"You'll stay in your own house," said Richard. "I told you, we're a team. We'll enjoy acting as your ostensible chaperones."

Samantha and Creek agreed. Nick caught Talty in a hug. "You bet. I'm sorry, guys. I act like a jerk sometimes."

Eyes shining, Talty grinned and hugged him back.

* * * * *

The fireplace in Brian's office blazed. Brian sat before it trying to remember when Jack's hair had turned white. In his mind, his uncle's hair was as black as a dinner jacket.

From the way Jack tilted each glass and let the whiskey trickle down the side, Brian knew trouble was brewing. At last Jack plugged the crystal seal into the decanter and handed Brian a half-filled tumbler. They clinked their glasses and sipped.

"Are we celebrating something, Jack?"

Jack set his glass on the table, and then his pipe was tumbling in his hands. "Maybe. An hour ago I got a call from our Minister for Foreign Affairs. The English ambassador requested a meeting with her this morning. Prince Geoffrey wants the Marriage Treaty resurrected and adhered to for the sake of justice and balance between our great nations."

The whiskey caught in Brian's throat. When he could speak, he punched the arm of the chair. "Let me understand you without the diplomatic gobbledygook. Geoffrey expects my daughter to marry John Wessex?"

"Authorized agents of both countries signed the treaty. I read it over before I came here. It states that the King of Ireland's marriageable daughter shall marry the King of England. The fact that we have the same daughter and a different king is irrelevant. Geoffrey is insisting we abide by the treaty."

Brian sprang from his chair. Alone with his uncle, he held no reins on his temper. He pounded one fist against the other, and then he did it again. "I'll tell that reupholstered weasel what he can do with his insisting. Send the English ambassador home, Jack. Give him twenty-four hours to vacate his embassy. Then I'll decide whether or not to burn it to the ground!"

"Calm down, Brian. Severing diplomatic relations isn't the answer. We need diplomacy most when relations are strained. Geoffrey's requests are lawful, not affronts that render it impossible for us to engage in diplomacy."

"You don't think what Roger Wessex pulled was an affront?"

"Unquestionably, but Geoffrey covered himself by denying any involvement. According to him, Roger's invasion was independent of and unsanctioned by the government of England. No casus belli there."

"I want them to know how displeased I am, Jack."

"Let's do it by presenting you as a dignified, if irate, head of state rather than an unhinged ding-a-ling."

Jack's good humor had Brian suspecting that Ireland's back wasn't against the wall. A few deep breaths helped him regain his composure. "What do you suggest?"

Sliding the pipe back into his pocket, Jack crossed his legs. "We can recall our own ambassador from London for consultations, a wonderfully ambiguous term. We can also summon the English ambassador to our Foreign Minister's office to hear our protests and remonstrations."

"I want him to hear the word 'No' loud and clear! The decent thing to do would be to leave Talty alone after all that's happened."

"It would, but a covetous man is always in want, and Geoffrey wants those oil wells." Jack picked up his glass and swallowed. He smacked his lips and curled them in a cunning smile. "So much trouble over a simple marriage treaty."

"What happens when we refuse?"

"Geoffrey can petition the World Court to impose sanctions against us for breach of a lawful treaty. The World Court can impose hefty fines. I believe it's some sort of percentage or formula, not a flat amount. They'd hit our Exchequer for a sizeable chunk, though."

Brian saw no way out. "Doesn't the World Court get tired of Geoffrey?"

"Not as tired as we do."

The crystal decanter sparkled in the firelight as Jack poured himself another shot of whiskey. He reached over to top off Brian's glass.

Brian shook his head. "I can't drain the kingdom's coffers. It's bad enough I emptied my own. Still, I promised Talty I'd never ask her to marry for political reasons again. I intend to keep that promise."

"Good man." Jack's grin widened. "I believe we can work our way out of this. I've asked Liam and Kevin to read that treaty to see if they notice the same thing I did. If they do, we'll call an emergency family meeting."

Jack's foxy grin began to irritate Brian. "Give me a hint, Jack."

"Geoffrey is giving us until Monday next to respond. If we don't agree by then, he'll sue. We're going to pull his plug, though. The phrase 'the King of Ireland's marriageable daughter' is our out. All we have to do is render Talty unmarriageable before Monday."

"What? How do you intend to do that?"

"It's quite simple. If she's already married, she can't be marriageable. I was thinking Saturday would be a perfect day for a wedding."

While Brian sat gaping, Jack savored his whiskey, lacing each sip with gentle chuckles.

* * * * *

Richard arrived at the centuries-old Dublin prison with Samantha and Nick to oversee the treatment of Roger Wessex and the two dozen followers arrested with him. As an English national himself—not to mention his being Princess Taillte's commanding officer—Richard's position as interim inspector was awkward. He doubted he could guarantee fair and impartial treatment to the man who'd played butcher to Talty, but his duty was to try.

He shuddered at the sight of the hideous snakes above the entrance to the prison. The repulsive symbol of constrained evil filled him with dread. Carved in stone, the snakes writhed together, necks fettered by the chains of Law and Order.

An aide led him and the others to the Prison Governor's office, where Aidan sat chatting with the Governor. Aidan rose and made the introductions with perfect protocol.

Richard kept his tone formal. "I'm surprised to see you here, Major Dacey."

"The King's Rangers are on standby to transport the prisoners."

"Transport them where?"

"To our facility on Rathlin Island," the Governor said. "Major Dacey has offered to conduct your first tour. Our medical officer is waiting to meet with Dr. Reed."

The Governor had ordered a secure area prepared for the English prisoners. Richard found the cells clean and warm. He identified himself and Nick to the prisoners—two he knew to be Bert Benson's men—and assured them that the Irish officials were carefully observing International Regulations concerning their treatment.

Roger sat sulking in his one-man cell. After several unsuccessful attempts at conversation, Richard left him to himself.

The tour ended. He and Nick left the cellblock. Aidan waited opposite the last cell.

Richard glanced inside when he reached it. Gordon Randolph glowered back at him.

$$*\ *\ *\ *\ *$$

Liam removed his glasses and rubbed his tired eyes. He'd scrutinized the treaty twice. Something in it pulled at him. After another cup of tea, he would read it again. "Can we say there's no specified time provision and too much time has elapsed?"

Kevin kept reading as he answered. "There's no time provision," he agreed, "but that would only be a valid lapse if one of the parties didn't accept the treaty. Both your father and Prince Geoffrey accepted the treaty, and representatives for Uncle Jack and Geoffrey signed it. I'm looking to see if we can offer additional consideration to waive our contractual obligations."

"I checked. The amount would be the same as the fines we'd have to pay. It's too bad Talty wasn't still married to Eric Yamada. She wouldn't be marriageable then."

Kevin glanced up. "What did you say?"

"Marriageable. The treaty doesn't exactly say 'capacity to marry,' but that's what it means. 'The King of Ireland's marriageable daughter shall marry the King of England.' Now, if she were still married to Eric—"

Kevin sprang from his chair and seized Liam's shoulders. "You're a genius, Li!"

"Am I? It's about time someone recognized it. What did I do?"

"Talty married Eric Yamada in a wedding put together so fast, our heads all spun. If she did it once, she can do it again."

Liam grinned. "Do you have someone in mind for her to marry?"

Kevin grinned back. "I think we might know an interested fella."

Liam crossed the room and opened the door. "Uncle Jack!"

$$*\ *\ *\ *\ *$$

The angry clack of Nuala's knitting needles was the only sound in Brian's conference room. Liam ignored it. Struggling to contain his joy for fear he'd give the game away, he scanned the faces around him. His father's was grave, while Uncle Peadar's usual jocular glow had mellowed to serene contemplation. Kieran looked tired. Uncle Jack and Kevin wore the only smiles. The women made no attempt to hide their fury over this latest outrage.

Liam thought Maura looked lovely, sitting there beside his enraged mother. His mother looked lovely too. And Peggy, Breege, and Nuala—lovely, lovely. There was the lovely Samantha Reed, coming in with Richard and Nick, exchanging lovely, quiet nods with everyone.

Aidan trudged in behind them. His brooding scowl wasn't lovely at all, though Liam paid him no mind. Only Neil and Talty were missing. By the time they arrived, the scene would be set. Things couldn't be lovelier.

Nuala's clacking stopped when Brian stood and spoke. "Thank you all for coming on such short notice. Richard, we've asked you to attend this family meeting not as ISF officers, but as Talty's friends. You've been an important part of her family for some time now."

Richard nodded politely. Brian continued, explaining Prince Geoffrey's ultimatum, which infuriated the newcomers, and further incited—or delighted—those who'd already heard it.

"We must render Talty unmarriageable at once," Brian said. "We've been discussing an expedited wedding to accomplish this. However, we have two problems. First, Talty knows nothing about it. She won't be pleased, though I'm sure she'll be angry enough to do whatever it takes to outwit Geoffrey. Second, even if she agrees, we have no husband for her."

Understanding brightened Aidan's face. He grinned at Liam, though he spoke to Brian. "Surely you have a long list of candidates, Uncle Brian?"

"No. We're asking those of you who know Talty well to help with that."

Eileen began to cry. "Why don't you let Talty choose this time?"

"I haven't seen her show such an interest in any man," Brian said. "Where is she, anyway?"

"She and Neil are on their way," Liam said. "When they get here, I'm sure everything will be just lovely."

CHAPTER THIRTY-SIX

Sacred Assignments

The troubled atmosphere in the conference room hit Neil right away. He touched Talty's elbow and nodded toward two vacant seats.

Brian stopped them. "Talty, come here, please."

Talty obeyed. Neil waited where he stood.

"Geoffrey Wessex is demanding that we honor the treaty we signed when you married Thomas. He's insisting you marry John. We have until Monday to respond."

Her trembling shoulders infuriated Neil. "You can't do this, Uncle Brian. Not again!"

Peadar's bellow blasted the room. "Neil! You'll not speak to your uncle so!"

The rebuke drew Neil's angry gaze. Peadar had raised his hand to his mouth, though not in time to hide a smile. His sly wink left Neil confused.

Talty's quivering voice broke the silence. "What did you tell him, Dad?"

"We instructed the English ambassador to relay our refusal. We intended to call our own ambassador home to show our displeasure, but Geoffrey expelled him before we could. It didn't take long for word to spread. The ambassadors of nearly every embassy in London have been called home—for consultations."

"What does it all mean?"

"It means the rest of the world is sympathetic to our situation, Tal. Even so, we signed a treaty. Geoffrey has the law on his side. But I've given you my word, darlin'. I won't ask you to marry for politics ever again. However, the World Court can impose sanctions if we refuse."

"Can we afford them?"

"We might not have to pay them. I'll let Liam explain."

Coward! Neil thought as Brian took his seat.

Liam sauntered over to Talty and snatched her hand to his lips. "The treaty states that the King of Ireland's marriageable daughter shall marry the King of England. You already married the fella, Tal, but we annulled that marriage. So we're back to square one."

Her lips tightened.

"Have faith, love. You have brilliant legal minds on your side. Uncle Jack, Kevin, and myself"—he folded an arm over his chest and made a slight bow—"have determined that if we can declare you unmarriageable by Monday next, we can render the treaty invalid."

"What? But…how?"

"By Monday we hope to say you already *are* married. We've been planning a lovely wedding for next Saturday. All you have to do is show up and marry someone." He waved his hand. "Anyone!"

Talty shot a murderous look at her father. "You're joking! What are you going to do this time, put an ad in the paper?"

Neil was about to object when Liam's wink caught his attention. Suddenly seeing the conspiracy, he smiled and tapped Talty's arm. "Tal? Will you marry me this Saturday?"

As he expected, her cheeks blazed. "I don't—we haven't—"

"Say yes." He tugged her hair. "They have to order flowers and things."

She swiped a hand at her glistening eyes. Her lips wobbled into an almost smile, and she nodded.

Neil spun toward Brian. "Uncle Brian, I love your daughter. We're going to be married next Saturday. We're hoping that you and Auntie Leenie will give us your blessing."

Brian scowled. "What? You're telling me, not asking?"

"You've given her away too many times. She's mine now. Are we all right with it, Uncle Jack?"

"Yes. The High Court has already granted the exemptions. We'll get everything signed this afternoon." Jack smiled at Talty. "Then all you have to do is decide what to wear, love."

Talty sniffed and held up her chin. "I have more to say than what I'll wear! I'll have a proper Irish wedding this time, one with real music and real dancing. I want fiddles and pipes, and bodhrans and harps. As for what I'll wear, I'll dress like a proper Irish princess, with lace on my gown and gold in my hair."

Joy crinkled Brian's face. "I believe we can arrange all that."

"We'll look at the gold combs and hairpieces tonight," Eileen said. "And we'll send for the dressmaker first thing in the morning."

"We have chefs coming from all over Europe to help with the food," said Peggy.

"And you'll have roses everywhere!" shouted Peadar.

"The jeweler is coming to show you his best rings," Kevin said.

The extent of the conniving astonished Neil. When the meeting was over, he would call Adam DeWitt and remind him to bring the band of roses.

Liam raised his hands. "We'll have a fine show, one we can pull together fast. No months of planning to have the pope and rock stars attend. We'll keep it simple."

"It isn't going to be as simple as you think," Kieran said. "People from all over the world are calling the Hall. They want to come to the wedding to show their support for Ireland."

Talty's eyes widened in amazement. "The whole world knew there was a wedding before the bride and groom did? How did you know I'd find a fella to marry me?"

Kieran's right eyebrow arched up. "I figured that fella I saw kissing you in the hangar the other night would oblige us."

That raised a round of good-natured teasing. Then Liam called for order. "All right, I think we've covered enough for now. As they say, a good beginning is half the work."

Neil closed his eyes and dared to hope for the second half.

* * * * *

Tired of the rain, Richard stared out the Prison Governor's window. If the deluge continued, the growing puddles would soon flood the exercise yard. He missed California's sunshine. He missed Catherine. He wanted to return to Mendocino to see her—but then he'd be missing Talty. He already was. He wished the Prison Governor would leave him alone so he could brood in peace.

"I'm not sure Lord Roger will be fare better in the medical wing," the Governor was saying. "Still, we'll do our best to look after him."

A rumble of thunder interrupted his droning. The arrival of Kieran Dacey and Bert Benson ended it. The Governor bobbed his head and departed. Richard saw Aidan standing by the door in the hall, as if on guard.

The thunder faded. The men shook hands. Richard nearly gagged at the reek of cigarette smoke emanating from Bert's clothing. When they took their seats at the small conference table, he sat as far from Bert as he could without seeming rude.

"I understand you and Bert know each other," Kieran said.

"Yes. I worked for Bert once. What's the crisis, gentlemen?"

A raspy cough prefaced Bert's answer. "During a walk around the exercise yard, one of my men overheard Roger Wessex and Andrew Mayne plotting an escape."

Kieran frowned. "How and when?"

"Two days from now, when you transport them to the ship that's to take them to Rathlin Island. It seems others are waiting to aid their escape."

"To where?" Richard asked. "England doesn't want them back."

"They can sail to Antarctica for all I care," said Bert. "Nevertheless, they're going to try."

"We'll push the transfer to tomorrow morning," said Kieran. "That should bollix their plans. And the captain of the *Cecilia* is one of your men."

Richard asked why they weren't using an Irish ship for the transport.

"Good question," Kieran said. "Geoffrey offered the *Cecilia* to show his disapproval of Roger's actions. King Brian accepted in good faith."

Bert sniffed. "Politics. Who can keep up? Well, we've had a dramatic few days."

Richard smiled at the understatement, and at Bert's fidgeting fingers. "I understand Admiral Mayne is negotiating for a lesser sentence."

"Yes," Kieran said, "though it doesn't concern the invasion. We've charged him with complicity in the murders of eight Irish fishermen during Geoffrey's seizure of Fargan. Mayne will swear to Geoffrey's part in the matter to save himself from a life sentence."

"It's fitting," Richard said. "Geoffrey will be disgraced, and John will be out from under his thumb."

"God save the King." Bert seemed keen to leave. His yellowed fingertips shook when he extended his hand.

Despite his distaste for the nicotine stains, Richard squeezed Bert's hand tight. "Take care, Bert."

✳ ✳ ✳ ✳ ✳

The rain didn't slow Aidan. He knew the way to Curragh Camp well and allowed the clicking windshield wipers to lull him into a reflective trance.

What he meant to do was wrong, but he couldn't remember the last time he'd seen Neil and Talty so happy. Geoffrey Wessex had unwittingly given them a chance they might never have had otherwise.

Aidan intended to see that they got that chance.

The rain had eased to a gentle mist by the time he reached Curragh Prison. He slowed the car to have a look. It wasn't a bad place, for a prison.

316

Of course, Roger and his friends would end their days in a facility with tighter security—a facility where they'd be alive, thriving even, learning new skills in personal development while they made shirts and gardened. Their continued existence would overshadow the lives of those they'd tried so hard to slaughter.

Aidan smacked the steering wheel and drove on.

Up ahead, a farmer herded a flock of sheep across the road. Aidan stopped. Roger had planned to herd the family onto the *Lady Grania* after he captured Clontarf Castle. He'd planned to tell them he was moving them to a temporary domicile so they could get their affairs in order before he exiled them from Ireland.

But the *Cecilia*'s first officer had told Aidan about the specialists who'd boarded the *Lady Grania* with Wessex. Aidan ordered a search. His men found enough P-4 in the engine room to blast the yacht to Greenland.

He dispatched two men to Curragh Camp to store the confiscated explosives in an ordnance depot. Be quiet about it, he told them. Don't let anyone log the stuff in.

He didn't want anyone to miss it when it disappeared.

Since he'd taken Gordon Randolph at Clontarf Castle, images of Jill's broken body had returned to torment him. When he saw Randolph in his jail cell, he swore he'd kill the man. How, he didn't know—until he heard about the escape plan that morning. His father had moved the transfer of the prisoners to the next day.

Things could go wrong when plans changed so fast.

Aidan remembered Talty's wedding night. He'd never forget kind old Auntie Deirdre's sightless eyes. Wessex had nearly decapitated her. And Talty. Oh, Talty.

His hands tightened on the steering wheel. It would never end as long as Wessex was alive. He'd give Neil and Talty—his cherished cousins and closest friends—the chance he and Jill never had. He wasn't sure how he'd do it, but Curragh Camp was still a few miles away. He had time to think.

The last of the sheep cleared the road. Aidan drove on, thinking.

✱ ✱ ✱ ✱ ✱

The captain of HMS *Cecilia* rewarded those crewmembers he knew to be King John's supporters by granting them shore leave. The crewmen took a water taxi to Dublin, leaving only a dozen men—all Roger's men, not counting the first officer—aboard the *Cecilia*.

First Officer Bradley expressed his alarm over the crew's departure. Didn't the captain realize the prisoner transfer had been moved to the next morning?

The captain apologized. He hadn't read the dispatch. He'd have his aide recall the crew at once.

* * * * *

Bevin Quinlan sat at her desk reviewing requisitions. Snippets of dark hair eluded their pins and fell over her forehead. Her blue eyes sparkled when she saw Aidan.

"Hello, darlin'," he said. "I'm glad you're here. I need a favor."

The sparkle faded. "I see. You haven't come to see me."

"Oh, but I have. If you weren't here, I'd have found you. I have a few items to add to the miscellaneous articles we sent down the other day, and I don't want them logged in just yet."

Bevin lifted the key ring from its hook. "That's what those fellas said when they brought the other things. What's going on?"

"Nothing for you to worry about. Give me the keys. I'll return them when I'm done."

Her glare said no. "I'm responsible for the keys. I'm coming with you."

He'd expected this. Bevin might love him, but she was a responsible army officer whom he wouldn't easily hoodwink. He smiled his most charming smile. "I want to put a few things with the stuff the fellas brought the other day. You can show me where."

"I can. Let's go." She jingled the key ring and headed for the door.

Ten minutes later, Aidan was looking over the P-4 that less than a week ago had been set to annihilate his family. Bars of plastique rested in a cabinet. Remote control timers and blasting caps sat beside them. Vaguely aware of the alarm on Bevin's face, he selected several six-inch bars and blasting caps and slipped them into his pockets.

"What are you doing, Aidan? I thought you were bringing things in, not taking them out."

Ignoring her, he searched the other cabinets. "Where are our own fine electronic timers? I have no use for these radio things. I don't want to set the stuff off by remote. I'd rather set it ahead and be done with it. Ah, here they are." The timers found their way into other pockets. The components of his firing train complete, Aidan closed the cabinet doors.

Bevin grabbed the front of his jacket and yanked hard. "Set what stuff? What game is this, Aidan Dacey?"

He eased her hands from his jacket. "I'm seeing to it that certain elements don't threaten my family anymore."

Her eyes grew wide. She pulled her hands from his. "You can't. It's

318

wrong! If you do this, you're as bad as them!"

"What if I told you that one of them was the captain of the English vessel that scuttled the *Fancy Annie* after his men murdered her crew? Murdered your own grandfather!"

Bevin gasped. Her eyes fluttered while she considered his words. "Aidan! Oh, Aidan, you aren't thinking you don't care what happens to you, are you?"

He let out a relieved breath. She wasn't going to stop him. "I won't tell you a word of a lie. I care about few things in this world, and you're one of them." He pecked her mouth.

She nudged him away. "Never mind your blarney and blathering. How will I explain this stuff being gone?"

"No one logged it in, remember?" His good-bye kiss not only left her breathless, it branded her an accessory. "Thank you, darlin'. I couldn't have done it without you."

Tonight he'd meet his father and Uncle Peadar at Clontarf to discuss the final security arrangements. He'd spend the night in the hangar and board the *Cecilia* at dawn.

Five minutes in the engine room was all he needed.

✳ ✳ ✳ ✳ ✳

The drive south was easy at four in the morning. Though plenty of time remained before sunrise, Neil kept an eye to the east. Before long, a tiny glow sparkled at the skyline. He turned onto an unpaved road and roused Talty from her catnap. "We're here."

Rubbing her eyes, she sat up in the seat beside him. "Where?"

"In Wicklow, near the beach. Come on."

A torch from the glove compartment lit their way. Holding hands, they came to a large sign: Private Property—No Trespassing.

"Maybe we shouldn't be here, Neil."

"It's early. No one will know."

He led her down to the rocky beach and sat her on a large, flat boulder. The last time he'd been here he'd gathered driftwood. Kneeling in the sand now, he set fire to the wood. Her cheeks glowed in the light of the flames. He sat beside her. "Are you warm enough?"

"I'm fine. Are you going to tell me why we're here?"

"I've always loved the beach. I've been visiting different ones. This is my favorite."

"We shouldn't be here. It's private property."

"We're doing no harm. By the time anyone comes, we'll be gone."

Their mouths melded while the fire popped and crackled. When it burned down, Neil added no more wood. Sunlight twinkled on the surface of the sea.

He took her hand. "Asking you to marry me in front of the whole family wasn't what I had in mind. I'd like to give it another try."

"I thought so." She smiled and waited.

"You told me you love the sunrise because it fills you with the promise of the day. I brought you here to see the sunrise. Not for the promise of the day, but for the promise of the rest of our lives. I love you, Talty. Will you marry me?"

Her eyes gleamed. She squeezed his hand. "You're the other half of what I am, Neil. I love you well, and I'll stand beside you always."

None of his dreams had been so sweet. While one hand stroked her cheek, the other retrieved the box from his pocket. When he opened it, the band of roses glittered in the dawn.

"Oh, Neil, it's beautiful! But we weren't supposed to do this. There wasn't time for presents, they said."

"I've had this for a while, darlin'. It was only a matter of time before I gave it to you." He plucked the ring from its case and slipped it on her finger. "We still have lots to discuss."

Talty stared at the ring as if she were dreaming. "Like what?"

"Like, what will happen with your ISF career? Where will we live?"

"I expect we'll live at Rowan Court. It's a fine place, right in town."

"But it has no garden. I know how much you love your garden in California. We should find a place with a garden."

"I can have something done with the gardens in Malahide."

"Those old things? Don't you want something you can design yourself?" He stepped away from the rocks and stomped the ground. "I thought maybe right about here for the herb garden. The landscape fella says you could even grow roses here, if they're the right sort."

The astonishment on her face delighted him. A few feet to the left, he stomped again. "The kitchen will be here, with a big window that looks out over the sea. You'll have your sunrise every day, girl."

"Neil! What have you done? You wanted a beach, so you bought one?"

"I did, though the beach is just a small part of it. I wanted the house built before we were married, but now we can plan it together."

Talty eyed the ring and then gazed lovingly back at Neil. "We'll do everything together, Neily. This is all so hard to believe. I keep thinking something will go wrong and spoil it all."

He hugged her. "Nothing will go wrong. I love you, Tal."

✱ ✱ ✱ ✱ ✱

As Roger had hoped, concerns about his mental health led to his transfer to the *Cecilia* apart from the other prisoners. After an early breakfast, the medical officer escorted him to a small office near the courtyard. An unmarked car waited outside.

The burly guard unsnapped a pair of handcuffs from his belt. "Come along, Your Grace. We're taking you to see a pretty boat."

Roger recoiled from the handcuffs. "Please. That isn't necessary."

Nevertheless, the cuffs snapped over his wrists. "Sorry, sir. Rules is rules. Don't you worry. I've got the master key to all the handcuffs right here." The guard patted his pocket.

Seething at the indignity, Roger took special note which pocket the guard patted.

The key wouldn't be there long.

CHAPTER THIRTY-SEVEN

A Rain of Fire and Blood

The unmarked prison car arrived at the Clontarf marina at seven on Friday morning. Roger recognized First Officer Bradley, the traitor whose pointing arm now guided the driver into a parking slot beside the boathouse.

HMS *Cecilia*'s captain waited beside the boathouse with two crewmen. The taller crewman opened the rear door for Roger and the medical officer. Despite his handcuffed wrists, Roger rose unaided from the car.

"Good morning, Your Grace," the captain said. "We'll take you to our finest cabin."

"I expect no less." Roger's part was to create confusion. He peered down his nose at the prison guard. "And now that I'm here, remove these outrageous shackles."

The guard wagged his head. "Sorry, sir. We can't remove them until you're in your cabin."

"Remove these manacles at once, do you hear? I refuse to move another step until you do. Remove these wretched appurtenances now!"

The captain stepped forward. "What harm can there be in allowing His Grace the dignity of his station? I'll see that nothing goes amiss."

The guard's face hardened. "I never broke the rules in all the years I've been a warder. I'm not about to start now."

The captain nodded. The crewmen drew weapons. "Now," said the captain. "Where is the key to the handcuffs?"

"In his left inside pocket." Roger backed up to allow the captain access to the guard. As he did, he swung his restrained fists. The medical officer crumpled against the boathouse wall.

"What is this?" Bradley demanded.

"Nothin' for you to worry about," said the shorter crewman. "We're just going to lock these men in the boathouse for a few hours."

Eyes wide, Bradley turned his head from the crewman to the captain. "Sir, I must protest—"

The captain's attention remained on the handcuffs he unlocked. "I thought you would. You'll be locked in with them, I'm afraid."

Roger rubbed his wrists. "That key will open all the other cuffs."

"We'll put it to good use shortly, Your Grace." The captain tucked the key in his shirt pocket and opened the boathouse door. "Inside, gentlemen, if you please."

A shove from behind sent Bradley and the prison guard tripping through the door. At the same time, the taller crewman pulled the medical officer to his feet.

Still breathless from Roger's assault, the officer scowled at his captors. "I'm disappointed in you, Roger," he said as the crewman pushed him through the boathouse door.

Roger turned away from him. "Get on with it."

The captain nodded. The crewmen stepped to the doorway. Their noise-suppressed pistols spit a dozen times.

"Are you sure you won't come aboard, Your Grace?"

"No, Captain. There's something I must see to first. If I'm not back before you get underway, leave without me. I'll join you on the Isle of Man." He pointed at the prison car. "I'll need the keys. They'd be in one of the other pockets. Where are the things I asked for?"

The taller crewman found the car keys. The shorter retrieved a rucksack from behind the boathouse. Roger took both keys and sack, hurried to the car, and drove away.

* * * * *

Aidan's request to conduct an early morning security inspection aboard the *Cecilia* aroused no suspicion. The Officer of the Deck greeted him by name and pointed him toward the area that would quarter the prisoners during the nine-hour voyage trip to Rathlin Island.

"I'd escort you myself, but we're short of crew. Shore leave, sir."

Aidan responded with a crisp smile. "No problem. I'm sure I can find my way."

His soft-soled shoes made no sound as he rounded the corner leading to the holding area. Glancing over his shoulder, he detoured into the hot, noisy, unmanned engine room and set his charges near the diesel engines and generators.

323

He'd calmly suggested the spot inspection the night before, during a strategy meeting with his father and Uncle Peadar. They'd approved the idea, believing the careful measures they were taking would prevent any intended escape. Aidan had sabotaged those measures as effectively as he had sabotaged the *Cecilia*.

Peadar believed the failure of HMS *Cecilia*'s captain to cancel his crew's shore leave resulted from a communications breakdown. Aidan was to have the captain recall his men. He didn't. He was also to warn the captain of a possible escape attempt, though he neglected to do this as well, wanting the prisoners to have every advantage for a successful getaway.

Aidan did the math. The *Cecilia* would leave Clontarf on the next high tide, this morning at half-nine. At an average speed of seventeen knots, she'd reach Rathlin Island in nine hours. He set the timers to go off at half-twelve, when the ship would be farthest from shore, off Dundalk Bay, fifty miles north of Clontarf.

Convinced that no one would discover his part in the ship's demise, he returned to the hangar. Bevin would say nothing—she'd helped him, after all—and no one on board the *Cecilia* would survive to say he hadn't done what he was supposed to do.

And that was when the doubts crept in.

Ridding the world of vermin like Wessex was one thing, but innocent men would be aboard that ship. Aidan hadn't thought of those men when his Swiss army knife had notched the blocks of P-4 to direct the blasts at the diesel engines.

He told himself he was avenging Jill's murder. Lying on his bunk in the hangar, he tried to conjure her smiling face instead of the rain-soaked, rose-covered corpse that haunted him. Disturbed that she was unclear in his memory, he closed his eyes to bring her face into focus.

It melded into Bevin Quinlan's face.

If you do this you're as bad as them!

No. She was wrong. She didn't know the grief his family had endured.

But she did know. Her own family had suffered from Wessex treachery.

Treachery that was in the past. Aidan was protecting his family from future harm.

If you do this you're as bad as them!

Aidan checked his watch. Eight-thirty. Just enough time to pull the blasting caps. He flipped his phone open and called Bevin.

She didn't answer. He left a message. "You were right, love. I'm going to fix it. I'm going to toss that stuff in the ocean." Strapping on his gun belt, he hurried to the dock.

Neil parked the Jaguar near the hangar and walked around the car to open the passenger door. Talty decided she'd allow him to spoil her a little, at least for now. She ran her thumb over the band of roses and smiled.

The tide was high, the breeze salty and warm. Screeching seagulls glided over the sunlit water. The raven-black Morrigan basked in the sunshine. Behind it, the Sea King rested on the mangled grass.

Neil put on his Ranger jacket. "Your father is already here. We're late."

"No, we're not. It's only twenty past nine."

Behind them a small sedan screeched into the parking lot. The door opened. A young woman in an army lieutenant's uniform rushed toward them, her pinned-back hair coming loose.

Neil remarked that she looked familiar.

"We met her at Curragh," Talty said. "She taught Aidan's classes after Jill died."

The woman wasted no words on hellos. "Where's Aidan?"

"At the dock, I expect," answered Neil. "What's the emergency, lieutenant?"

Talty feared it was more than a romantic quarrel. "Tell us while we walk over. Bevin, isn't it?"

"Yes, ma'am. Sorry. Bevin Quinlan." Her heels clicked on the pavement. She nearly passed them in her press to find Aidan.

"I'm Neil Boru, and this is Talty Boru."

"Yes, I know. You're Aidan's cousins."

Even with some new calamity looming, Talty smiled. To Bevin Quinlan, Princess Taillte and the Duke of Leinster were merely Aidan's cousins. "We are. Now, what's this all about?"

"Yesterday, Aidan took some P-4 from Curragh to blow up that boat."

Neil stopped cold. His eyes bugged. Talty's mouth opened so wide she tasted the salty air. She spun and scanned the scene below.

HMS *Cecilia* sat at the dock, ready to get underway. A unit of King's Rangers stood near Brian, who conversed with Kieran and Richard. Nick's arms waved as he talked to Samantha. Peadar waited near the gangway with a man whose insignia marked him as the ship's captain. Four English seamen stood near them. More of *Cecilia*'s crew waited on deck to receive their human cargo. Flanked by uniformed guards, handcuffed men walked toward the ship from a shuttle bus bearing the Irish Prison Service logo.

Neil shaded his eyes and searched the crowd. "Where's Aidan?"

"There!" Bevin pointed to the gangway. Aidan and Richard were boarding the ship.

Neil started running but froze at the sound of gunshots. *Cecilia's* crew had fired rifles into the air. "Get down!" he yelled, snatching his pistol from inside his jacket.

Talty had already pulled Bevin to the ground. Neil crouched in front of them. In horrified silence, they watched the scene unfold.

As the crew aimed their rifles at the small crowd, the four seamen near the gangway seized Aidan and Richard, disarming them and jamming pistols against their necks. The prisoners sprinted up the gangway. Brandishing his own weapon, the captain backed up after them, his shouted words lost in the breeze. The seamen pulled Aidan and Richard onto the ship. Another burst of rifle fire, and the gangway lifted. *Cecilia* cleared the dock.

"It's going to blow up!" cried Bevin.

Neil tucked his gun away and wrenched her to her feet. "What did Aidan do? What did he tell you?"

"He took explosives and timers from the ordnance depot." She looked away. "I unlocked it for him. He said he'd see to it that certain elements didn't threaten his family anymore."

Feeling dizzy, Talty rose. "Did he say what time it would go off?"

"No."

Neil released Bevin's wrists. "I expect it will be somewhere between Clontarf and Rathlin Island. And you didn't think to tell anyone, lieutenant?"

"Please, sir! I'm telling you now. He said the man who killed my grandfather is on that boat. I don't know if it's true, or if he was coddin' me. He just—well, he caught me unawares."

"Your grandfather?" Neil's tone softened. "Who was he?"

"His name was Matt Foley. He was the captain of the *Fancy Annie*."

"Oh, no. Aidan wasn't coddin' you." Neil stared at the departing ship.

Talty stepped beside him. "What are you thinking? If we try to contact the *Cecilia* and tell them there's a bomb on board, they won't believe it."

"I need Dan. We have to get Aidan and Richard off that boat without letting anyone know about those explosives. Aidan will be in serious trouble if it gets out."

"He already is. Wait till I get hold of him."

The *Cecilia* was leaving the marina. When she passed the *Lady Grania's* berth, her 40 mm cannons boomed. Neil pushed both women down. The crowd dropped to the ground as well, helpless to stop the guns from blasting the king's yacht to pieces. Then, as abruptly as it started, the bombardment ended. Aided by wind and current, *Cecilia* put on a burst of speed and made her cowardly escape.

"You bastards!" Talty hoped no one had been aboard the *Lady Grania*, though that seemed unlikely. "Maybe Aidan had the right idea after all."

"Maybe." Neil's lips were tight and colorless. He scanned the angry crowd. "There's Dan. Get to the hangar, Tal. Try to figure out what Aidan was thinking. Get on the radio and let me know. Tell my father we might need the Sea King." He sprinted away.

Talty glanced at the ring he'd given her only a few hours ago. "Be careful, Neil," she whispered. She managed a smile for Bevin. "Can you hold out in those heels?"

Fingers shaking, Bevin brushed a clump of hair from her forehead. "I'll do, ma'am."

Talty spotted her uncle in a flurry of Rangers. Nick and Samantha were with them. She and Bevin reached the marina just as the wail of sirens pierced the air. Ambulances and fire trucks rushed into the boatyard.

"Uncle Peadar!" Talty shouted over the din. "Nick! Is everyone all right? We saw what happened. What did they tell you?"

"We're all right," Peadar said, his voice deadly calm. "That gobshite captain said he'd kill Aidan and Richard if we tried to stop them. He threatened to fire missiles at the shore. We must disable those missiles. I sent Neil and Dan after them."

"But Aidan—"

"Who are you, young lady?"

Despite her bedraggled appearance, Bevin stood erect when Talty introduced her. "Neil wants the Sea King on standby, Uncle."

Peadar summoned Rory and Barry. "Get the Sea King ready to follow Neil and Dan, though I don't know who the devil will fly the thing."

Rory scratched his ear. "That's surely a problem, sir. We have no other pilots here at the moment."

Nick smacked his chest. "I can fly the Sea King blindfolded."

Peadar refused. "You can't become involved. You're an ISF officer."

"So am I," Talty said, "and that's our CO out there. Nick goes."

Samantha nudged between them. "You'll need a doctor along in case there's casualties."

"Heaven help us," Peadar muttered. "Go! And see that you all get back here in one piece."

The Morrigan rose from behind the castle. It hovered and then veered out to sea in a sendoff of good luck shouts. The sight heartened Talty. The helicopter's weaponry was more than a match for *Cecilia*'s.

The Morrigan would hunt the cowards down—and she always caught what she hunted.

If only Aidan and Richard weren't aboard.

*****

Aidan rocked on a wooden stool and watched Richard pace. Roger's men had taken their guns, though they'd been in too much of a hurry to search their clothes before locking them in the bare-bones cabin. Aidan's Swiss army knife would make short work of the lock on the door. Before it did, he owed Richard an explanation.

"We can get out of the room easily enough, Richard. It's getting off the ship before it explodes that will be the trick."

Richard whirled. "What?"

Aidan explained how he'd set the plastic explosives in the engine room. "But I changed my mind, you see. I was on my way to pull the timers. I just didn't get there in time."

"Bloody hell! We have to warn the crew!"

"All right." Aidan got up and banged on the door. "Hello out there! There's a bomb in the engine room. The ship's going to blow up!"

Silence. Aidan pulled out his Swiss army knife. "Time to go."

"We could try for the engine room and defuse the charges."

"We could. We might even have time, but we have no weapons except my wee knife here. Tell you what. You're a big fella. You go first, clear a path through Roger's eejits with your bare fists, and I'll follow along behind, nice and easy."

Richard's darting eyes reflected his racing thoughts. "We passed a row of rolled-up dinghies on deck. If we can get one inflated and into the water, we can get the hell out of here."

"How fast can you row?"

"With a ship about to explode behind me, faster than you'd believe. Do you have a better idea?"

"I might. Wessex used a rigid inflatable with an outboard to hijack the *Lady Grania*. It's still on deck, under a tarp. I believe two strong lads like us could hoist it over the side. The water is cold, but it's summer, and we'd only be wet for a minute or two."

"Your P-4 will take the engines with it. We can't outrun a detonation of that magnitude."

"Maybe we can. Lambay Island isn't far. You can see it there." Aidan pointed to the window. "I'm betting Neil will come after us in the Morrigan. He'll toss us a line, and we can have him alert the *Cecilia* about the P-4, if anyone will listen. Will that do?"

Richard nodded toward the door. Aidan had it unlocked in seconds.

*****

Talty and Bevin raced to the hangar. They had little time: Brian and Peadar were right behind them.

Talty switched on the radio and set it to the Morrigan's frequency. "Get the maps in that desk drawer, Bevin. Find Ireland's east coast."

Bevin's efficiency impressed Talty. The maps only snapped and rustled for a moment.

"Here it is. What are we doing, ma'am?"

"Figuring out when Aidan's surprise will occur. If I were going to blow up the *Cecilia,* I'd do it as far offshore as possible." She ran her finger over the map from Clontarf to Rathlin Island. Then she tapped the Irish Sea, east of Dundalk Bay. "Right here."

"How long will it take the ship to get there?"

"The trip is a hundred and forty nautical miles. *Cecilia* is a Verburg. She can sail twenty, maybe twenty-two knots if they push her, but they wouldn't for a trip like this. So we'll say seventeen knots, a nice, comfortable cruise. Nearly nine hours. If Aidan set the timers to go off here"—Talty pointed to Dundalk Bay—"she'd get there three hours after she left Clontarf."

"Half-twelve," whispered Bevin.

"Yes." Talty's watch read nearly eleven. She switched on the radio. "Hangar C to Sachem One. Come in Sachem One."

Neil's voice crackled back. "Sachem One here. What have you got?"

"A look at the map suggests the party will be off Dundalk at half-twelve."

"That makes sense. Good work, Hangar C. We have the target on radar. She just passed Lambay Island and is on course for Man. We should have visual soon. I'll try to raise them and get them to stop."

"You can't!" Bevin cried. "They said they'd kill Aidan if anyone tries to stop them."

"We are aware of the situation," Neil said after a brief pause. "Sachem One out."

Talty placed the handset on its hook and inspected Bevin. Her hair was hopelessly tangled. Mud stained her wrinkled uniform. Her stockings were torn, and her tear-streaked face quivered with heartache and exhaustion.

"Go and fix yourself, Bevin. You'll find clean clothes and things in my locker, the last one on the right."

"All right." She turned to go and stopped. "Will they? Can they?"

"My commanding officer is a clever man. So is Aidan. They won't give up. They'll find a way. When they do, Neil and Nick will be there to help."

Trying to smile, Bevin disappeared into the locker room. Talty hoped Richard and Aidan were being as clever as she'd painted them.

Counting to three, Aidan and Richard heaved the inflatable over the side. Aidan checked his watch. "Let's get after it before it floats away."

"What's going on here?" Gordon Randolph asked behind them.

Adrenaline surged through Aidan's veins like an electrical current. "Go, Richard. I'll just be a minute." Giving Richard no time to respond, he lunged at Randolph, knocking him against the steel wall behind him.

Randolph recovered quickly, kicking back at the wall to catapult himself at Aidan. Aidan easily countered the attack. As he did, he caught a glimpse of Richard's worried face.

"Go, Richard! I'll be right there."

Richard went over the side.

* * * * *

Smoke wafted into the hangar, a grim reminder of the wrecked *Lady Grania* and her slaughtered crew. Talty debated whether or not to tell her father about the P-4. If she did, nothing would change—except that Aidan would be safer on the *Cecilia*. She said nothing.

Brian looked defeated. Kieran sat beside him, furious over the discovery of the bodies of the two prison guards and *Cecilia's* first officer, worried beyond words about Aidan.

Peadar barked orders into the telephone. The air traffic controllers on either side of the Irish Sea would reroute all aircraft from the area. The Coast Guard would divert all vessels from *Cecilia's* path. The police had arrived at the marina to help the Rangers contain the press and the curious.

The radio hummed. Neil's steady voice drew all eyes. "Sachem One to Hangar C. Come in."

Talty grabbed the handset. "This is Hangar C, Sachem One."

"We are southeast of Lambay Island and have visual contact with the target. We have an inflatable in the water off the target's aft deck. Request Code One SAR support."

Aidan and Richard must have found a way to get off the ship! Trying not to grin—the funereal mood in the hangar helped—Talty shot her uncle a silent question. When he nodded, Kieran ran outside and signaled the Sea King to deploy.

Talty spoke calmly into the radio. "Sea King Three is on its way, Sachem One. Have you contacted the target?"

"Affirmative, Hangar C. Target is hostile, but our monitors are clean."

Peadar took the handset. "This is Gabriel Two, Sachem One. Continue shadowing the target. Watch your missile launch monitor. If it even blinks, take the target out."

"Roger that, Gabriel Two. We are locked on the target."

"We'll monitor communications. Good luck, Sachem One. Hangar C over and out."

*****

Neil's watch read eleven forty-five. He glanced at the gunnery station in the Morrigan's nose, where Dan worked the controls with serene efficiency.

"Aren't we too close to use the missiles, Neil?"

"Not if it's the only way to stop them from firing theirs." Neil scanned his monitors, trying to ignore the stab of guilt that threatened to run him through for not telling Dan what Aidan had done. At least he would spare Dan from having to fire the death-dealing Akumas. The missile controls were on Neil's flight control grip.

"Missile launch detector activated," said Dan.

"Put the false guidance signals on standby. Keep the jammers on. They can see us, but I don't want them to pick up the Sea King yet. I'm going to try to raise her again."

"Don't be so polite this time."

Neil didn't intend to be. He opened the hailing frequency. "This is Air Corps Sachem One calling HMS *Cecilia*. Do you copy, *Cecilia*?"

Static hissed through the cockpit. "This is HMS *Cecilia*. Turn back, Sachem One. We have hostages. Our missiles are locked on the Town of Dundalk, and we will fire. We've locked our guidance system onto your aircraft as well. Turn back."

Neil pressed the mute button. "Pleasant fellas. Keep your eyes on the detectors, Danny. I don't want to miss my wedding tomorrow." He released the button. "This is Air Corps Sachem One. *Cecilia* is in our field of fire. Put down your arms and surrender, or we'll blow you out of the water."

Neil eyed the inflatable below him, rocking in the swells at the rear of the ship. It was too far down to tell who was in it. He switched on the optical sensor and turned up the magnification. Richard sat near the dinghy's outboard.

"I've got Richard, but I don't see Aidan. Where's the Sea King?"

"Coming up behind us," Dan said. "Fast." He pointed to the inflatable. "Look, Neil."

Water splashed near the dinghy. Someone on the *Cecilia* had fallen overboard.

*****

Randolph aimed a roundhouse punch at Aidan's head. Aidan dropped to evade the attack. Then he sprang up and smashed his fists into Randolph's ears, a double-barreled blow meant to rupture eardrums.

Randolph howled and struck Aidan's chest. Aidan took the punch, giving way just enough to give him room to drive an elbow into Randolph's jaw. Randolph staggered.

Richard shouted, but Aidan refused to leave Randolph alive.

"You're better at killing girls, aren't you! Get up, you gick!"

Blood poured from Randolph's mouth. Venom blazed in his eyes. He shot a left-hand slap at Aidan's head. Aidan moved sideways to avoid it, and stepped right into the stomach punch Randolph had intended. The blow robbed him of breath and knocked him backward. Randolph's fist slid into an uppercut that smashed his jaw. Aidan teetered and nearly fell.

Randolph twisted Aidan's arm. Aidan yanked his arm—and Randolph— back toward him and rammed his other hand into Randolph's face.

Randolph grunted but didn't let go. He shoved. He pushed. He forced Aidan back. The ship's rail dug into Aidan's spine. He tried to heave Randolph away. Randolph squeezed against him, bending him over the railing to break his back.

Aidan relaxed and rocked until he and Randolph both toppled overboard. Gripping and squeezing, Aidan held Randolph's head beneath the water. Randolph thrashed. He finally went limp. Aidan kicked his corpse away. Teeth chattering, he swam through the frigid water to the inflatable.

* * * * *

The optical monitor showed Richard pulling Aidan into the raft. Neil pushed the radio to the Sea King's frequency. "This is Air Corps Sachem One calling Sea King Three."

Nick Tomasi's cool, competent voice crackled in the receiver. "This is Sea King Three, Sachem One. You now have buddies on station."

Despite the gravity of the situation, Neil smiled. "We have two other buddies on that inflatable, Sea King Three."

"Heads up!" Dan shouted.

Shells from *Cecilia*'s rear-mounted guns blasted through the inflatable's hull. The stricken dinghy tossed Richard and Aidan into the water.

"Bastards!" At a touch of Dan's hand, hundreds of rounds erupted from the Morrigan's nose, strafing *Cecilia*'s aft deck, destroying the guns and killing the gunner.

"Nice shooting, Sachem One!" shouted Nick. "Can you take out those forward guns too? A guy on a winch line would sure make an easy target."

"Affirmative, Sea King." Neil had already veered toward the ship's forward deck. "Take those fuckin' guns out, Danny."

Dan's hand moved again. The Morrigan's automatic cannon reduced the forward guns to useless chunks of metal.

Nick whooped. "Now we're sucking diesel!"

Dan hit his mute button. "That leaves their missiles."

Neil had no misgivings now about firing the Akumas, though he'd do his best to get Aidan and Richard out of harm's way first. He checked the missile launch detector. "They haven't locked on us yet. Even if they had, a missile strike this close would bowl them over. I don't think they'd be stupid enough to fire."

"I think their fuckin' mooring balls are altogether loose."

Smiling grimly, Neil checked the optical monitor again. Richard held onto Aidan, who appeared hurt. The current was sweeping them out to sea. "Get them out of there, Sea King Three."

"Roger, Sachem One," said Nick. "You're our guardian angel."

Neil checked his watch. Twelve-ten. "Imperative that you waste no time, Sea King Three."

* * * * *

Richard surfaced gasping, choking, and expecting the second round of gunfire to end his life. He suddenly realized the gunfire was the Morrigan's, blasting *Cecilia's* aft guns. Closing his eyes in gratitude, he scanned the debris around him. Aidan was nowhere in sight.

Richard dove. The salt water stung his eyes, yet he searched and saw a human form drifting below the surface. He rose for air and tore through the water, hooking his elbow around Aidan's neck. Desperately kicking, he reached the surface.

Aidan was unconscious, but he coughed. Richard held him close, not only to keep from losing him, but also to share their combined body warmth in the chilly water. At least the current was sweeping them away from the ship. Still, if the *Cecilia* blew... He tried not to think about that.

Sweeping down again like the huge black raven in Liam's story, the Morrigan destroyed *Cecilia's* forward guns and veered away. The Sea King hovered behind her.

Richard was shivering now, struggling to hold onto Aidan, straining to keep both their heads above water. Surely they'd see him.

* * * * *

"This is Gabriel Two calling Sachem One. Come in, Sachem One."

Talty prayed her uncle hadn't chosen a critical moment to raise the Morrigan.

"This is Sachem One"

"What's your status, Sachem One?"

"We are monitoring the target for hostile intent and guarding Sea King Three. One man is on the winch line now. One is already up."

Peadar yielded the handset to Brian. "This is Wolfhound One, Sachem One. Once Sea King Three is clear, order *Cecilia* to surrender. If she refuses, release your ordnance."

"Say again, Wolfhound One."

"If they refuse to surrender, you will release your ordnance. Do you copy?"

"Affirmative, Wolfhound One. Sachem One out."

Talty glanced at the clock. Twelve twenty-five. She hoped, as she suspected her father did, that *Cecilia* would refuse to surrender.

* * * * *

Twelve twenty-eight. Ever so gently, Neil drew the cyclic toward him to back away from the *Cecilia*. "This is Air Corps Sachem One calling HMS *Cecilia*. We have you in our line of fire. Put down your arms and surrender."

"This is Admiral Andrew Mayne. You're running out of fuel, Paddy. Give up. You've got your boys. Turn around or we will fire our missiles."

Neil's thumb slid over the flight control grip. He aimed two Akumas at *Cecilia*'s engine room. "You're bluffing, Mayne. You haven't got the cacks."

Dan's head jerked at the provocation. The launch detector shrieked. The pulsing green blip on the screen flashed. Neil fired and swerved away.

Cecilia shivered and disintegrated. Seconds later, the explosion thundered through the air. A second blast churned the sea and set Neil struggling to counter the shock waves.

"Mary and Joseph!" Dan shouted. "That was bigger than Hoy's Neck! I can't believe two little missiles could blow up a ship like that. And you aren't even going to give us a hint, are you, Neil?"

Dan had suspected something all along, but Neil couldn't tell him that the Akumas had had help from Aidan. "They must have hit the engines, Danny. We'll have a look for survivors and go home."

CHAPTER THIRTY-EIGHT

Closing Ranks

Suppressing a yawn, Neil stepped away from the window to let the day nurse draw the blinds. The light hurt Aidan's eyes. Tape and white gauze covered a gash on his forehead that had taken twenty-eight stitches to close.

"I'm fine, Neil," he murmured from his hospital bed. "Really. Just a little headache."

"Are you? That's good." Neil spoke in a soothing tone, relieved that his cousin was as well as anyone who'd nearly drowned, smashed his head, and suffered the initial stages of hypothermia could be. "Samantha is seeing about healing the cut on your head."

"It's nothing. I'm only having them fix it so's I can come to your wedding tomorrow. I'm fine, really."

"I'm glad to hear it. Because as soon as you can stand again, I'm going to beat you senseless. What the hell were you thinking, pulling a stunt like that? Do you know how much danger you put everyone in?"

Aidan turned away. "Sorry, Neil. I expect I'm for it with the old fellas."

"We didn't tell them. Talty and I are the only ones who know. And your girl Bevin."

"She's not my girl." Aidan sighed miserably. "She might have been, but now she thinks I'm bog slime. Richard knows too. I had to tell him, so he'd have an incentive to get off the ship."

"I expect that did it."

"He's all right?"

"Yes. He's going home soon."

"Good. I did try to get the stuff off the boat, but it didn't work out."

"Maybe it did. Roger and his pals are gone. No complaints there."

335

The door opened. Samantha tiptoed in. "How are you feeling?"

"His head hurts," said Neil.

"I'll bet. Well, I have good news and bad news. Here's the good news: I tracked down the bioaccelerator we left here after you got yourself shot, Neil. The doctors used it today to heal a little girl with third-degree burns. She's good as new. Not one scar."

Neil shook his head in amazement. "That's a grand thing. What's the bad news?"

"Treating the girl drained the battery pack. I called Creek at the lab. He's been working on a new fuel cell to replace the batteries. If someone can go get a few of them, we'll have Aidan looking his handsome self lickety-split."

"You can really fix my head?"

Neil laughed and gently tousled Aidan's hair. "Now that would be a miracle. I'll get them, Samantha. We can't have Aidan miss the wedding."

"I'll let Creek know you're on your way." She waved and left.

"Now I can come to your wedding." Aidan sighed again, louder this time. "All alone."

"Call your girl and have her come with you."

"I told you, Neily. She's not my girl."

The door opened again. Talty eased into the room. Neil got a quick kiss, Aidan a sympathetic smile. "Hey, Aid. Howya?"

"I'll do, Beauty. You're a good girl to come by. Shouldn't you be getting your hair done or something?"

Talty rolled her eyes. "Once my mother and Jenna get their claws into me, they'll never let go. 'Try this on again, Talty. Your nails are a disgrace, Talty. What a shame we don't have time to perm your hair, Talty.' I'll stay away as long as I can, thank you."

"I'm driving up to the lab to pick up fuel cells for the bioaccelerator," Neil said. "Take a ride with me."

The door opened yet again. Bevin Quinlan peeked in. Neil had never seen such terror on Aidan's face.

"Come in," said Talty. "We were just leaving."

Aidan grabbed Talty's hand. "You don't have to go just yet, do you?"

Bevin approached the bed. "They can go or stay for all I care. I only came to see were you dead or alive, then I'll be off myself. You don't seem any worse for the wear."

"Oh, but I'm feeling just awful."

"Good. You deserve it. You lied to me, Aidan Dacey!"

Talty started to object. Neil tapped her arm and shook his head. He inched toward the door.

"I only did what I thought I had to do," Aidan practically whimpered. "I meant no harm."

"No harm? Coddin' me with one hand and stealing things off the shelf with the other. 'Who else would I ask, love? You're one of the few things I care about, love.'"

Aidan seemed to shrivel in the bed. "I'm sorry, Bevin. I did think about what you said, and I tried to fix the harm. I don't suppose you'll believe that, though."

"I don't suppose I'd ever believe another word you say." She bent and pecked his mouth. "Good thing you left that message on my answering machine."

Neil's hand was on the door. "We'll be going now."

Aidan didn't hear him. "What message? Oh, that. Well…"

Talty laughed all the way to the car. "She'll keep him in line, I think."

"I hope so. Let's get those fuel cells. I don't know about you, but I'm melted."

*****

Bearing different license plates now, the missing prison car merged into the traffic behind the Jaguar. Roger never lost sight of it. He knew who was in it: Talty Boru, who'd murdered his faithful Philip, and her lowborn cousin, whom the Irish were calling a hero for slaughtering Andrew, Gordon, and dozens of Roger's loyal supporters.

All day he'd listened to the radio broadcasts. Everyone believed he'd been aboard the *Cecilia*. No one would interfere while he completed his business here.

The Jaguar's left directional blinked. Roger slowed and followed it. When it swerved into a car park, he drove on. Just up the road, he stopped and turned back.

*****

Talty played with Neil at avoiding puddles on the walkway to the lab. The building was dark. The only lights shone from Creek's basement workshop.

Loving Neil's arm around her, she eyed the rooms on the upper levels. "We can leave him downstairs for an hour or so. The living quarters have cozy beds."

"And they call us poor fellas rascals. Talty darlin', no one enjoys a good bout of loving more than I do, but if I lie down now I'll fall asleep. You must be tired yourself. We've both been up since three this morning."

"I see how it is. We're not even married yet, and you're already pretending you're all tuckered out." Talty tapped the security keypad. The

337

lock clicked. They entered the building.

Neil bussed her forehead. "The only pretending I'm doing now is to be awake. I'll make it up to you soon enough."

They descended the concrete staircase to Creek's largest lab. Off-key humming drew them inside. Talty stiffened at the sight of the Peregrine Portal sparking and snapping in the center of the room.

Creek knelt beside it, tapping this and twisting that. Tomato sauce stained his wrinkled shirt. Grease smudged his cheek. The scraggly scientist grinned and rose to greet them. "I hear you two have had a busy day."

Neil stepped forward to shake hands. Talty threw her arm out. "No! Don't go near it!"

"There's nothing to worry about." Creek pointed to a lever behind him. "The transpulsion switch is off. The portal is closed tight."

Despite his assurances, Talty's stomach wouldn't stop fluttering. "I thought you were sending that thing back to Fort Pinard. What are you doing down here, Creek?"

"My amazing staff and I have been developing a new type of microfuel cell that uses lutanium instead of hydrogen. Our miniature version can plug into the bioaccelerators more easily than the battery packs we've been using. They work so well, I thought I'd try them on some of the other doodads we have around here."

"And you chose this thing?" She jumped when the portal sparked.

"Well, it's the only thing that has a spot to plug the fuel cells into." He held his tools up. "At least it does now. Pretty soon we'll generate enough electricity to run this whole place. And I happen to know where we can get plenty of lutanium."

A buzzer sounded from somewhere in the building. Creek's shoulder twitched. "That's dinner. I get the best pizza from a place down the road."

Neil offered to get it for him.

"No need. I could use the exercise. I'll grab those fuel cells on my way back." Humming away, Creek left the lab.

Neil stared mesmerized at the Peregrine Portal. "Talty, is that thing what I think it is?"

"Yes," she whispered. "He should've sent it back by now."

"It doesn't matter. You're never going through it again. Come here."

His loving embrace held no lust. For several luscious moments, she snuggled against him, secure in his arms.

"How sweet," said an English voice.

Neil pulled Talty behind him. "Wessex. So you're alive."

"I'll be alive long after you and your whore cousin." He raised a pistol.

Neil shouldered Talty sideways and lunged. He grabbed Roger's arm and chopped it down against the thigh he raised. Cursing, Roger dropped the gun and kicked. Neil sidestepped and swung at Roger's head.

Roger ducked just in time. Then he sprang back up and spit in Neil's face. Neil instinctively wiped his eyes and didn't see the punch that knocked the breath from him, though he blindly grabbed the offending arm and twisted until Roger bellowed.

Amid the ruckus of grunts and growls, Talty snatched Roger's gun from the floor and rolled to her knees, poised to shoot, but Neil was in the line of fire. He'd maneuvered in close to counter Roger's skilled kicks and was dishing out a brutal barrage of slaps and pokes.

Roger pounced and slammed Neil against the wall. The bang stunned him. He stood defenseless while Roger's squeezing hands crushed his throat.

Neil seemed to deflate. Suddenly he propelled his shoulder up and broke Roger's grip. Then he spun and drove both elbows into Roger's solar plexus. Roger stumbled. Eyes wild with rage, he regained his balance.

Talty was afraid to shoot. She could attack Roger herself—and was most tempted to do so—but a better idea presented itself.

She tossed the gun on the counter and wrenched the portal's transpulsion switch. The crackling sparks intensified to a pulsing glow. The gateway was open. "Neil! The portal!"

Neil shoved Roger through the humming gateway. His momentum nearly sent him through too. Talty tackled him to the floor just in time.

Roger disappeared in a swarm of sparks. Moments later, a man's shrieks pierced the room from the other side of the portal.

I'd never allow anyone who didn't have the proper neural baseline frequencies to go through the portal. If they didn't, they'd die the way Zev did.

Talty felt no sympathy for Roger Wessex. Still, she buried her face against Neil's chest until the wailing died away.

Neil lurched to his feet and pulled the transpulsion lever. The humming stopped. "You are *never* going through that thing again, Tal. Get the gun. Let's find Creek."

Slipping the pistol into her purse, Talty hurried with Neil to the main lab. A chair had been jammed under the doorknob. Neil wrenched it away and opened the door.

Creek sat at a table in the corner. He'd finished his pizza and root beer and was paging through a technical journal. "It's about time you found me. The door got locked somehow. I couldn't open it, so I figured I'd eat my supper." He set the journal aside and walked to a cabinet. "I have the fuel cells right here."

Neil took the box. "Thank you, sir. We'll get these to Samantha."

"You should be more careful when you open the door for deliveries," Talty said. "We'll see you tomorrow, all right?"

"I wouldn't miss it for the world, Miss Talty. Nick has our uniforms all spiffed up. You know, he can probably do something for yours, Neil. It looks a little ragged."

Exhausted but smiling, Neil opened the door. "Good-night, Colonel."

✱ ✱ ✱ ✱ ✱

Geoffrey had lost. By this time tomorrow, Taillte Boru would be married. He rubbed his throbbing forehead. What was John saying?

"…that I'm going to attend to offer our best wishes to Princess Taillte on the occasion of her marriage."

"You stupid boy." Geoffrey pounded the desk. "I forbid you to go."

"I'm not a stupid boy, uncle. I'm the king, and I forbid *you* to interfere in my activities, or in any government activity from this day forward. You have no authority. I'm the representative of the people's sovereign power."

Had John raised his voice? Geoffrey tried to laugh at his nephew, but something was wrong with his lips. "You don't know what you're doing."

"I know exactly what I'm doing. I'm attempting to preserve what goodwill remains between England and Ireland. There's no need for us to steal their oil wells. We can negotiate."

John's face grew fuzzy. Geoffrey thought he really must visit the eye doctor. "After all I've done for you, you simpleton! What do you know of government, you and your crayons?"

"I deal with more than crayons. I attend hearings at Parliament and the House of Lords. I support charities and run committees."

The boy sounded…threatening? Geoffrey jumped up. Too fast. He reeled and leaned on the table. "Don't challenge me. I'll tell everyone what a half-wit you really are."

John planted his hands on the desk and leaned until his face, a man's face, determined and tough, was level with Geoffrey's. "Listen, Uncle. Do you remember Bert Benson? The MI6 man whose duty it is to protect the sovereignty of the king? He showed me a letter written by an officer who was on the *Coulter* when you stole Fargan from Ireland. The letter describes how you yourself shot the captain of that fishing boat and ordered your men to gun down his crew. And you said Roger was bad! I ought to turn *you* over to the Irish!"

Nausea bubbled in Geoffrey's stomach. He choked and grew dizzy, and as he collapsed, he heard John shouting for help.

CHAPTER THIRTY-NINE
A Major Diplomatic Advance

Sunlight streamed through the stained-glass windows of St. Columcille's Cathedral. Carnival colors washed over the foyer, where King's Rangers in full dress uniform stood guard over Talty and her father. Maura and Nancy chatted in a corner, their flowing blue gowns rustling with each move they made. From the other side of a heavy wooden door, the King's Piper tuned his Great Pipes. Talty found the primal caterwauling soothing.

She'd last seen Brian in his imposing naval uniform at Liam's wedding, and before that, the day she married Thomas. The suit still fit him well. He was a handsome man, her father.

Talty looked splendid herself today. The dressmaker's staff had handsewn pearls into the weightless lace of her sumptuous ivory gown. Despite Jenna's pronouncement that diamonds were an unsuitable match for pearls and lace, Talty wore her treasured Fianna pin on her collar.

Jenna might have backed off over the Fianna pin, but she would fuss over Talty's hair and face until the last moment. Talty didn't mind. She was representing Ireland today and couldn't have her tiara falling off. Ethereal and understated, the heirloom headpiece matched the gown perfectly. An ancient craftsman had wrought the gold into a wreath of tiny leaves and roses. Lustrous pearl droplets graced the fine golden strands that crisscrossed the top.

A side door opened. Dashing in his dress uniform and bearing no signs of his recent injuries, Aidan entered the foyer. "Look at you, Beauty. There are no words! You'll have them shading their eyes when you walk by. If you're ready, they're all set inside."

Aidan retreated through the door. Maura and Nancy hefted their flowers and bussed Talty's cheeks. Brian linked arms with her. Jenna set a huge bouquet, a mix of Princess Taillte and Ace of Hearts roses, in her other arm. The glowing aide then summoned the piper. Pipes droning, the traditionally clad musician led Maura, then Nancy into the church.

Holding her father's arm, Talty stepped onto the roll of white silk that covered the aisle all the way to the altar. As Peadar had promised, roses filled the church, casting their gentle perfume over the packed cathedral.

Talty recognized many heads of state. She knew the uniforms, if not the names, of the Irish Defense and International Security personnel who stood at attention in their assigned pews.

They passed the senior officers of the *Kincora*'s crew. And there was Kiyoshi, whose smiling face wore no mask today. In the next pews, Creek stood grinning beside Richard, Nick, and Samantha. The Daceys beamed when she passed. Kieran and Breege gave little waves. Nuala blew a kiss; Jack winked. Bevin stood with them, radiant in a peachy frock.

Arm in arm in the next row, Peadar and Peggy offered tender smiles. And in the front pew—for this wedding, there were no set sides for families of the bride and groom—Eileen stood alone. Talty smiled; her mother responded with a nod and a quivering lip.

At last, father and daughter reached the steps to the altar. The boys stood on the right side, Kevin on the top step, Liam on the middle. Enticing in his Air Corps uniform, Neil descended from the first step. He bent his knee and kissed Brian's hand, and then he stood and kissed Talty's fingers.

The piping stopped. Brian pecked Talty's cheek. She curtsied, and Neil knelt again, both offering formal obeisance to their king. When they rose, Brian shook Neil's hand and whispered, "I'm fiercely proud of the two of you," and he took his seat beside Eileen.

Clutching Neil's arm now, Talty climbed the steps to a small, unadorned altar where the officiating Brehon waited. At her request, the ceremony would be simple and nonreligious. The family had only chosen the cathedral for its capacity to hold more than one thousand guests.

And so, Talty wondered why the velvet prié-dieu remained at the front of the altar. She and Neil would not be kneeling today.

They stopped before the Brehon, a dignified gentleman in a three-piece suit and horn-rimmed glasses. Nancy took Talty's bouquet and set it on an elaborate stand.

The Brehon adjusted his microphone. "Good afternoon, and welcome. We are here today to join Neil and Talty in a marriage that has special significance not only for them, but for the Kingdom of Ireland. Neil and Talty, I might be the officiator here, but the power to sanction this union truly lies with you. Your hearts have already done that. Now place your hands on this Oathing Stone and swear that love before these honored witnesses."

The Brehon raised a square of blue limestone from the altar. Talty and Neil rested their fingers on it.

"Will you, Neil Ryan Christopher Boru, take Talty to be your wife? Will you live in truth with her, pledging your protection and love, surrendering yourself to her care, and joining your life to hers in a marriage of equals forevermore?"

Neil's answer rang through the church: "I will."

The Brehon rephrased his questions for Talty. She forgot the hundreds of watching eyes. "I will."

Kevin delivered the rings. Once the ritual exchange was completed, Talty relaxed. All that remained was the pronouncement that she and Neil were husband and wife.

"Neil, Talty, please kneel for the blessing."

What was this? Neil seemed surprised too, but he drew her down to the prié-dieu.

"For this most unusual wedding," said the Brehon, "we have a most unusual blessing. I understand no one has used it for centuries."

Where had it come from? The beatific smile on Liam's face gave Talty her answer.

The Brehon adjusted his glasses. "When the spirits of warriors seek each other in companionship and love, we as well as they are blessed. From the beginning of time, the warriors of Ireland have guarded the fruit-strewn mountains and showery woods that are our heritage. We have no fear that our enemies will rouse the swift seas. Our land is free of invaders, for you are strong in warlike deeds. Like lions fierce and furious, you protect us. You are our battle shields, our swords. Our elders and our children are safe from harm. Our cattle roam free, and our brimming pots bubble on their hooks.

"Avengers of a faithful people, we have seen you rise in battle and lift your red-tipped spears against aggressors. You have triumphed over proud giants, and yielded the green and glorious plains of Tara to none.

"Terror goes before you. Death is behind your backs. Your voices shake the sky. Your chariots roll on the open plain to scatter the battalions of the foe. Bright weapons glint in the air. Enemies count their wounds. You have fed their corpses to the ravens. You have thrown them into the sea again and again"—the Brehon paused for effect—"and yet again.

"But for all the might in your spears and swords and shields, remember that none of these is as mighty as the love you bear for each other. We invoke the blessing of our ancestors on this union of warriors. Stately and strong may you pace through your banquet hall. Mouth to mouth, skin to skin, may you reach out your hands to each other in kindness, as you raise your arms without mercy against our enemies.

"Laoch and Banlaoch, rise as one." The Brehon removed his glasses. "By the power invested in me by the Kingdom of Ireland, I declare you husband and wife."

Applause and cheers filled the cathedral. Neil held Talty's hands and kissed her mouth. She laughed at her own burning cheeks and took her bouquet from Nancy, the cue for the piper to return and lead the bridal party down the aisle.

In the foyer, Liam ushered the newlyweds to a side room, giving them each a hug as he did. "Wait here till we get everyone outside," he said, and he closed the door.

Neil smiled with joy—and relief. "We did it, Tal. I'm so proud of you. You look so beautiful. And Maura and Nancy. I had all I could do not to burst out laughing when you were all coming up the aisle. Liam was making the most obscene noises under his breath."

Talty chuckled. "Where do you suppose he dug up that old blessing? Is it real?"

"If Liam got it, it's real. It sounded like whoever wrote it, wrote it just for us."

"Oh, he was a real romantic, him and his corpse-fed ravens."

"A fitting poem for a lady with a gunship named the Morrigan."

They were kissing when Liam reopened the door. "Ah, getting right to it. Good man, Neil. 'Mouth to mouth, skin to skin…' I'm feeling right poetic today."

Talty feigned annoyance at the interruption. "What is it, Liam?"

Liam's hands flew to his chest. "'Such were her eyes that where her glance fell, all was bright.' The honor guard is ready. Let's get it done."

A roaring crowd greeted Talty and Neil outside the cathedral. Barry, Dan, Rory, Packy, and Jimmy Gallagher made up the left portion of the honor guard. Talty didn't know the first four ISF officers, but to her delight, Ron Chambeau stood at the end of the row.

"Center Face!" Jimmy shouted. "Draw Sabers!"

Ten swords rose in the air with astounding precision.

"Arch Sabers!"

The swords clanged together. Neil and Talty kissed and walked beneath them, symbolically entering their new life together. In one neat click, the guards returned their swords to their scabbards. Applause and shouts burst from the crowd.

A lazy smile appeared on Ron's face. "Congratulations, Major Princess."

Talty smiled back, unable to speak above the crowd's shouts of blessings and good wishes. With the rest of the family, she and Neil approached the police barriers, shaking hands and chatting with the people until the limousines arrived to whisk them off to Clontarf Castle.

* * * * *

Winking at his daughter and son-in-law, Brian squeezed Eileen's hand and stepped up to the rose-bedecked podium. Eyes turned. Conversation ceased. Soon the crackle of fire was the only sound in the great hall.

"Good evening, everyone. I hope you're all having a wonderful time. I know I am. We're all happy you came to our party. This is a great day for Neil and Talty, and we wish them grace and gladness in their new life."

He waited until the cheers and whistles faded away. "It's a great day for Ireland as well. There's an old Irish saying: 'In times of trouble, friends are recognized.' Even a blind man would recognize our friends today. The kindness you've shown by coming here has blessed us.

"My father told me once, 'There are three things proper for one who has received kindness: Thanks, remembrance, and reciprocity.' Thanks I surely have, though no words can express what your support means to me and my family. Remembrance? We Borus never forget our friends. Reciprocity? If you haven't overeaten, we're going to teach you how to dance!"

Laughter trickled through the hall. At Brian's nod, the band readied their instruments.

"May the hands you've stretched to us in friendship never be stretched in want. May tonight's fun in some small measure repay the generous gift of time and comfort you've given us today. And may the blessing of each day be the blessing you need most."

The band began with a joyous fiddle riff. One by one, pipes, guitar, and bodhran joined in. Brian strutted to the center of the dance floor and raised his arms to the delighted bride.

"Talty Boru, come dance with your daddy!"

* * * * *

When the first waltz played, Richard claimed a dance with Talty, who'd danced every dance and was flushed and breathless. He waltzed her to an exit, snatched two flutes of champagne from a passing tray, and swept her into the drawbridge room.

She collapsed on a rugged wooden bench in a puff of silk and lace. Even in her wedding finery, she didn't look the least bit out of place among the

345

medieval trappings on the old stone walls. Not Talty.

He handed her a glass. "I thought you'd like to hide for a few minutes."

"I do need to catch my breath. I never realized you were such a fine dancer, Richard."

"I'm pleased to surprise *you* for a change. I'm going to miss my good friend Christy. I might never have a decent cup of tea again."

"Nick makes wonderful tea, and Christy will always be around. Don't forget. I have an investment in that big old house. I intend to visit often."

"You'll at least have to come for your things. No self-respecting princess would dream of starting life in her new palace without her tanto knife and her Viking bow."

Talty stared at her bubbly wine. "Are we in trouble over it all?"

"I've spoken to our superiors in Brussels. They've scheduled a court of inquiry, and they won't accept your resignation until it's concluded. I think it's more out of curiosity than to decide if we've broken any rules. I'm honestly not sure we did."

"Well, *you* didn't. I'm afraid I've been..."

"You've been caught in a conflict I wouldn't wish on anyone, darling. You did what you thought was right. When we finally do part brass rags, you'll have an honorable discharge, if I have my way." He took her glass and placed it beside his on the bench.

"Thank you, Richard. You're a good friend."

He smiled. "I always will be. Fighting Vikings and lions together creates a special bond."

They returned to the hall. Neil stood near the door. He beamed when he saw them. "I see you've been looking after my wife, Richard."

"I must say, I'm relieved to be handing her off to you. She does have a tendency to get into mischief."

Talty ignored their joking. "Kieran's coming this way, and he doesn't look happy."

He was barreling straight toward them. When he reached them, he said, "Stroll over to Brian nice and easy. John Wessex came by to say hello. Remember to smile."

The crowd parted for the newlyweds. Side by side, Richard and Kieran followed.

✳ ✳ ✳ ✳ ✳

With Eileen at his side, Brian approached King John and his retinue and clasped his neighbor's hand. "John! You honor us. Please, come in."

"Thank you, sir. You remember my cousin, Lady Claudia?"

Brian kissed the hand of the woman who'd nearly become his sister-in-law so many years ago. "I certainly do. Thank you for coming, Claudia."

She smiled and said, "We must apologize for missing the wedding. Our uncle is quite ill."

Despite his differences with Geoffrey, the news saddened Brian. "We're so sorry to hear that. Nothing serious, I hope."

"A stroke, I'm afraid," said John. "He's aware of his surroundings, but can no longer swallow. The doctors had to give him a permanent feeding tube."

"How awful," said Eileen.

John nodded. "I'm sorry for him, yet I believe his actions concerning the marriage treaty were wrong. I've ordered the withdrawal of his lawsuit from the World Court."

Before Brian could respond, Neil and Talty approached. Neil's expression dared anyone to upset his bride. Talty's face masked her feelings well, though Brian detected anxiety in her eyes.

John extended his hand to Neil. "I've come to offer my congratulations to you on this happy occasion, sir. I wonder if I might dance with your lovely wife?"

Neil turned his head. "Talty?"

She responded with a cordial smile. "I'd be honored, Your Majesty."

Neil offered his arm to Lady Claudia, and they waltzed beside John and Talty. The members of the Boru clan paired off to dance.

Jack and Nuala passed Brian on their way to the floor.

"Well done, Brian," said Jack. "A major diplomatic advance, this waltz."

Nuala agreed. "A blessing three times over."

Perhaps, thought Brian. He only knew that the blessings he'd received this day were the blessings he needed most.

ACKNOWLEDGMENTS

A Band of Roses was several years in the making, and I am deeply grateful to the readers and writing professionals who have offered invaluable feedback along the way.

Sincere thanks to:
My incomparable writing group, Dave, Heather, John, and Kathleen, for their outstanding critiques and unwavering optimism.

John Bubar for his gracious help with aviation and military terminology.

David Duford for his archery lesson and expert hunting advice.

County Clare historian and genealogist Dr. Hugh W.L. Weir, author of *Hugh Weir's Brian Boru*, for his kind encouragement.

My treasured aunts, Kathleen and Geraldine O'Brien, for so generously allowing me access to their astounding library of old Irish books.

ABOUT THE AUTHOR

Boston, Massachusetts native Pat McDermott writes romantic action/adventure stories set in Ireland. *Glancing Through the Glimmer, Autumn Glimmer,* and *A Pot of Glimmer* are young adult paranormal adventures featuring Ireland's mischievous fairies and an Irish royal family that might have been. The Glimmer Books are "prequels" to her popular Band of Roses Trilogy: *A Band of Roses, Fiery Roses,* and *Salty Roses.* Her first contemporary romance, *The Rosewood Whistle,* features Ireland's music and myths.

Pat's favorite non-writing activities include cooking, hiking, reading, and traveling, especially to Ireland. She lives and writes in New Hampshire, USA.

For more information, or to contact Pat, visit her website:
http://www.patmcdermott.net/

Also by Pat McDermott

FIERY ROSES - BOOK TWO in the BAND of ROSES TRILOGY

Irish Kings still rule the Emerald Isle, and part of the kingdom is burning...

In the thrilling sequel to *A Band of Roses*, a major discovery of offshore gas ensnares Irish Crown Princess Talty Boru and her Royal Consort, Neil in a web of blackmail and murder. When the locals of rural County Mayo object to plans to run pipelines over their pristine bogs, an arsonist tries to change their minds. One of his fires triggers a chain of events that sends newlyweds Talty and Neil to an ancient world at the mercy of a waking volcano. Their fledgling marriage comes under fire as they struggle to outwit a tyrant with a shocking secret and find their way back to Ireland. While they do, King Brian locks horns with a ruthless oil tycoon trying to bully his way across the bogs. The resulting conflict proves fatal for the Boru clan, whose members again close ranks to thwart the latest threat to the kingdom they are sworn to protect.

SALTY ROSES - BOOK THREE in the BAND of ROSES TRILOGY

A ride aboard luxury submarine leads to oceans of trouble for Ireland's Crown Princess...

From an Ireland that might have been to the perils of parallel worlds, warrior princess Talty Boru has outwitted all sorts of scoundrels. A wife and mother at last, the dynamic heir to the Irish throne believes her days of exotic adventure are done and dusted. Yet her royal duties seem endless, and a day off with handsome husband Neil is looking good. Former naval officer Talty eagerly accepts an eccentric billionaire's invitation for a jaunt aboard his luxury submarine, but as she and Neil dive beneath the waves to view an eerie shipwreck, a sinister plot unfolds. An unknown enemy lures them to an ancient tomb and sends them to a world infested with treacherous pirates. Talty takes charge of a pirate ship and its mangy crew, while Neil matches wits with a steamy temptress who jeopardizes his wedding vows. As he and Talty battle to save their marriage, they learn that the door to parallel worlds swings both ways...

Made in the USA
Middletown, DE
07 August 2015